HARSH TIMES

HARSH TIMES

Mario Vargas Llosa

TRANSLATED FROM THE SPANISH BY
ADRIAN NATHAN WEST

FARRAR, STRAUS AND GIROUX
NEW YORK

Farrar, Straus and Giroux
120 Broadway, New York 10271

Library of Congress Cataloging-in-Publication Data
Names: Vargas Llosa, Mario, 1936– author. | West, Adrian Nathan, translator.
Title: Harsh times : a novel / Mario Vargas Llosa ; translated from the Spanish by
  Adrian Nathan West.
Other titles: Tiempos recios. English
Description: First American edition. | New York : Farrar, Straus and Giroux, 2021.
Identifiers: LCCN 2021025307 | ISBN 9780374601232 (hardcover)
Subjects: LCSH: Guatemala—History—Revolution, 1954—Fiction. | United States.
  Central Intelligence Agency—Fiction. | Political violence—Guatemala—History—
  20th century—Fiction.
Classification: LCC PQ8498.32.A65 T5513 2021 | DDC 863/.64—dc23
LC record available at https://lccn.loc.gov/2021025307

Designed by Abby Kagan

Our books may be purchased in bulk for promotional, educational, or business use.
Please contact your local bookseller or the Macmillan Corporate and
Premium Sales Department at 1-800-221-7945, extension 5442, or by email at
MacmillanSpecialMarkets@macmillan.com.

www.fsgbooks.com
www.twitter.com/fsgbooks • www.facebook.com/fsgbooks

1 3 5 7 9 10 8 6 4 2

TO THREE FRIENDS:

Soledad Álvarez,
Tony Raful, and
Bernardo Vega

Harsh times they were!

—SAINT TERESA OF ÁVILA

I'd never heard of this bloody place Guatemala until I was in my seventy-ninth year.

—WINSTON CHURCHILL

BEFORE

THOUGH THEY ARE UNKNOWN to the broader public, and occupy a minor place in the history books, the people with the greatest influence over the destiny of Guatemala and, in a way, over the entirety of Central America in the twentieth century, were Edward L. Bernays and Sam Zemurray, two men who could not be more dissimilar from one another in terms of origins, temperament, and vocation.

Zemurray was born in 1877, not far from the Black Sea, and being a Jew in a time of vicious pogroms across Russian Territory, he fled to the United States, where he arrived along with one of his aunts at fifteen years of age. They took refuge in the home of a relative in Selma, Alabama. Edward L. Bernays was also from a family of Jewish immigrants, but they were wealthy, from the upper class, and boasted an illustrious figure among their numbers: Bernays's uncle, Sigmund Freud. Putting aside their Judaism—and neither was particularly devout—the two of them were quite different. Edward L. Bernays styled himself a sort of father of public relations, and if he didn't invent the profession, he did take it (at Guatemala's expense) to unanticipated heights, making it the central political, social, and economic weapon of the twentieth century. This much there was no denying, even if his egoism compelled him to pathological degrees of exaggeration. They met for the first time in 1948, and began working together that same year. Sam Zemurray asked for an appointment, and Bernays received him in his small office in the heart of Manhattan. Most likely, the enormous and badly dressed brute, with his five-o'-clock shadow, open collar, faded blazer, and work boots made a poor impression on Bernays, known for elegant suits, scrupulous diction, Yardley cologne, and aristocratic manners.

"I tried to read your book *Propaganda*, but I didn't get much out of it," Zemurray told the publicist by way of introduction. He spoke a labored English, as though hesitating over every word.

"But the writing is quite plain, any literate person can grasp it," Bernays objected.

"Could be it's my fault," the other man admitted, not discomfited in the least. "Truth is, I'm not much of a reader. I hardly went to school back in Russia and I never completely got English, as you can tell. It's even worse when I write letters, they come out filled with misspellings. I'm more interested in action than the life of the mind."

"Well, if that's the case, I'm not sure what I can do for you, Mr. Zemurray," Bernays said, making as if to stand up.

"I won't waste much of your time," the other interjected. "I'm head of a company that brings bananas from Central America to the United States."

"United Fruit?" Bernays asked, examining his shabby visitor with greater curiosity than before.

"Seems we have a bad reputation in the United States and Central America. In the countries where we operate, in other words," Zemurray continued with a shrug. "And word is, you're the man who can fix that. I'm here to hire you as the company's director of public relations. Or something along those lines, you feel free to choose the title. And the salary as well, to save us time."

Such were the beginnings of the relationship between two men who were poles apart, a refined publicist and aspiring academic and intellectual and the boorish self-made impresario Sam Zemurray, who had started out with savings of one hundred fifty dollars and had built a company that made him a millionaire, despite his appearance. He hadn't invented the banana, of course, but it was thanks to him that in the United States, where few people had tried that exotic fruit, it now formed part of millions of Americans' diet and was beginning to make inroads into Europe and other parts of the world. How had he managed it? It is hard to say objectively, because in Sam Zemurray's life, fact and legend mingle. This brash entrepreneur seemed less the product of the American business world than of the pages of an adventure story. And unlike Bernays, he wasn't at all ostentatious, and rarely spoke about his life.

In the course of his journeys, Zemurray had discovered the banana tree in the forests of Central America, and with a fortuitous instinct about the commercial potential of its fruit, he began transporting it in motorboats to New Orleans and other North American cities. It was successful from the beginning. So much so that growing demand turned him from a mere vendor into a cultivator and international banana producer. This was the beginning of United Fruit, a company which, by the beginning of the 1950s, extended its reach into Honduras, Guatemala, Nicaragua, El Salvador, Costa Rica, Colombia, and a number of Caribbean islands, generating more dollars than the vast majority of firms in the United States or in the rest of the world. The empire was unquestionably the work of a single man: Sam Zemurray. And now many hundreds of people depended on him.

To achieve all this, he had worked from dawn to dusk and dusk to dawn, traveling throughout Central America and the Caribbean in dire conditions, wrangling over terrain at gun- or knife-point with other speculators like himself, sleeping hundreds of nights in open fields, devoured by mosquitoes, waylaid more than once by the ravages of swamp fever, bribing authorities and hoodwinking peasants and ignorant natives, doing deals with corrupt dictators whose greed or stupidity had gradually enabled him to acquire properties whose area in hectares now exceeded that of a respectably sized European country, creating thousands of jobs, laying down railroads, opening ports and connecting barbarism with civilization. At least, this was what Sam Zemurray said when forced to defend himself from the attacks leveled at United Fruit—La Frutera, which people all over Central America had christened the Octopus—attacks brought not just by the envious, but by his own North American competitors, rivals he'd never given a fair shake in a region where he exercised a tyrannical monopoly in the production and commercialization of the banana. His triumph was based, in the example of Guatemala, on absolute control of the country's sole port to the Caribbean—Puerto Barrios—as well as of the electrical systems and the railway that spanned the coasts of two oceans, which belonged exclusively to his company.

They were complete opposites, but they made a good team. Bernays helped a great deal to improve the company's image in the United States, to make it presentable to the upper echelon of Washington politics, to build ties between it and the self-styled aristocrat millionaires of Boston. He had come to publicity indirectly, thanks to his good relations with a wide range of persons, especially diplomats, politicians, newspaper and radio and television station owners, businessmen, and high-level bankers. He was an intelligent, hardworking, likable man, and one of his first achievements was organizing a U.S. tour for Enrico Caruso, the celebrated Italian singer. Bernays's open and refined manner, his culture, his accessible demeanor pleased people, and he gave the impression of being more important and influential than he was. Naturally, advertising and public relations had existed before his birth, but Bernays had raised the profession, which every company depended on but disdained, into a sophisticated intellectual discipline, an extension of sociology, economics, and politics. He gave lectures and classes at prestigious universities, published articles and books, presented his occupation as the most representative pursuit of the twentieth century, synonymous with modernity and progress. In *Propaganda* (1928), he had written a prophetic paragraph, which would, in a certain way, pass on to posterity: "The conscious and intelligent manipulation of the organized habits and opinions of the masses is an important element in democratic society. Those who manipulate this unseen mechanism of society constitute an invisible government which is the true ruling power of our country . . . it is the intelligent minorities which need to make use of propaganda continuously and systematically." Bernays would apply this thesis, which certain critics considered the very negation of democracy itself, with great effectiveness in Guatemala a decade after beginning work as public relations consultant for United Fruit.

His advice did much to clean up the company's image and garner it support and influence in the political world. The Octopus had never bothered to present its considerable industrial and commercial activities as something beneficial to society in general, let alone the "savage countries" where it operated and which—according to Bernays—it was helping to emerge from barbarism, creating jobs for thousands of citizens, raising their standard of living, and in this way bringing them into the fold of modernity, progress, the twentieth century, civilization. Bernays convinced Zemurray that the company should build schools in its dominions, take Catholic priests and Protestant preachers onto the plantations, set up first-aid centers and other projects of that ilk, give scholarships and travel grants to students and teachers, and he would publicize all this as incontrovertible evidence of the modernizing influence they were exerting. At the same time, through rigorous planning and the help of scientists and technicians, he promoted the consumption of the banana at breakfast and all hours of the day as indispensable for health and the formation of strong, athletic citizens. It was he who brought to the United States the Brazilian singer and dancer Carmen Miranda (the Chiquita Banana girl of stage and screen), who would prove a hit with her hats of banana bunches and would use her songs to popularize, with remarkable efficiency, the fruit that the advertiser's exertions had made a staple in North American homes.

Bernays also extended and deepened United Fruit's political influence in Boston. The richest of the rich in that New England city where the company began had more than money and power; they had prejudices, specifically against Jews like Zemurray, who had won control of the company from the Brahmins, and so it was no mean feat to get Henry Cabot Lodge to accept a post on the board of United Fruit, or for John Foster Dulles and his brother Allen from the white-shoe legal firm Sullivan & Cromwell in New York to agree to work with the company. But Bernays knew that money opens doors and that not even racial prejudice can resist it, and he managed to cement these strained ties after the so-called October Revolution of 1944 in Guatemala, when United Fruit started to sense danger in the wings. Bernays's ideas and relationships would be extremely useful in toppling the alleged "communist government" in Guatemala and replacing it with a more democratic one—that is, a more docile one, more congenial to their interests.

Alarms began going off during the mandate of Juan José Arévalo (1945–1950). Not because Professor Arévalo, defender of the muddled ideal of "spiritual socialism," had taken action against United Fruit. But he did oversee the passage of a labor law that allowed workers and peasants to form unions, and this had never been permitted in the company's domains up to that time. Zemurray and the other directors caught wind of it. In a heated meeting of the board in Boston, it was agreed that Bernays would visit Guatemala, assess the situation and future prospects, and get a sense of how dangerous events there could be under the first government in the history of the country to emerge from truly free elections.

Bernays spent two weeks in Guatemala, staying at the Hotel Panamerican in the center of the city, not far from the National Palace. As he didn't speak Spanish, he relied on translators to interview landowners, soldiers, bankers, members of congress, policemen, foreigners who had long resided in the country, union leaders, journalists, and employees of the United States Embassy and of United Fruit. He did his job well, despite suffering from the heat and the mosquitoes.

At another meeting of the board in Boston, he offered personal reflections on what, in his judgment, was taking place in Guatemala. He relied on notes for his presentation, and spoke with the ease of a good professional and without an ounce of cynicism:

"The danger that Guatemala should turn communist and become a beachhead for a Soviet infiltration of Central America that would pose a threat to the Panama Canal is remote and for the moment, I would say, inexistent," he assured them. "Few people in Guatemala know what Marxism or communism are, even among the stray elements calling themselves communists who founded the Escuela Claridad to disseminate revolutionary ideas. The danger isn't real, but it is convenient for us that people believe it exists, above all in the United States. The real danger is another one. I have spoken with President Arévalo and his closest advisers in person. He is as anticommunist as you and I. Proof is that the president and his supporters have insisted that the new Constitution of Guatemala forbid the existence of political parties with international connections. They've declared on numerous occasions that 'communism is the greatest threat faced by democracy,' and they closed down the aforementioned Escuela Claridad and deported its founders. And yet, contradictory as it may seem to you, Arévalo's boundless love for democracy represents a serious threat for United Fruit. This, gentlemen, is something good for you to know, but not to say aloud."

He smiled and looked theatrically at all the members of the board, some of whom smiled back politely. Then, after a brief pause, he continued:

"Arévalo would like to make Guatemala a democracy like the United States, a country he admires and considers a model. Dreamers are dangerous, and it is in this sense that Dr. Arévalo is dangerous. His project has not the least chance of being realized. How can you turn a country of three million inhabitants, most of them illiterate Indians who have just emerged from paganism or are still in the grips of it, where there must be three or four shamans for every doctor—how can you turn such a place into a modern democracy? A place where, moreover, a white minority made up of racist landowners and speculators detests the Indians and treats them like slaves. The military men I've spoken to seem to be living in the nineteenth century as well, and could stage a coup at any moment. President Arévalo has suffered a number of military rebellions already, but he's managed to quash them. Now then. Though his efforts to make his country into a modern democracy strike me as vain, let's not deceive ourselves: any advancement he makes in this direction will be highly detrimental to us.

"You realize that, don't you?" he went on, after another pause to take a few sips of water. "Let me give you a few examples. Arévalo has approved a labor law that permits the formation of unions in businesses and farms and allows workers and peasants to join. And he has drafted an antimonopoly law based on already existing legislation in the United States. You can imagine what a measure to ensure equal competition would mean for United Fruit: if it didn't ruin us completely, at the least we'd be looking at a major decline in revenues. Our profits are not just the result of our hard work, our commitment, the money we spend to prevent diseases, or the forest we clear to plant more banana trees. They also come from our monopoly, which keeps competitors away from our territories, and the privileged conditions we work under, with no taxes, no unions, none of the risks and dangers those things imply. The problem isn't just Guatemala, which is a small part of the world we operate in. It is the contagion spreading to other countries in Central America and to Colombia if this idea of becoming a 'modern democracy' were to catch on there. United Fruit would be forced to deal with unions and international competition, to pay taxes, to guarantee health insurance and offer retirement plans for workers and their families, and it would be subject to the hatred and envy prosperous, well-run companies inevitably arouse in poor countries—especially if they're American. The danger, gentlemen, lies in setting a bad example. Not so much communism as democracy in Guatemala. Though it will likely never materialize, any achievements in this direction will mean a loss and a step backward for us."

He stopped speaking and examined the perturbed or inquisitive faces of the board members. Sam Zemurray, the only one not wearing a tie, looking out of place among the elegant gentlemen seated together at the long table, said:

"Fine, you've given us the diagnosis. Now how do we cure the disease?"

"I wanted to let you catch your breath before continuing," Bernays joked, taking another sip of water. "Now I will discuss the remedies, Sam. It will be a long, complicated, costly process. But it will kill the infection at the root. And that could mean another fifty years of expansion, profitability, tranquility for United Fruit."

Edward L. Bernays knew what he was talking about. The treatment meant working simultaneously on the United States government and North American public opinion. Neither of them had the least idea that Guatemala existed, let alone that it constituted a problem. That was, in principle, a good thing. "We are the ones who have to enlighten the government and public opinion about Guatemala, and to do it in such a way as to convince them the problem is so serious, so grave, that it must be taken care of immediately. How? With subtlety and good timing. Organizing things so that public opinion, which is essential in a democracy, pressures the government to act in order to head off a serious threat. What threat? The very same one I have just told you Guatemala *doesn't* represent: the Soviet Trojan horse sneaking through the U.S.A.'s back door. How do we convince the public that Guatemala is a country in which communism is already a reality, one that will soon become the first satellite of the Soviet Union in the new world if Washington fails to act? With the press, radio, and television, the main resources that inform and orient the citizenry, in free countries as well as enslaved ones. We must open the eyes of the press to the danger looming just two hours by plane from the United States, right on the doorstep of the Panama Canal.

"It would be best if all this were to occur naturally, without anyone planning or steering it, especially not one of us, with a stake in the matter. The idea that Guatemala is on the verge of passing into Soviet hands shouldn't come from the Republicans, from the right-leaning outlets in the United States, it would be better if it came up in the liberal papers, the ones the Democrats read and listen to, the center, even the left. That's the way to get the broader public's ear. All this will seem more realistic if we have the other side doing our work for us."

Sam Zemurray interrupted him to ask:

"So what are we going to do to convince those bullshitting hacks on the left?"

Bernays smiled and paused again. Like a skilled actor, he looked solemnly at each of the members of the board.

"That's why you have the king of public relations on your side. Me," he joked, devoid of all modesty, as if he were wasting his time trying to convince this group of gentlemen that the earth was round. "This, gentlemen, is the point of having so many friends among the owners and managers of America's newspapers and radio and television stations."

They would have to work nimbly, with discretion, to keep the media from feeling used. Everything needed to appear spontaneous, like a natural process, to give the appearance that the free press, with its progressive agenda, was discovering these "scoops" and sharing them with the world on its own. They would have to carefully massage the journalists' normally fevered egos.

When Bernays was done talking, Sam Zemurray asked for the floor again:

"Please, don't tell us how much this escapade you've just described in such detail is going to cost us. We've already had enough trauma for one day."

"I'll leave that aside for now," Bernays agreed. "What's important is that you all remember one thing: the company will earn far more than it could ever spend on an operation like this if we manage to delay for another fifty years Guatemala's becoming a modern democracy of the kind President Arévalo's dreaming of."

What Edward L. Bernays proposed at that memorable board meeting of the United Fruit Company in Boston was carried out to the letter, confirming, it must be said in passing, his contention that the twentieth century would mark the advent of propaganda as a basic instrument of power and of the manipulation of public opinion in democratic societies as well as authoritarian ones.

Little by little, toward the end of Juan José Arévalo's mandate, but much more during the government of Colonel Jacobo Árbenz

Guzmán, Guatemala began appearing frequently in the American press, in reports in *The New York Times*, *The Washington Post*, or *Time*, which described the growing danger to the free world of Soviet influence in that country, whose successive governments, though they worked to present an appearance of democracy, were infiltrated by communists, fellow travelers, and useful idiots. Their methods stood at odds with the rule of law, pan-Americanism, private property, and the free market, and stoked class war, hatred of social distinctions, and hostility against independent businesses.

Newspapers and magazines in the United States that had never before taken an interest in Guatemala, Central America, or even Latin America as a whole sent correspondents to Guatemala, thanks to Bernays's connections and his agile maneuvering. They were lodged at the Hotel Panamerican, where the bar became a hub for international journalists who would go there to receive file folders filled with documentation confirming what they'd been told—that unionization was becoming an instrument of conflict, and private businesses were under siege—and they got interviews, arranged or facilitated by Bernays, with landowners, entrepreneurs, priests (even the archbishop himself), journalists, opposition leaders, pastors, and professionals who gave detailed accounts of how the country was becoming a Soviet satellite that international communism intended to use to undermine the influence and interests of the United States throughout Latin America.

At a certain point—just when Jacobo Árbenz's government had initiated its land reform program—Bernays's machinations with the owners of the newspapers and magazines were no longer needed: these were the days of the Cold War, and there was now real worry in political, business, and cultural circles in the United States. On their own, the media wanted correspondents on the ground to tell them about the situation in that tiny nation infiltrated by communism. The pinnacle of this had been a dispatch published in 1950 by the United Press, written by the British journalist Kenneth de Courcy, which announced that the Soviet Union was intending to build a submarine base in Guatemala. *Life* magazine, the *New York Herald Tribune*, the

Evening Standard in London, *Harper's Magazine*, the *Chicago Tribune*, *Visión* (in Spanish), *The Christian Science Monitor*, and countless other publications devoted page after page to revealing, through concrete facts and testimonials, Guatemala's gradual slide into communism and submission to Soviet rule. There was no conspiracy: propaganda had simply imposed an amenable fiction atop reality, and it was this that became the subject of the benighted North American journalists' reports, and few of them ever realized they were marionettes in the hands of a brilliant puppet master. This explains what drove a personage as distinguished on the liberal left as Flora Lewis of *The New York Times* to write her fulsome accolades for the American ambassador in Guatemala, John Emil Peurifoy. Then again, this was the low point of McCarthyism and the Cold War between the United States and Russia, and that helped render this fiction plausible.

Sam Zemurray died in November of 1961, shortly after his eighty-fourth birthday. With his millions, he had retired to Louisiana, and still couldn't quite believe that everything Edward L. Bernays had planned in that faraway meeting of the United Fruit board in Boston had come so precisely to fruition. Nor did he suspect that despite winning that particular battle, La Frutera, as it was known to the south, had begun to disintegrate, and that in a few years its president would end his own life, that the company would then disappear, and that nothing would be left of it but memories, bad and worse.

I

Miss Guatemala's mother came from a family of Italian immigrants named Parravicini. After two generations, the surname was shortened and Hispanicized. When the young jurist, law professor, and attorney Arturo Borrero Lamas asked for the young Marta Parra's hand in marriage, rumors started circulating in Guatemala's high society because, to all appearances, this offspring of Italian tavern keepers, bakers, and pastry chefs failed to measure up to the status of the handsome young man whose venerable family, professional prestige, and fortune made him the favorite of all the well-bred girls of marrying age. With time, the gossip died down, and when the wedding was held in the cathedral, officiated by the city's archbishop, nearly everyone who mattered was in attendance, some as invited guests, others as onlookers. The eternal president, General Jorge Ubico Castañeda, was there, arm in arm with his gracious wife, in an elegant uniform spangled with medals, and amid the multitude's applause, they had themselves photographed with the bride and groom standing before the facade.

With regard to descendants, the marriage was an unfortunate

one. Martita Parra became pregnant each year, but however much she took care of herself, she only gave birth to a series of skeletal boys who emerged half dead and succumbed in a matter of weeks or days, in spite of the best efforts of the city's midwives, gynecologists, and even witches and shamans. After five years, these endless frustrations abated, and Martita Borrero Parra came into the world. Even in the crib, she was beautiful, lively, and vivacious, and they nicknamed her Miss Guatemala. Unlike her brothers, she survived. And how!

She was born scrawny, nothing but skin and bones. What people noticed, even from those very early days when they were having Masses said for the newborn so her fate would be different from her brothers', was the smoothness of her skin, her delicate traits, her big eyes and that tranquil gaze, firm and penetrating, which settled on people and things alike as though determined to engrave them in her memory for all time. A disconcerting, frightening stare. Símula, the K'iche' Maya Indian who would be her nursemaid, prophesied: "This child will have powers!"

Miss Guatemala's mother, Marta Parra de Borrero, got little joy from her daughter, the only one of her children to survive. Not because she died soon afterward—no, she would live to ninety and end her days in a nursing home with little idea of what was going on around her—but because, after the girl was born, she was left weary, mute, depressed, *touched* (as they used to say then to speak euphemistically of the mad). She spent whole days immobile at home, not uttering a word; her maids Patrocinio and Juana fed her by hand and massaged her to keep her legs from atrophying; she would only emerge from her silence in occasional fits of tears that ended in exhausted oblivion. Símula was the only one she communicated with, in gestures, or else the servant simply guessed her whims. With time, Dr. Borrero Lamas forgot he had a wife; days would pass, then weeks, without his entering her bedroom to kiss her on the forehead, and every hour he wasn't at his office, pleading before the court, or giving classes at San Carlos University he devoted to Martita, whom he fussed over and adored from the day of her birth. The girl grew up by her father's side. On the weekends, when his home was filled with highborn friends—judges, landholders, politicians, diplomats—who came to play *rocambor*, a card game popular a century before, he would let Martita run free among his guests. Her father liked to watch how she pinned his friends in her verdigris eyes, as if determined to extract from them some secret. Anyone could pat or tickle her, but with the exception of her father, she was reluctant to respond with a kiss on the cheek or any other show of affection in return.

Later, recollecting those first years of her life, Martita had hardly any memory—as if it were a flame that flared up and died out—of the political turmoil that overtook the conversations of those gentlemen who came by on the weekends to play a card game from another era. She heard confused acknowledgments, around 1944, of the unpopularity of General Jorge Ubico Castañeda, the grandee strewn with medals and gold braid, and now civilian and military movements and student strikes were working to depose him. They achieved this in the famous October Revolution of that same year, when another military junta rose up, presided over this time by General Federico Ponce Vaides, whom the protestors would overthrow in turn. Then, at last, there were elections. The upper-crust devotees of *rocambor* were terrified that Professor Juan José Arévalo might win; he had just returned from exile in Argentina, and the men said his "spiritual socialism" (what might that mean?) would bring catastrophe to Guatemala: the Indians would raise their heads and start killing decent people, the communists would take over the landholders' fields and would send the children from good families off to Russia to be sold as slaves. When they said these things, Martita would always wait for the reaction of one of the good men who attended these weekends filled with *rocambor* and political gossip: Dr. Efrén García Ardiles. He was handsome, with bright eyes and long hair, and he often laughed, calling his fellow visitors paranoid cavemen. In his judgment, Professor Arévalo was more of an anticommunist than any of them, and his "spiritual socialism" was merely a symbolic way of saying that he wished to make Guatemala into a modern, democratic country, lifting it out of the poverty and feudal primitivism it was mired in. Martita remembered the arguments that arose: the patricians browbeat

Dr. García Ardiles, calling him a red, an anarchist, a communist. And when she asked her father why that man was arguing with all the rest of them, her father would respond: "Efrén is a good doctor and an excellent friend. It's too bad he's harebrained, and a leftist!" This made Martita curious, and she decided one day to ask Dr. García Ardiles what it all—leftism and communism—was about.

By then she was attending the Colegio Belga-Guatemalteco (Congregation of the Holy Family of Helmet), where all the finer families of Guatemala sent their girls to be educated by Flemish nuns, and she was winning awards for academic excellence and getting top marks on her exams. It was no great effort for her, she just needed to concentrate a bit, drawing on her abundant natural intelligence, knowing that As on her report card would bring her father great pleasure. How happy Dr. Borrero Lamas felt on the last day of school, when his daughter climbed the stage to receive recognition for her application and her impeccable behavior! And how they applauded the girl, the nuns and everyone else in the audience.

Did Martita have a happy childhood? She asked herself this many times in the years to follow, and she answered yes, if happy meant a tranquil, ordered life, without upsets, as a girl surrounded by servants and pampered and protected by her father. But the lack of a mother's love saddened her. Only once a day—it was her hardest moment—did she visit that lady who always lay in bed and paid her no mind, even though she'd given birth to her. Símula would take the girl to give her a kiss before bed. She didn't like this visit, the woman struck her as more dead than alive; she looked at her with indifference, offered no response to the kiss, there were times when she would even yawn through it. Martita didn't especially enjoy her friends, the birthday parties she would attend with Símula as a chaperone, or her first dances when she was in secondary school and the boys were already flattering the girls, sending them notes and pairing off with their first loves. She preferred the weekend evenings that stretched on into the late hours and the gentlemen who played *rocambor*. Above all, she enjoyed her private talks with Dr. Efrén García Ardiles, whom she would pepper with questions about politics. He told her that, despite the patricians' complaints, Juan José Arévalo was doing right, trying to finally achieve justice in the country, especially among the Indians, who were the great majority among Guatemala's three million citizens. Thanks to President Arévalo, he said, Guatemala was finally becoming a democracy.

Martita's life took a tremendous turn at the end of 1949, on the day she turned fifteen. The entirety of the old neighborhood of San Sebastián where she lived took part, in a way, in the celebration. Her father threw her a quinceañera party of the kind typical for daughters of the better families in Guatemala, to signify her entrance into society. The house, with its spacious vestibule, ironwork bars on the windows, and lush garden in the heart of the colonial quarter, was decorated with flowers and wreaths and filled with light. The archbishop himself held a Mass in the cathedral, and Martita attended in a white dress with tulle frilling and a bouquet of orange blossoms in her hand. The whole family was there, uncles and aunts and cousins she was seeing then for the first time. There were fireworks in the street and a huge piñata full of candies and dried fruits that the young guests fought over joyfully. The maids and waiters looked after the attendees in folk costume, the women with colorful huipils embroidered with geometric figures, pleated skirts, and dark sashes, and the men in white pants, bright shirts, and straw hats. The Equestrian Club provided the banquet and hired two orchestras, a traditional one with nine marimba players and a more modern one composed of twelve music teachers who played the dances fashionable at the time: the bamba, the waltz, blues, tango, corrido, guaracha, rumba, and bolero. In the middle of it all, Martita, the honoree, fainted while dancing with the son of the United States ambassador, Richard Patterson Jr. She was carried off to the bedroom and Dr. Galván, who was there to accompany his daughter, Martita's friend Dolores, took her temperature and blood pressure and rubbed her down with alcohol. She soon regained consciousness. It was nothing, the old doctor said, a sudden drop in blood pressure, the fault of her overexcitement that day. But she spent the remainder of the evening maudlin and absent.

When the guests had gone and the night was well along, Símula approached Dr. Borrero. She whispered they should talk alone. He took her to his study. "Dr. Galván is wrong," the servant said. "A drop in blood pressure, how ridiculous. I'm sorry to put it this way, Doctor, but it's best I just come out with it: the girl is expecting." Now it was the master of the house who went faint. He stumbled over to a chair; the world, the shelves full of books, spun around him like a carousel.

Despite her father's pleas, demands, and threats of the worst punishments imaginable, Martita, showing signs of the enormous character that would take her far in life, roundly refused to say who was the father of that child now forming inside her womb. Dr. Borrero Lamas nearly lost his senses. He was deeply Catholic, sanctimonious, even, and yet he considered agreeing to an abortion when Símula, seeing his desperation, told him she could take the girl to a lady specialized in "sending the unborn to limbo." But after turning the matter over in his mind and consulting with his friend and confessor, the Jesuit Father Ulloa, he chose against exposing his daughter to such a risk. Nor was he willing to go to hell for committing this mortal sin.

The knowledge that Martita had ruined her life tore him to pieces. He was forced to disenroll her from the Colegio Belga-Guatemalteco because the girl vomited constantly and fainted. Otherwise, the nuns would discover her pregnancy and naturally a scandal would ensue. It hurt the lawyer to realize that his daughter's lapse would preclude her finding a suitable husband. What serious young man from a good family and with a bright future ahead of him would allow a fallen woman to take his name? Neglecting his firm and his classes, he devoted the days and nights following the discovery of his daughter's pregnancy to trying to ascertain who the father was. No one had been courting Martita. A dedicated student, she hadn't seemed interested in flirting with young men like other girls her age. Wasn't that strange? Martita had never had a sweetheart. He had kept a close eye on her comings and goings outside school hours. Who had gotten her pregnant, where, how? The thing that seemed impossible at first slowly wormed its way into his mind, and he decided to confront it, at once believing and disbelieving. He loaded five bullets into his antique Smith & Wesson revolver, which he had used just a few times, for target practice at the

Hunting, Sport Shooting, and Fishermen's Club, or bored on one of the hunts his friends dragged him off to.

He showed up unannounced at the house where Dr. Efrén García Ardiles resided with his aging mother in the neighborhood bordering San Francisco. His old friend, who had just returned from the office where he passed his afternoons—he worked in the morning at San Juan de Dios General Hospital—received him immediately. He took him to a small, shelf-lined room filled with primitive K'iche' Maya objects, masks, and burial urns.

"Efrén, you're going to answer me a question," Dr. Borrero Lamas said very slowly, as if he had to extract the words from his mouth one by one. "We went to school together with the Marists, and despite your eccentric political ideas, I consider you my closest friend. In the name of our longstanding friendship, I am hoping you won't lie to me. Are you the one who got my daughter pregnant?"

He watched as Dr. Efrén García turned white as a sheet of paper. He opened and closed his mouth several times before responding. When he did, he stammered, and his hands shook:

"I didn't know she was pregnant, Arturo. Yes, it was me. It's the worst thing I've done in my life. I will never stop regretting it, I swear to you."

"I came here to kill you, you son of a bitch, but you're so repugnant, I can't bring myself to do it."

And he began to cry. Sobs shook his chest, and tears washed down his face. They were together for nearly an hour, and when they said their goodbyes in the doorway, they neither shook hands nor clapped each other on the back, as was their custom.

When he reached his home, Dr. Borrero Lamas walked straight to the bedroom where his daughter had been kept under lock and key since the day she fainted.

He remained standing in the doorway as he spoke to his daughter, in a tone that didn't admit reply:

"I've spoken with Efrén and we've reached an agreement. He will marry you, so that the baby in your stomach will grow up with a good name, not like those whelps a dog gives birth to in the street. The

21

marriage will be held at the estate in Chichicastenango. I will speak to Father Ulloa, who will officiate. There will be no guests. A notice will be printed in the paper, and afterward, announcements will be sent round. Up to that point, we shall go on pretending we are united as a family. Once you have married Efrén, I will not see you again, I will not concern myself with you, and I will look for a way to disinherit you. In the meanwhile, you will remain locked in this room and you will not sct foot outside."

All that he said came to pass. The rushed marriage of Dr. Efrén García Ardiles with a girl of fifteen—twenty-eight years younger than he—gave rise to rumors and innuendo that circulated back and forth and held the whole of Guatemala City in suspense. Everyone knew Martita Borrero Parra was marrying because the doctor had gotten her pregnant, and this was unsurprising, coming from a trafficker in revolutionary ideas; and everyone sympathized with the upright Dr. Borrero Lamas, whom no one had since seen smile, or go to parties, or play *rocambor*.

The wedding took place on a remote property of the bride's father, a coffee farm on the outskirts of Chichicastenango, and he served as one of the witnesses; the others were workers from the fields, and since they were illiterate, they signed with an *X* or a simple downstroke before receiving a few quetzales in return. There was not even a glass of wine to toast to the married couple's happiness.

Bride and groom returned to Guatemala City and went straight to the house Efrén and his mother shared, and all the good families knew that Dr. Borrero, having fulfilled his promise, would never see his daughter again.

In the middle of 1950, Martita gave birth to a boy who, at least officially, was born in the seventh month of her pregnancy.

II

You've got to tame your nerves, one way or another," Enrique said, rubbing his hands together. "Before I get started, these things always put me on edge. But when the moment arrives, I calm down and I take care of it, and that's that. What about you? Does that happen with you?"

"I'm the opposite," the Dominican said, shaking his head. "I'm nervous when I wake up, when I go to sleep, when I get out of bed. When I have to act, I'm even more nervous. Being high-strung is just my natural state."

They were in the offices of the Dirección General de Seguridad, which took up one corner of the Palacio del Gobierno, and from its windows, they could see Constitution Plaza with its leafy trees and the facade of the Guatemala City Cathedral. It was a sunny, still-cloudless day, but the rain would come down that afternoon and would likely go on filling the streets with puddles and rills all through the night, just as it had all week.

"The decision's taken, the plans have been made, and the people who matter are committed. You've got the permits and tickets in your pocket, for you and for the lady. Why should anything go wrong?" the other man said, talking very softly now. And smiling, though without a jot of humor, he changed the subject: "You know what's good to calm your nerves?"

"A nice swig of dry rum," the Dominican said with a grin. "But at the whorehouse, not in this miserable office, with all these ears around us, that's what they say where you come from when they're talking about snitches, right? Ears! I like the sound of that. Let's go to Gerona, to that place run by the gringa with the dye job."

Enrique looked at his watch:

"It's only four in the afternoon." He looked dismayed. "It'll be closed, it's still early."

"We'll kick the door down if we have to," the Dominican said, standing up. "That's all there is to it. Fate has chosen. We're having a nice drink together to kill time. My treat."

As they were leaving, crossing the room full of desks, the civilians and soldiers stood to salute Enrique. He didn't linger, and as he was out of uniform, limited himself to nodding at them briefly before departing. A car was waiting for them by one of the side doors, manned by the ugliest chauffeur in the world. He hurried them to their destination, the gringa's whorehouse, which was closed as predicted. A lone street sweeper limped over to inform them that it only opened "when it was dark and rainy out." But they knocked at the door all the same, and went on doing so harder and harder until they heard a clanking of keys and chains and it drew open slightly.

"Gentlemen, already?" the woman with the still disheveled platinum-blond hair said, recognizing them with surprise. Her name was Miriam Ritcher, and she forced her accent a bit so she would sound like a foreigner. "The girls are either still asleep or having breakfast."

"We're not here for the girls, Miriam, we're here to have a drink," Enrique said, cutting her off rudely. "Can we come in, yes or no?"

"For you all, it's always yes," the gringa said, shrugging, resigned. She opened the door the rest of the way and stood back, curtsying, to let them through. "Gentlemen, after you."

At that hour, dim and empty, the bar room looked sadder, shabbier than when the lights were up, the music loud, the boisterous clientele in attendance. Instead of pictures, the walls were lined with posters advertising liquor brands and the coastal rail line. The friends sat at the bar on two tall stools, lit their cigarettes, and smoked.

"The usual?" the woman asked. She was wearing a housecoat and slippers. Arrayed this way, hair unkempt and without makeup, she looked a hundred years old.

"The usual," the Dominican joked. "And if it's possible, a tasty gash to lick."

"You know quite well I don't care for vulgarities," the mistress of the house grumbled as she served their drinks.

"Me neither," Enrique said to his friend. "So show a bit more respect when you open your mouth."

They said nothing for a moment, and then Enrique asked suddenly:

"I thought you were supposed to be Rosicrucian? What kind of religion allows you to talk all crass like that in front of a lady?"

"Lady—I like that," the woman said on her way out, not bothering to turn and look at them. She disappeared behind a door.

The Dominican thought for a moment and shrugged.

"I'm not even sure it's a religion: maybe it's just a philosophy. I met a wise man once, and they told me he was Rosicrucian. In Mexico, not long after I got there. Brother Cristóbal. He gave off this feeling of peace that I've never felt again. He spoke very calmly, slowly. And he seemed to be inspired by angels."

"What do you mean, inspired?" Enrique asked. "Are you talking about one of those holy men who walk around the streets half crazy, mumbling to themselves?"

"He was wise, not crazy," the Dominican said. "He never said Rosicrucian, he said the Ancient Mystical Order Rosae Crucis. It made you feel respect for it. It arose in ancient Egypt, in the pharaohs' days, as a secret brotherhood, hermetic, and it survived through the centuries outside the public eye. It's widespread in the Orient and in Europe, so they say. Nobody here knows what it is. Not in the Dominican Republic, either."

25

"So you are or aren't a Rosicrucian?"

"I don't know if I am or not," the Dominican said, abashed. "I never had time to learn about it. I just saw Brother Cristóbal a couple of times. But it left an impression on me. From what I heard, it seemed like the religion or philosophy that suited me best. It gave you a great deal of peace and didn't meddle around in people's private lives. And when he spoke, he transmitted something: tranquility."

"Honestly, you're a strange bird," Enrique said. "And I'm not talking just about your vices."

"As far as religion and the soul go, I'll give you that," the Dominican said. "A man who's different from the others. I am, and I'm honored to be so."

III

I NEED A DRINK, he thought. And he wriggled away from the embraces, his ears tormented by shouts of *Viva!* and loudspeakers chanting his name, whispered to María Vilanova—"I have to go to the bathroom"—and pushed his way through the people on the balcony and back into the Palace. He ran to the office he had occupied as Arévalo's minister of defense. After locking the door, he hurried over to the cabinet behind his desk, where he kept his whiskey locked up. His pulse racing uncontrollably, he opened it and poured a glass half full. His body was quivering, especially his hands. He had to clutch the glass in all ten fingers to keep it from falling and splashing whiskey all over his pants. *You're an alcoholic*, he thought, scared. *You're killing yourself, you'll wind up like your father. You can't let that happen.*

For Jacobo Árbenz Guzmán, the suicide of his father, a Swiss pharmacist residing in Quetzaltenango, the mountainous highlands region in the west of Guatemala where he was born on September 14, 1913, was an unfathomable mystery. Why did he do it? Were things going badly at the pharmacy? Did he have debts? Was he bankrupt? His father was an immigrant who established himself in those hills still bearing traces of their Mayan heritage and married a local teacher, Miss Octavia Guzmán Caballeros, who always kept the reason her husband took his life hidden from her son (and perhaps didn't know it herself); only years later would Árbenz discover that his father, an inscrutable man, was suffering from a duodenal ulcer and gave himself morphine injections to combat the pain.

Why did he not drink the glass of whiskey he clutched in his hands, for which he had been yearning for so long? It frightened him that he'd spent the entire victory ceremony obsessed with having a drink. *Am I already an alcoholic?* he asked himself again. With all the work he had ahead of him! With the hope so many Guatemalans had invested in him! Was he going to disappoint them with his miserable craving for liquor? And yet, even if he couldn't drink it, he also couldn't bring himself to pour the glass of whiskey he held, slightly trembling, in his hands, down the sink.

As a boy, as a teenager, Jacobo had lived there in the highlands, where the Indians languished in poverty and were bled mercilessly by the landowners, and from an early age he realized Guatemala had major social problems with inequality, exploitation, and poverty; but later, he would say it was only thanks to his wife, the Salvadoran María Cristina Vilanova, that he became a man of the left.

From a young age, he was passionate about sports—gymnastics, swimming, soccer, horseback riding—and it was probably for this reason that he chose a military career. His family's difficult economic situation after his father's death likely played an important role as well.

Even as a boy, he stood out for his good looks, his academic brilliance, and his athletic achievements, as well as for his long silences and the subdued, retiring, and austere character he had inherited from his father. When he entered the Politécnica, Guatemala's military academy, with top exam scores, midway through 1932, he was spoken of as a young man with a promising future. The cadets were given ranks during their years of study; Árbenz attained first sergeant, the highest in the Politécnica's history. He became the cadets' standard-bearer and a champion boxer.

Was it there that he discovered his predilection for drinking? He recalled that it was the main diversion of the cadets as well as the officers and their subordinates. What his classmates and teachers valued most highly were neither good grades nor an impeccable service record, but an ability to hold one's liquor. *Morons,* he thought.

He was still a schoolboy when he met the beautiful and intelligent María Cristina Vilanova. She had come to Guatemala for a visit, and they were introduced at a fair held on November 11 in honor of the reigning dictator, General Jorge Ubico Castañeda. Árbenz was very pale that day, because he had just left the hospital after a motorcycle accident. There was a mutual attraction, and when the girl returned to San Salvador, they wrote each other feverish declarations of love. In her brief autobiography, she tells how they spoke during their courtship of romance, but also of more serious subjects, "like chemistry and physics." María Cristina, born in 1915, belonged to one of the so-called fourteen families of El Salvador; she had studied in the United States, at the College of Notre Dame de Namur in Belmont, California, she spoke English and French, and she would have gone on to university if she'd been allowed, but it was forbidden since, according to the prejudices of the time, a decent girl didn't do such things. She supplemented her studies with reading, with a passion for literature, politics, and the arts. She was a restless young woman with progressive ideas, worried by economic and social conditions in Central America, and she spent her free hours painting. Despite resistance from María Cristina's family, she and Jacobo Árbenz decided to marry, and did so soon after he had received the rank of second lieutenant. They took their vows in the church in March of 1939. To do so, the groom had to confess and take his first communion—his education had been secular up to that point. As a wedding present, the couple received a villa from María's family, Finca El Cajón in the town of Santa Lucía Cotzumalguapa in the Escuintla Department.

María, of course, was the first to notice his penchant transforming to a vice. How many times did he hear his wife say, "That's enough, Jacobo! You're slurring your words, don't drink any more!" And he always obeyed.

The marriage was a happy one, and María Cristina's culture and sensitivity had a deep effect on the young officer. She brought him into the orbit of intellectuals, writers, journalists, and artists from Guatemala and elsewhere in Central America whom he wouldn't have known otherwise; among them were more than a few who called themselves socialists and radicals, people who railed against the military dictatorships (like General Ubico's) spreading through Central American countries, who wanted democracy for Guatemala, with free elections, freedom of the press, political parties, and reforms that would raise the Indians from the servile position they'd been forced into since colonial times. The problem with these artists and intellectuals, he thought, was they all had the same taste for drink as he; he learned a great deal in his meetings with them, but they nearly always ended in drunken revels. He went on staring, hypnotized, at the slightly yellowish liquid in his hands.

María Cristina would be roundly criticized later for having consorted with two foreign women reputed to be communists during their time in Guatemala: the Chilean Bravo Letelier, who would later become her secretary, and the Salvadoran Matilde Elena López. But she was not a woman to let sniping intimidate her, she did as she liked without caring what others said, and that part of her personality was what her husband most admired about her. He hadn't yet thrown his whiskey in the sink, but he hadn't drunk it either. His thoughts were elsewhere, but his eyes were focused on the drink. Outside, in Constitution Plaza, the hurrahs and the loudspeakers went on calling his name.

Jacobo Árbenz and María Vilanova had three children, two girls and a boy: Arabella, born in 1940, María Leonora in 1942, and Juan Jacobo in 1946. She accompanied her husband through his career as an official at the various military installations where he served, in places like San Juan Sacatepéquez and San José Castle. Those were years when his prestige grew, and with it, his status as a leader among his comrades in arms. She was delighted when recognition came to him in the capital, at the Glorious and Centenary Polytechnic School, where he was appointed captain, overseeing a company of cadets, and later made professor of science and history.

They lived for a long time in boardinghouses, because his modest income of seventy dollars a month didn't suffice to rent an apartment; but in time, with his various promotions, they were able to take up residence in Villa Pomona, on the corner of Calle Montúfar and Avenida de la Reforma, surrounded by stands of tall trees in a yard ample enough to give them the feeling of living in the country. There they continued meeting with the same group of artists and intellectuals, many of whom had been persecuted and even sent into prison or exile for their political ideas, among them Carlos Manuel Pellecer, who would pass through the Military Academy and go into exile in Mexico for opposing the Ubico government, and José Manuel Fortuny, the journalist, politician, and graduate of the Escuela Normal Para Varones, who would go on to direct the PAR (Revolutionary Action Party), a leftist academic movement, before cofounding the communist Guatemalan Party of Labor.

But I never got drunk, vomited, or made a scandal like so many of the losers I knew when they downed a few too many, he thought. No one ever noticed he was drunk. He had a talent for covering it up. And he would stop drinking when he felt that tingle in his head and noticed he couldn't pronounce his words without swallowing a letter or drawing out the vowels. He would fall silent and wait there tranquilly, neither moving nor taking part in the chitchat or discussions, until that invasive tingle slowly died away.

General Jorge Ubico Castañeda remained thirteen years in power, until 1944. Prior to the Second World War, he had shown clear sympathy for Hitler and the Nazis. He recognized Franco's government in the midst of the Spanish Civil War, and more than once he had attended gatherings held by the Falangists in their blue uniforms, throwing up the fascist salute, in front of the Spanish Embassy in Guatemala. But he was prudent and an opportunist, and was among the first to break off relations with Germany at the outbreak of WWII, and to ingratiate himself with the United States, he even issued a declaration of war.

The year 1944 marked the beginning of protests against the dictatorship in Guatemala. The first to participate were the students from the venerable San Carlos University, and for the most part, public opinion, the workers, the field hands, and the young would follow suit in due time. Then-captain Jacobo Árbenz was one of the most influential military men to persuade the army to request the dictator's resignation; later, when Ubico stepped down and left the government in the hands of General Federico Ponce Vaides, who threatened to follow in his predecessor's footsteps, Árbenz pushed them to rebel against this intrigue. Ponce Vaides resigned after substantial popular protests against succession by appointment and the decisive intervention of the army, encouraged by two officers, Major Francisco Javier Arana and Captain Jacobo Árbenz, to support the uprising against the dictatorship. A junta was then established, composed of the two soldiers Arana and Árbenz and a civilian, the businessman Jorge Toriello. As agreed, the junta convened a constitutional assembly and organized elections for the presidency and congress. These were the first genuinely democratic elections in Guatemala's history. The movement that made them possible would come to be known in the future as the October Revolution, and it ushered in a new era in the country. The winner of the elections was a distinguished (albeit deeply vain) educator and thinker, Juan José Arévalo. He had been living in Argentina in exile, and when he returned to Guatemala to announce his candidacy on September 3, 1944, he was received with immense jubilation. His victory over General Federico Ponce Vaides was devastating, with 85 percent of the electorate voting in his favor.

Jacobo Árbenz, an enthusiastic supporter of Arévalo's candidacy, became his minister of defense, rising to the rank of major. He played a decisive role in keeping Arévalo in power for four years and enabling him to carry through the political and social reforms he had proposed. It's said he had to face down some thirty attempted coups, and that it was thanks largely to Árbenz's energy and his influence over his fellow soldiers that they were contained in time or defeated through military action. Some of these were overseen by an obscure officer with the nickname Hatchet Face, Lieutenant Colonel Carlos Castillo Armas, a man of the same age as Árbenz, whom the latter recalled, if only slightly, as a nebulous figure who passed through the

Military Academy without distinction. Despite his insignificance, this tenacious adversary would later become his mortal foe.

How many minutes had passed since he'd shut himself up in his office at the Palace? At least ten, and the glass of whiskey was still quivering slowly in his hands. He was soaked through with sweat. He felt remorseful and disgusted, as he always did before and after drinking, though he hadn't taken a single sip and suspected he wasn't going to do so.

Predictably, María Cristina Vilanova continued to collaborate closely with her husband during his years as Arévalo's minister of defense. She wasn't just there to be looked at, though tradition and law had assigned this role to the wives of presidents and ministers up to then. She was her husband's chief confidante and, according to Árbenz himself and many of those they kept company with, her opinions were always listened to and often prevailed over those of other advisers.

During Arévalo's time in office, a rivalry arose between Jacobo Árbenz and Colonel Francisco Javier Arana, head of the armed forces, who aspired to take over as president. An intelligent, affable man of the people—he had been a common foot soldier and rose to become an officer without passing through the Military Academy—Arana played a decisive role in toppling the dictator Ubico. In return, he had received a promise from the two parties affiliated with the Árbenz government—the Popular Liberation Front and the National Renovation, which would later merge into the PAR—that they would support his presidential candidacy in the 1950 elections. After Juan José Arévalo became head of state, Arana worked to mitigate certain social reforms and impose a measure of prudence on the democratic regime's economic policies, weakening those measures that generated controversy. According to rumors put out by his opponents and denied by those close to him, Colonel Arana began to conspire against the government, preparing a coup d'état which, while not replacing Juan José Arévalo, would turn him into a figurehead without any power to speak of. Soldiers loyal to the government revealed that Arana was assigning key posts to his allies, among them Hatchet Face, chief of the Fourth Military Zone. In a meeting of the Council of Ministers, with the president of the congress, writer Mario Monteforte Toledo, in attendance, the decision was taken to arrest him.

On July 18, 1949, Colonel Arana arrived at the National Palace and requested that President Juan José Arévalo hand over a shipment of weapons that the Caribbean Legion—a group of volunteers who had brought José Figueres to power in Costa Rica and was attempting fruitlessly to invade Trujillo's Dominican Republic—had returned to the Arévalo government, weapons that had yet to be placed at the armed forces' disposal. Those in the press hostile to the government spread rumors that Arévalo was planning to distribute these weapons to so-called popular militias. The president informed Arana that the shipment lay in a government building known as El Morlón, which had once been Ubico's weekend residence and was now the army's Officers' Club. It was near Lake Amatitlán, some twenty miles from Guatemala City. Colonel Arana departed from the Palace in the company of the chief of staff, whom Arévalo had instructed to deliver the cache into the army's hands. Behind him was a group of policemen and soldiers with Major Enrique Blanco of the Civil Guard at the head, with orders to arrest Colonel Arana as he returned from the handover.

The army leader was ambushed at Puente de la Gloria, a small bridge crossing the Michatoya River. There was a firefight between the two groups, and Arana and Major Blanco were both killed. The political opposition would blame the former's death on Colonel Árbenz, who had allegedly observed the whole scene through binoculars high up on the lookout at the Parque de las Naciones Unidas. Even today, historians still argue about what actually took place, and it remains one of those mysteries that permeate the history of Guatemalan politics. Whether intentional or accidental, Blanco's death would cast a disgraceful shadow on Colonel Árbenz's public life, with his adversaries accusing him of planning the assassination to eliminate an inconvenient rival. It was also the chief pretext employed by Colonel Castillo Armas, who viewed himself as Arana's disciple, to renew his insurgency against Arévalo's government, which he claimed was serving a secret communist agenda.

At any rate, on the evening of July 18, 1949—the very day of Arana's death—there was a military uprising that shook Arévalo's government and, for a few hours, came close to toppling it. The Honor Guard regiment, the air force, and the Fourth Zone under the leadership of Colonel Castillo Armas mobilized against the main government offices. Other military divisions and bases remained loyal to the minister of defense, Jacobo Árbenz, who led the resistance against the mutiny. There were shoot-outs and deaths, and for several nights, the outcome was uncertain. Carlos Manuel Pellecer, head of the cultural outreach missions under Arévalo, organized civilian groups that helped the soldiers push back the revolt of Arana's forces, which were led by Mario Méndez Montenegro. At dawn, the rebel forces yielded, their commanders took shelter in foreign embassies, and the coup was defeated.

When all this was over, Árbenz shut himself away to drink alone, at this same desk, just like right now. He remembered how exhausted he was: he took one shot after another until he felt that tingle in his head. A tingle more intense than usual, and then he started heaving and had to run to the bathroom to vomit. Now he had brought the glass to his lips and wetted them, but without drinking a drop. He felt a profound self-loathing.

During the years of the Arévalo government, Árbenz forged a close relationship with the barrister José Manuel Fortuny, leader of the Revolutionary Action Party that would hand him the presidency. Since his student days, Fortuny had worked doggedly to depose Ubico. He would become one of Árbenz's closest advisers. By then, Fortuny had distanced himself from the PAR and was focusing his energies on the Guatemalan Party of Labor. It never amounted to much, and it was never proven that it received financing from or was otherwise aided by the Soviet Union, but the implication was pervasive in the national and foreign press and was taken as evidence of Árbenz's communist leanings (the existence of which was never proven). In his memoirs, dictated years afterward, Fortuny states that the leaders of the Guatemalan Party of Labor, himself included, had little knowledge of Marxism at the time. Árbenz and Fortuny, despite their occasional disagreements over policy, would collaborate during the former's presidency, above all on Decree 900, the Agrarian Reform Law. Fortuny recalls that he wrote all of Árbenz's speeches, including his resignation, though this last assertion is debatable. There were suggestions that the president had taken on Carlos Manuel Pellecer and Víctor Manuel Gutiérrez as governmental advisers: two men whose efforts at organizing the workers and field hands into unions and federations had given them a reputation as revolutionaries.

When Juan José Arévalo's administration ended in 1950, the parties and organizations that had backed his government supported Jacobo Árbenz as his successor. His election was a resounding victory, with 65 percent of the votes in a field of nine candidates. His program rested on five pillars: a highway to the Atlantic, a Caribbean seaport in Santo Tomás de Castilla, the Jurún-Marinalá hydroelectric plant, a refinery for imported crude oil, and, first and foremost, agrarian reform.

It was March 15, 1951, and Árbenz still held the glass of whiskey in his hand. Outside, in Constitution Plaza, thousands of Guatemalans had gone on celebrating his victory. He wasn't going to disappoint them. He got up, walked to the bathroom, threw the whiskey in the toilet, and flushed. As long as he was Guatemala's head of state, he decided, he wouldn't touch another drop of alcohol. He kept this promise stringently until the day of his resignation.

IV

W HAT I DON'T GET IS YOUR STUBBORNNESS," Enrique
said. "Wanting to get the woman out of all this and cart
her off to San Salvador. What's the point?"

Not a single noise was audible from the street: either no cars were
passing or the boleros were drowning out the motors and horns.

"I've got my reasons," the Dominican replied curtly. "You need to
respect them."

"I respect them but I don't understand them, and still, I've done
everything you've asked," Enrique reminded him. "I took away her
guards, they'll be gone tonight after seven. But listen. It would be
good for her to get caught up in all this, too, to sow a bit more confusion. Anyway, don't fool yourself: Guatemalan society has taken sides
in this little civil war over the president and his lover, they're all with
Palomo, not with the other one. We're very Catholic here. It's not like
in your country, where Trujillo can drag anyone he wants into bed
without consequences."

They were both chain-smoking, and the ashtray in front of them
was full of spent butts. A cloud of smoke floated over their heads.

"I'm perfectly aware of that," the Dominican said. "People here, especially the upright married women, don't like their president to have lovers. Maybe that's why Guatemalans are so bad in the sack?"

"Stop with the drivel and answer me. Why do you want to take her?" Enrique pressed him. "It's better for us if she's mixed up in this, it will make things more chaotic when word gets out. Don't forget, you're leaving afterward, but I have to stay. And I need to take precautions."

They had drunk two glasses each of rum, and the brothel was still empty and forlorn. Miriam, the madam with the immense head of platinum hair, had vanished, and a circumspect Indian was sweeping the scattered sawdust from the floor, gathering it in his hands, and dumping it into a plastic bag. He was a small, rickety creature, and he hadn't once turned to look at them. He was barefoot, and his cotton shirt, torn and mended in places, revealed patches of dark skin inside. The owner had put on a stack of records, a collection of boleros sung by Leo Marini.

"The plan's all set, there's no need for you to go complicating things. You know perfectly well how up in arms people will be as soon as the news gets out," the Dominican said. "Why are you so set on getting that poor girl wrapped up in it to boot?"

"Poor girl?" Enrique said with an abrupt laugh. "You're badly deceived. She's a snake, a witch if you've ever seen one, with that innocent face of hers. No matter what she looks like, there's nothing she's incapable of. Otherwise she would never have gotten to where she is."

"You won't change my mind," the Dominican said. "No point in trying. A plan is a plan. We have to do as we agreed. Don't forget, there are lots of people involved in this."

"It would make things way easier for me, my friend," the other went on as if he hadn't even heard. "This is very serious business, and that means it's essential that there be the maximum degree of confusion when they start looking for the guilty parties. We need to throw out all kinds of clues that lead nowhere. To distract people. Think it over."

"I've thought it over, and I'm afraid I can't help you here," the Dominican said. "No is no, my friend."

"May I know why?"

"You may," the Dominican said, irritated, after a moment. He paused, gathered his energies, and let loose: "Because I've wanted a piece of that gash for a long, long time. Since the first day I saw her. Is that reason enough for you, or do you need more?"

Instead of answering, Enrique, who had listened to him with a surprised expression, laughed again. When he was done, he said:

"Honestly, I didn't see that coming." He shrugged his shoulders and affirmed, by way of conclusion: "Vices are one thing, duty's another. You know it's not good mixing business with pleasure."

V

C OLONEL CASTILLO ARMAS, Hatchet Face to those close to him, found out the mercenaries from the Army of Liberation had started arriving in Tegucigalpa from all the hell they were raising in the city's bars, whorehouses, gambling dens, and taprooms. The press and radio in the Honduran capital were filled with tales of the disgraceful behavior of those Cubans, Salvadorans, Guatemalans, Nicaraguans, and Colombians, even a few "Hispanics" from the United States. It was a poor endorsement of the forces proposing to save Guatemala from the clutches of Jacobo Árbenz's communist regime. When Howard Hunt, his contact in Florida, upbraided him for these headaches, Castillo Armas asked to go to Miami to speak in person with those members of the CIA who had contracted these so-called soldiers without looking deeply into their backgrounds; but Hunt, ever evasive and mysterious, told him it wasn't convenient for him to be seen around those parts. The general relieved his ill humor by lambasting anyone who came across his path in that house in the suburbs of the Honduran capital that served as his headquarters. He had always had a nasty disposition. From a young age, when his classmates at the Military

Academy had nicknamed him Caca, making creative use of his initials, he'd had the habit of secretly devising baroque, overwrought, generally insulting sobriquets for the people who sent him into tantrums. For these uproarious mercenaries he chose the name "fleabags." Right away, he instructed the handful of Guatemalan soldiers who had deserted on his behalf to fine those guilty for disorder, and, if their infractions were grave enough, their contracts were to be canceled. But since it was their Stepmother—the CIA—who paid the Army of Liberation's salaries, his orders had little effect.

It was an outright scandal that such a thing was only happening now, after Eisenhower had taken office in 1953 and the United States had finally resolved to set aside political intrigues and to remove Árbenz by force, as Hatchet Face had been urging. With Truman in power, it had been impossible to convince the gringos that military action alone—action of the kind that the CIA had undertaken in Iran not long before, to liquidate Prime Minister Mohammad Mossadegh's regime—would put an end to the communists' growing influence in Guatemala. But at last, thanks largely to the new Secretary of State, John Foster Dulles, and his brother, the new CIA head, Allen Dulles, both former representatives of United Fruit, the North Americans had decided to give the armed invasion the support Castillo Armas had sought ever since he'd escaped from the dank, decrepit Central Penitentiary of Guatemala into exile in Honduras. The Stepmother, the CIA, had backed Operation PBSuccess, as they dubbed it, from the beginning, and they were the ones who entrusted Hunt and others to support it on the ground. In the early days of the Army of Liberation, when they were still gathering troops, the mercenaries' scandals in Honduras were a provocation to President Juan Manuel Gálvez (the Sleaze), who had been hesitant to support the planned coup; he only ceded in the face of great pressure from the American government and United Fruit, which was even more powerful in Honduras than in Guatemala. Castillo Armas was certain this would suffice for the gringos to come to an agreement at last with President Anastasio Somoza to begin training the mercenaries on Nicaraguan territory. So why the hell were the negotiations taking so long? He had spoken with Somoza and was certain the general was fully behind the invasion.

It's the gringos who are slowing everything down, he thought. From his office he could see a landscape dotted with trees and pastureland, the outline of one of those dun hills that surrounded Tegucigalpa, and farther off, peasants in straw hats bending over their crop rows. He couldn't complain about the house United Fruit had set him up in, or the workers or the cook they paid for, they took care of the upkeep as well, even his driver and the gardener. It was good the gringos had finally decided to act, but they shouldn't try and do everything themselves, pushing him aside—not when he'd risked his life bringing to light the communists' infiltration into Guatemala from the time of Colonel Francisco Javier Arana's assassination through the three years of Árbenz's administration. He had complained to the management at United Fruit, but they tried to convince him that the best thing was to keep his distance from the Americans, so the journalists on Árbenz's side wouldn't accuse him of being a mere tool of the Stepmother. He didn't buy it: being kept out of the major decisions made him feel like a patsy of Washington and the CIA. *Sons of bitches!* he thought. *Puritan scum!* He closed his eyes, sucked in a deep breath, and tried to calm his ill mood, remembering that soon he would depose (and maybe even kill) Jacobo Árbenz (the Mute). He'd hated him since they were cadets at the Politécnica. Back then, it was for personal reasons: Árbenz was white, handsome, and successful, whereas Castillo Armas was poor, a bastard, his Indian features a sign of his humble origins. Then Árbenz had married María Vilanova, a beautiful, rich Salvadoran, while his own wife, Odilia Palomo, was a homely teacher as destitute as he. But it was their political differences that were fundamental.

It enraged him that he couldn't communicate with the CIA or its intermediary, Howard Hunt, who disappeared for long stretches—Castillo Armas hadn't heard from him for months—without giving the least indication of where he'd gone; he couldn't even reach the people from the State Department in charge of preparing the invasion. He felt humiliated, degraded, ignored in matters crucial to his country. For a long time, before Howard Hunt came on the scene, his only contact was Kevin L. Smith, the director of United Fruit in Honduras. Smith was the one to tell him *they* had finally settled on him to lead the Army of Liberation. The very same Smith took him to Florida in his private plane, to the former Naval Reserve base at Opa-Locka, eleven miles north of Miami, where he would oversee Operation PBSuccess. There he met Colonel Frank Wisner, the CIA's Deputy Director of Plans, hired by Allen Dulles to supervise the project of overthrowing Árbenz. He was, as Castillo Armas understood things, Howard Hunt's immediate superior. Wisner told him he had been chosen over General Miguel Ydígoras Fuentes (the Toady) and the lawyer and coffee grower Juan Córdova Cerna, and it was he who would take the lead in liberating Guatemala. What he didn't tell him was the words Howard Hunt had used to defend his candidacy: "Mister Caca looks a bit Indian, and don't forget, the vast majority of Guatemalans are Indians. They'll love him!"

His euphoria at his appointment was brief, quickly overshadowed by the infinite precautions the gringos took before every step. Their hope was to keep up appearances so the UN couldn't accuse the United States of being the true agents (and above all, financiers) of the future war of liberation in Latin America's first communist republic beholden to Moscow. As if you could just cover it up! For Castillo Armas, the gringos' scruples were all a product of their religious puritanism. He told his men this often, in every meeting where they gathered in his office: "The gringos' puritanism makes them dawdle, and when they finally do take action, they move at a snail's pace." He didn't really know what he meant by that, but he felt proud of himself for saying it, and he considered it a weighty, philosophical insult.

In contrast, his gratitude toward the president of Nicaragua, Anastasio Somoza, was without limits. Somoza was a real ally, generous and aware of everything that was at stake. He had allowed the soldiers of the Army of Liberation to train in his country—he even offered El Tamarindo, one of his haciendas, and Momotombito Island for the purpose—and he'd authorized the CIA to take off from Nicaraguan airports to throw leaflets over Guatemala's cities and bomb strategic targets once the operations had begun. He'd let the military campaign run its command center out of Managua. The CIA had already placed its airmen there, along with the North American soldiers who would dictate the invasion's strategy. Somoza had named his son Tachito liaison between his government and the American administrators who would map out battles and acts of sabotage. Trujillo (the Spider) was a different matter. He'd been generous with his armaments and his money, but Castillo Armas didn't trust him. The powerful and vain Dominican caudillo made him nervous, even afraid. His nose told him if he depended too heavily on Trujillo in his struggle for liberation—he had already received sixty thousand dollars from him in person, apart from two more consignments of cash and arms through intermediaries—he would have to pay a high price in return once in power. The only time the two men had spoken, in Ciudad Trujillo, he'd been repelled by the man's smarmy way of eliciting recompense once victory had been achieved. Moreover, he was aware that the Generalísimo's preferred candidate to decide the destiny of a future Guatemala was his friend and confidant General Miguel Ydígoras Fuentes.

Everything was well underway, but Hatchet Face remained more or less in the dark. He had the unpleasant feeling that the gringos were hiding their intentions *ex professo*, because they didn't trust him or quite simply didn't respect him. Frank Wisner had even upbraided him for exaggerating the number of volunteers he'd recruited for the Army of Liberation in Guatemala: he promised five hundred and had delivered just shy of half that. This was how the CIA began recruiting fleabags from assorted Latin American countries: the men now causing so much disorder in Tegucigalpa. The best thing would be to cart them all off to Nueva Ocotepeque until they could begin their training in Nicaragua. He called Colonel Brodfrost of the U.S. Army, Frank Wisner's second-in-command and his new contact in Managua, who assured him that they would start training at the hacienda and on the island that upcoming Monday, and that he would begin the transfer of soldiers from the Army of Liberation to Nicaragua that very afternoon. The CIA had sent Howard Hunt to another country on a new mission, and he wouldn't see him around there anymore, he said.

And to save Wisner further inconvenience, Brodfrost told Castillo Armas he would be his sole contact from then on.

Another major problem had been Radio Liberación, the underground radio station. The gringos had bought a powerful transmitter that would allow the station to reach every region of Guatemala, even though they were broadcasting from Nueva Ocotepeque, a Honduran city not far from the border. When Castillo Armas tried to name the station director, Brodfrost informed him that the CIA had already chosen one, a gringo by the name of David Atlee Phillips (the Invisible Man). Radio Liberación was meant to coordinate its broadcasts with the Army of Liberation, which Castillo Armas represented, but still, he never managed to speak to Phillips personally. From its very first transmission, on Saturday, May 1, 1954, there were problems. The colonel had asked for the programs to be recorded inside Guatemala, but was told they would be produced instead at the Panama Canal, where the CIA had set up a "logistical center" devoted exclusively to the invasion of Guatemala at France Field, the U.S. military installation. Weapons flowed from there along with the recordings; the tapes were sent directly to Nueva Ocotepeque with the approval of Phillips. The colonel was horrified when he heard the first broadcast: only one of the speakers had a Guatemalan accent; the rest (including one woman) were Nicaraguans and Panamanians, as their cadences and turns of phrase made instantly apparent. Castillo Armas's complaints reached central command, but nothing was done until the fourth or fifth day, by which time many Guatemalans and Árbenz's government knew that Radio Liberación's broadcasts came not from *somewhere deep in the jungles of Guatemala*, but from outside the country, at the behest of interests outside the country. And who could be behind all that except the Americans?

What had functioned well was the campaign on the radio and in the press accusing the Árbenz government of having turned Guatemala into a beachhead of the Soviet Union with plans for taking control of the Panama Canal. That had been the work not of the U.S. government or the CIA, but of United Fruit and its publicity genius, Mr. Edward L. Bernays. Castillo Armas's jaw dropped as he listened to him explain how publicity could change a society's way of thinking or suffuse it with hope or fear. In Guatemala, it had worked perfectly. With United Fruit's money, Bernays had managed to convince North American society and even the government in Washington that Guatemala was already in the grips of communism and that Árbenz was personally pulling the strings. Colonel Castillo Armas felt that things would have gone much better if United Fruit alone had been in charge. But alas!—as Generalísimo Trujillo had told him that time—everything had to pass through the Stepmother and Washington.

All those precautions the CIA and the State Department took to keep the United States free from suspicion of instigating the upcoming invasion were pointless in Castillo Armas's eyes. Árbenz and his minister of foreign affairs, Guillermo Toriello, would level accusations against them at the UN with or without proof. Why waste time with measures that would slow down their plans and allow errors like the one made with Radio Liberación? It took whole days to send the tapes from Panama to Nueva Ocotepeque. Then, unexpectedly, the president of Honduras, Juan Manuel Gálvez, announced the station had been discovered and that they would have to close it down or move it out of the country. The CIA decided to take it to Managua. Not only did Somoza not object, he arranged a location for them. Later, without offering Hatchet Face the least explanation, the CIA decided to move it again, and began sending its clandestine broadcasts from Key West, Florida.

The weapons for the Army of Liberation took a similar meandering trajectory before reaching Honduran territory, where the invasion would begin. They were stockpiled at the U.S. military base in Panama, and from there, the airplanes the CIA had purchased for the Army of Liberation transported them to various points along the Honduran border. The expeditionary forces would begin their march from there. Some of these weapons and explosives were airdropped into Guatemalan frontier villages where—in theory, if less in practice—clandestine sabotage and demolition groups had gathered. There were numerous problems with the Army of Liberation's fleet. Castillo Armas had always imagined these planes would come from the Guatemalan air force, whose men would desert their base in La Aurora to join him. But an exultant Brodfrost told him one day that Allen Dulles had gotten approval from his brother John Foster and perhaps even from President Eisenhower to buy three Douglas C-124Cs on the international market for Operation PBSuccess. They would drop leaflets and acquaint the civilian population with the purpose of the invasion. And once it began, they could take weapons, food, and medicine to the Liberationist forces and bombard the enemy. Just as with all the other preliminaries, the gringos wouldn't let Castillo Armas send a single airman under his command to accompany the buyers, let alone to look for crewmen. The colonel was further displeased to discover that one of the pilots hired to fly the Army of Liberation's planes was an adventurer and psychopath named Jerry Fred DeLarm (the Nutcase). He was good behind the stick, but was known throughout Central America as a smuggler and a blowhard. When he was in his cups, he liked to brag at the top of his lungs about his unlawful jaunts, saying he'd take off and land wherever he damn well pleased, no matter what measures a country took to supervise and protect its airspace.

Mr. Caca wasn't the only one to feel slighted by the gringos' rudeness; the same was true for the small group of Guatemalan officials who had deserted, either from friendship with the colonel or from irritation at Árbenz's reforms, and constituted the rebels' General Staff. His stomach in knots, Castillo Armas told them the *puritan gringos'* prudence was due to the delicate diplomatic situation Washington would find itself in if the United Nations confronted it with conclusive evidence that it had invaded a small country like Guatemala, deposing a government elected by the people. The gringos were bunglers in the best of cases. But they couldn't forget that these "bunglers" were the ones giving them the weapons, the airplanes, and the money that made this invasion possible. Castillo Armas said these things, but even he didn't believe them, and he shared his officers' frustration and skepticism.

And if all this weren't enough, the colonel's headaches multiplied dramatically with the testimony of Rodolfo Mendoza Azurdia, head of the air force, the highest-ranking officer to join the Army of Liberation and the holder of an important post in the Árbenz government. Castillo Armas had gone to receive him in person, embracing him at the airport in Tegucigalpa, aware of the complex machinations Colonel Mendoza—who had been Árbenz's deputy minister of defense until the day before—had employed to escape Guatemala and make common cause with the forces of freedom.

Mendoza Azurdia and Castillo Armas had attended the Military Academy together, but they hadn't been friends. Assigned to different garrisons, they had seen each other little and had pursued their careers separately. Hatchet Face's two prior attempts at subverting the governments of Arévalo and Árbenz had failed to draw Mendoza in. And so he was surprised when this leader of the diminutive Guatemalan air force, whom he'd numbered among Árbenz's allies, sent him an emissary who discreetly informed him that he was considering quitting the government and fleeing Guatemala. Would he be welcome in the ranks of the Liberationists? Castillo Armas responded that they would receive him with open arms. And at the airport in Tegucigalpa, in plain sight of the journalists, he congratulated Mendoza Azurdia for his bravery and his patriotism. The attacks the official press levied against him would be his highest endorsement in the Guatemala of tomorrow.

Castillo Armas's hair stood on end when Colonel Mendoza revealed to him and his general staff the intimate secrets of Árbenz's government. He was getting stabbed in the back, and this time by the person he least expected: the new U.S. ambassador in Guatemala, John Emil Peurifoy, whose confirmation he had celebrated because the CIA had informed him that John Foster Dulles had handpicked him for his hardness. He'd won the nickname the Butcher of Greece for his exemplary work helping the monarchist soldiers crush the communist guerrillas. To make matters worse, after presenting Árbenz with his credentials, Peurifoy had handed him a list of forty communists employed in Guatemala's public administration, demanding they be expelled from their posts and imprisoned or shot. Apparently, this gave rise to a diplomatic uproar. Since that time, Guatemala's leftist press had attacked Ambassador Peurifoy, referring to him as the Viceroy and the Proconsul. No one knew that the leader of the Liberationists had privately taken to calling him the Cowboy.

What most worried Castillo Armas was that, according to Colonel Mendoza, Peurifoy had immediately begun conspiring with officers in the army, inviting them to the U.S. Embassy or meeting them at the Officers' Club, the Equestrian Club, or in private homes. He demanded they undertake an "institutional coup," overthrowing Árbenz or forcing his resignation and imprisoning all the communists who were turning the country into a Soviet satellite—exactly the same thing that had happened in Greece. Mendoza Azurdia told him Ambassador Peurifoy took a dim view of Castillo Armas's planned invasion and thought a civil war could bring bad consequences, because it was far from evident, once military operations were underway, that the Liberationists would triumph. There were many imponderables, he said, and the invasion could easily founder. It was safer, from his perspective, to infiltrate the army and encourage it to pursue a coup on its own. In the most recent meeting between the gringo ambassador and the Guatemalan heads of the military, the latter, with Colonel Carlos Enrique Díaz (the Dagger) as their spokesman, told him that in principle they accepted the idea of an institutional coup, but with two conditions: first, that Castillo Armas surrender and bring his military projects to an end, and second, that he occupy no post in the government that would come after Árbenz. Ambassador Peurifoy seemed to be in agreement, and he sent extensive telegrams in code to Mr. Allen Dulles and the Secretary of State John Foster Dulles seeking their approval of his strategy. Carlos Castillo Armas felt the thing he had been building up scrupulously for all these years now crumbling to pieces. He'd end up a fifth wheel if the ambassador got his way. That was when he started hating the Cowboy almost as much as the Mute.

These discoveries had made him anxious, but the CIA, in the form of Colonel Brodfrost, soon lifted his spirits: the invasion would cross the Guatemalan border and initiate military actions against Árbenz at dawn on June 18, 1954.

VI

EVERYONE SPILLS IN THE END," the Dominican said. "If the thing tonight goes south and they catch us, you and me will end up singing like canaries."

"I won't," Enrique said firmly, smacking his hand softly on the bar. "Know why? Because it wouldn't do any good. They'll kill us either way. In a case like that, it's best just to deny everything or keep your mouth shut till the end. Lesser of two evils, you know."

"I don't have the experience you have," the Dominican said after a pause. "But still, when I was in Mexico doing those police classes I told you about, they gave me a book. What do you think it was called?"

Enrique turned and looked at him without a word.

"*Chinese Tortures*," the Dominican said. "The Chinese are famous as merchants and for building the Great Wall. But what they've really got a knack for is torture. No one's invented as many tortures or ones as terrible as they have. When I was saying everyone spills in the end, that book about the Chinese is what I had in mind."

Leo Marini's boleros had come to an end, and the Indian had

disappeared, without looking at them even once, after sweeping the sawdust off Miriam the Gringa's brothel floor. The two of them had the run of the place. With the music gone, you could hear a car pass now and again in the distance. It had probably started raining, the Dominican thought. He didn't like the rain, but he did like the rainbows that filled the Guatemala sky with colors when the showers were over.

"Cheers," Enrique said. "To the Chinese."

"Cheers," the Dominican said. "To tortures that get you to talk."

They took a sip of rum, and Enrique recalled:

"I've seen people who could stand the worst torture. People who'd rather die than give names or addresses or implicate their companions. Some of them went crazy first, it's true. So when I tell you what I'm telling you, it's because I know about it firsthand."

"It's not that I don't believe you," the Dominican responded. "I'm just telling you, if you'd had my *Chinese Tortures* book with you, those tight-lipped heroes would have talked, they would have told you everything they knew and even some things they didn't know."

"You never change, do you?" Enrique said, laughing. "Always the same thing: torture, women whose gash you licked or want to lick, and the Rosicrucians, whatever they are. You know what you are? An obsessive. Not to say a pervert."

"Could well be," the Dominican agreed, shrugging. "You want to know something? Times when I've had to make a guy talk, using force, I like to sing. Or recite poetry, Amado Nervo, my mom loved him. I don't usually go in for that kind of thing. Singing, reciting. The mood never strikes me. Only when I've got to hurt someone and make him talk. That *Chinese Tortures* book kept me under a spell for I don't know how long. I read it and reread it, I dreamed about it, I can remember the illustrations to a T. I could draw them out right now. That's why I can promise you that none of those heroes would have stayed mum if you'd had my copy of *Chinese Tortures* on you."

"I'll ask to borrow it next time," Enrique said. He smiled and looked at his watch. Then he continued: "If you want time to stop, all you've got to do is look at your watch."

"Have another drink and don't look at your watch," the Dominican said, grabbing his glass and raising it. "We've still got a good stretch ahead of us."

"To Chinese tortures," Enrique said glumly, lifting his in turn, keeping his eyes on his watch.

VII

GENERALÍSIMO TRUJILLO LOOKED AT HIS WATCH: four minutes to 6:00 a.m. Johnny Abbes García would be there at six on the dot, the hour the two of them had agreed on. He'd probably been sitting in the anteroom for some time now. Should he have him shown in? No, better to wait until six exactly. Generalísimo Rafael Leonidas Trujillo was a maniac, not just for punctuality, but also for symmetry: six meant six, not four till six.

Had he been right to foot the bill for that myopic, big-bellied journalist, with his flabby build and his camel's gait, so he could attend those peculiar courses in police science in Mexico? He found out a thing or two beforehand: that his father was an upstanding accountant and he a slightly bohemian two-bit reporter covering horses; he had a little program about equestrian sports on the radio; he hung around with scribblers and poetasters, artists and free spirits (anti-Trujillo types, probably) at the Gómez pharmacy on Calle El Conde in colonial Ciudad Trujillo. He'd been heard to boast of being a Rosicrucian. People had seen him once or twice at the whorehouses, asking the girls for a discount on his preferred aberrations, and on race days he showed up bright and early at the Perla Antillana hippodrome. When the Generalísimo received a letter from him asking for assistance to travel to Mexico to attend courses in police science, he had a premonition. He gave him an appointment, saw him, listened to him, and decided right away to help him, with the vague sense that this pudgy mass of human ugliness concealed something, someone, he could take advantage of. He was right. At the same time that he was passing him a monthly stipend so he could eat, sleep, and go to class, he asked him for reports on Dominican exiles in Mexico. Abbes García performed meticulously, finding out what they did, where they met, and how dangerous each of them might be. He made friends with them, even got drunk with them, all the better to betray them. He even found a couple of Cubans on the lam—Carlos Gacel Castro, who liked to introduce himself with the line "Greetings from the ugliest man in the world," and Ricardo Bonachea León—willing to lend a hand when the Generalísimo decided that the truly dangerous elements would best have an accident or perish in a supposed holdup. Abbes García, Gacel, and Bonachea worked together impeccably, giving orders and determining the best places and times to fake a hit-and-run or quite simply liquidating a threatening exile in an ambush. But what the Generalísimo would ask of the ex-journalist this time was something more delicate. Would he be up to it?

Though he was only thinking indirectly of Colonel Carlos Castillo Armas, president of Guatemala, still, it was enough to make his blood boil and froth bubble from his mouth. This had happened to him since his youth: rage made the saliva build up, and he'd have to spit. But since there was nowhere to do it here, he swallowed. *I need to get myself a spittoon*, he thought. He'd proposed celebrating the Liberationists' victory with Castillo Armas in Guatemala's National Stadium, which ex-president Juan José Arévalo had built at the so-called Olympic City. The poor idiot refused, arguing *the times aren't right for that kind of spectacle*. He'd even sent his minister of foreign affairs, Skinner-Klee, and his chief of protocol to explain why such an event was unbecoming. Trujillo didn't let them speak, and gave them twenty-four hours to leave the Dominican Republic. The mere memory of that ungrateful nitwit Castillo Armas turned the Generalísimo's stomach.

"Good day, Your Excellency," the scrawny colonel said, standing at attention, clicking his heels, and raising his hand to his forehead in a salute, even though he was out of uniform. It was obvious that the new arrival felt out of place.

"Good day, Colonel," the Generalísimo said, shaking his hand, then pointing toward an armchair. "Have a seat, we'll talk better here. First of all, welcome to the Dominican Republic."

He'd made a mistake with the good-for-nothing Castillo Armas, the Generalísimo had no doubt about it. That bony, consumptive-looking colonel with the Hitler mustache and sheared skull hadn't done even one of the three things asked of him, but snubbing Trujillo's proposals wasn't enough—now he was talking bad about his family. The psychiatrist Gilberto Morillo Soto, Dominican ambassador in Guatemala, had written in a detailed and explicit report: "President Castillo Armas, besotted after several drinks, dared to entertain the audience at the expense of your son, General Ramfis, inciting laughter with the following words, which I quote literally (I beg Your Excellency's pardon for these crudities): *What's impressive about fucking Zsa Zsa Gabor or Kim Novak if first you've got to give them a Cadillac, a diamond bracelet, or a mink coat? Anybody can be that kind of playboy!* Instead of departing in outrage, I remained behind to see if he would continue mocking your esteemed family. And indeed, Your Excellency, he did, and went on doing so for the rest of the evening."

The Generalísimo felt one of those jabs of rage that struck him every time he found out someone had spoken ill of his children, his siblings, or his wife—not to mention his mother. The family was sacred to him; whoever slighted them had to pay. *And you'll pay, you bastard*, he thought. *And General Miguel Ydígoras Fuentes will be where you're sitting.*

"I'm here to ask for Your Excellency's help," Colonel Castillo Armas said in a thin, quavering voice. He was gaunt, haggard, tall, a bit hunchbacked, the very antithesis of military bearing. "I've got the men and the support of the United States and the Guatemalan exiles.

All the army needs to join the cause of liberation is for me to make my move."

"Don't forget the support of United Fruit and Somoza, they count for something, too," the Generalísimo reminded him with a smile. "So what do you need me for?"

"Because your endorsement is the one that matters most to the CIA and the State Department, Your Excellency," the colonel replied, hurried and unctuous. "They told me that themselves: 'Go see Trujillo. He's the number one anticommunist in Latin America. If he's on board, we're on board, too.'"

"Yes, they've asked me several times." The Generalísimo smiled and nodded. But then his mien turned serious once more. "Obviously I'll help. The communist Árbenz has to go as soon as possible. The best thing would have been to get rid of his predecessor, Arévalo, he was another communist, not to mention a know-it-all. I warned the gringos, but they didn't listen. They're naive, sometimes even obtuse, but what can you do, we need them. I suppose they've come to regret it."

Now it was six on the dot, and just then, knuckles rapped respectfully on his office door. A gray head of hair and a servile smile, belonging to Cristósomo, one of his assistants, leaned in.

"Abbes García?" the Generalísimo said. "Show him in, Cristósomo."

A moment later, the man entered, with that extraordinary disjointed gait of his, as if he were crumbling apart with each step. He wore a checked jacket, a slightly ridiculous red tie, and brown shoes. Someone would have to teach this fool to dress better.

"Good day, Your Excellency."

"Take a seat," the Generalísimo ordered him, getting straight to the matter at hand. "I called you because I'm going to entrust you with a very important task."

"At your service, Your Excellency, same as always." There was a kind of dissolute perfection in Abbes García's voice—did it have something to do with his days as a radio announcer? Most likely yes. That was something else the Generalísimo knew about him, that he'd been an announcer and a current events analyst on some third-rate radio station. Was he really a Rosicrucian? Apparently that reddish handkerchief he was blowing his nose into just then was a symbol of that religion.

"Everything is coming together quickly, Your Excellency," Colonel Castillo Armas said. "All we need are instructions from Washington to get underway. I've recruited most of the men we need. We'll train at one of President Somoza's haciendas in Nicaragua, and also on an island there. And in Honduras. We wanted to expand to El Salvador, but President Óscar Osorio has scruples and still hasn't given us his authorization. The gringos are putting pressure on him, though. What we need is a bit of cash. Those puritan gringos are a little tightfisted."

He laughed, and Trujillo noticed he did so without making noise, wrinkling his lips and showing his teeth. A mirthful glow illuminated his rat's eyes.

"It's that son of a bitch Castillo Armas," Trujillo said, his eyes turning glacial as they did when he spoke of his enemies. "Thanks to me he's been more than two years in power, and he hasn't kept a single one of his promises."

"You say the word and I'll obey, Your Excellency," Abbes García said, bowing his head. "Whatever needs to be done will be done. I promise you that."

"You're going to Guatemala, as a military attaché," Trujillo said, looking him in the eyes.

"A military attaché?" Abbes García said, surprised. "I'm not a soldier, Your Excellency."

"You are though, you have been since the beginning of the year," Trujillo said. "I drafted you into the army with the rank of Lieutenant Colonel. There are your papers. Morillo Soto, our ambassador there, has already been informed. He's waiting for you."

He watched Abbes García's stare as it transformed from one of surprise to pleasure, satisfaction, astonishment. For God's sake, the poor bastard had on blue socks. Was that a Rosicrucian thing, too? Apparel mixing every color of the rainbow?

"You'll have all the necessary weapons," Trujillo told the

Guatemalan, as if it were no great concern. "And all the cash you need, too. Since I had an inkling of what you were after, I have here a little advance payment, sixty thousand dollars, in this bag. Let me give you a piece of advice, Colonel."

"Yes, of course. I'm listening, Your Excellency."

"Stop chasing grudges with General Ydígoras Fuentes. You two need to understand each other. You're on the same side, don't forget it."

"I'm speechless, Your Excellency," Colonel Castillo Armas murmured, amazed everything had turned out so easy. He'd thought he'd have to sugarcoat things with Trujillo, negotiate, haggle, beg. Then and there, he pinned him with the moniker the Spider. "I know you two are friends. The problem is that General Ydígoras doesn't always play by the rules with me. But we'll come to an understanding sooner or later, I assure you of that."

The Generalísimo smiled, satisfied he'd made an impression on the soldier from Guatemala.

"I'm only going to ask three things of you, once you're in power," he added, observing how slovenly the Colonel looked in his civvies.

"Consider them done, Your Excellency," Castillo Armas interrupted him. He had begun gesticulating, as if speaking at a rally. "In the name of Guatemala and our Liberationist crusade, I thank you for your generosity with all my heart."

"As soon as I leave here, I'll pack my bags, Your Excellency," Abbes García said. "I've been in Guatemala before, I know a few people there. Carlos Gacel, the Cuban guy who helped us out so much in Mexico, among others. Remember?"

"Try to get to the president, take him my greetings. Ideally you'll manage to become friends with Castillo Armas. The best way to do so is through his wife—or better still, his mistress," the Generalísimo said. "I have the reports Morillo sends me. I don't know if he's any good as a diplomat, but he's a first-class informant. Apparently the president has gotten his hands on a rather young lover, a certain Marta Borrero. Pretty, they say, and bold. It seems Martita has caused strife among his supporters. A civil war, almost, between the followers of the first lady, Odilia Palomo, and those of the inamorata,

Miss Guatemala. That's what they call her. Try to reach her. Generally speaking, a lover has more influence than a legitimate spouse."

He laughed, and Johnny Abbes García laughed, too. He had started scribbling in a small notebook, and Trujillo realized that the fingers of the newly minted lieutenant colonel from the Panamanian army were of a piece with his body and face: thick, rounded, and knotty, like those of an old man. And yet he was young, he couldn't be past forty.

"The first thing is to get General Miguel Ángel Ramírez Alcántara behind bars," Trujillo said. "You know him, I assume. He was leader of the Caribbean Legion that tried to invade the Dominican Republic. That was the doing of that bastard Juan José Arévalo. It wasn't enough for him to break off relations with Franco's Spain, Somoza's Nicaragua, Odría's Peru, Pérez Jiménez's Venezuela, and me. No, he wanted to invade us, too. We killed a good number of the intruders, but Ramírez Alcántara got away. And now he's walking free in Guatemala under the protection of President Árbenz."

"Of course, Your Excellency. I know him very well. That will be the first thing I do once I'm in power. Of course. I'll send him back here in wrapping paper."

Trujillo didn't laugh. He'd narrowed his eyes and was looking at something in the emptiness, talking all the while in a sort of monologue:

"He's out there running loose around Guatemala, bragging about his exploits," he repeated in an icy rage. "Especially about trying to overthrow me. He failed, the invasion failed, and we made a lot of that scum pay with their lives. But General Ramírez Alcántara got away, and now it's time for him to pay for what he did. Don't you think?"

"Of course, Your Excellency," Castillo Armas affirmed with a nod. "I know very well who General Ramírez Alcántara is. Consider it done. Don't think twice about it."

"I want him alive," Trujillo interrupted. "No one should touch a hair on his head. Alive and kicking. I'm holding you responsible for his life."

"Of course, Your Excellency. Lovers always do come in handy,"

Abbes García said, his laughter this time a little forced. "I learned that in those police science courses I took in Mexico, the ones you've made so much fun of."

"Safe and sound, just as you say," Castillo Armas added. "So what are Your Excellency's other two conditions?"

"They're not conditions, they're requests," Trujillo clarified, wrinkles appearing between his brows. "Friends don't place conditions on each other. Instead they ask for and perform favors. And you and I are friends, isn't that right, Colonel?"

"Of course, of course," his visitor agreed hastily.

"I asked him to bring me Ramírez Alcántara," Trujillo said with irritation. "And when the Liberationist revolution worked out and they arrested him, I believed he would. But that son of a bitch Castillo Armas dragged things out with this song and dance. And now he's let him go. Him—the leader of the Caribbean Legion. Now he's a loyal follower of the Castillo Armas regime. A dog who tried to take me out! Have you ever in your life heard of such a betrayal?"

"Tell me the other two," Colonel Castillo Armas said with an imploring, almost puling face that the Generalísimo found risible. "They will be the first things I will do, Your Excellency. Anything to please you. My word of honor."

"An official invitation as soon as diplomatic relations between our countries are reestablished," Trujillo said gently. "Don't forget, Arévalo's government was the one to break them. I've never been to Guatemala. I would love to get to know your country. And, if possible, the Order of Quetzal. Somoza already received it, no?"

"There's no need to mention any of this, Your Excellency," Colonel Castillo Armas affirmed. "I would have done all that first thing even without your asking: reestablish the relations the communists broke off, invite you to our country, award you the supreme rank of the Order of Quetzal. How glorious it will be for Guatemala to receive you with the highest honors!"

"He didn't do any of the three," the Generalísimo murmured, clicking his tongue. "When he won, I proposed a big ceremony at the

National Stadium in Guatemala, with him and me together, to celebrate his victory. He dug around for stupid pretexts to refuse."

"He's envious of you, sir," Abbes García decided. "That's the explanation. He's an ingrate and a lowlife, or so it seems to me."

The Generalísimo shot one of those inquisitive looks that always so discomfited those who spoke with him. Once more, he inspected the man from head to toe.

"You'll need to go get some uniforms made," he said finally. "Two right away: one for day-to-day use, and one for parades. I'll give you the address of my tailor, Don Atanasio Cabrera, in Ciudad Colonial. He'll take care of it in a couple of days if you tell him it's urgent. Let him know I sent you and that the Palace will take care of the bill."

"With respect to weapons, Your Excellency," the Guatemalan interjected, "is that something we could talk about now?"

"I'll send you a ship with everything you need," the Generalísimo replied. "Machine guns, rifles, revolvers, grenades, bazookas, heavy artillery. Even people, if you need them. Just let me know a safe harbor in Honduras where they can dock. When you leave, there will already be waiting for you two trusted men from my army, you can present your request for weapons to them."

Colonel Castillo Armas's astonishment didn't flag. His mouth was open, his tiny eyes glimmered with satisfaction and gratitude.

"I'm overwhelmed by your generosity and efficiency, Your Excellency," he purred. "The truth is, I can't find the words to thank you for all you've done for us. For the Guatemalan people, I mean to say."

Trujillo felt contented. The little man was in his pocket.

"And then that traitor Castillo Armas goes and gets drunk and starts running down my family," he exclaimed, furious and tense. "Do you realize? He was a no one, and it's thanks to me and the gringos he's in power. He's let it go to his head. He thinks he can make jokes about me and my family, about Ramfis, to get a laugh? This can't go on."

"It certainly can't, Your Excellency," Abbes García said, rising.

Trujillo smiled, scrutinizing him: no doubt about it, this spanking-new lieutenant colonel in the Dominican army had not the least shadow of military bearing. That was one thing he had in common with Castillo Armas.

"They tell me you're a Rosicrucian," the Generalísimo said. "Is that true?"

"Yes, Your Excellency, it's true," Abbes García said, uncomfortable. "I don't know much about it yet, but the Rosicrucians, well, I like them. Maybe it would be better to say it suits me. It's not so much a religion as a life philosophy. I was initiated into it by a wise man up in Mexico."

"You can tell me about it later, when you've got more time," Trujillo interrupted him, pointing toward the door. "In exchange, I'll teach you a lesson in how to dress a bit less flamboyantly."

"May the Lord bless you and keep you safe, Your Excellency," Colonel Castillo Armas said in leaving, saluting one more time from the office doorway.

VIII

"IT's ALMOST SIX," the Dominican said. "I checked out of the San Francisco Mansion, I've got my bags in the car. Any chance I could wait things out at your place?"

"At my place? Afraid not, my friend," Enrique said with a shake of the head. "It would be reckless. You'd have been wiser to hold on to your hotel room until evening."

"Don't worry about it," the other man said tranquilly. "I'll kill time wandering around downtown—it's the only thing worth looking at in this eyesore of a city. Should we go over the target's agenda one more time?"

"No need," Enrique replied. And yet, closing his eyes, he did so, virtually reciting it: "This morning, the president kept rigorously to his program. He received the United States ambassador and met with a commission of Indians from Petén. He dictated some letters, gave a speech at the Mexican Embassy, and had lunch at the first lady's place. This afternoon, he has a reunion with a group of businessmen to try and encourage them to bring home the money they took overseas under Árbenz and invest it in the country."

"The birthday party of your brother, the defense minister—" the Dominican began.

"It's still underway, and will be keeping the whole cabinet busy, so no need to worry about that," the other man interrupted him. "Everything will turn out perfectly. Unless . . ."

"Unless what?" the other asked, uneasy.

"Unless a miracle occurs," Enrique responded with a strained giggle.

"Ah. Well, fortunately, I don't believe in miracles," the Dominican said with a relieved sigh.

"Me neither," said Enrique. "I was just trying to fuck with you. And calm my nerves a bit. They're on fire, you know."

"Let's get out of here, then."

The Dominican left a few banknotes next to a bottle of rum, which they had nearly drained in the hours they'd spent there. The brothel remained dismal and deserted. Miriam the Gringa hadn't reappeared and was surely still applying her makeup slowly to try and look a bit less depleted for the nighttime, when the place was filled with noise, music, and people.

Once outside—an invisible drizzle was falling, the sky was cloudy, and the thunder was audible farther off over the chain of mountains—they saw two cars waiting for them, each with a chauffeur behind the wheel. The one parked next to that of the ugliest man in the world was also driven by a Cuban. His name was Ricardo Bonachea León. He'd arrived recently from Mexico, where he'd been the Guatemalan's faithful collaborator, and he was already employed by the Guatemalan state security services alongside him.

Enrique and the Dominican nodded to each other by way of goodbye, not bothering to shake hands. Enrique got into the car with the ugliest chauffeur in the world. The Dominican got into the other. He ordered his driver:

"Take a spin downtown, but don't go down the same road twice, Ricardito. I need to be at the door of the cathedral at seven on the dot."

IX

MUCH LATER, during his itinerant exile, when his memory
would turn to the three and a half years—no more—that
he'd been in power, Jacobo Árbenz Guzmán would remember as the most important experience of his time in office those
weeks in April and May of 1952 when he presented his draft of the
Agrarian Reform to the cabinet before sending it to the Congress of
the Republic. He was well aware how important—even essential—it
was for the future of Guatemala, and before it was put into effect,
he wanted it analyzed by supporters and adversaries alike in a public
forum. The press reported on the proceedings in extraordinary detail.
They were held in the National Palace, and people followed them on
the radio in every corner of the country.

It was a subject that stirred friends and enemies alike, and him
more than anyone—no doubt about it. It was the matter where he
had concentrated the most energy, the one he had studied most, the
one he struggled most to make a reality in—to use his words—"a rigorous law, without political bias, perfect, beyond debate." How could
he have imagined that law would lead to the fall of his government

and the deaths of hundreds of Guatemalans, with others imprisoned or expelled from the country while he and his family lived hand-to-mouth in exile ever after!

There were three public debates, each lasting several hours, the third dragging on past midnight. The participants paused briefly at midday for a tortilla or a sandwich and something to drink—but no alcohol—before proceeding with the day's agenda through to the end. Not only were his supporters there, but also many from the other side. The president had been emphatic: "Everyone should come. Starting with the lawyers from United Fruit, the directors of the AGA (the General Association of Agriculturalists), representatives of the landholders, and also, naturally, the National Federation of Farmworkers. Along with them, journalists from the press and the radio, including foreign correspondents." Everyone. He made the same demands of his backers, some of whom—like Víctor Manuel Gutiérrez, secretary general of the Confederation of Workers' and Farmers' Unions—would have preferred to avoid so much controversy concerning the law, fearing the government's enemies would use those debates to dynamite the proposal. Árbenz wouldn't give, though: "We must listen to all opinions, those in favor and those against. Criticism will help us improve."

He practiced self-criticism and rarely sought excuses for his mistakes; to the contrary, if they were pointed out to him, he was happy to rectify them. He was intent on acting in such a way that his own limitations wouldn't affect his actions in the government, but with the benefit of hindsight, he admitted he had done many things wrong. Still, he was proud of his conduct in those debates, the way he defended each of the law's proposals and responded to the various objections. The so-called specialists and technicians wanted to neuter the law, filling it with exceptions, exemptions, and compromises that would have left land ownership in Guatemala in the same state it had been in for centuries. But he didn't allow it. His resolve, sadly, hadn't accomplished much, and had likely exasperated his enemies.

Árbenz was sure the Agrarian Reform would change the very basis of the economic and social situation in Guatemala, building the foundations for a new society where capitalism and democracy would lead to justice and modernity. "This will bring opportunities to all Guatemalans, not simply to the insignificant minority who enjoy them now," he repeated several times in the course of those discussions. His wife, María, was a severe critic of all he said and did, but even she congratulated him. With tears in her eyes, she clutched his arm and said to him, moved: "You did very well, Jacobo." His ministers and his friends in Congress agreed with her unanimously: he'd never looked more eloquent than during those debates. But he didn't convince his foes: afterward, the opposition of the property owners grew more rabid and determined.

As a young man, Árbenz hardly thought about the troubles in his country: the situation of the Indians, the scattering of rich people and the masses of the poor, the marginal, almost vegetative life led by three-fourths of the population, the light-years' distance between indigenous groups and the well-off, the professionals, the farm and company owners, businessmen and merchants. It took him a long time to grasp that only a handful of his compatriots had access to the fruits of civilization and that the social root of the problem would have to be dealt with if the situation was to change, so that all Guatemalans could have a share in what up till then were the privileges of the minority. Agrarian Reform was the key.

He wasn't ashamed to say that he had finally understood what country he was living in—a country very beautiful, with a rich history, but full of terrible injustices—thanks to María Vilanova, the woman whose beauty and elegance had made him fall in love with her the first time he saw her. He would fall even deeper when he found out how sensitive and intelligent the girl with the vivacious eyes, svelte figure, and slender nose really was. Despite coming from a well-off Salvadoran family, she was aware from a very young age of the backwardness of Central America, of the blindfold Árbenz and so many others wore when it came to the social problems of the countries there.

María Vilanova revealed to him, before he'd even made second lieutenant at the Military Academy, all the things he didn't know, shut away as he was in a world of weapons, chants, strategies, codes, local heroes, battles—the same as his classmates, who were thoroughly ignorant of the racial prejudice afflicting their society, which not only ignored but actively despised the millions of Indians on whom civilization had turned its back.

María Vilanova had opened an unknown world to him, one of centuries-old injustices, bigotry, and indifference, but possessed of a hidden strength that could be awakened and mobilized to revolutionize Guatemala, El Salvador, and the whole of Central America. She told him about learning, when she studied in the United States, how far Latin America had been left behind, about the enormous inequalities that divided social classes in its countries, and the few—not to say nonexistent—opportunities the poor had there to escape their condition and receive the kind of education that could help them get ahead in life. That was the big difference between them and a modern democracy like the United States. Thanks to her, Árbenz was able to overcome the watertight prejudices that dictated social conduct and relationships in Guatemala, where whites—or those who thought themselves white—viewed the Indians as no better than animals. And since that time, when he and María were only dating, he tried to get past his ignorance and puncture these commonplaces, studying sociology, political theory, and economics, spending sleepless nights figuring out what could be done to pull his country—and all of Central America—from the depths it was mired in, transforming it so that one day it could be like the democracy of the United States, which had opened María Cristina's eyes and cleansed her of her prejudices.

Already in those early years as an officer in the armed forces, Jacobo Árbenz, like María Cristina and the group of civilians he'd befriended thanks to her, had reached the conclusion that the key to change, the indispensable instrument for beginning the transformation of Guatemalan society, was land reform. They would have to change the feudal structures that reigned in the countryside, where the peasants—the immense majority of Guatemalans—worked for white and mestizo landowners for miserable wages, while the large estate holders lived like colonizers in the days of the encomiendas, enjoying all the benefits of modernity.

But what about United Fruit, La Frutera, the infamous Octopus? It was a gigantic company that had corrupted Guatemala's governments—particularly its dictators—in exchange for exploitative contracts that no modern democracy would find acceptable. They were even exempted from paying tax. Unlike many of his extremist friends, Jacobo Árbenz was convinced the Octopus shouldn't be expelled from Guatemala: to the contrary, La Frutera had to be brought under the yoke of the law, made to pay taxes, respect its workers, allow the formation of unions. They would need to make it into a model, so as to attract other American and European firms that would be essential for the development of the country's industry.

Árbenz would always remember the endless arguments he had with the friends he had made thanks to María Vilanova. They would meet once a week, at least, and sometimes twice, usually on Saturdays at someone's house or at the pension where Jacobo and María resided. They debated, listened to discussions, and commented on books or political news while they ate or had drinks. They were people from various professions—journalists, artists, professors, politicians—of a kind Árbenz had never encountered before. They revealed to him aspects of life in the country he had been ignorant of, social and political problems, the baleful consequences of civil war and dictatorship—the current one, Jorge Ubico Castañeda's, among them—and the ideas of democracy, free elections, an independent, critical press, socialism. He argued with them hair, tooth, and nail, railing against communism and defending capitalist democracy. "Like in the United States," he kept repeating. "That's what we need here."

María had a weakness for impecunious painters, musicians, and poets, people with bohemian tendencies. Árbenz didn't care so much for them. They meant less to him than the journalists and university professors with whom he could discuss politics. Among them, Carlos Manuel Pellecer and José Manuel Fortuny, whom he came to consider friends, if it can be said that Jacobo Árbenz, with his habitual reserve and his obstinate silences, ever managed to have a close friend. He felt an affinity for Fortuny and Pellecer, shared their concerns, enjoyed their frankness, their indifference to material things, maybe even their nonchalance and the disorder they both lived in (*Opposites do attract*, he thought more than once). Árbenz never considered himself a socialist, and he always took an ironic view of Fortuny's attempts to better himself intellectually by reading Marxist thinkers (whose books he could never find in Guatemala, ordering them instead from Mexico and spending on them the salary that barely permitted him to eat) and his commitment to one day founding a communist party in Guatemala. Despite their differences, the truth remained that Fortuny's advice, ideas, and above all his superior grasp of politics were of great use to him when he took power.

He met Fortuny during the October Revolution of 1944. At twenty-five, he was, albeit only slightly, the younger of the two. At the time he was a reporter for *Diario del Aire*, a radio program overseen by the poet Miguel Ángel Asturias, and he had a reputation as a bohemian, intelligent, brave, full of nervous energy. It seems he had entered the Escuela Normal at twelve, but he gave up on the idea of becoming a teacher, and would likewise abandon his studies in the law school of San Carlos University in favor of journalism, which better accorded with his somewhat dissolute nature. He wrote for a number of newspapers and magazines, and his political activism against the Ubico dictatorship brought him problems with the regime, so that, for a time, he was forced to go into exile in neighboring San Salvador. There, he continued working as a journalist.

For his part, Pellecer had been a student of Árbenz at the Military Academy, and was later exiled in Mexico. On his return to Guatemala, he worked to form unions and cooperatives and collaborated intensely with Juan José Arévalo's government, bringing cultural programs to the country's hinterlands. He knew a great deal about the agrarian question and helped Árbenz to grasp it. (Years later, he would become a zealous anticommunist and would even put himself at the service of military dictatorships.)

Hearing these friends talk, Jacobo Árbenz discovered how much he didn't know. Fortuny and Pellecer believed, like him, that land reform was the first, indispensable step to pulling Guatemala out of its morass and turning it into a democratic society. It would bring an end to discrimination and violence. It would fill the back country with schools. Indigenous boys and girls would learn to read, would grow up with running water, electric light, and roads. Thanks to dignified work with decent salaries, they would be better fed and clothed. Was it an impossible dream? No, he told himself at the start of his administration: with work, commitment, and will, it could certainly be done. Two years later, he would start asking himself if he hadn't been overly optimistic.

What Árbenz appreciated in Fortuny was all the things he wasn't: his heterodox, undisciplined spirit, his brilliance, his constant engagement with culture in all its forms, his fleeting enthusiasms for authors, thinkers, films, and singers, his good appetite, his relish as he downed drink after drink. He was like a different self, one not defined by the mania for order, promptness, discipline, and rigor. During their long discussions—particularly when they got heated—María would often intervene to calm them down. They frequently disagreed, especially when Fortuny turned to the subject of socialism and said, if he had to choose between the United States and the Soviet Union, he would prefer the latter. Jacobo and María stood up for the United States. With all its defects, they said, it remained a free, prosperous country, while the Soviet Union was a dictatorship, even if it did take the Allies' side in the war against Hitler and Nazism.

When the October Revolution came and Ubico fell along with Federico Ponce Vaides, the general he had hoped would succeed him, Juan José Arévalo rose to power, and Árbenz became his minister of defense, interrupting his economics studies and with them his thinking about land reform. His post left no time for them. In essence, his responsibility was to keep politics from driving the army apart and to prevent incitement to conspiracy: the eternal story of Central America. He met with his colleagues in the military, visited the barracks, explained to the men the fundamental importance of President Arévalo's measures and reforms, and removed from command any officers who showed signs of insubordination. Even in those years, Fortuny and Pellecer lent him a hand from Congress, where both had been elected as representatives. In private, though time was often short, they continued to exchange ideas. Beyond that, Fortuny wrote speeches for him and advised him on the leading issues of the day. He had assumed leadership of the two parties that supported Arévalo, the Popular Liberation Front and the National Renovation Party, when they decided to merge into the PAR.

That Fortuny was pragmatic and a realist despite his communist inclinations became clear to Árbenz during the fierce polemics unleashed by the Agrarian Reform. Fortuny brought the full weight of his intellect to bear on the matter, combating not only the rabid lawyers of the AGA but also the leftist extremists who intended to collectivize all the country's estates, stripping them from the landowners by force and redistributing them as state-controlled farms as they had done in the Soviet Union. Fortuny agreed with Árbenz that this was insanity, and would provoke immense opposition inside and outside the country's borders, especially in the United States. Nor was it certain to work. He had studied the land reform carried out by President Paz Estensoro in Bolivia, which Árbenz criticized fiercely for its focus on the state rather than on the peasants. More interesting, for Árbenz, was the solution Chiang Kai-shek's government had arrived at in Taiwan, where they had distributed land in small plots, with the same respect for the capitalist system he hoped to spread among the campesinos of Guatemala.

Árbenz never spoke so much as he did in those public debates at the National Palace in April of 1952. Those who knew him intimately and were aware of his habitual reserve, his silences, were stunned to see him defending his project with such palpable vigor, proclaiming that only unproductive fields would be expropriated from the large landholders, with usage rights rather than ownership conveyed to the peasants, to prevent them from selling them back to their former proprietors. In addition to providing the campesinos with land, the state would offer them technical assistance and financing for the acquisition of machinery to increase agricultural output. Owners would be paid for their land in accordance with the value they themselves had assigned it on their tax returns.

Fortuny assisted him greatly in Congress during the debates surrounding the law, which was finally passed, with amendments, on June 17, 1952. That day, there were grand celebrations across the country, but despite his friends' attempts to coax him into raising a glass, Árbenz didn't break his promise not to drink a drop of alcohol so long as he was in power, instead observing the occasion with fruit juice and water.

A complication, unforeseen by Jacobo Árbenz, was the land seizures, the invasions of farms and fields, including properties the law had protected because their owners worked them responsibly. The press was largely in the hands of the opposition, and with *La Hora* and *El Imparcial* at the forefront, they denounced these invasions in scandal-ridden reports, exaggerating the violence they led to and accusing the government (following the North American line) of imitating the principles and even following the orders of the Soviet Union. The affected parties turned to the courts, which often ruled against the government, demanding that they remove the invaders by force and compensate the victims financially. In some cases, the trespasses led to injury and death. Víctor Manuel Gutiérrez, secretary general of the Confederation of Workers' and Farmers' Unions, gave his word to Árbenz that neither he nor anyone in the upper ranks of his organization had encouraged these invasions, but police reports and military intelligence confirmed that the leaders of the peasant syndicates were provoking the Indians into occupying the estates, principally in the most populous regions, where there was little fallow land but a multitude of poor, unemployed campesinos. They had provided them with clubs, spears, even firearms in some cases. The newspapers and radio stations were vociferous in their condemnation, magnifying the events and using them as unequivocal proof of the communist tenor of the Agrarian Reform law, which had already led to violence and could soon produce massacres of landowners and the abolition of private property. Árbenz spoke often on the radio and throughout the country, condemning the land seizures, which he decried as irresponsible and counterproductive; the reforms, he stressed, had to be carried out within the bounds of legality, without harming those who had shown respect for the law, and he affirmed that all who had participated in the incursions would be brought before the court and sentenced by a judge. But things didn't always happen that way, and at times, the best intentions crashed up against more complex realities.

Árbenz would always remember his bewilderment in May 1951, when the opposition gathered a crowd of more than 80,000 to protest the government's decision to replace the Sisters of Charity at the National Home for Orphans with social workers and teachers. Then there were the accusations that the government was imprisoning members of the opposition without a court order and beating and torturing prisoners. When he first heard this, he was outraged. He had given very specific instructions against abuses or any violence whatsoever toward inmates to Major Jaime Rosemberg, chief of the Judicial Police, and Rogelio Cruz Wer, head of the Civil Guard. And yet, eventually, they had occurred, and later, when the threat of an invasion by Castillo Armas with the United States' backing appeared on the horizon, human rights, freedom of expression, and tolerance of criticism weighed less on his conscience than the more important question of his government's survival.

One night, Jacobo and María Vilanova lay in bed, talking in the darkness. Out of nowhere, his wife said, "When a snowball falls from the top of a mountain, it can set off an avalanche."

It was true. At last, the Indians had awakened, but they were impatient, and they wanted all the reforms to take place right now. But was it the Indians, really, the mass of peasants, or was it small groups of agitators from the city inciting the raids? Or was it possible the landowners themselves, in cahoots with La Frutera, were behind them, hoping to later malign the government as extremist?

His friends had congratulated him for the way he'd defended his project in the three public hearings. Even adversaries in the press had recognized his courage and seriousness in responding to his enemies. But *El Imparcial*, *La Hora*, and the rest of the papers went on declaring that the law would be the start of communist revolution in Guatemala.

Perhaps Árbenz's greatest surprise came in those exhilarating days after Decree 900, as it was popularly known, went into force. It had passed through Congress with a few minor amendments. The foreign press attacked it, the United States especially, and accused his government of bowing to the Soviet Union, conspiring to create a communist fifth column in Central America that would threaten the Panama Canal, a strategic center for navigation and free commerce for the entire American continent.

In his shock, he had many unanswered questions: How was this possible? Did his country not have a free press? How could all of them agree in promoting this distortion, this caricature, of what his government was doing? Was American-style democracy not the model for what he was trying to put into practice? Did feudalism exist in the United States? Weren't the spirits of free enterprise, of open competition and private property the very things his Agrarian Reform law wished to promote? He had naively believed the United States would be the greatest advocate for his policy of modernizing Guatemala and pulling it out of the Stone Age.

Convinced that there was nothing to be done, that dispelling the lies was having no effect, that his and his ministers' declarations were pointless, and that the PR campaign launched against him had indelibly shaped reality, Árbenz became worried about a different problem: the army. All that propaganda was meant to help the enemies of the revolution inside the country's borders to turn toward the army, undermining their loyalty to the government so that they would conspire to commit a coup d'état. Would that miserable Hatchet Face lead it? Impossible. No one in the military respected him, he had always been a gray figure, lacking in prestige, incapable of leadership, a crackpot whom the landowners and the Octopus used like a battering ram against his regime. Colonel Carlos Enrique Díaz, head of the armed forces and a trusted friend, assured him that the army remained loyal. But things began to change among his fellow soldiers when a new United States ambassador hit Guatemala like a cyclone, replacing the gentle, well-mannered Mr. Patterson and Rudolf E. Schoenfeld. His name was John Emil Peurifoy and he had come—he said so himself, without the least trace of embarrassment—to put an end to the communist menace that Jacobo Árbenz's government represented for the Americas.

X

A T A QUARTER TO SEVEN, Ricardo Bonachea León left him at
the doorway to the cathedral. It was starting to get dark,
and the streetlamps in Constitution Plaza had just gone on,
casting a pallid glow. There were few people beneath the tall mango,
jacaranda, and palm trees. The bootblacks and food and knickknack
vendors were starting to depart.

It occurred to the Dominican that he'd never been inside Guatemala's cathedral, and since it was open, he decided to use the fifteen
minutes at his disposal to take a look. It was immense and imper-
sonal, bigger but less warm, less welcoming than the one in Ciudad
Trujillo. Its many altars were better lit than Constitution Plaza. In
a side chapel, he saw the replica of the Black Christ of Esquipulas
that Archbishop Mariano Rossell y Arellano had ordered made, since
they'd been unwilling to lend him the original, so he could parade
it through the country as part of the anticommunist crusade against
Árbenz's government. He was a piece of work, this archbishop; not
for nothing had he received the public honors President Castillo Armas had bestowed on him. Had he really named the Black Christ of

Esquipulas general of the National Liberation Movement, dressing it in military uniform for the occasion? Strange things happened in this country.

Few people were worshipping in the cathedral pews. How many shocks had that church withstood? No doubt many: Guatemala was plagued with volcanoes, earthquakes, and tremors. Not long after his arrival there, he remembered he had felt the ground shake on a visit to Antigua, which had been the country's first capital, until an earthquake rendered it unviable. He recalled the sudden feeling of danger as his feet slipped, the ground shifted, and a hoarse, menacing sound emerged from the bowels of the earth. Around him, people went on walking and talking as if nothing were happening. It lasted only a short while, and soon enough he felt the ground go still beneath his toes. He breathed easier. It had been terrifying. He had thought he would relive there the earthquake that had destroyed half of Ciudad Trujillo in 1946, provoking a tidal wave that left 20,000 Dominicans homeless. Would things go off smoothly that night? Yes: their plan was good, everything would work out perfectly. He relaxed. Only much later, when the whole thing was finally over, would he realize his pants were damp, and that he'd pissed himself.

He strolled through all the chapels. At the last of them was a group of people kneeling and praying aloud, their heads lowered, their faces sad. It smelled of incense. Compared with the Dominican Republic, Guatemala certainly was a somber country.

When he returned to the cathedral's doorway, Enrique was already there waiting for him in uniform.

"Good evening, Lieutenant Colonel," he greeted him in jest, bringing his right hand to his peaked cap.

They parked at Constitution Plaza, now deserted, without exchanging a word. The National Palace, ordered built by the dictator Jorge Ubico in one of his worst paroxysms of grandeur, stood there before them, with heavy columns, hundreds of lamps, waterfalls, a mural dedicated to Fray Bartolomé de las Casas. Despite housing virtually every ministry and the security services directorate, much of it remained empty.

"I don't suppose we'll take the front door," the Dominican said, a weak attempt at a joke meant to relieve something of the tension that was overwhelming them.

Walking on, they veered left onto Sixth Avenue, which ran alongside the Palace. A few yards ahead, on the left side of the street, was the Mexican Embassy, a large colonial house now shrouded in darkness. They were both surprised to find neither soldiers nor guards outside the doors. They continued in silence, in almost utter darkness, until they reached the corner, where they turned right, reaching the entrance to the Casa Presidencial, the residence of Castillo Armas, close to the old evangelical church. Enrique stopped there and gestured for the Dominican to hold still. He removed a key from his pocket, and his companion watched as he felt his way along the wall, looking for a small door half concealed by greenish paint. When he found it, Enrique looked for the lock. He had to force it a bit, then the door opened. They entered a garage. Enrique closed the door behind them and locked it. He raised a hand, motioning for the other man to stick close to him.

We're inside now, the Dominican thought. *There's no turning back.* He was jittery, feverish, as he'd been in other extreme situations, and to feel safer, he stroked the grip of the revolver dangling from his belt.

Enrique guided him down solitary, shadowy hallways, and they passed a small courtyard with a single acacia and an adjoining garden. They encountered not a single guard on patrol. So the order had worked. Enrique stopped and stretched out an arm so the Dominican would do the same.

"This must be where our poor little soldier is," he murmured.

The addition of the word "poor" struck the Dominican as in bad taste.

XI

S HE DEPARTED IN SECRET, too quiet for the servants to hear, wrapped in a blanket that covered her and gave her a form- less appearance. Naturally, she took nothing, not even a sewing needle from the house she was fleeing and had sworn she would never return to. She regretted, at least somewhat, abandoning her child, but she'd made her choice and was trying not to think about it. There would be time enough for that later.

It was late. A soft rain was falling, invisible but persistent, and there was no one in the streets of downtown Guatemala City. She knew perfectly where she wanted to go. Only twelve blocks separated the neighborhoods of San Sebastián and San Francisco. She covered them quickly, wrapped in the cape that gave her the look of one of those ghosts that inhabit the night in the folktales of the Guatemalan In- dians. The few passersby she crossed paths with didn't bother her; indeed, those shadows and silhouettes sidestepped her, frightened. Only a stray dog looked her in the face, on the sidewalk, not barking but flashing its teeth.

When she reached the studded door of the colonial mansion, there was no doorbell. She pounded the bronze knocker two, three times, forcefully. It took time, but she was lucky—it was Símula who opened up. She waved her into a foyer full of echoes, with old stone walls and a deep coffered ceiling, and hugged and kissed her without uttering a word. Martita felt her maid's tears soaking her face. While Símula caressed her in the dim light of the room, Marta, breathless from anguish, asked her:

"Is Papa here? I want to see him. Tell him I've come to ask for forgiveness on my hands and knees. I'll do what he asks of me, as long as he wants. Make him listen to me, for pity's sake, for compassion's sake, in the name of all the saints. Tell him I'm begging him."

Símula shook her head, trying to dissuade her, but seeing her so desperate, she soon turned serious and agreed, making the sign of the cross over herself.

"It's all right, dear, I'll go tell him. You sit here. Hopefully God, the Black Christ of Esquipulas, and the Virgin of Guadalupe will make this miracle occur."

Marta sat on the stone bench that ran along the walls of the foyer and waited, febrile, for Símula to return. She remembered how she had left her child behind while he slept and would probably never see him again. What would happen to him? What would fate bring him? She felt her entire body trembling, but it was too late for regret. In the shadows, she could see the statues in the garden of her former home, the jacarandas, the acacias, the thick-trunked mango, and past the servant's quarters, she glimpsed the kitchen, the laundry, the cage where the dog was most likely locked up for the day, the pantry stuffed with provisions. Would her father forgive her? Could she go back to living here? Her heart withered from sorrow.

At last, Símula returned. Her silence, her teary eyes, her crestfallen expression made plain to Martita that Dr. Arturo Borrero Lamas had refused her, despite her pleas.

"He told me to tell you he no longer has a daughter," she muttered, her voice rasping. "That his daughter died, and that she's buried together with her siblings. That if you didn't leave, he'd have his servants remove you by force. May the saints watch over you, Marta, my child!"

Símula sobbed and crossed herself. Taking Marta by the arm, she walked her toward the door that led to the street. As she opened the old, heavy door, she moaned:

"Go, my dear. May Christ protect you and your child as well, the poor creature. I promise you I will go see him from time to time."

She crossed herself one last time, and made the sign of the cross over Miss Guatemala's forehead as well.

When the door closed behind her, Marta noticed the rain was thicker now; big drops were pounding on her face, and she heard thunder farther off, over the chain of mountains. She stood still, getting soaked, not knowing where to go. Should she return to her husband's home? No, never: she had no doubts there. Kill herself? Not that, either: she refused to let herself be defeated. She clenched her fists. There was no turning back. Following a sudden impulse, she started walking. She was drenched, but determined.

Fifteen minutes later, she walked past the enormous National Palace, then around it, taking Sixth Avenue toward the Casa Presidencial. Water was dripping from her head to her feet, and she shook as she passed the evangelical church. But she was calm again as she reached her destination. She didn't hesitate as she approached the team of soldiers guarding the entrance to the massive edifice, which was surrounded by fences and, past them, a high wall full of shadow-darkened windows. She stared back at the soldiers, none of whom took their eyes off her:

"Which of you is boss?"

The soldiers looked at each other, then gave her a thorough examination.

"What can we do for you?" one of them finally asked brusquely. "Don't you know stopping here is prohibited?"

"I need to speak with the president of the republic," she replied in a loud voice. She heard laughter, and the soldier who spoke to her before took a step toward her.

"Keep walking, babe." His voice was menacing now. "Go get some sleep, you'll catch cold out here in the rain."

"I am the daughter of Dr. Arturo Borrero Lamas and the wife of Dr. Efrén García Ardiles, two friends of the president. Go tell him I want to talk to him. And mind your manners with me or it will cost you dearly."

The giggles disappeared. Now, in the half-light, the eyes of the soldiers revealed worry and surprise. They must have been asking themselves if she really was who she said or if she was out of her goddamned mind.

"Wait here, miss," the soldier who had called her *babe* earlier now said. "I'll call the supervisor."

Time passed interminably, and the soldiers from the detachment never stopped eyeing her, some furtively, others not concealing their crudity. The rain was heavy now, and ricocheted against the occasional decrepit car with bright headlights rounding the corner. Finally, the soldier from before returned with another man, an officer, most likely, judging by his uniform, which was different from theirs.

"Good evening," he told her as he approached, raising his hand to his visor. "What can we do for you here?"

"I'd like to talk to the president," she said, her voice showing a confidence she didn't actually feel. "Tell him it's Marta Borrero Parra, daughter of Arturo Borrero Lamas and wife of his friend Efrén García Ardiles. I know it's late. I wouldn't bother him at this hour if it wasn't deeply urgent."

The officer stood there silent for a moment, scrutinizing her.

"The president receives no one without an appointment," he finally declared. "But, well, we'll see. I'll go and ask. You stay here."

The wait was so long that Marta imagined the officer would never return. The blanket she was wrapped in was now soaked with water. She was shivering.

At last the officer returned and motioned for her to follow him. Martita sighed, relieved.

They stepped into a hallway dimly lit by weak lights. In one room there was a man in civilian clothes, smoking, who stared her up and down.

"My apologies, I have to make sure you're not armed."

She agreed. The officer moved his hands over her entire body, taking his time, squeezing her. The man in civilian clothes, more Indian than mixed, with a mocking smile and suggestion in his eyes, kept his cigarette tucked in his mouth, inhaling smoke and blowing it out.

"Come with me," the officer said.

Again they crossed deserted hallways and a small courtyard with potted flowers and creepers where she saw a cat slip past. She noticed that it had suddenly stopped raining. The officer opened the door to a room bathed in light. She could make out Carlos Castillo Armas sitting at a desk. When he saw her enter, he stood up and walked toward her. He wasn't a tall man, his hair was very short, and his ears were pointed. He was so thin you could see the bones poking through his face and arms. He had rat's eyes and a rather preposterous toothbrush mustache. He was dressed in khaki pants and a short-sleeved shirt that revealed his hairless arms. Marta felt his roving stare, which paused for a moment on the blanket covering her.

"Are you really Arturo's daughter and Efrén's wife?" he asked her from a few feet away.

Martita nodded and, as though in reply to an unuttered question, showed him the ring on her finger, adding:

"We were married five years ago."

"Might I know what you're doing here at this hour of the night without asking for an appointment beforehand?"

"I didn't know where to go," Miss Guatemala confessed. She could feel the tears welling, but she told herself, *I'm not going to cry.* She didn't want to put on a show, playing the poor, defenseless woman. And she managed not to. At first her voice quavered, but it turned resolute as she decided to tell all. "I've escaped from Efrén's home. My father married us by force, because Efrén got me pregnant. I can't bear to live with him any longer. I left without anyone seeing me. I went to my father's house, but he rejected me. He had them tell me his only daughter had died, and that if I didn't leave, he would have the servants throw me out. So it occurred to me I might come here and tell you my story."

Colonel Castillo Armas watched her a long time with his shifty rat eyes. He seemed unsettled, unsure he'd heard her right. Finally he stepped toward her and took her by the arm:

"Have a seat, you must be tired," he said, his intonation more cordial now. Something in him had softened. Did he believe everything she'd said? "Come here."

He pointed toward a sofa. Martita let herself fall on the cushions, and only then did she realize how exhausted she was, and that if she'd stayed standing much longer, she would have collapsed. Intermittently she shook from the cold. Castillo Armas sat down next to her. Were those his civilian clothes or his uniform? The khaki pants and the black ankle boots had an official air about them, but not the brownish-gray short-sleeved shirt. His leaden, unquiet eyes examined her with curiosity.

"You still haven't told me why you've come here, why you're here with me. Your name is Marta, no?"

"I don't know what I'm doing here either," she confessed, noticing that she was stumbling over her words. "I thought my father would forgive me. When I heard the words that I was dead to him, my world came crashing down. I'm not going back to Efrén. Our marriage was a lie, we only did it to please my father and maintain appearances. For me, it's been a five-year-long nightmare. I didn't know where to go, and then it struck me I could turn to you. I've heard many times you and Efrén were friends."

The president nodded.

"We played soccer together as boys," he said in a high, slightly shrill voice. "As I recall, Efrén wasn't a communist in those days; to the contrary, he was a devout Catholic. Same as your father. Tell me everything, from the beginning. That will be best."

And that is what Martita did, for a long time, rubbing her arms when she got chills but never stopping her tale. She told him how, on those weekends devoted to *rocambor*, where her father allowed her to be present, she was surprised by the hostility the political beliefs of that sober doctor, Efrén García Ardiles, aroused, and she began to talk more often to him, asking him questions about politics and noticing the way her father's friend with the *obstinate* ideas (to use Dr. Borrero's term) had begun to look at her, cautiously so the other gentlemen playing cards would fail to notice; the kind of look reserved not for a curious girl, but for a soon-to-be woman. And she told him how he got her pregnant.

"If you like, Martita, since you're so inquisitive, so curious about politics, you could come by my house now and again. After school, perhaps. That would be a better place than here for me to educate you about all the things you wish to know. I've realized you're a girl with a lively intellect."

"But, Doctor, Papa would never give me permission to go to your home."

"There's no reason for you to tell him," Efrén said, lowering his voice to a whisper, looking around, nervous. "You could stop by after class. Tell Arturo you're going to study and do your homework at a girlfriend's house, for example. What do you think?"

She accepted his little game, not so much from curiosity about politics as for the risks it entailed. She liked that more than politics, and indeed, though she didn't know it yet, taking risks would become her watchword throughout the course of her life.

And so she did it. When she repeated to Castillo Armas the lie she'd told her father—that she was going to the home of her friend Dorotea Cifuentes to do the assignments given by the nuns from the Colegio Belga-Guatemalteco—when she told him how, once she'd arrived at Dr. Efrén García Ardiles's home and he would show her into his office, she could see a tiny, very peculiar light shining in the colonel's minuscule eyes, an avid grin, as if her story had inspired in him an intense yearning to know more, to hear the whole thing in precise detail.

"Call me Efrén, Martita," the doctor had told her on one of those afternoons. "Or do I seem that old to you?"

They were in his diminutive study overflowing with books and medical journals. They had just filled up on cups of hot chocolate and pastries. On the rug were small painted stones, which García Ardiles explained he had dug up himself years ago on an archaeological expedition to the forests of Petén, keeping them less for historical than for aesthetic reasons.

"No, Doctor, it isn't that, it's just that it embarrasses me. I don't know you well enough to call you by your first name yet."

"You're so innocent, Miss Guatemala," Efrén replied, stroking her face with an anxious expression. "You know what I like most about you? That profound, unwavering look of yours, as if you were digging deep inside a person and stealing their secrets."

At a certain point in her long confession, Martita noticed that Castillo Armas was smiling sympathetically and even with affection. At another, she realized he had placed a hand on her knee absentmindedly and had begun stroking it. Then Martita knew that her daring gamble in coming to the official residence of the head of state, brazenly asking the guards at the door to let her in to speak to the president, had paid off.

XII

A NOISE CAME FROM THE SHADOWS in the hallway: somebody was coming down the stairs. A soldier with a rifle in hand. Enrique stepped forward to meet him, and when the soldier saw his uniform with its lieutenant colonel's braid, he stood at attention and saluted, surprised.

"Who are you?" Enrique asked him energetically.

"Romeo Vásquez Sánchez, at your service, sir," the boy said, clicking his heels. His bearing was firm, and he stared straight ahead.

Even in the darkness, the Dominican could see that he was very young, hardly old enough to be drafted.

"I'm on watch upstairs on the terrace, sir," he added, now slightly more relaxed. He explained to his superior, "I was coming down to see if the other soldiers were here. They still haven't shown up, which is strange, sir. The guard changed at seven, as always. But no one's here, and apart from me, there's no one else in the residence. Except for the cook and the maids, I mean. And the detachment outside by the front door."

"Yes, that is strange, I'll find out what's going on right now,"

Enrique told him. "The president's house can't be unprotected, not even for a minute."

"It's never happened before, sir," the soldier added, remaining at attention. "That's why I decided to come down."

"I'll take care of it," Enrique said. "Go back to your post and don't move from there. Upstairs, on the terrace, right?"

"Yes, sir." And he repeated, disconcerted, "Nothing like this has ever happened before, sir."

He saluted, turned back, and made his way up the stairs, with Enrique behind him. The Dominican remained hidden in the murk of the hallway. He listened closely, trying to sense what was going on upstairs, but not a sound came through. After a short while, there was a thud, as though someone had fallen to the floor. A long silence followed, and he seemed to hear the pounding of his heart. Finally he saw Enrique coming down the steps with the soldier's rifle in his hand.

"Ready," he heard him say, passing him the weapon. "He never saw it coming."

"I didn't hear the shot," the Dominican whispered.

"My pistol's got a silencer," Enrique said. He flicked his lighter to check the time on his watch. "I don't think they'll be long now."

Then the Dominican watched as he calmly lit a cigarette and blew the smoke out in rings. He seemed serene.

XIII

I T'S NOT JUST GUATEMALA *that's lost its mind,* Dr. Efrén García Ardiles thought. *It's not just myself and all my countrymen who have lost our minds. The entire world has. The United States above all.* He turned off the radio. The parade had just ended, and according to the announcer, thousands of North Americans had cheered Colonel Carlos Castillo Armas in New York, and he in turn, deeply moved, thanked them for the rain of confetti and streamers, standing up in a convertible alongside his wife, the urbane, well-mannered Odilia Palomo de Castillo Armas . . .

It was the beginning of 1955, and the nights were cool; in the day-time, heavy winds blew through on certain afternoons, driving away the birds that flew down to drink from the rills and puddles in the old city in Guatemala. But the inclement weather hadn't demoralized Dr. García Ardiles, nor his family situation, nor even the departure eight months ago of his wife, who was now President Castillo Armas's lover. It wasn't the crying of that barely five-year-old boy who bore his name and surname in the next room over and was, to all indica-tions, his son. Nor his library, ransacked by the new inquisitors: three policemen had come and decimated it, two in plainclothes and one in uniform. They told him his name had appeared on a "blacklist" and they had orders to search his home. The books they took with them were a ridiculous jumble that gave away the poor men's ignorance and their bosses' stupidity. No—what had sunk him into despondency was the great success of President Castillo Armas's tour of the United States, which he had just heard reported on the radio.

After the triumph of the Liberationist revolution, toward the end of 1954, Dr. Efrén García Ardiles was held for fifteen days in a military prison following two days in an internment camp where by a miracle alone (or was it by order of Castillo Armas?) he escaped the beatings and electrical charges that elicited shrieks from the union leaders and unlettered peasants who had no idea what was happening to them. At San José Castle, no tortures were carried out, only executions by firing squad. In the two weeks he spent there, Efrén counted six at least. Or were they feigned, to terrify the political prisoners? His wife, Marta, barely greeted him when he returned home. Was she already planning the escape she would make months later?

In just two weeks, Guatemala had shed its skin. Every trace of the government of Jacobo Árbenz seemed to have disappeared, and in its place was a frantic country where the hunt for real or alleged communists had become a national obsession. How many people had sought asylum in Latin American embassies? Hundreds, maybe thousands. And for nearly three months, at the behest of the CIA, it was said, asylum seekers were refused safe conduct on the grounds that they were *assassins and communist agents who could be carrying compromising documents that proved the Soviet Union's intention of turning Guatemala into a satellite state.* Day after day, week after week, the market sellers, led by Concha Estévez, who had been a supporter of Árbenz but was now a fanatical follower of Castillo Armas, had protested in front of the embassies of Mexico, Chile, and Brazil, demanding they turn hundreds of asylum seekers over to the police to be tried for their crimes in Guatemala. The Apostolic Nunciature declared that they would give up their protectees, but in the end they refused, reportedly because of protests from the ambassadors of Mexico, Brazil, Chile, and Uruguay. It was further rumored that hundreds or thousands of people had fled into the countryside or were hiding out in the homes of friends or in the mountains, waiting for the hysteria to die down. The *Diario de Centro América* of June 24 reported that numerous members of the Agrarian Committees of Chiquimula, Zacapa, and Izabal had been assassinated, and at the end of 1954, the National Committee of Defense Against Communism published a list of 72,000 individuals it confirmed were employed in Guatemala by the Soviet Union, adding that the list could eventually expand to include up to 200,000 people. The Mexican ambassador, Primo Villa Michel, raised his voice in disapproval after his attempts to plead the case of certain exiles was met by the newly appointed minister of education for Castillo Armas's regime, Jorge del Valle Matheu, with the reply: "We're a dictatorship, and we'll do what we damn well please."

There were unverifiable innuendos of all sorts, among them that the government had handed out machine guns among the landlords so they could dole out justice on their own if the campesinos continued to occupy the lands ceded them through the Agrarian Reform, now that all efforts at expropriation and redistribution had been revoked. What had happened to all those thousands of Guatemalans who had filled up Constitution Plaza just weeks before, hailing Jacobo Árbenz and the October Revolution? How could the feelings of an entire people change? García Ardiles didn't understand.

Soon after his rise to power, Castillo Armas had created the National Committee of Defense Against Communism, appointing as its director José Bernabé Linares, an assassin and torturer who led the secret police during the thirteen years of General Jorge Ubico Castañeda's dictatorship—a man whose name alone brought chills to Guatemalans of a certain age. The Committee was responsible for the book burnings in the street, which spread across the country like an epidemic. It was as though colonial times had returned, when the Inquisition preserved religious orthodoxy through blood and fire. All the public libraries and some private ones, like his own, were purged of Marxist manuals, anti-Catholic and pornographic books (for good measure, they had requisitioned all his books written in French), the poems of Rubén Darío, and the tales of Miguel Ángel Asturias and Vargas Vila. At San José Castle, García Ardiles was interrogated day and night by young officers who wanted to know what contacts he'd had with Russia or among atheist communists. "I've never met a communist in my life," he repeated dozens of times in those two weeks. "Nor any Russians, so far as I remember." Eventually, they believed him, or maybe not, but they let him go, possibly following orders from above. Could they have come from Castillo Armas, his old soccer teammate? The anticommunism that had swept the country was like one of those plagues that drove European cities mad with fear in the Middle Ages. By the time Efrén left prison, it had gotten worse.

The new government had returned to United Fruit all those fallow lands nationalized by the Agrarian Reform law under Árbenz and abolished the tax on the owners of latifundia, nationals and foreigners alike. The police and the army took back the estates that had been parceled out among half a million peasants; when necessary they used force, suppressing the agricultural cooperatives, the campesino federations, and—absurdly—even a good number of fraternal organizations founded over the past ten years to care for the patron saints of the villages. Archbishop Mariano Rossell y Arellano had been decorated for his support of the Liberationist revolution, and had proclaimed the Christ of Esquipulas *General of the Army of National Liberation*, fitting him with the corresponding gold braid. In Guatemala, history was racing backward toward tribalism and absurdity. *Will they bring back slavery next?* Dr. Efrén García Ardiles asked himself. The quip wasn't humorous in the least to him. The persecution of those who had collaborated in one way or another with the governments of Juan José Arévalo and Jacobo Árbenz went full steam ahead, despite the former's discreet attempts, over the following months, to distance himself from his successor. Following the instructions of the United States, the harassment of Guatemalans in exile, starting with the former president Jacobo Árbenz, had worsened. Many governments refused permission to allow the exiles to work, and Castillo Armas's administration increased its requests for the extradition of exiles, accusing them of felonies and thefts.

Dr. García Ardiles had lost his post at San Juan de Dios General Hospital, and no patients came to his private practice anymore. He'd already had a bad reputation for his ideas, but after his imprisonment, he was utterly discredited. He was never again invited to the houses of the better families in Guatemala. Or perhaps it was his hurried secret marriage to Marta, the young daughter of Dr. Borrero Lamas, that had made him a pariah? Both things, surely. He tried without success to find work in the new Roosevelt Hospital. For a year, he practiced medicine without charge, ministering to the poor and insolvent. He lived from his savings, selling the few valuables he still held on to. Fortunately, his mother's mental state no longer permitted her to understand what was happening around her.

As a young man, Efrén had been a practicing Catholic and had occasionally spent time in the Marist monks' seminary. But a year and a few months ago, he had stopped taking communion and going to confession. It was, to be exact, on June 18, 1954, the day the forces of Castillo Armas's Liberationist Army had invaded Guatemala, crossing the border with Honduras and attacking the small garrisons to the east, at the same time as the planes of the Army of Liberation—the "sulfates," as the city dwellers called Castillo Armas's Liberationist planes, because their presence made the helpless people on the ground empty their bowels in fear—bombarded the troop detachments and Guatemala City itself. And since his young wife had left him, he'd also stopped believing in God. The ferocious, truculent way the Catholic Church, especially Archbishop Rossell y Arellano, supported that crusade in print and in sermons in every parish disgusted him. He was appalled by what the archbishop had done with the Black Christ of Esquipulas. Naturally, the Church applauded Castillo Armas's celebration of the closure of Guatemala's Grand Masonic Lodge with a military parade. Now Efrén was no longer sure he believed in anything. In his free time, instead of reading Saint Augustine or Saint Thomas Aquinas as he was used to, he perused Nietzsche, one of the authors who had mysteriously escaped the flames. *We're all mad*, he repeated from time to time. How was it possible that the administrations of Juan José Arévalo and Jacobo

Árbenz Guzmán, determined to bring feudalism in Guatemala to an end and make the country into a liberal, capitalist democracy, had provoked such hysteria from United Fruit and America? The indignation among the Guatemalan landholders he could understand, they were people frozen in the past; he could even understand La Frutera, which had never paid a cent in taxes. But Washington! Was this the democracy the gringos wanted for Latin America? Was this the democracy Roosevelt had imagined with his Good Neighbor Policy for Latin America? A military dictatorship at the service of a handful of greedy, racist latifundistas and a big Yankee conglomerate? Was that why the sulfates had bombed Guatemala City, killing and wounding dozens of innocents?

All that had torn his life to pieces, demolishing his hopes and his faith. Or did it start earlier, with his ill-fated adventure with the daughter of a former classmate and intimate friend? Yes, that had been the beginning of the end. Was the fault his, or was he rather the victim of the unconscious lust of the girl, who drove him out of his mind? Was Miss Guatemala innocent or diabolical? At times, he was ashamed to see himself searching for excuses for what had been, pure and simple, a lecherous adult's exploitation of a girl. And then remorse would eat away at him. He hadn't seen Dr. Arturo Borrero Lamas again since that mockery of a wedding at the finca in Chichicastenango. But he knew his former friend had shut himself away, even closing down his practice. His only professional activity was the law classes he taught at San Carlos University. He was rarely seen at social events, and had naturally put an end to the *rocambor* games that once filled his home with friends on Saturday afternoons. Until Marta left, abandoning him and the child, she and Efrén had slept in separate beds, and they hadn't made love once since Father Ulloa had presided over their wedding. Was that even a marriage?

In a bitter, dejected mood, he had spent the past days following the official trip of the president of the republic, Colonel Carlos Castillo Armas, to the United States. The local press and radio described his tour day and night, as if it were an event of global significance. Was that what had driven him to such despair? And why? What was the nerve touched by that specific event? Were there not a thousand worse outrages in the world? He had witnessed the extraordinary reception the president received through radio and newspaper reports. Not only Guatemala had lost its mind, the United States had, too. Or was he the one who had lost his mind, who failed to understand what was happening, he and the half a million Indians Árbenz had given land to and who were now losing it in a rain of bullets? Since President Eisenhower was in the hospital following a heart attack, Vice President Nixon was the one to greet Castillo Armas and his wife at the airport in Washington, surrounded by dignitaries from the U.S. government. In homage, he received the obligatory twenty-one-gun salute, along with a well-attended military parade. In speeches and editorials— even in *The New York Times!*—Castillo Armas was spoken of as a hero, the savior of freedom in Central America, an example to all the world. That was the essence of all the addresses welcoming him across that great country to the north. When he stepped out onto the street, he was greeted by applause and requests for autographs, bystanders took his picture, ordinary people thanked him for liberating his homeland. From what, from whom? Dizziness forced Dr. García Ardiles to close his eyes. How was it possible that this insignificant little man and his so-called Liberationist revolution had so impressed the United States? And not just the government: prestigious universities, Fordham and Columbia, had named him *doctor honoris causa*. He'd been taken to Fitzsimmons Army Hospital in Colorado so President Eisenhower could embrace him in person and thank him for pulling Guatemala away from the clutches of the Russian bear. How many communists were there in the country apart from the three or four congressmen from the Guatemalan Party of Labor, which couldn't have had more than sixty members and which had been closed as soon as the counterrevolution triumphed? Very few. He didn't know how many, but it couldn't be enough to amount to anything. Dr. García Ardiles had a clipping of the speech Nixon had delivered at a state dinner saluting the *brave soldier* who had led his country's uprising against *a corrupt and mendacious communist dictatorship*. What uprising? Who were the people who had risen up? Castillo Armas had appeared before Congress in Washington, and the senators and representatives had applauded him uproariously in a joint session.

Was history nothing more than this fantastical repudiation of reality? The conversion into myth and fiction of real, concrete events? Was that the history we read and studied? The heroes we admired? A mass of lies made truth through vast conspiracies of the powerful against poor devils like him and Hatchet Face? Was that band of masqueraders the heroes the people revered? He felt something like vertigo, and his head seemed on the verge of exploding. *Maybe you're being unjust with Castillo Armas,* he considered, still in a daze. *He was the one who saved your life and got you out of that prison where you would have rotted to nothing. Ingrate. With your failures in life, your personal and professional frustrations, you dare to insult your old friend, the one you played soccer with on Saturdays. Maybe you're the envious one?* But no, it wasn't envy. His defects, which were doubtless many, had never included rancor at the triumphs of others.

Dr. Efrén García Ardiles again heard crying in the neighboring room, from that boy who bore his name. Was he really his son? Officially, yes. Because of his name, and because he was the child of Martita Borrero Parra, now known as Marta García Ardiles, a girl he slept with when he shouldn't have. He would pay for his wrongdoing for the rest of his life, he was certain of it. But was he the guilty one? Again he was trying to look for excuses, blaming that poor girl for his own shortcomings. He had recognized the newborn because he was a decent man, even if impregnating a fifteen-year-old girl implied the contrary, revealing him to the world as a vile abuser, a contemptible pedophile. Was his own life a farce, just like Castillo Armas's? He felt the urge to cry, just like the little boy the serving girl was trying to hush in the neighboring room. He was a normal child who would soon turn six years old. His grades at the kindergarten were good, and he kept himself amused playing alone, with his miniature tenpins or his spinning top. He hadn't even been baptized. He was registered at city hall under the name Efrén, but Símula, who came to see him now and again, always called him Trencito.

The little desk where the doctor passed the better part of his day was covered in books, even after the Liberationists' ransacking. Not just medical texts, but philosophy, which had been his other passion ever since his years as a student. Now he could hardly read. He tried, but he lacked the concentration of before and the excitement he'd once harbored, when he believed that the reading of good books, apart from being a pleasure, was an enrichment of a man's awareness and sensitivity, and made him a more complete person. Castillo Armas's official visit to the United States had worsened the neuroses that had overtaken his life since the time when, to his disgrace, he had begun responding to the questions about politics the beautiful Miss Guatemala had posed to him on those weekends when *rocambor* games were played in the home of his former friend Arturo. It didn't matter that she'd left him. He had never loved her. *And she never loved me*, he thought. But whether or not he was to blame, what had happened had been the beginning of his downfall, his plunge into an abyss from which he was sure he would never emerge.

He and Carlos Castillo Armas were of the same age or, at least, of the same generation. Efrén had met him when they were still boys attending their respective schools. He and Arturo studied with the Marists, at San José de los Infantes, but since the Catholic schools that educated the sons of Guatemala's decent families refused entry to children born out of wedlock, to bastards like the scrawny, weak, and maudlin boy named Castillo Armas, the most he could do was wander around the Marists' soccer field on Saturdays and Sundays. Carlos himself had told him his story, saying his mother and father weren't married: his father had another family, his real family, and Carlos and his mother were just people he *took care of.* His father had tried to have him admitted to the Marist school, but they rejected him as a child born in sin. That was why he attended the public school. He repeated all this naturally, without shame or rancor. Efrén felt sympathy for him, and convinced his friends to let the boy play soccer with them on the weekends they devoted to sports. *It's thanks to that bit of kindness, perhaps, that I'm alive*, he thought. *That's the proof you weren't the scoundrel people thought you were, especially Arturo.*

The Carlos from back then had seemed like a good person, Efrén recalled. It had saddened him to see the young man suffer discrimination from an unjust society, to see him relegated to second place, marginalized for the sins of his parents (*Look who's talking, Efrén*), not even entitled to inherit his family's properties, which would end up in their entirety in the hands of his legitimate brothers. His gawky frame and his far from athletic movements boded ill for his military career. And so Efrén, who saw him out and about—they used to go to the cinema, to the Lux, the Capitol, or Variedades to see Mexican cowboy films, movies starring María Félix, Elsa Aguirre, or Libertad Lamarque, and to watch the national soccer championship—was surprised when Carlos told him he would be applying to the Politécnica. Him, a cadet? Practical considerations must have led to the decision. In the sanctimonious, prejudice-ridden high society of Guatemala, he would never have been able to carve out a path for himself or become successful when all the affluent families had rejected him because of his shameful birth. Every door would have been closed to him. At the Military Academy, he was the classmate of Jacobo Árbenz, the very same president he'd deposed and whom he'd humiliated, after Árbenz had spent three months in hiding, a refugee in the Mexican Embassy, by forcing him to strip naked at the airport and be photographed on his way into exile, *to be sure he wasn't carrying valuables*, as the government press—which was now the only press in the country—stated. Then he had expropriated all of his wealth, from the Finca El Cajón to his personal savings accounts.

When Carlos was a cadet, they seldom saw each other. From time to time, on his free days, Carlos would call Efrén, who was busy with his medical studies, and if they had money, they would meet to drink a beer and talk at the Granada or, if money was tight, at a tiny bar next to the Mercado Central. Their friendship was distanced, intermittent. Efrén knew Carlos had made a mediocre showing in the army. He invited him to his graduation, and that day Efrén met Carlos's mother, Josefina Castillo, a humble woman in a huipil embroidered with a quetzal and a long skirt held up with a rustic sash, who cried when they handed her son the second lieutenant's sword. His father, naturally, was absent from the ceremony.

They stopped seeing each other, and much later, Efrén found out that in the period of the October Revolution of 1944, which ended with Professor Juan José Arévalo coming to power in the first free elections in Guatemala, Carlos had spent eight months in the United States at the U.S. Army Command and General Staff College in Fort Leavenworth, Kansas, learning counterinsurgency tactics. He would see him again a while after his return to Guatemala, when they had named him director of the Politécnica. Thereafter, they would occasionally run into each other at social gatherings, say hello, quickly share what was going on in their lives, tell a joke or two, and make a promise to call, which they never did. When Carlos married Odilia, Efrén received word of it along with an invitation, and he sent them a nice present. What sort of career had Carlos had in the military? A rather elusive one, moving from one base to the next all across the country, promoted slowly for time served, nothing glamorous; a far cry from classmates like Jacobo Árbenz or Francisco Javier Arana, who even then were spoken of as leaders in their field and likely future presidents.

The next thing Efrén knew about Carlos was that he had taken the side of Arana in his feud with Árbenz, in recompense, perhaps, for the protection Arana had offered him in the army. And when they assassinated Colonel Francisco Javier Arana in that strange skirmish on July 18, 1949, at Puente de la Gloria, Carlos, by now a lieutenant colonel and chief of the Mazatenango garrison, accused the government and specifically Jacobo Árbenz of complicity in the killing. He had a fleeting moment of stardom as leader of an attack on the La Aurora garrison on November 5, 1950. The attempt failed, several died, and the caudillo was gravely wounded. By a miracle, he escaped being buried alive. Thinking he was dead, they were taking him to a pit already full of bodies when Castillo Armas groaned, letting the soldiers know he was still breathing. (*It would have been better if they'd buried him*, Dr. García Ardiles thought. But he immediately corrected himself: *In that case, you'd already be dead or imprisoned for God knows how long*.) He was saved, but Juan José Arévalo's government expelled him from the army and the judges condemned him to death. The sentence was delayed several times. His escape from the penitentiary on June 11, 1951, was celebrated throughout the country. There were two versions of the story. His supporters claimed that he and his companions had lived an adventure hardly less extraordinary than that of the Count of Montecristo, digging a long, secret tunnel that took them to freedom. His enemies said the fugitives had paid off their jailers in quetzals and had walked out the prison doors without any risk to themselves. He took shelter in Colombia before moving on to Honduras, where he devoted himself body and soul to conspiring against the government of Jacobo Árbenz. It was there that he founded the so-called National Liberation Movement and made a pact with General Ydígoras Fuentes and a shrewd civilian, Dr. Córdova Cerna, a former lawyer for the Frutera and one of Arévalo's collaborators and ministers who, so it was said, had changed ideologies following the tragic death of his son in an opposition protest. Purportedly the United States, or better said, President Eisenhower's Secretary of State John Foster Dulles and his brother Allen, head of the CIA, had chosen Castillo Armas to lead the counterrevolution because he lacked Ydígoras Fuentes's aristocratic background and because Córdova Cerna, the one with the brains, ideas, and prestige, was found to have throat cancer around that time. Then again, they may have believed Carlos was the most docile and malleable of the three, and his skin and facial features were those of an Indian rather than a mestizo. Was that all it took to be president of the Republic of Guatemala and a hero to the free world? Feted in the United States, with prizes and applause, dubbed an example for the rest of Latin America by the most prestigious newspapers?

The boy had finally calmed down, and a strange peace reigned in that mundane little house in the San Francisco neighborhood where Dr. Efrén García Ardiles was feeding his pessimism and neuroses. Grabbing a coat and his umbrella, he set off to take a walk through the city center. He would come back tired, soaked, perhaps a bit calmer.

XIV

T HE HALL WAS STILL DARK AND DESERTED, except for the dim light at the end, where Enrique had told the Dominican the kitchen and dining room lay.

"They're taking their time," Enrique said, using the flame from his lighter to take another look at his watch.

The Dominican didn't answer. It wasn't hot, but he was sweating. He hadn't been in such a state of effervescent expectation, of exacerbated apprehension, since his years in Mexico, when he had to take part in some of the assassinations covered up as accidents under orders from Generalísimo Trujillo. But he was sure that this was much more important than anything he'd ever done to please El Jefe. Fortunately, Enrique was there to guide things. Would it all turn out as he'd hoped? Enrique was immensely ambitious, and he thought that in the resulting vacuum, his dream of becoming president of the republic would become a reality. The Dominican had his doubts, and Mike Laporta did too. But then, nothing was impossible in this life. Was it true that President Castillo Armas had given him that dreadful nickname, the Lug?

"There they are," he heard Enrique whisper.

To his right, a door had just opened, a spurt of light brightened the garden with its lone acacia, and two people came through, walking toward them slowly. To get to the dining room, they would have to walk in front of the two men, almost grazing them.

"Give me the rifle," he heard Enrique say.

"I'll do it," the Dominican replied immediately, thinking this would better accord with the Generalísimo's wishes. And he repeated, to encourage himself, "Me."

"Then take it off safety," Enrique said, bending toward him to do it himself. "There."

The couple was now crossing the small garden, and the Dominican heard the woman exclaim, her surprise mixed with indignation, "Why haven't they turned the lights on? And where are the servants?"

"And my guards?" the man shouted.

They stopped and looked to all sides. The man turned, apparently deciding to run back into the house he had just emerged from. In the darkness, the Dominican took aim and fired. The shot was loud and echoed through the corridor. He fired a second time, and the woman screamed and started crying hysterically. She had fallen to the floor next to the man lying there.

"Come on, quick," Enrique said, grabbing his companion's arm and dragging him off. He dropped the rifle on the floor and went along. With quick steps, almost running, they retraced the path they had taken to enter the Casa Presidencial. When Enrique opened the little door hidden in the wall on that corner of Sixth Avenue, they saw the black car there driven by the Cuban Ricardo Bonachea León.

"There's your ride," Enrique said. "I'll give you an hour to get the woman out of here. Not a minute more. An hour, then I'm ordering her arrested."

XV

THE DOMINICAN REPUBLIC'S NEW MILITARY ATTACHÉ in Guatemala, Johnny Abbes García, arrived in the country clandestinely. He hadn't notified the ambassador of his arrival. He caught a taxi at La Aurora airport and ordered the chauffeur to take him to Sixth Avenue, to the San Francisco Mansion, a seedy hotel that he would soon turn into his center of operations. He asked the man at the front desk if there was a Rosicrucian temple in the city, and on receiving a disconcerted, uncomprehending stare in reply, he continued, "Don't worry about it."

After unpacking the little clothing he'd brought in his suitcase and hanging it in the old wardrobe in his room, he called Carlos Gacel Castro on the phone, anxious that the only person he knew in the country might not be around. But he got lucky. Carlos answered the phone himself. He was surprised to hear Abbes García was in Guatemala, and immediately accepted his invitation to dinner. He would pick him up at San Francisco Mansion at eight that night.

Carlos Gacel Castro was Cuban, not Guatemalan. Abbes García had met him in Mexico when Trujillo was footing the bill for him to take those classes in police science and spy for the Generalísimo on the Dominican exiles residing in the land of the Aztecs. Gacel Castro, himself an exile, was well acquainted with these people.

Carlos's boast that he was the ugliest man in the world had endeared him to Abbes García: compared with such a monster, anyone was presentable, even him. Gacel was tall, muscular, pale, with a fleshy, malproportioned face covered in pockmarks, massive ears, nose, and mouth, and orangutan hands and feet which, viewed against his garish tropical dress, made him a tacky, repellent figure. Worst of all were his icy yellowish eyes that probed others, especially women, with aggressive impertinence. He swaggered like a goon, flaunting his physique, in tight pants that showed off his buttocks. He'd been a gangster in Havana, gotten blood on his hands, and had to leave the country to keep from going back to prison, where he'd already done his fair share of time. When Abbes García met him in Mexico and began employing his services, he hadn't wanted to know much about all that. Gacel was eternally broke, so Abbes managed to get Trujillo to send him a small monthly stipend, along with the occasional gratuity when, apart from informing, he took part in violent actions against some exile or other, always careful not to leave any clues. With time, Gacel had to leave Mexico as well, because the government was about to extradite him to Cuba, where the courts were clamoring for him. That was why Johnny Abbes was able to get his number. Gacel had gotten a job here in the security services as a part-time snitch and part-time bruiser under the leadership of Lieutenant Colonel Enrique Trinidad Oliva.

Gacel came to pick him up at eight o'clock precisely, and they had dinner at a tavern, starting with a few beers and moving on to tortillas and roasted chicken with chilies. When the Cuban found out his friend was now a lieutenant colonel and his country's soon-to-be military attaché in Guatemala, his eyes lit up. He hugged him to congratulate him.

"If I can do anything for you, I'm at your service, pal," he said.

"There certainly is something," Johnny Abbes replied. "I'm going to put you on the payroll for two hundred dollars a month, more for special tasks. Now, let's go somewhere you can really take the country's pulse."

"Old habits die hard, no, compadre?" Gacel replied. "Don't get your hopes up though. The whorehouses in this country are like a morgue."

Brothels were the former horse racing journalist's great weakness. He visited them assiduously to gather information, and they gave him a feel for what was going on in town. He felt good, comfortable, at ease in those flea traps dense with smoke and the stench of alcohol and sweat, in the company of tipsy, aggressive men and women you didn't have to pretend with, who responded to orders: *Open your legs and give me that asshole, whore, I'm here to have fun.* It wasn't easy to get the hookers to suck his cock, he had to negotiate every time, and often they flat-out refused. But none of them objected when he wanted to suck on their gash. That was his weakness. A dangerous weakness, sure, he'd been warned about it more than once: "You could get syphilis or who knows what infection. Almost every one of those whores has got the drip, crabs, or something." But he didn't care. He liked risk, any risk, but especially this one, which came with pleasure attached.

Gacel knew the cathouses in Guatemala City like the back of his hand. Most were scattered around the rundown Gerona neighborhood. They weren't as rowdy or violent as the ones in Mexico, and were light-years away from the ones in Ciudad Trujillo, with their spirited merengues, deafening music, and intrepid Dominican hookers, lusty phrases ever on the tip of their luscious tongues. The girls here were surlier, more distant, some of them were Indians who blabbed in their dialects and could hardly get out a word of Spanish. Gacel took Abbes to a bar-cum-bordello on a narrow street in Gerona overseen by Miriam, a woman with a long mane she dyed red or platinum blond, depending on the occasion. Abbes bedded a black chick from Belize who spoke to him in a mix of Spanish and badly mumbled English. She was delighted to part her legs and let him drive his tongue into that red, humid cavity with its succulent stench.

When Gacel left him at San Francisco Mansion at dawn, Abbes García had learned two things about Guatemala: first, no one had a

good word to say about President Castillo Armas and in all the political gossip he heard, there wasn't a single person who would give a
quetzal for his life. Second, even if Guatemala's whores left a lot to be
desired, Zacapa rum was just as good as the Dominican Republic's.

He waited two more days before presenting himself at the embassy.
But he didn't waste those forty-eight hours. He was working, getting
the lay of the land in that unknown city full of unknown people. He
read all the newspapers from cover to cover, *El Imparcial*, the *Diario
de Centro América*, the *Prensa Libre*, and *La Hora*, listened to the news
on Radio Nacional, TGW, and Radio Morse, and walked ceaselessly
through the streets, squares, and parks, stopping in occasionally at
the cafés and cantinas he came across. He conversed with people, and
though it wasn't easy—many of them looked at him askance when
they heard his foreign accent—he got bits of information out of them.
At night he returned to his hotel, weary and certain of something
he'd already guessed at that first evening in his conversations with
Carlos Gacel Castro: no one liked Castillo Armas, many thought he
was a flunky, lacking character and authority, a consummate mediocrity only respected by a handful of friends, most of them opportunists
and ass-kissers. Not even his anticommunist convictions were all that
firm; word had it that he was talking now about giving back some of
the lands they had taken from the Indians. He hadn't done it yet, but
the rumors were spreading, probably thanks to his enemies. Everyone
said his lover kept him under a spell, and that Marta was the one who
called the shots, even at the highest level of government. How different from Generalísimo Trujillo! Who in the Dominican Republic
would dare say a word against him the way everyone here did against
Castillo Armas, even in the cantinas! That was the reason for all the
disorder, the uncertainty in Guatemala City, that was why no one
seemed to think things could go on like this indefinitely.

On the third day, he showed up at the Dominican Embassy. His
sudden appearance surprised everyone, starting with Ambassador
Gilberto Morillo Soto, a renowned psychiatrist at home who was already aware of Abbes's promotion. They had been waiting for him,

they would have gone to the airport to pick him up if they had known the hour of his arrival.

"Don't worry, Ambassador," Abbes García responded. "I wanted to take a look around town, make a few contacts, before getting to work."

Morillo Soto showed him the office he had prepared for him in the embassy building. Abbes García thanked him, at the same time letting him know he wouldn't come there often, as his mission demanded he spend much of his time on the streets or traveling in the country's interior. For now, he said, he would like to interview two high-level figures in the Guatemalan government, to convey his personal greetings: Carlos Lemus, the civilian head of the security services, and Lieutenant Colonel Enrique Trinidad Oliva, chief of the various bodies charged with public order and safeguarding the regime.

Both of them gave him an appointment almost immediately. His interview with Carlos Lemus left him disappointed—he struck him as a bureaucrat, incapable of independent thought, so timid he refused to give a personal opinion about anything and only responded to questions with commonplaces and evasions—but he took a great liking to Lieutenant Colonel Enrique Trinidad Oliva. He was a tall, wiry man, with dusky skin and an enormous crocodile mouth. From the first, it was evident he was a person of action, ambitious, resolute. His responses were clear because he thought for himself, and like Abbes García, he was willing to take risks and to talk openly, without reservations.

Abbes García took him a bottle of Dominican rum—*So you can see, Lieutenant Colonel, it's as good as the finest Zacapa*—and they opened it immediately. Though it wasn't yet midday, they toasted and drank two or three glasses each in the course of their conversation. Afterward, Trinidad Oliva invited him to lunch at El Lagar, a restaurant that served traditional Guatemalan cuisine.

Trinidad Oliva was a great admirer of Generalísimo Trujillo and could recognize, having been there himself, how he had transformed the Dominican Republic into a prosperous, modern country with the best armed forces in the entire Caribbean. *Your boss is a man of character*, he affirmed. *A great patriot. And he's got a pair of balls as big as an elephant's.* He paused, lowering his voice, then added: *We could use some of that around here.* Abbes García laughed, and Trinidad Oliva laughed, too, and from that moment, it was clear that they were friends, maybe even accomplices.

They saw each other the next morning and the morning after, and soon, apart from drinking and eating together, they were going whoring at establishments of a rather higher class than the ones Carlos Gacel Castro frequented. From their many outings, Abbes García drew a number of conclusions that he passed along to the Generalísimo in detailed reports: Lieutenant Colonel Trinidad Oliva was a man who was aiming high. He felt the government had unfairly pushed him aside. He'd been imprisoned under Jacobo Árbenz for conspiring against the regime and had no love for Castillo Armas, which meant he could be key to their project. Then again, it was hard to get a sense of his position in the armed forces, an institution apparently rife with divisions, with groups conspiring one against the other. That was the reason Castillo Armas's government was unstable, held together by stopgaps, prone to collapse at any moment, whether from outside action or through erosion from within. Another important thing: Marta Borrero Parra, nicknamed Miss Guatemala, a young and very beautiful woman, did indeed have the president mesmerized, and she exercised a great deal of power over him. He had given her a house and consulted her about everything, people said, including matters of state. Abbes García would therefore try to meet her as soon as possible, to establish a relationship advantageous to his diplomatic maneuverings in the country. The fact was that the principal division that existed in the government—incredible as it seemed—was between the supporters of the first lady, Mrs. Odilia Palomo, and those of the president's mistress. This rivalry might make conditions favorable to his undertaking. Johnny Abbes sent all his reports to the Generalísimo in coded messages.

While wandering the city in constant search for information, the lieutenant colonel discovered that another of the topics of the day was the debate on the opening of casinos, which the government had announced with the intention of encouraging tourism, but which the Catholic Church had declared its opposition to. Archbishop Mariano Rossell y Arellano himself had railed against gambling, which he said would extend corruption, vice, and crime, attracting gangsters and mafiosos to Guatemala just as it had in Havana. The arrival of casinos had turned their sister nation of Cuba into one big brothel, a hotbed of criminals and fugitives from North America.

Abbes García was struggling with these controversies when Gacel Castro told him Ricardo Bonachea León had escaped from Mexico to Guatemala and that he needed his help, having entered the country covertly. Bonachea León was an expatriate gunman in Mexico, where he had occasionally collaborated with Abbes García and Gacel Castro spying on Dominican exiles. Trujillo had ordered him to liquidate one of them, Tancredo Martínez, the former Dominican consul in Miami, who had run away to Mexico seeking asylum. Bonachea León made a mess of it, going to the insurance company where the target worked and shooting him square in the face. He maimed him terribly, but the man survived. That was his reason for absconding to Guatemala, and now he needed a hand. Abbes García talked with Lieutenant Colonel Trinidad Oliva, who not only arranged papers for him, but even said he could offer the Cuban certain jobs in the same line as Carlos Gacel Castro that would earn him a living.

At one of their weekly lunches, the Dominican made a bold offer to his Guatemalan friend: the two should open a casino together. The dark, wiry officer stared at him, disconcerted.

"You and me, half and half," Abbes García went on. "I've got no doubt it's a solid business, one that will bring in a good deal of cash."

"Have you seen the commotion in Guatemala about this issue of casinos?" Trinidad Oliva asked, carefully measuring his words. "Castillo Armas ordered the Beach and Tennis Club closed and expelled the owners, a couple of gringos, from the country. And the archbishop will fight any other casinos tooth and nail."

"Hearing that is what gave me the idea," Abbes García said. "If worst comes to worst, they could be casinos exclusively for foreigners, if that will mollify the archbishop. Let him save the citizens; the tourists can go to hell: more than one priest thinks that way. Who gives the permits to open a casino? You, right?"

"It's dicey," Trinidad Oliva said, turning grave. "I would need to consult the president."

"Consult him, no worries. Besides, even if we are the owners, there's no reason for your name or mine to appear anywhere. Don't you know someone who could serve as a front man for us?"

The lieutenant colonel reflected for a moment.

"I've got the perfect person," Trinidad Oliva said. "Ahmed Kurony, the Turk. He deals in jewelry, precious stones, shady business. They say he moves contraband, he's some kind of gangster, that much is obvious."

"There you go then. Sounds like our guy."

But the operation fell through, and only deepened the antagonism between Castillo Armas and Enrique Trinidad Oliva. When the Lug told the president he was going to authorize a casino for Ahmed Kurony, the president categorically forbade it. He had enough problems with the Catholic Church, he explained, and not only with the casinos. At the archbishop's instigation, many priests had been pounding the pulpit and railing against *men who keep concubines and call themselves Catholics*, and he'd just heard that the cathedral would soon be holding a week of prayer to prevent the devil's taking hold of the city through the casinos; so for now, another gambling den was out of the question, especially if a known contrabandist and thug like the Turk was going to be behind it. Didn't this Ahmed Kurony have a nasty reputation? And so Trinidad Oliva had to tell Abbes García:

"For now, we'll need to forget that plan. In the future, we'll see."

Getting to Miss Guatemala was more difficult. The famous Marta rarely set foot outside, never mind going to gatherings or high-society cocktail hours; she only met with trusted friends, and Abbes García wasn't invited. But one afternoon, at a reception at the Colombian Embassy, he was lucky enough to run into her. As soon as he saw her, he was certain Generalísimo Trujillo's intuitions were correct: that woman would be essential for what he had come to Guatemala to do.

Laying eyes on her, the lieutenant colonel realized she was a woman he would like to be with. She was prettier than the legends circulating about the president's lover had led him to believe. And very young: to all appearances, hardly more than an adolescent. Not tall, but marvelously proportioned, with a natural coquettishness in her way of dressing—she wore a sinuous skirt that showed off her shapely legs and ankles, sandals, and a blouse that revealed her shapely chest—and when she walked, she moved her shoulders savvily and each step made her buttocks and breasts quiver. What was most attractive about her was her strangely tranquil gaze, which forced her interlocutors to look down, as though the gentle insolence of those penetrating, greenish-gray eyes had caused them to flag and admit defeat. Abbes García did the impossible to win her favor and strike up a friendship with her. He praised her, congratulated her, asked if he might pay her a visit; she said yes, and even gave him a date: next Thursday at five in the afternoon. That night at the brothel, as he got hot and ejaculated with a run-of-the-mill tramp, he kept his eyes closed and dreamed of undressing Miss Guatemala and having his way with her.

On the lieutenant colonel's first visit to the house Castillo Armas had given his lover, not far from the Casa Presidencial, Miss Guatemala sealed her friendship with Johnny Abbes García. An odd current of sympathy united Marta and the Dominican. He brought her gifts, sent her flowers, thanked her fulsomely for receiving him. He told her that, since his arrival in Guatemala, he had heard from all quarters about the sway she held over the president and how the most important things Colonel Castillo Armas had done for his country were thanks to her advice. As they drank their tea, he told her of the marvels Trujillo had carried out in the Dominican Republic and invited her to come see them herself whenever she liked: she was always welcome as the Generalísimo's guest. She could enjoy the beaches, the music, the tranquility, and when she learned to dance to the merengue, she would realize it was the happiest music in the world.

After that visit, he wrote a detailed report to his leader about his relationship with Miss Guatemala, including an enthusiastic description of her physical attributes. At the same time, he said: *That is not the end of her attractions. Despite her youth, she possesses obvious intelligence, a great deal of curiosity, and political intuition.* In his response, Generalísimo Trujillo told him the relationship was an opportune one and that he should cultivate it. But for now, he needed to make contact with the CIA's man in Guatemala, a gringo who called himself Mike and had some kind of association with the Yankee embassy. He should look for him there, or leave his name and address for Mike to get in touch with him.

Abbes García was still living in the San Francisco Mansion, the same drab hotel he'd checked into on arrival. He had lunch and dinner out, and at night, if he had no other commitments, he'd go with Gacel and Bonachea León to some brothel or other. A routine life, in appearances, but at their core his activities had no other goal than fulfilling the task Trujillo had set him.

Just as Abbes García was asking himself how to get in touch with this gringo whose name was probably something other than Mike, he received (not through the Dominican Embassy, but at the hotel where he was staying, which no one but Gacel was supposed to know) an invitation to dine at the Hotel Panamerican two days later from a gentleman whose card read: *Mike Laporta. Specialist in climate, biogeography, and the environment. United States Embassy, Guatemala.* How the hell had he found out his address? Undoubtedly, here was proof the CIA was functioning as it should.

Mike Laporta couldn't look more like a gringo if he tried, but he spoke good Spanish, with a slight Mexican accent. He must have been somewhere between forty and fifty. His blond hair was thinning, and he had a heavy, strapping build, with red hair on his arms and chest. He wore glasses to correct a short-sightedness that lent a certain vagueness to his stare. His manner was natural, sympathetic, and he seemed to know everything about Guatemala and Central America in general. But he didn't make a show of it, indeed he had a timid, discreet air about him. Abbes García asked him how many years he'd been there, and he waved one arm as he replied curtly, "Quite a few."

Mike confirmed what Abbes García already knew in broad

outlines, but added numerous details about the various factions the army was divided into, and revealed that several conspiracies were already afoot. He surprised him by saying that among Castillo Armas's presumptive successors, the one with the best chance was Miguel Ydígoras Fuentes. He was living outside the country at present, apparently prevented from returning on the instructions of Castillo Armas, who feared him. Despite his retirement, he still had many supporters among the officers and enlisted men, and the Guatemalan people admired his spirit, energy, and strength of character. The same reasons Castillo Armas refused to let him return.

"What I mean to say is, he has everything this president doesn't," Mike concluded. "I suppose Generalísimo Trujillo will be pleased to hear that."

"It's true, he has a very fine impression of General Ydígoras Fuentes, the two men are friends," Abbes García said. "But what interests Trujillo in any case is what's best for the Guatemalans."

"Of course," Mike said, with a sardonic little laugh. "I'm under the impression General Ydígoras is a great admirer of Trujillo as well. He considers him a model."

They talked about this and that, and the Dominican confessed to the gringo that though he'd been in Guatemala for several months now, he hadn't managed to arrange a private meeting with President Castillo Armas. As if remembering something all of a sudden, Mike told Abbes García he wanted to ask an important favor of him. What? Could he introduce him to Martita, Miss Guatemala, the president's beloved?

"Yes, of course, I'd be happy to," the Dominican said. "How strange that you don't already know her."

"She's not an easy woman to meet," Mike told him. "The president is deeply jealous, he won't let her go out alone. Only with him, at receptions and dinners, and apparently even that's very rare. Rarer than a bishop's funeral, as they say around here."

"So she's the one who really holds the power," Abbes said. "Not Mrs. Odilia Palomo."

"Of course," Mike affirmed, then adding immediately afterward, "at least, that's what people say."

"I would be very happy to introduce you to her," Abbes said. "We could go visit her one afternoon. You'll notice she's quite a beauty."

"Hopefully she'll see us." Mike sighed. "Up to now, all my attempts have failed."

She did see them, at her home, and offered them each a cup of tea with sweets made by the Clarist sisters. Seeing Marta's perplexity as she looked at his card, Mike explained his profession and his responsibilities at the embassy: he advised the National Meteorological Service on the latest advances in weather forecasting and on the best policies for protecting cities from the seismic shifts so frequent in this country covered in volcanoes.

As he left, Mike asked Miss Guatemala if he, too, could come visit her again.

"Not too often," she replied frankly. "Carlos is quite jealous, and a man of the old school. He doesn't like me seeing other men, even in the company of their wives, if he isn't here."

They laughed, and she added with a flirtatious smile:

"It would be best if you come see me together."

And so they did. Every two or three weeks, Johnny Abbes García and the man whose name wasn't Mike and who was probably not even a meteorologist came to the home of the president's lover, with bouquets of flowers and boxes of chocolates, to have tea with pastries made by the Clarist sisters. Their conversations, anodyne at first, turned increasingly to politics.

Abbes García noted that on each visit, as though inadvertently, Mike subtly extracted information from the young beauty. Did she realize? Of course she did. Abbes García found out for certain one afternoon when Mike left the two of them alone for a few moments to go to the bathroom. Lowering her voice to a whisper and pointing to the departing American, Marta said:

"That gringo's from the CIA, right?"

"I've never asked," Abbes said. "Anyway, if he was, he'd never admit it."

"He's trying to get things out of me, like I'm an idiot and I don't realize it," Martita said.

On the way out of Miss Guatemala's house, it struck Abbes García that he should warn Mike, and he told him what Marta had said. The gringo nodded.

"Of course she knows who I work for," he said, giggling once more. "She even asked me for money for the information she's giving me. She and I have a deal. But perhaps it would be best if you and I didn't discuss such delicate matters."

"Understood," Abbes García said. And he made the sign of the cross over his lips.

They went to see a cowboy film at the Variedades. The gringo loved them. It was a slow one, featuring the lovely Ava Gardner and plenty of shoot-outs. When they left, they went to dinner at a small Italian restaurant. They had a glass of rum to finish, and Abbes García indecorously proposed to Mike that they end the night at a whorehouse.

Mike's face flushed purple, and he looked at him severely.

"My apologies, but I never go to such places," he said, grimacing with disgust. "I'm faithful to my wife and my religion."

XVI

"I NEED TO MAKE A PHONE CALL," the Dominican said. "Let's go to the Hotel Panamerican first."

It was nearby, so Ricardo Bonachea León wheeled a while through the solitary downtown streets before stopping in front of the bar of Guatemala City's main hotel. Outside, everything was tranquil. The Dominican imagined the uproar that would break out as soon as people heard the news: the phone calls, the gossip, the military patrols that would take to the streets, arresting people left and right. Enrique's office at the National Palace would be the center of that feverish agitation. Hopefully things would work out for him as he wished: he genuinely appreciated the Guatemalan, though something deep down told him it would be hard for him to make it to the presidency.

Inside, it was almost empty, with just two tables occupied and a single man at the bar, smoking and drinking a beer. A marimba was playing on the radio. The Dominican motioned for the barman to give him a token for the phone and pour him a glass of rum. He closed the door to the booth and dialed. The line was busy. He hung up, waited, and dialed again. It was still busy. He called two more times: always busy. Now not just his hands were sweating, but also his forehead and neck, and on his back he could feel the damp soaking through his shirt. He called a fifth time, thinking, *His phone's broken. Just what I needed.* But this time he heard Mike's voice after the second ring.

"It's done," he told him, trying and failing to talk naturally. "I'd like to request that you call Marta as soon as possible. She needs to take a car right away. Gacel should be right outside her door."

There was a long silence.

"Did everything go well?" Mike finally asked.

"Yes, fine. Make that call, please."

"You're sure her escorts are gone?"

"Sure," the Dominican said, impatient. "In three-quarters of an hour, Enrique will give the order for her arrest. So she needs to leave right now if she doesn't want to go to jail. Tell her."

"I talked with her on the phone yesterday, I've prepared her," Mike said. "Don't worry. And good luck."

The Dominican stepped out of the booth and stopped at the bar to take a sip from his glass of rum. The barman looked at him, not sure whether to say something to him or keep quiet. Finally he decided:

"Excuse me, sir," he said. And lowering his voice, he pointed toward the man's zipper. "Your pants are wet."

"Ah, yes, you're right," Abbes stuttered, looking dismayed at the spot.

He paid and went outside.

"Ready, Ricardito," he said, getting into the car parked at the door of the Hotel Panamerican. "Put the pedal to the floor and don't stop till we get to San Salvador."

XVII

M ISS GUATEMALA TURNED BLISSFULLY under the linen
sheets in her big colonial bed. With one eye, she saw the
alarm clock through the white gauze of the mosquito net-
ting: seven in the morning. Normally she woke at six, but last night,
Carlos had burst into her bedroom very late, after an intense day of
work, and woke her, overexcited, to make love. Then they had rolled
around a long time, caressing each other, while she listened to him
curse and complain (*Just imagine, those measly sons of bitches*) about
the intrigues and ambushes he thought he was constantly uncovering
among those who were supposed to be his closest and most loyal collaborators. Now he was even suspecting Lieutenant Colonel Enrique
Trinidad Oliva, his general director of security.

Martita turned back around in the bed, still pleasantly drowsy.
She was naked, she hadn't put her nightgown back on, and the linen
sheets were cool against her body and seemed at times to be sending her little electrical pulses. How would that soft, tubby Dominican, the military attaché, make love? She had never seen another
human being less handsome than Johnny Abbes García, but even so,

or perhaps for that very reason, he intrigued her. She thought of him frequently ever since they'd met. Why? What was there in him deserving of the curiosity he aroused? His ugliness? *Are you some kind of pervert?* she asked herself. *He's got a bad reputation, that's what I hear,* Carlos had told her the day she'd managed to arrange a meeting between the two men. *He's involved in some kind of shady business with Trinidad Oliva. The Lug asked me for permission to open a casino, with the idea of promoting tourism. I said no, and now it turns out he just went ahead and did it himself, with that military attaché as a partner, using a notorious front man, Ahmed Kurony, a Turk who deals in contraband. Bastards. They won't get away with it, I'll tell you that.*

Shady business with casinos? Partner and sidekick of Trinidad Oliva, Carlos's chief of security? What was that all about? Abbes García was a mysterious guy, he had a hidden plan, something seamy was guiding his steps, his projects and actions. That much Martita was sure of. But what, exactly? What were these dark intentions about? Politics? Finance? Was he with the CIA like Mike? Had he approached her and become her friend solely to get the meeting with the president that would take place that morning? No, it couldn't just be that. Maybe the explanation for all those visits and gifts over the past few weeks— flowers, perfumes, bits of folk art—was simply that he liked her, that he was dreaming of making love to her. Wasn't that the case with many of her hangers-on? Even with Carlos and his jealousy! Miss Guatemala touched herself down there, between her legs, and saw that she was wet. Did the memory of that horrible man excite her? She laughed at herself a moment, in silence. She had time. Abbes García would be there at nine thirty in the morning, his appointment with the president was at ten, she herself would take him to Carlos's office. The National Palace was just a ten-minute walk from the house Castillo Armas had set her up in that first night when, in a bold gesture dictated by desperation, she went to ask him for help and he made her his lover.

The truth was, he had behaved well with her. Marta couldn't complain. He had quickly arranged a divorce from her husband. She hadn't seen Efrén García Ardiles again. All she knew was he was depressed and practically in hiding, jobless and demoralized after she abandoned him and his mother died, no longer practicing medicine, anxious that the government not put him back in prison. Símula told her Efrén was teaching school now and that he had grown closer to Trencito, the boy who bore his name. Their boy. Martita didn't like to think of the child she'd abandoned. But slowly she had managed to push him out of her mind, and when, in spite of everything, he appeared in her thoughts, he did so only as the son of her ex-husband. She smiled, remembering the look on the face of the minister of justice when he received an order from the president to *issue a divorce to the aggrieved party forthwith*, freeing her from the abusive marriage inflicted on Marta by her father, the prideful Arturo Borrero Lamas—another man who seemed to have withered away and vanished from public life. The minister complied without her needing to move an inch or consult with judges, notaries, or lawyers. In less than a week, the judge had dissolved their union, making her a single woman again. Just like that. Had Carlos issued the order because he wanted to marry her? Martita was certain he did, if he could ever divorce his wife. But that wouldn't be easy. Odilia Palomo de Castillo Armas posed as a devout Catholic and had the support of the archbishop and priests, who now were in control of everything. This Odilia was ferocious. She defended what she considered her rights with everything she had. Martita laughed, her face pressed into her feather pillow. There was a civil war raging in Guatemala between the supporters of the first lady, Odilia Palomo, and those of Martita Borrero, the mistress. Who would win? Now Miss Guatemala turned serious: it was going to be her. She looked at her nails: she would have liked to bury them in her rival's throat. She was fully awake now, and it was time to get up. She called Símula—she had brought her to work there, and her father had put up no resistance to her leaving—and asked her to prepare her breakfast and a hot bubble bath.

A half hour later, breakfasted, bathed, and dressed, she looked at the day's newspapers. She had always taken an interest in politics—hadn't that been what attracted her ex-husband when she was still a girl?—but it had grown immensely since she'd been with Castillo Armas. On all the front pages was the motto of the Liberationist revolution: *God, Fatherland, and Freedom*. Politics were now the center of her life. She knew her social and economic status depended on it. Thanks to politics, she had achieved the power she enjoyed. And politics would decide if it lasted or disappeared like a mirage. For now, all she had to do was make a phone call to a minister or a colonel and her recommendations were immediately accepted. So much so that, as her circle of fawners had reported to her, people—and not just the communists and Liberationists—were saying that Castillo Armas was nothing more than a lovesick clown and his mistress was the one sitting on the throne. That Miss Guatemala made the important decisions, and could do so thanks to the perversions and depravities she performed for the colonel at night in bed. She had dominated him with her sensuality, beguiled him with her witchcraft. In the depths of her heart, she liked the rumors and hearsay, even if this idea that she was deadly and imperious was false.

Was it true she had so much power over Carlos? If not, the military attaché from the Dominican Republic, Abbes García, wouldn't have needed her help to get an appointment with the president. He could have gone through the Lug, Lieutenant Colonel Enrique Trinidad Oliva, the security chief. Weren't they friends? Carlos described them as accomplices and said they were making a fortune from that casino of theirs. And yet, when Abbes needed an appointment, he'd turned to her. If it was true she had all this power, she should use it to secure a life for herself. Her future was a persistent worry for her, however much she believed in herself. It wasn't assured—it wouldn't be without money, and she had none, however generous Carlos was with her, however comfortable the life he gave her was. If her relationship with Castillo Armas ended, she would be left with nothing but her miserable savings account. And Mike's little envelopes wouldn't save her from poverty, either.

At nine thirty sharp, Símula came to tell her the military attaché from the Dominican Embassy was at the door. She ordered her to let him in.

"You're punctual," she said, extending him a hand with her usual sauciness.

Abbes García had removed his uniform cap, and his elongated head gleamed with pomade as he bent over to kiss her hand. That took her aback: no one kissed women's hands in Guatemala.

"It's not polite to keep a lady waiting," the lieutenant colonel said with a smile. "Let alone the president of the republic. You don't know how thankful I am that you've arranged this appointment, Miss Borrero."

"Don't call me Miss, it makes me sound old," she replied, likewise with a smile. "Just call me Marta, I've told you that before."

The lieutenant colonel had hired a limousine and liveried chauffeur to take them to the National Palace, though it was close enough that they could walk. Martita told the two guards who escorted her to wait at the doors to the palace. When they arrived, Martita saw that the banner reading *God, Fatherland, and Freedom* had been replaced by an even larger one—with the same slogan that had appeared on countless posters throughout the city since the triumph of the Liberationist revolution. The lieutenant colonel recalled that the Dominican Republic had adopted the same motto under the leadership of Juan Pablo Duarte when they were fighting to emancipate themselves from the Haitian occupation.

When they recognized her, the detachment of guards let them pass without the usual pat-down. Inside, the aide-de-camp, a young lieutenant, saluted them, clicking his heels and bringing his hand to his peaked cap. He guided them to the president's office and opened the door for them himself.

Castillo Armas got up from his desk as soon as he saw them enter.

"I'll leave you two here to talk . . ." Martita said.

"No, don't go, you can stay." The president stopped Miss Guatemala. "There are no secrets between you and me, correct?"

He turned and gave Abbes García his hand.

"A pleasure, Lieutenant Colonel. We meet at last. You can imagine how busy affairs in this office keep me."

"Generalísimo Trujillo has asked me to convey his warmest greetings," Abbes García said, putting out his soft, fleshy hand and bowing courteously to the Guatemalan leader.

Castillo Armas guided his two visitors to a row of red velvet arm-chairs that occupied an entire corner of his office. When a waiter in a white jacket appeared, he offered them coffee, soft drinks, and iced water.

"How is His Excellency the Generalísimo?" Castillo Armas asked. "I'm a great admirer of his, as you know. Trujillo is a guide and example to all of us in Latin America. And not only because of his success in defeating so many communist conspiracies bent on overthrowing him. More than that, he has known how to bring order to the Dominican Republic and to develop the country remarkably."

"The admiration is mutual, Your Excellency," Abbes García said, bowing once more. "The Generalísimo thinks highly of your crusade for liberation. You saved Guatemala from becoming a Soviet colony."

Martita was growing bored with these exchanges of gallantry between the two officials. *It's like they're Japanese*, she thought. Was this all Abbes García was after when she got him this appointment with Carlos? An exchange of compliments?

As if he'd read her thoughts, the Dominican lieutenant colonel turned grave, bent down slightly toward the president, and murmured:

"I know you're a very busy man, Your Excellency, and I don't want to waste your time. I've asked for this appointment to convey to you a message from Generalísimo Trujillo. Since it's a very serious matter, he asked me to speak to you in person."

Marta, who had been observing a painting of Mayan pyramids surrounding a lake, held still. She focused all her attention on what the Dominican was saying. Castillo Armas leaned in soberly toward his guest.

"You can speak freely here. Don't worry about Marta. She and I are one and the same. She can be quiet as a grave if need be."

Abbes García nodded. He had lowered his voice so much, his words were little more than a sigh. His eyes were fretful, and a vein in his forehead swelled, seeming to divide it in two.

"The Generalísimo's secret service has detected a conspiracy to murder you, Your Excellency. It's been underway for some time, with instructions and funding coming from Moscow."

Martita noticed the firmness in Castillo Armas's face, which didn't even turn pale.

"Another one?" he murmured, grinning. "Every single day the Lug— Lieutenant Colonel Trinidad Oliva of the intelligence services, I mean— you two are friends if I'm not mistaken—comes to me with one."

"This is an international conspiracy," Abbes García continued, as if he hadn't heard him. "Of course, former presidents Arévalo and Árbenz are behind it. But the Russians are the real planners, and they likely chose the men meant to carry it out. All of international communism is behind the scheme. Not to mention Moscow's gold."

During a pause, Castillo Armas took a slow sip of water.

"Is there proof?" he asked.

"Of course, Your Excellency. Trujillo would never send you information of this kind if he hadn't verified every last point. Naturally, our intelligence services have been spending their days following every step of the plot."

"I'm well aware people want me dead, and they have for some time," Castillo Armas said, shrugging. "We drove the reds out of power, and that's not something they'll easily forgive. All that remains to be seen is who defeats whom."

"Exactly," Abbes García interrupted him, turning his palms outward. "The Generalísimo has asked me to tell you something else. That he has the means to bring an immediate end to this episode."

"Might I know how?" the Guatemalan leader asked, surprised.

"Cutting off the problem at the root," Abbes García said. He paused, then added, staring straight at the president: "Liquidating Arévalo and Árbenz before they liquidate you."

Now Miss Guatemala's heart skipped a beat, and she thought it had stopped. Her hands began to sweat. Less because of what Abbes García had said than for his glacial, cutting tone, his vicious, unshifting stare as he pinned the Guatemalan leader with his bulging eyes.

"Trujillo understands that for you, it will be difficult to take such radical steps," the Dominican said, moving his right hand in a circle to drive home his words. "But back in Ciudad Trujillo, we've made all the preparations for this kind of operation. You won't have to intervene at all, Your Excellency. We won't speak of this issue again. You won't be informed of the preliminaries of the plan or when and how it is carried out. You won't even have to see me again after today, if that's how things must be. All you have to do is give us your approval and forget about it."

A long silence fell over the office when Abbes García stopped talking. Marta's heart was pounding faster and faster. On Castillo Armas's desk, among the stacks of papers, was a document framed in glass with the initial motto of the revolution—*God, Fatherland, and Family*—coined, it was said, by Archbishop Mariano Rossell y Arellano, with the colors of the Guatemalan flag. Later, someone had changed *Family* to *Freedom*. Martita's attention was so acute now, she thought she could hear all three of them breathing. The president had lowered his head in reflection. After a few seconds that seemed like centuries, she saw him smile a moment, and finally he muttered:

"Please thank His Excellency for this offer, Lieutenant Colonel." He spoke as if he were counting the syllables of each word. "He's a generous man, as I'm well aware. His help was essential in the crusade I had the honor of leading."

"There's no need to give me an immediate answer," Abbes García said, bending forward again. "If you'd like to think it over, consider, there's no problem, Your Excellency."

"No, no, I prefer to take care of things now," the leader replied bluntly. "My answer is no. Those two are better alive than dead. I have my reasons, and eventually I will explain them."

He seemed on the verge of adding something, but he then closed his parted lips, not uttering another word. His eyes had wandered off to some indeterminate point in space.

"Perfect, Your Excellency," Abbes García said. "I will communicate your response to the Generalísimo immediately. And, it goes without saying, I will have all the reports about Arévalo and Árbenz's plans, that is to say, Moscow's plans, sent over to you."

"I appreciate it. Don't forget to extend my thanks to President Trujillo for his proposal," Castillo Armas added, standing up in a way that made clear their meeting was over. "I know he's a good friend, someone I can trust. I wish you a pleasant stay in my country."

Abbes García and Miss Guatemala stood up as well. Castillo Armas shook his visitor's hand.

"Good luck with your work in Guatemala," he said. Then, turning to Marta, less formal now, he added: "I'll try to have lunch at home. But don't wait for me. You know my time is not my own."

She and the lieutenant colonel departed from the National Palace in silence. Once they were outside, before stepping into the car, Abbes García whispered to her:

"I don't know if it was a good thing for you to hear that conversation, miss. But there's nothing to be done, this may have been my one opportunity to pass Generalísimo Trujillo's message along to the president in person."

"I didn't hear anything, and I don't remember anything," she said severely. "You don't need to worry about that."

They said nothing while the vehicle drove them back to Miss Guatemala's home. The lieutenant colonel got out first to open the door for her. When he said goodbye, Miss Guatemala noticed his hand was hot and moist, that it held hers longer than was prudent, and that he looked at her a long time, boldly, almost obscenely. She shivered.

XVIII

LIEUTENANT COLONEL ENRIQUE TRINIDAD OLIVA crashed into
his office and shouted from the doorway:
"Someone's assassinated the president! Activate emergency
measures! Close the borders! We need patrols at all strategic points!
Put the military bases on lockdown! No exceptions!"

For a moment, he saw how perplexity immobilized the civilians
and soldiers, who looked at him without managing to do anything.
They were frightened, stunned, some standing, some sitting at their
desks. A second later, all were on their telephones, sending his orders
out across the country.

"Apparently it was one of the soldiers escorting him," the lieutenant colonel said. "I need to speak with the head of the presidential
guard immediately."

"Yes, sir, right away," one of his secretaries said, a young man in
civilian clothes and glasses, with a pencil behind his ear, who dialed
the number and passed him the telephone.

"This is Lieutenant Colonel Enrique Trinidad Oliva, Director
of Security," he said as soon as he'd grabbed the receiver, shouting

so that everyone in the office could hear him. "Who am I speaking with?"

"This is Major Adalberto Brito García," the voice on the other end replied. "The news is confirmed, sir. A soldier from the presidential guard is the guilty party. Apparently he's committed suicide. According to the medical examiner, who showed up on the scene immediately, the president received two bullets to the chest. One of these was fatal."

"Have you arrested any suspected conspirators?" the lieutenant colonel asked.

"Not yet, sir. We're going through the Palace room by room. I've ordered everyone to stay on the premises until further notice. The dead soldier's name is Romeo Vásquez Sánchez. He seems to have killed himself immediately after committing the murder. Almost all the ministers are here. The president of the congress, Mr. Estrada de Hoz, also just arrived."

"I'll be over there soon to put emergency measures in place," Trinidad Oliva said. "Keep me informed of any developments. Wait— how is Odilia?"

"The doctor has given her tranquilizers. Her dress is covered in blood. Don't worry—I'll keep you up to date."

Enrique Trinidad Oliva walked over to his second-in-command, Ernesto Eléspuru, who stood when he saw him approaching. He was pale, and asked him in a low tone:

"Was it the communists who killed him? I could have guessed it."

"Who else if not them?" his boss said. "At any rate, we need to start arresting suspects immediately. You take charge of that. I've got a list for you here. Don't let anyone get away. You answer to me on this."

"No need to worry, I'll send the order out right away."

Lieutenant Colonel Trinidad Oliva, now on his way out, turned around and walked back.

"Have Marta Borrero, the president's girlfriend, arrested, too," he ordered his subordinate. "Now."

Commander Eléspuru stared at him, perplexed.

XIX

F OR MARTA, the day of July 26, 1957, started off not bad, but very bad. She'd had nightmares, had barely slept, and the first thing she saw when she opened her eyes was a black cat on the windowsill looking at her with diabolical green eyes. A shiver ran from her head to her toes, but she was quick to react. Pulling aside the mosquito net, she grabbed a shoe and threw it at the cat with fury. When it struck the windowpane, the creature scurried off.

The bad dreams, the bad night weighed down on her body, but she got up and went to the bathroom, where she leaned against the vanity. She felt her hand slip over the small mirror resting there, and it crashed on the tile floor, breaking into a thousand pieces. Now she was completely awake. *A black cat, a broken mirror*, she thought with a tremor. An unlucky day. A day when she'd do best not to leave the house, because something bad could happen to her, anything, an earthquake, a revolution, any catastrophe imaginable: devils were running loose and they could do whatever they wished.

She put on her robe and asked Símula to make her breakfast and draw her a hot bath. While she drank her tea, eating a tortilla with a small dish of beans, she flipped through the day's newspapers. The phone rang. Margarita Lavalle, the justice minister's wife and a close friend of hers, was calling to ask if they could go together to the party being thrown by defense minister Juan Francisco Oliva that night to celebrate his birthday.

"Carlos didn't tell me anything about the party," Marta replied. "He always forgets these things. Or maybe they sent an official invitation to Odilia?"

"No, no," Margarita assured her. "I just spoke with Olinda, you know she's on your side and she told me she'd invited you, not his wife."

"If that's the case, then I'm happy to go with you," Miss Guatemala said. "Carlos will most likely be home for lunch. I don't know if he'll prefer we leave straight from here or if he'll go from the National Palace. Either way, we can attend together, obviously."

The war between Martita and Odilia, the wife of Colonel Castillo Armas, had taken on disturbing proportions. The wives of the ministers were now being drawn in: Margarita, wife of the justice minister, was one of Miss Guatemala's fervent defenders, and apparently the defense minister's wife (her name was Olinda? All Marta could remember of her was her enormous jostling behind) was also on her side. Deep down, this skirmish stroked her vanity, but things were starting to look dangerous. Even Mike, that strange gringo, had told her: *This little war between you and Mrs. Odilia Palomo is getting ugly. I don't think it's good for anyone. Don't you agree?*

Martita laughed, remembering the gringo. Was his name really Mike? *Let's just say he calls himself Mike*, Abbes García had told her the day he introduced them. And added, without further explanation: *It's a fake name, obviously.* Everything about him was mysterious, but she had no doubt he was with the CIA. He never asked her about big secrets (even if he had, she couldn't have revealed any), just gossip, trifles, chatter. One day she'd joked that if he wanted her to keep supplying him with information, she'd need to pass him an invoice. To her surprise, the next time they saw each other, Mike handed her an envelope, saying she deserved to be compensated, since he was taking up so much of her time. *I've never known how to give a woman presents*, he said, *not even my wife. I think it's better if they buy them for themselves.* She hesitated, wondering whether she should throw him out, but in the end, she accepted. It was a dangerous game, she knew, but she liked danger, and those envelopes enabled her to have a little money of her own. Was it strange? Of course it was, very strange. Her life was strange nowadays, thanks mostly to that Dominican lieutenant colonel and the gringo whose name wasn't Mike.

Carlos came for lunch at midday. His mood was unbearable. When she told him Margarita had called to ask if they could go to the party together that night, all he said was, *What party is this?* Then he carried on ranting about the Lug: he did nothing, knew nothing, was a damn loafer, and worse, he hid things. He could well be a traitor, like so many others. It seemed to Marta that the presidency, far from making him happy, had embittered Carlos. He was always irritable, stressed, obsessed with intrigues and conspiracies among everyone around him.

A few minutes later, poking at his ground beef and rice, he turned to her and asked her again, with no change in his testy demeanor:

"What party is this again?"

"The defense minister's. It's at his home, they're celebrating his birthday. A fancy affair, according to Margarita. All the ministers and their wives are invited."

"But not me. Doesn't that strike you as rude?" Castillo Armas asked with a shrug. "All the ministers are invited to a party, but the president gets passed over. Do I have another traitor in my cabinet? Before now, I always assumed Juan Francisco Oliva was one of my most loyal men. But of course, I could be wrong. He *is* Trinidad's brother, that would explain everything."

"You're right, it's very odd," she agreed. "Margarita told me your wife wasn't invited, either. Apparently Olinda, the minister's wife, has taken my side."

Castillo Armas seemed not to hear her. He was pensive, his face furrowed.

"Every day, more and more unexpected things are happening," he said. "I don't think Oliva is in the right post. That's too much responsibility to entrust to a fool like the Lug. Let alone to a potential traitor."

"You're thinking of firing your security director?"

"I don't trust him anymore." Carlos was pallid, and instead of eating, he just stirred his ground beef and rice back and forth with his fork. "I've been noticing suspicious things about him for some time. He's not shooting straight with me, he's envious, he mucks things up. A resentful man is always dangerous."

"Can you tell me why you distrust him all of a sudden? He used to be your friend," Marta said. But she saw that Castillo Armas was once again lost in thought. His growing worries were eating away at him, absorbing him day and night. What had he learned? What had put him in such a mood? She watched him as he got up brusquely before drinking the strong cup of coffee he always had at the end of his meal.

"I'm going," he said, leaning over mechanically to kiss her on the head. He hurriedly put on the jacket he had thrown on an armchair and bounded toward the front door.

What the hell was happening in Guatemala? Marta had not the intuition, but the certainty that the black cat and the broken mirror were a foretaste of something ominous that could have devastating effects on her life. Was Abbes García's sudden departure for another country also a sign things were going south? What in the hell was about to happen?

The Dominican military attaché had showed up at Marta's house two days before without warning, at three in the afternoon, when she had just awakened from the brief nap she usually took after eating.

"A thousand pardons for bursting in like this unannounced," the lieutenant colonel said, taking her hand in the entryway. "I'm here to say goodbye."

He was in civilian clothes, a jacket and tie, with a bulky suitcase in his hand.

"Government mission," he explained. "They're sending me to Mexico for a few days."

"So it's a work trip?"

"Yes," he said hastily, rolling his bulging eyes and passing his tongue over his dry lips. "I'll be back in two or three days at most. Anything you would like from Mexico?"

"It's kind of you to come say goodbye," Martita said, blinking. "Have a nice trip. And I wish you success on whatever mission it is they've assigned you."

She motioned for Abbes García, who was still standing, to take a seat, but he replied that he was in a rush. His manner was grave, and his face became stern when he continued, lowering his voice slightly:

"You know, Marta, how highly I think of you."

"The feeling is mutual, Lieutenant Colonel," she said with a smile.

Abbes García didn't laugh. He glanced around, as though trying to verify no one was listening in.

"I tell you that because, if something were to happen in my absence, I want you to know you can always count on me. As a faithful, loyal friend. For anything."

"What is it that might happen, Lieutenant Colonel?" Marta asked, unsettled.

"In our countries, unexpected events are a fact of life," Abbes García said, with a smile that was more like a grimace. "I don't want to upset you, far from it. But if, while I'm gone, you need help of any kind, call Mike, or call Gacel. I've written both their numbers down for you on this piece of paper. Don't lose it. You can call them anytime, day or night. See you soon, my friend."

He handed her the piece of paper, kissed her hand, and left. Marta hadn't thought much of the lieutenant colonel's strange way of saying goodbye to her before—she had taken it for mere gallantry on the part of an admirer. But on that day full of strange occurrences, it suggested something darker. What was the reason for his sudden departure, for giving her those telephone numbers? She looked in the drawer of her vanity—the two numbers were still there. She was holding the paper in her hand when Símula came to tell her Mike wanted to see her.

He was dressed as always in jeans and a plaid shirt, the sleeves rolled up to reveal his hairy arms. He spoke fluent, almost perfect

Spanish. Abbes García had told her he was a meteorologist associated with the United States Embassy and that he wanted to meet her to find out more about the social and political situation in Guatemala. Marta still found it disturbing how, after conversations that involved gossip as well as political matters, he would pass her those envelopes full of dollars as though it were the most natural thing in the world. But she justified it with the thought that at least she was making money of her own. She had nothing else, apart from what Carlos gave her for the upkeep of the house, and that was the bare minimum. But this time, Mike wasn't there to talk politics or gossip. He was warning her. He did it with eerie directness, as he did everything.

"I'm here to alert you, Marta," he told her with a hint of alarm in his pale eyes. "As you well know, you have many enemies. On account of your situation, your relationship with the president, that is. And there may be difficult or unusual moments in store for you."

"What does that mean, Mike?" Marta interrupted. She didn't want to seem frightened, but she was.

"Pack a bag with whatever's absolutely indispensable," Mike said, glaring at her and lowering his voice. "Be ready to leave if it comes to that. At a second's notice. I can't say any more. Don't breathe a word of this to anyone. Especially not to Colonel Castillo Armas."

"I don't keep anything from Carlos," she reacted, unnerved.

"This you're going to keep from him, it's for you to know, no one else," he said sternly. "I'll call you or come get you if it comes to that. Do not leave this house for any reason. Don't have anyone in, either. I will come here, or Carlos Gacel Castro will come on my behalf. You've met him, correct? The ugly one—that's what everyone remembers about him. What I'm telling you is for your own good, Marta. Believe me. I have to go. See you soon."

The gringo left without shaking her hand. She was stunned, speechless. She didn't even have the chance to ask him what was the meaning of those orders he'd given her. Anyway, who was he to be giving her orders? Had this gringo lost his mind? What was happening in Guatemala? It occurred to her the president must be in danger, and that it was her obligation to do something about it. This was serious, and there was no doubt some kind of conspiracy was underway. Maybe a coup d'état. How did Abbes García and Mike know? She picked up the phone, but she wavered before dialing. What if it was too late to tell him? Besides, Carlos knew nothing about Abbes García and Mike's visits. He would want explanations, concrete details, his constant jealousy would make him suspicious. She saw the trouble it could cause her. She was drowning in doubts, and anxiety left a pasty feeling in her mouth.

She was torn for the rest of the afternoon. Should she call Carlos or not? At a certain point, not really conscious of what she was doing, saying nothing to Símula and still uncertain whether to phone Carlos at the Palace, she filled a suitcase with all the things she'd need for an unexpected journey, including the envelopes of dollars she'd received from Mike. Her mind was a whirlwind, her heart was in her throat. Could this be the last day of her life? Was it true that there were people who wanted to kill her? That was exactly what the gringo had implied. And all this was associated in her mind with Abbes García's mysterious departure for Mexico two days ago. The fear remained with her from the afternoon to nightfall.

Around five, Símula came to ask if she should serve her tea and pastries. She was surprised to find Marta looking so pale. Did the poor thing feel ill? Marta shook her head. But she was beside herself, and didn't dare to say another word, fearing Símula might detect her turmoil and the shock she'd received.

Soon she received a call from Carlos's office at the Palace.

"Are you sure Margarita told you there was a party at the minister of defense's house?" he asked.

"Do you think I'm crazy enough to invent such a thing? I'm absolutely certain," she responded. "Why are you asking?"

"I just spoke with him and he denied it," Carlos said. "Margarita really said to you . . ."

"She told me exactly what I told you," she said angrily. "Could we go to the dinner together. And that Odilia wasn't invited. Why would I make up such nonsense?"

"It's not you, but someone's fabricated this entire story, apparently," Carlos said.

"Maybe it's his wife, the one with the enormous behind—Olinda, isn't that her name? Maybe she's planned a surprise party for his birthday and he doesn't know about it."

"Perhaps," Carlos said. "Juan Francisco seemed genuinely confused. If it's true, then we've fucked up Olinda's plans."

"This morning, I saw a black cat as soon as I opened my eyes," Martita blurted out. "And when I went to the bathroom just afterward, I broke a mirror."

"What's that supposed to mean?" the president said with a forced giggle.

"Seven years of bad luck, that's what," Martita said. "I know you don't believe in that stuff, you think it's stupid."

"Of course it's stupid," Castillo Armas replied. "Anyway, don't worry yourself."

"I don't believe in it, either, but even so, I'm afraid," Marta confessed. "Are you coming tonight?"

"I'd like to, but no, I can't," Carlos said. "I have a lot of work, I'll be here all evening. I'm meeting with a group of businessmen here at the Palace. I'm trying to convince them to invest here. I'll see you tomorrow. There's a lot going on, I'll tell you about it soon enough."

When Marta hung up, she was quaking as if from an attack of malaria. Her eyes were filled with tears. *You have to calm down*, she ordered herself. *You need to keep a cool head if you don't want them to kill you.*

She called Margarita, but she wasn't home. Or was she not picking up? She tried several times. The servants offered conflicting excuses. How could it be that Margarita had called her to accompany her to the defense minister's party if Juan Francisco told the president there was no such party? Was all that somehow related to Mike's visit and his bizarre instructions? To pack a bag with whatever she might need? Had she been right to hide all this from Carlos? Apparently the Cuban with the face of an outlaw would be coming to pick her up—Carlos Gacel Castro, he was called, the one who worked with Lieutenant Colonel Trinidad Oliva and was Abbes García's driver. To take her where? Now she decided she would call the Palace immediately and tell Carlos everything. She had to. But as soon as she picked up the receiver, she faltered and decided against it. Mike had told her *especially* not to speak to the president. Why did that gringo who wasn't named Mike take those kinds of liberties with her? Why did he give her money? Had she been wrong to traffic in hearsay with him?

She was in this anguished state when Símula came to her room to ask if she'd like to be served dinner. She looked at her watch: 8:00 p.m. She said yes, but when the food came, she didn't take a bite. She brushed her teeth, put on her nightgown, and got into bed. Her body ached, and she felt profoundly fatigued, as if she had walked for hours on end. She was falling asleep when Símula returned to her room with fear in her eyes to tell her the gringo was on the phone for her. He had said to wake her up, that it was urgent. For the rest of her life, she would never forget that brief conversation with Mike.

"What is it, Mike, what is it?"

"Gacel is coming to pick you up. He'll be there in three or four minutes. Wait for him at the door. Your guards are gone, they've been called away."

He seemed self-assured when he spoke, but Martita could sense that he was making a great effort not to give away his tension.

"Where is he taking me? I don't trust that ugly bastard."

"Right now, your life depends on him, Marta."

"I'm going to call Carlos and tell him everything," she said.

"Someone's made an attempt on the president's life. We don't know if he's dead or just badly wounded," Mike said dryly. "Lieutenant Colonel Trinidad Oliva may issue an order to arrest you for conspiracy to commit murder, Marta. If that happens, they probably won't detain you—they'll just kill you. Whether you live or die depends on you alone. They took away the escorts assigned to your home this afternoon. That's a bad sign. Go outside and get in Gacel's car, Marta."

He hung up. She didn't hesitate a second. She dressed hastily, took down her suitcase, and with Símula behind her, crossing herself insistently, she hurried through the living room, shocked to find the guards who watched over the house day and night were gone. She cracked the door. The soldiers who protected her outside were gone, too, just as Mike said. The guard shack was empty. Why had they taken away her escort? There was a black car parked next to her house. One of its doors opened, and she saw Gacel's horrible face peek out. He looked nervous. Without saying a word in greeting, he grabbed her suitcase and threw it into the trunk. Then he opened the back door to let her in.

"Hurry, miss, hurry," she heard him say.

When the car pulled away, Marta realized she had forgotten to say goodbye to Símula. The car passed through the deserted downtown streets with its headlights off. Everything seemed calm.

In future days and years, Marta would often recollect that car hurtling with its lights off through the dim streets of San Francisco, the oldest neighborhood in Guatemala City. She didn't know she would never set foot there again, or anywhere else in that country she was abandoning in a daze, with no clear idea of what was going on around her. She wouldn't forget how, perhaps for the first and last time in her life, she had known fear, panic, a terror that crept into her bones and made her skin damp. Her heart was pounding like a kettledrum, and she felt it might rise out of her throat at any moment. Was it true they had tried to kill Carlos? Why not? Wasn't the history of Guatemala full of murdered politicians and presidents? How many heads of state had been assassinated? And could she believe that Lieutenant Colonel Trinidad Oliva had given the order to arrest her? For conspiracy to commit murder! Her! My God, my God! This had to be one of Odilia's intrigues. She must be in cahoots with the security services director; people had told her the Lug had a weakness for Carlos's wife. Or was Mike trying to frighten her to get her offstage? She had never been much of a believer, but now she prayed to God with exceptional fervor to take pity on her, a poor, defenseless little woman, alone in the world, fleeing who knew where. What if this was the real ambush, and the creep driving the car at breakneck speed was the one assigned to kill her? It was possible, anything was possible. He'd take her to an empty lot, dump four bullets in her, and leave her body stretched out for the dogs, rats, and vultures to eat.

"What's happening, what's happening?"

"There's a patrol," Gacel said. "Don't move and don't say a word, miss. Let me handle it."

A barrier was blocking the road, surrounded by helmeted soldiers with rifles. She saw an officer with a lit flashlight approach the car, a revolver in his other hand. Gacel lowered the window and showed him some papers. The officer shone his light on them, examined them, approached the back window, and looked directly at her, blinding her with the glare. Then he returned the papers to Gacel without a word and gave an order to the soldiers. They pulled away the barrier to let the car through.

"Thank God, thank God," Miss Guatemala babbled. "What did you show them?"

"A pass from the Security Directorate," Gacel said in his unmistakable, singsong Cuban accent. "Here in the city, Lieutenant Colonel Enrique Trinidad Oliva is in charge, so I don't think we'll have any problems. The danger is at the border. Pray to God we get through."

"At the border?" she said. "Can you tell me where you're taking me?"

"To San Salvador," Gacel said curtly, before repeating, "Pray to God we get through, if you believe in Him."

To San Salvador? She had never had a passport, she had never left Guatemala. How would she get into San Salvador? And what would she do there? The only money she had was in the envelopes Mike had given her. She had them in her suitcase, but they didn't amount to much, and would only keep her afloat a short time. What would she do in San Salvador without even identity papers? Why was that nameless gringo protecting her? Everything had turned mysterious, perilous, confusing.

"Once we get over the border, you can sleep awhile, miss," Gacel said. "Hopefully Abbes García has already gotten through. In the meantime, we'll pray to get across. Even if I'm not much of a believer in the afterlife, either."

I'm so scared I can't pray, Marta told herself. But that didn't keep her from falling almost immediately to sleep. She had nightmares of being stalked by death in the form of wild beasts, abysses, traps that opened before her and left her no option but leaping into the darkness. One question kept revolving through her mind: Why had Gacel said that? Hadn't Abbes García said he was leaving for Mexico two days ago? Why was he wondering then whether or not he'd crossed the border to El Salvador?

"This is the hardest part," she heard the driver say. "Stay still."

She woke up right away. She saw lights, a long row of trucks and buses, and a military outpost with men in uniforms and civilian clothes. Gacel parked the car and got out with a sheaf of papers in his hands. He walked off without uttering a word, toward a wooden shack where the drivers of the buses and trucks parked by the roadside had lined up. The wait seemed interminable. The night was dark, starless, and soon it started to rain. The uneven sound of the raindrops on the car hood made her shudder. Finally, Gacel reappeared with an official in a plastic raincoat with a flashlight in his hand. Gacel opened the trunk and the official bent over and leaned in to inspect it. Would he interrogate her afterward? No, the official left without even looking into the back seat. Gacel got in, turned the key in the ignition, and sighed with relief. They drove very slowly across the bridge. The rain was fierce now, pounding like bullets against the car's frame as it climbed a high hill.

"You can sleep easy now, miss," Gacel said, not bothering to conceal his satisfaction. "The danger's past."

But Marta couldn't close her eyes again. The road was full of potholes, and her head struck the backrest with each one. How many hours had passed by the time they pulled into the big city? Three, four, five? She had no idea, she had lost all sense of time. There was still no light in the sky.

Gacel must have known San Salvador well because he never stopped to ask for directions from any of the occasional passersby circulating on the streets like shadows. The first rays of dawn began to appear on the horizon. It had stopped raining.

Finally, the car stopped at the door to a hotel. Gacel stepped out to remove her suitcase and help her out. As soon as they went inside, Marta saw Abbes García in civilian clothes sitting in one of the armchairs near the door. He looked as if he'd only just arrived. When he saw her, he got up and strode toward her. Instead of taking her to reception, where a lone woman stood observing them, he grabbed her by the arm and dragged her into the hall. He clapped Gacel on the shoulder to say goodbye, and opened a door once they'd reached the end of the corridor. Marta saw a bed and an open closet with a cluster of empty hangers. There was a suitcase, unopened. So Abbes García really had just arrived.

"I don't have my own room?" Marta asked.

"Of course not," Abbes García replied, a grimace deforming his pudgy face. "One bed is enough, especially for two people who really care about each other. Like you and me."

"I need someone to tell me what's going on in Guatemala," she said. "What's going to happen."

"You're alive, that's what matters for now," Abbes García said, the tone in his voice changing. "So here's what's going to happen next. I'm going to put it up your ass and make you squeal like a piglet, Martita."

Even more than the curse words she heard the Dominican utter for the first time, she noticed that at last the Dominican lieutenant colonel was no longer calling her miss.

XX

THE ÁRBENZ GOVERNMENT threw me in jail for anticommunism!" Lieutenant Colonel Enrique Trinidad Oliva screamed. Then he raised his hands to show his handcuffs. "Now you've got me locked up like an animal. What kind of aberration is this? I'm begging you to tell me."

Colonel Pedro Castañino Gamarra, an army lawyer and the man in charge of military justice, paid him no attention. He continued flipping through papers as if he were in his office alone. He was nearly bald, with a thick mustache like a Mexican cowboy. He was dressed in his uniform, with thick glasses to correct his myopia. Slanting light entered through the broad windows of the barracks housing the Honor Guard, and the sky outside was overcast. Farther off, in the courtyard, there were soldiers standing in formation.

"And what's worse, I'm accused of plotting to assassinate the president!" the lieutenant colonel roared, feeling drops of sweat drip down his forehead. "I demand more respect for my position and rank. I took part in the peace treaty negotiations in San Salvador. I was a member of the transitional government. The president nominated me to be head of security. I demand respect and consideration. Why won't you let me speak with my brother, Colonel Juan Francisco Oliva, who was Castillo Armas's minister of defense? Why won't you let me see my family? Or are all of them in jail, too?"

Colonel Castañino Gamarra had lifted his head, removed his glasses, and looked at the other man impassively. He didn't speak until the lieutenant colonel fell silent.

"You are not under arrest for participating in any conspiracy," he said aridly. "Don't pay attention to what people are saying. Your family is fine, they are going on about their lives. So calm down. You are under arrest for using the assassination as a pretext to exercise powers beyond the scope of your authority. Moving around military leaders, granting and revoking authorizations, ordering the arrest of honorable people without the least reason for doing so. And for declaring a state of siege without consulting your superiors. What got into you? Did Castillo Armas's death make you lose your mind?"

"I was only fulfilling my obligations!" the prisoner screamed, furious. "I had to find the president's killers. That was my duty, do you not understand that?"

"You overstepped your limits," the military justice chief replied, in a monotone voice, as though repeating a text from memory. "You thought of yourself as the new president of the republic, and you committed numerous abuses without the least justification. That is why you are here."

"I demand respect for my position and my rank!" the lieutenant colonel screamed, showing his handcuffs again, incensed. "This is an intolerable humiliation. Ridiculous. You haven't even allowed me to meet with my lawyers!"

The two of them were alone in the room. Castañino Gamarra had asked the guards who brought the prisoner in to leave after forcing him into a seated position in front of the desk. Outside, through the windows, the soldiers in formation were now beginning to march. The officer in charge of them took the lead, and was striding with great conviction. His lips were moving, but his shouts didn't reach them.

"Calm down a little," the colonel said, a bit more affable now. "This is not an interrogation. There are no minutes being taken, there's no stenographer. Do you not see that? This is a private conversation, it won't make it into the papers, there won't be a single trace of it anywhere. So relax."

"A private conversation?" Trinidad Oliva said sarcastically, showing his cuffs a third time.

"The army wants to offer you an opportunity," the colonel said, lowering his voice a bit. He looked around, as though to assure himself they really were alone. "Calm down and listen closely. I'm warning you, this offer will not be repeated, and if you reject it, you will have to accept the consequences."

"What's the offer?"

"You will present your resignation to the army, on whatever pretext you choose. Say you're exhausted, overwhelmed by what happened to the president, it doesn't really matter. And accept the charges for exceeding your mandate and abusing your position as director of security services with your appointments and your illicit arrests."

The colonel paused to measure the effect of his words. Trinidad Oliva had gone pale. In his few days as prisoner, he had lost weight, his features were gaunt, his forehead covered in wrinkles. Sweat coated his temples and cheeks.

"There will be a brief trial, very discreet, without any public spectacle. No press, I mean," the colonel proceeded slowly. He wanted to see the effect of his words on the captain. "You'll serve a couple of years in a military prison where you'll be treated in accordance with your rank. And you will get to keep your pension."

"You think I would accept such a flagrant insult?" the lieutenant colonel bellowed, once again inflamed. "Two years in prison? For what crime? For performing the duties of a director of security as assigned me by the president of the republic?"

The chief of military justice looked at him with a slightly mocking gaze. There was irony and a bit of contempt in his voice as he responded:

"I assure you, an open trial with journalists present is not in your interest, Lieutenant Colonel. The army is doing you a big favor in making this offer. Think about your future, don't be a fool and decline it."

"I'm the victim of an outrage, and I want, I demand an explanation!" Trinidad Oliva clamored, wrathful, never ceasing to show his handcuffs to the chief of military justice, who had by now lost his patience, and spoke again in severe, even aggressive terms:

"If you refuse this offer, a real trial awaits you, in front of a military tribunal. Your role in the assassination will come to light before the public. Everyone will know your lies. Among them that the killer, the soldier whose alleged diary you discovered, killed Castillo Armas to avenge his communist father. Vásquez Sánchez had no father. He never met him, he was the son of a single mother. Moreover, this diary, which you made famous, where the soldier explains the reasons he will commit suicide after murdering the president, is fake from beginning to end. Army investigators, two graphologists, have examined it closely. Both agree it's an inept fabrication. That soldier couldn't have written it, he was practically illiterate. Will it suit you to have all these fairy tales you've invented scrutinized in a public trial? Resign, accept the two years in the brig, which is a thousand times better than a common jail. Otherwise, you might spend the rest of your life behind bars. Incidentally, did you know that the deceased liked to call you the Lug? I wonder why that might be?"

XXI

COLONEL CASTILLO ARMAS OPENED HIS EYES, as he did every day, without need of an alarm, at exactly 5:30 in the morning. Even if he had gone to bed late—which he was forced to do often as president of the republic—his body was used to rising with the first light of the day, and had been since his cadet days at the Politécnica. To keep from waking Odilia, he tiptoed to the bathroom to shave and shower. When he saw his lean face in the mirror, with bags under his eyes, his pajamas sagging at the shoulders and waist, he realized he'd lost weight again. No wonder. With his headaches—a daily occurrence for three years now—and the imbeciles and traitors surrounding him, it was normal that he start to waste away. Eating had never been a passion of his; drinking was another matter. But lately food had begun to disgust him, and he'd had to force down a bit of fruit at breakfast or the tortilla with beans and chilies he had at midday whenever he wasn't called to an official luncheon. At night he made himself eat one dish, at least, along with the two glasses of rum he drank to relax and forget the bitter taste of those days that had long been filling him with frustration and rage.

While he shaved and showered, he asked himself once more when everything around him had started to crumble. It wasn't like this three years ago. Not at all. He remembered his arrival in Guatemala City from El Salvador after the peace negotiations with the armed forces, by the side of Ambassador John Peurifoy, that enormous gringo he had so mistrusted at first but who later behaved so admirably with him. The poor man had died in a collision, an assassination maybe, during his new posting as ambassador to Thailand, along with his son, who was riding in the car. May God have mercy on them both in heaven! He remembered the crowds who greeted him at La Aurora airport with hurrahs, applause, voices coming through loudspeakers. Like a king! That was how the civilians and soldiers had received him, friends and enemies, too, and the entire Guatemalan press. Right away, they had begun praising him, attending to his every wish, kissing his boots, begging for posts, ministries, promotions, contracts. Traitors! Rabble! Maybe it was on that very day, in the midst of his being welcomed, that things had started to go bad. Was that not the site of the first clash between the cadets from the Politécnica and the fleabag volunteers of the Army of Liberation? But there in the multitude, the incident passed unnoticed by many, himself included.

Three years later, everyone was conspiring against the government behind his back. He knew that very well. They wanted to eliminate him. Of course they did. Even his own director general of security, the Lug, a man he had entrusted with the country's entire special forces, the police, the military, thinking he'd watch his back better than anyone. He was sure of it: Enrique was plotting against him, too. His brother, the defense minister Juan Francisco, had admitted it (*I don't know what the hell Enrique's gotten into, you know he's always been a loose cannon. The truth is, we barely see each other anymore*). Lieutenant Colonel Enrique Trinidad Oliva was sharpening his knives, preparing to stab him in the back when the time came. But he wouldn't let him. Better still, very soon he'd be crushing him like the cockroach he was. All he needed was someone trustworthy to put in his place. He'd make him choke on his treason, humiliate himself, fall on his knees begging forgiveness. And he would brook no excuses for betrayal. Not for any of them. He swore to God!

As he dressed, he remembered his duties for the day. The delegation of natives from Petén wouldn't take long. At ten, he'd be meeting with the U.S. ambassador. He knew why: he'd be asking him for moderation and prudence. Some paradox! Now they want moderation and prudence, before it was an iron fist, doing away with all the real and imagined communists, the useful idiots and fellow travelers, the unionists and heads of the peasants' leagues, the intellectual sellouts and the exiled artists, the militants and cooperativists, the terrorists, Freemasons, even the leaders of fraternal orders. And above all, no exit visas for the people hiding out in the embassies, starting with Árbenz, the Mute! To jail with them! And if there weren't enough real communists, make up more, invent them to please those puritan know-nothings.

There was a ceremony at the Mexican Embassy, but he would only stay ten minutes, to read an address. Hopefully that text, by Mario Efraín Nájera Farfán, his consultant on judicial, diplomatic, and cultural questions, wouldn't be riddled with incomprehensible jargon or anything too hard to pronounce. Then he would receive dispatches and reports until lunchtime. Would he go to Miss Guatemala's house? Yes. He missed the serenity of mealtimes with Marta, just the two of them, chatting about anything, really, other than the present, and being able to nap for fifteen minutes afterward in the cozy wicker chair by the fan, gathering his strength before his afternoon and evening obligations began. Afterward, he would receive assorted ministers to take care of loose ends, plus the women's delegation from Catholic Action sent by Mariano Rossell y Arellano, his former friend and collaborator, and his number-one enemy ever since he'd been with Marta. It would be the usual refrain: he would need to be on guard, because the evangelicals were penetrating too deeply into Guatemalan society, especially among the poor, unlettered Indians. He would let them jabber and complain for a quarter hour's time, and then he would send them off with the appropriate reassurances: *Guatemala will be closing its doors to the evangelicals, what were they thinking, they're the last thing we need.* At nightfall, he had a meeting at the National Palace with the most important businessmen in the country. At the same time, Odilia would be representing him at an assembly devoted to education. They needed urgently to convince better-off Guatemalans to invest more in their country, to bring home the money they had stashed away in the United States. He would also have to give one more speech written by Mario Efraín Nájera Farfán. Would he go sleep afterward at Miss Guatemala's? It had been at least a week since he'd made love to her, he calculated. Or was it two? He no longer had a good head for remembering things, even the important ones. He might or might not do it tonight, it would depend on how tired he was, he decided.

When he was getting ready to leave, he heard his wife asking him, still groggy, if he would be home for lunch. Without stopping to wish her a good morning, he said no, he had official business to attend to. He walked out quickly, to avoid having to speak with Odilia. His relationship with his wife had been in crisis since he found out, a few weeks before, that she'd met with the military chiefs at their private casino without saying a word about it to him. When he questioned her about it, she turned nervous, hemmed and hawed, refused to admit it was true. Only when she heard him raise his voice did she confess: they'd invited her to discuss a *delicate and urgent* matter.

"So you think it's fine for you to meet with military men conspiring behind my back?" he asked, even louder.

"There was no conspiracy," Odilia said, holding her ground, her posture and stare defiant. "Those soldiers are your friends, they're loyal to you and they're worried about your situation."

"What situation?" Castillo Armas said, feeling rage blind him, but trying to keep himself from smacking her.

"That lover you've taken, who is now the biggest scandal in all of Guatemala!" she screamed. "And it's not just the military that's worried. The Church is, too, and so is every decent person in the country."

He was speechless. Until now, Odilia had never dared to mention Miss Guatemala in any of their fights. He hesitated a moment before responding.

"I don't have to answer to anyone for my private life!" he shouted violently. "Get that through your goddamn head for once."

"You do have to answer to me, I'm your wife before God and the law." Odilia's eyes and voice were filled with lightning. "You'll pay dearly for this scandal with that whore. That's why I met with the officers. They're worried, and they say this situation's bad for you and bad for the government."

"I forbid you to attend any further meetings with traitors!" he yelled, trying to bring all of this to a quick end. "And if you do, I warn you, you'll face the consequences."

He walked out, slamming the door behind him.

"Go to hell!" he heard Odilia shout from back in the bedroom. That was the first time Castillo Armas truly considered leaving his wife. He would pay whatever was necessary to annul his marriage in the Church and marry Marta and go live with her. With her he was happy, after all. Miss Guatemala had made him lust again, had made him feel like a man in bed. Who were those officers Odilia was meeting with? Neither shouting nor threats had compelled her to name names. He knew some, but he wasn't sure of the rest. And that imbecile the Lug had concealed all this from him. Obviously that meeting was an outright conspiracy. Those bastards were planning a coup. Obviously.

The meeting with the natives from Petén went better than expected. He thought they'd come to protest the expropriation of their lands, the dead and wounded from their clashes with the police and the landowners. But no, all they wanted was for the government to restore a church burned in a fire caused by a lightning strike and a subsidy for the friars and two local brotherhoods. Surprised, the president promised them everything they asked.

The meeting with the U.S. ambassador was more complicated. It was about United Fruit—what else? The U.S.A. recognized the efforts the government was making to compensate the company for its many losses under the Arévalo and Árbenz governments, and it was happy the Guatemalan courts and Congress had seen that it was best for the country to revoke the offending laws and restore their former accords. But what about the company's expenditures to rebuild its destroyed facilities, replace damaged machinery, legal costs, all they'd spent on unjust fines, onerous and arbitrary duties, etc., etc.? The company didn't expect the state to pay all this, but at the least the losses should be shared, following a review carried out by some neutral, prestigious firm both sides had agreed on. A bit sourly, Castillo Armas reminded the ambassador that all of that lay in the judges' hands and that his government would respect the courts' findings and pay whatever damages they assessed.

The ceremony at the Mexican Embassy lasted only half an hour, per his request. He read a speech in which Mario Efraín Nájera Farfán gave free rein to his usual baroque expository leanings, and on more than one occasion, he got lost among the verbiage so pleasing to that gentleman who had ignored the president's preference for clear, simple texts, ones that wouldn't create problems for him, throwing at him words he didn't know the meaning of. (Once again, he told himself he would have to get the man's attention, even threaten him with dismissal if he kept on giving him trouble with these disquisitions.)

Afterward, he dictated correspondence until lunchtime. He arrived at Marta's house at around 1:30, but he didn't enjoy the physical and emotional relaxation he ordinarily found eating with his beloved. He was irritated to discover that the head of the armed forces had organized a dinner to celebrate his birthday and had invited all the ministers in the government, but had failed to invite the president himself.

In the afternoon, back at the Palace, he phoned the minister of defense, Colonel Juan Francisco Oliva, and reproached him, half joking, half serious, for not asking him to the party. Colonel Juan Francisco Oliva said there had to be a mistake, and his surprise seemed sincere. It was true that July 26 was his birthday, but he was absolutely not throwing a party of any kind. To the contrary, he and his wife would be having dinner with their children, as a family, without a single guest. What kind of rumors were these? Who had come up with such a scenario?

The president called Marta, who was shocked, and assured him Margarita Lavalle, the wife of the minister of justice, had asked her to attend the festivities with her, and she wasn't the type to make things up. At first, Castillo Armas concluded that Colonel Juan Francisco Oliva had indeed organized a party, but that he would cancel it once the president heard he wasn't invited. Now he and his wife must be phoning the ministers trying to explain why they'd called it off. So Juan Francisco, feeling he'd done something wrong, would be left without a birthday party. Well done! But then something strange slipped into his mind, and the explanation appeared less and less convincing. He had a bad taste in his mouth the rest of the day because of it, and it confirmed his suspicions that he was surrounded by people he couldn't trust.

The evening's work weighed on him. At the meeting with the economic experts and the finance minister, he couldn't concentrate, despite his best efforts. This had happened frequently over the foregoing weeks. He was losing his head, no matter how he tried to make sense of those reunions, where the technocrats talked of loans, Guatemala's ratings at the IMF, the World Bank, and the Economic Commission for Latin America and the Caribbean, and other things where he felt at a complete and utter loss, and to make it worse, not one of these experts made the least effort to help him understand what the hell they were talking about. Fortunately, the minister seemed at ease with the figures and jargon, which not only confounded the president, but also bored him. He put on a serious face, kept his eyes on whoever was talking, feigned thorough concentration, and would, very occasionally, dare to comment or formulate a question, as general as possible to avoid looking like a dimwit. Even so, he saw now and again the startled, mocking faces of the experts, which let him know his intervention had missed the mark.

Did he regret it all? No, of course he didn't. If another situation arose like the one his country had been in before, he would rise up in arms again, fight, put his life on the line against the communists and their allies, the killers of Colonel Francisco Javier Arana, his friend and mentor. Some, including the gringos, were forgetting very quickly all that he had risked to save, among other things, United Fruit, which Árbenz, the Mute, wanted to see on the chopping block. Now the gringos were asking him for *moderation* against the same leftists that had them up in arms before. Yes, Colonel Carlos Castillo Armas had reasons to be disappointed. Especially with his military colleagues. He didn't have faith in a single one of them anymore. Least of all the Lug, that traitor he had so readily trusted. He was surely among the officers who had met with Odilia to talk about Miss Guatemala. Was his brother, Juan Francisco, there, too? They'd found the perfect pretext to remove him from power. But since all of them were hungry, they couldn't agree on a leader for the conspiracy. Everyone wanted to be president. For the moment, that had saved him. The insolence! Digging around in his private life, that was the last straw. As if all of them didn't have lovers, too, on the state's payroll, naturally.

When the conference with the economists was done, he had to oversee a meeting of representatives who would inform him of the latest developments concerning the laws then passing through Congress. He didn't feel as lost with them as he did with the others. But he couldn't concentrate with the congressmen either, or offer any reasonable opinions about the matters they'd come to consult with him over. His mind was incapable of staying attentive to what they were saying apart from brief stretches interrupted by the memory of that mysterious birthday dinner for the minister of defense that wasn't taking place. Why had Margarita Lavalle made that call to Marta? To get the president to ruin things for Juan Francisco Oliva by calling and asking why he wasn't invited? What had really happened? It was stupid, a trifle, probably, but there was something there, something in that confusion he would like to clear up. Was it an attempt, perhaps, to put Miss Guatemala in a compromising situation? To kidnap her, blackmail him, and force him into resigning? That was something he'd been afraid of from the moment they'd met, and it was why he had placed her house under permanent guard and forbidden her from going out alone.

When the congressional delegation left (without receiving any clear instructions from him), two secretaries appeared with a pile of letters. Requests, always requests, of all kinds from all parts of the country, generally from humble, impecunious people wanting help and begging shamelessly for money. For a few more hours, he dictated messages and acknowledged the receipt of various reports. At seven thirty, he felt the urge to cancel what remained of his agenda and go home. He was ill at ease, frustrated, dead tired. The prospect of seeing his wife depressed him, but he would forgo arguing with her and get into bed early. He would take his usual pill to get to sleep. The doctor had warned him against more than two or three Nembutals a week, but he downed one every night, because without them, he couldn't sleep a wink.

He couldn't leave yet, though. Out there in the waiting room were the ladies of Catholic Action, sent, of course, by the archbishop, another adversary hoping to be rid of him at all cost. He had them sent in, ready to cut them off if they had the temerity to touch, even indirectly, on the subject of Miss Guatemala. But the Catholic ladies avoided the issue. They were there to convey to him the worries besetting *Catholic Guatemala*, the vast majority of the country, in view of the systematic penetration of Protestant sects, so-called missionaries loaded with dollars who came here to build churches and indoctrinate the Indians; their houses of worship were more like circuses, with grotesque song-and-dance routines featuring black hordes meant to seduce the ignorant natives, after which they would campaign for divorce and a thousand other anti-Catholic practices, even abortion. If the government didn't put a stop to this aggression against the Catholic church, which was the religion of 99 percent of the population, Guatemala would soon be in the Protestants' hands.

The president listened attentively, took notes while the ladies spoke, and at the end assured them that the very next day he would order the responsible ministries to get to work on the issue. It was, as they said, a grave matter. He shared their concern. There was no doubt the influx of evangelical pastors had to be stopped. Guatemala was a free country now; it had liberated itself from communism, and it couldn't fall into some other quasi-pagan barbarism. Eventually the ladies from Catholic Action left, and he was certain each of them had the name Miss Guatemala in their head, though no one had dared to mention her. He knew perfectly well that in their private conversations, these people referred to Marta by the moniker the priests had invented to disparage her: *the palace slattern*. He'd consulted the dictionary and discovered with indignation that *slattern* was a synonym for whore.

He closed the day with a meeting with businessmen in the Palace's great hall. He had called them there himself, and he was surprised so many showed up: more than a hundred, maybe even a hundred fifty. The address was clearer and more substantive than the one at the Mexican Embassy. In detail, he described the economic progress the country was making and encouraged the businessmen, landlords, and industrialists to take a patriotic risk and invest in Guatemala to speed its recovery.

When he entered the Casa Presidencial, his wife, now home from the assembly on education, was shut in the bathroom getting her manicure and pedicure. He was so tired, he lay down in bed as soon as he'd removed his jacket and shoes. He fell asleep immediately. He had a strange dream in which, as he tumbled slowly into a dark hole, he was talking to someone concealed head-to-toe in a blanket and with the mask of a horned animal. This person told him he had to put his life in order and regain his lost joy. He tried but failed to recognize the voice. *Who are you? Tell me your name, let me see your face, I'm begging you.*

Soon his wife woke him. "Dinner's ready," she said. And she added, by way of reproach, "You've been asleep for nearly an hour."

He got up and went to the bathroom to refresh himself, washing his hands and face with cool water. They had to cross a small garden with a single acacia, then enter a hallway, to reach the dining room from the bedroom. No sooner had they stepped out than the colonel noticed something strange, but his wife was the first one to speak:

"Why haven't they turned the lights on?" she asked. "And where are the servants?"

"And my guards?" he exclaimed. They kept walking, but none of this made sense.

Why was everything dark? And where were the soldiers who stayed put in the garden twenty-four hours a day in front of the vestibule that led out to the street?

"Felipe! Ambrosio!" Odilia called for the butlers, but they neither responded nor appeared.

They were now in the passage that led to the dining room. It was dark there, too.

"Don't you find all this odd?" Odilia said, turning to her husband.

At that moment, Carlos Castillo Armas realized something, and he was turning to run to his bedroom and grab the machine gun he kept next to the nightstand when the shot rang out behind his back and made him stumble and fall facedown. As he felt the second shot blow through him, he could still manage to hear Odilia's hysterical screams.

XXII

M ANY TIMES, ex-Lieutenant Colonel Enrique Trinidad Oliva thought it would have been best for him to accept the proposal the chief of military justice, Pedro Castañino Gamarra, had made him on behalf of the Guatemalan army. But would they really have let him off with two years in a military prison, with special treatment and a pension, if he'd tendered his resignation?

Probably not. But maybe he wouldn't have spent the five years following their discussion passing through military and civilian prisons all across Guatemala, an arbitrary, idiotic, humiliating, and incomprehensible pilgrimage, a sadistic via crucis with no other purpose than to make him suffer and pay for a crime that technically he hadn't committed. Wasn't it the Dominican who twice pulled the trigger of the rifle that killed Castillo Armas? And any of those colonels, lieutenant colonels, majors, and captains would have done the same, and they were happy that someone had done it—starting with the despicable General Miguel Ydígoras Fuentes, who was now enjoying the presidency, though of course he didn't deserve it.

In those five years, he was ignominiously expelled from the army, without the right to a pension of any kind, for the worst of all crimes—treason to the Fatherland; his wife and children had abandoned him, moving to Nicaragua to escape the shame his name brought upon them; but first they'd sold his home, emptied his accounts, left him poorer than a beggar. They'd forgotten him, never visiting and never sending him food once the first few months of his imprisonment were past. His parents and siblings had forgotten him, too, as if he were the family's shameful secret.

But the worst thing was, there had never been a trial of any kind, he was never convicted, could never defend himself, even the lawyers in charge of his case at first—the ones who pretended, at least, to represent him—abandoned him when he couldn't pay them another cent, because his wife and children and other family members had left him utterly destitute.

For five years, he had lived among murderers and thieves, filicides, matricides, and patricides, perverts and pedophiles and degenerates of all kinds, illiterate Indians with no idea why they were in jail; he'd eaten the scraps the prisoners were fed, had punched, kicked, and bitten to defend his manhood when the perverts tried to take it from him in those overcrowded, promiscuous, vermin-ridden pigsties where inmates didn't even have their own cells.

For those five years in prison, the ex–lieutenant colonel had eaten nothing but shit: dingy, watery soup, filthy crusts of bread, rice full of weevils, in some places even crickets, toads, turtles, ants, and snakes. In the early days, on nights when his cravings got the better of him, he'd been forced to masturbate like a schoolboy. Later he lost the appetite for sex, and with time, he became impotent.

After two or three years of asking at every prison they sent him to, he realized they would never bring him before a judge, let alone give him a proper trial, and thinking the rest of his life would go on this way, he decided to kill himself. Even that wasn't easy in a Guatemalan prison. He made a noose with his shirts and pants and tried to hang himself while his cellmates slept, wearing nothing but his underwear. The result was grotesque. He tied the makeshift rope to a beam in the ceiling and wrapped it around his neck, but for his efforts all he got was a ridiculous bump on the head when he lifted his legs and the moth-eaten beam snapped in two. In the darkness, he couldn't help but laugh at how the injustice that was preying on him even deprived him of the right to suicide.

When the bailiff told him one fine day in the prison at Chichicastenango that he was the beneficiary of an amnesty, the news didn't move him. He was a skeleton, he spent the days clawing at his head trying to crush the lice, his hair and beard were long and matted, his shoes, shirt, and pants were threadbare and torn. They put him on the street without a cent in his pocket, with nothing but the tattered clothes on his back. He didn't even have an ID card. Fortunately, no one would recognize him. He was a different human being.

Weeks later, he arrived in Guatemala City by begging, sleeping in the rough, stealing fruits and vegetables from gardens to feed himself. He didn't know where to go or what to do. He survived the journey doing humiliating odd jobs: weeding farmland, clearing rocks and rubble from the road, for cash that seemed to dissolve in his hand. In the capital, he stayed in a shelter for the poor and needy run by an evangelical church. There, after years, he managed to take a bath with soap. He changed into clothes less ragged than those he'd had on, a gift from the people running the institution. He shaved and cut his hair. The mirror reflected an old man's face, though he was barely over fifty.

He got by for a long time doing occasional manual labor, and as a security guard, street sweeper, or night watchman for the pharmacies and markets. Then one day, passing a casino, he remembered that jeweler with the bad reputation, Ahmed Kurony, the Turk, the one he and the Dominican had made front man for their casino. He wrote him a letter asking for work, and incredibly, the Turk answered, giving him an appointment. He was dumbstruck when he saw the ex–military man enter his office. He took pity on Enrique after hearing his story, which he told in very broad strokes. Of course he could find him something to do, he promised, and would help him with identity documents as well. Surprise of surprises, he came through! Soon, Trinidad Oliva was appointed head of security for the clandestine gambling establishments that the Turk Kurony oversaw in Guatemala's capital.

XXIII

W HEN MISS GUATEMALA RECEIVED that invitation
from General Héctor Bienvenido Trujillo Molina, better known as Negro Trujillo on account of his mulatto
features, she was well established in Ciudad Trujillo, as the Dominican capital was then known. She had taken a long time to figure out
that the country possessed a president of the republic, elected and
reelected with an impeccable show of legality, who was not Generalísimo Rafael Leonidas Trujillo Molina, Benefactor and Patriarch of
the New Fatherland. No, the president was his brother, a puppet the
country's lord and master had installed to placate the North Americans who, after giving him their unconditional approval, had lately
reproached him for the eternity he'd spent in office and the utter lack
of any hint of democracy in the country since he'd risen to power in a
coup d'état in the year 1930. And it was 1960 now! Like Marta, most
of the people living in the Dominican Republic were more or less unaware that apart from Generalísimo Rafael Leonidas Trujillo, there
was a president, or the appearance of one, there to satisfy the gringos'
requirement of a democratic facade. The Dominican Republic was

their adoptive child, but recently, the two countries weren't getting along.

Marta showed the invitation to Colonel Abbes García, who'd gotten a promotion years back and was now the powerful head of the Military Intelligence Service (SIM). He examined it at length, scratching his dewlap and pinching together his brows. In a low voice, he warned her:

"Be careful, Martita. Negro Trujillo isn't a bad guy, but he's an idiot. He's got nothing to do except stand around like an ornament at whatever ceremonies the Generalísimo thinks are too boring to attend, and his life is devoted to listening to the private conversations of families in houses we've bugged and screwing his friends' wives. If you show up to that appointment, prepare yourself for the worst."

Abbes García had gotten a little fatter since she met him: his fitted uniform now swelled at the belly and emphasized the ridges of fat on his arms and buttocks; he had a growing double chin and his puffy face made his bug eyes even more prominent. As the absolute head of the country's secret police and espionage services, he was feared and hated wherever he went. Though Marta was his mistress, and hadn't dared to be with another man as long as she had been, she saw less and less of him. She would always remember that first night of love-making (could she even call it that?) with the then–lieutenant colonel from the Dominican Republic in that hotel in El Salvador where he had promised, with thuggish vulgarity, to fuck her in the ass and make her scream. He wasn't the savage lion he boasted of being; he had a stunted penis and ejaculated early, and the act was finished no sooner than it had begun, leaving her and the other women he slept with rather frustrated. The only thing he really liked was sinking his head between a woman's legs and licking her. Did he even sleep with his wife, Lupe, a mannish Mexican who walked around with a revolver, letting the handle stick up intentionally out of her purse? Marta wondered, and it made her smile. Lupe was a wreck with her big tits, wide hips, fleshy ears, and cruel, immobile eyes. There were all kinds of nasty rumors about her. They said she went with Johnny to all the brothels in Ciudad Trujillo and liked to whip the whores before she let them pleasure her. Marta had been introduced to her once or twice, and the three of them had gone out together to play roulette at the Hotel Jaragua. Marta was generally fearless, but she felt uncomfortable and apprehensive around the Mexican, who had nevertheless treated her kindly the whole time. It was known that Lupe accompanied Abbes García to La Cuarenta and other penitentiaries where they tortured and killed suspected conspirators or agitators working against Trujillo. It was said that in these torture sessions she was even crueler than her husband.

"How did you ever wind up marrying such an ugly woman?" Marta asked Johnny one night when they were in bed.

He didn't get angry. Instead he turned serious, and reflected for a while before responding. In the end, his answer was vague:

"What we have isn't love, it's complicity. Sex isn't what brings us together, not our hearts, either: it's blood. That's the strongest bond there can be between a man and a woman. Anyway, I doubt I'll be with Lupe much longer."

And it was true: she soon found out the colonel had divorced Lupe and married a Dominican named Zita. Since he never mentioned the subject, Marta acted as if she didn't know. She still saw him, but less and less often.

Had Abbes García been good to her? Undoubtedly, if it was actually true that he had saved her life back in Guatemala the night they killed Castillo Armas and that miserable lieutenant colonel Enrique Trinidad Oliva, the real killer, according to Abbes García, tried to have her arrested for complicity in the murder. Here in Ciudad Trujillo, he had set her up in a modest pension on Calle El Conde in the colonial city the day they arrived by private plane from El Salvador, and three years later, he was still paying for it from his own pocket, since her salary at La Voz Dominicana hardly covered anything and she was barely able to get by. In the early days, Abbes García would spend the night with her once or twice a week, taking her out occasionally to the cabarets and casinos and giving her money to bet on roulette. But in the past few months, he'd been kept away by the invasion attempts and terrorist attacks against the regime, financed by Venezuelan president Rómulo Betancourt and Fidel Castro's Cuba, or so he said. All that perplexed Marta, and though she didn't tell anyone, she had the feeling the Trujillo regime was plagued with internal weaknesses, irrespective of its solid appearance, and that its enemies at home and abroad, like the church and, now, the United States, were slowly undermining it. The harshest blow had come from the OAS (the Organization of American States), at the recent meeting in Costa Rica in August 1960, when the member countries, with the United States at the lead, chose to impose a trade embargo on the Dominican Republic and break off diplomatic relations.

Her radio programs had made her a well-known figure, but money remained her greatest preoccupation. Abbes García took care of her room and board, but she had left Guatemala with little more than the clothes on her back. The dollars she'd saved thanks to that gringo whose name wasn't Mike were only enough to buy a few clothes and other absolute necessities. Fortunately, Abbes offered her the job at La Voz Dominicana, a new radio station where he was an investor, before her first month in exile was out. That income, however scant, was a blessing for her. Not just that: more than a job for her, opinion journalism would become a profession, and her public face over the years. At first, she contributed brief commentaries that she would write and rewrite several times before reading them into the microphone. Soon these were reduced to notes she would use to improvise. She had a knack for it, and would often get impassioned, raise her voice, even break out in sobs. She talked about current affairs and politics in Central America and the Caribbean, with ferocious tirades against real and alleged communists. Communist, communism—those were words that for her embraced a vast swath of people of assorted ideologies and characters; all it took to be a communist was an attack or criticism leveled against the dictators, strongmen, and caudillos dead or alive—men like Trujillo, Carías, Odría, Somoza, Papa Doc, Rojas Pinilla, Pérez Jiménez, and all the South American despots present and past—whom she defended and lauded without exception. Her perennial subject, of course, was Guatemala. There was no end to her venomous assaults on the military junta that replaced Castillo Armas after his assassination. But her most unhinged invective was directed toward the so-called Liberationists, the companions and followers of Castillo Armas who had invaded Guatemala from Honduras in 1954. For a long time, she accused them of being his killers. Her worst harangues were reserved for Colonel Enrique Trinidad Oliva, Castillo Armas's chief of security, now locked up in some prison in Guatemala. She accused him not only of overseeing the conspiracy to kill Castillo Armas, but also of contriving to blame the assassination on the communists and protect the true criminals. She immediately rejected the Guatemalan authorities' contention that the foot soldier Romeo Vásquez Sánchez was the guilty party. The secret diary where he confessed to being a communist she denounced as a farce, and along with it his alleged suicide, which she swore was meant to protect the real culprits.

Her programs made her very popular in the Dominican Republic. People recognized her on the streets and asked for her autograph or a photo with her. Her attacks on the Guatemalan Liberationists—the *traitors* as she called them insistently—were brutal. Her acid broadcasts gave her the immense pleasure of meeting Generalísimo Trujillo in person. One morning, Abbes García appeared at the offices of La Voz Dominicana just as she was emerging from the studio and told her: *Come with me, you're going to meet El Jefe.* He took her to the National Palace, where they were whisked immediately into the Generalísimo's office. She was dumbstruck when she saw the man with the imposing, gentlemanly bearing, well dressed, with gray hair on his temples and sideburns. His penetrating stare made her eyes fill with tears.

"Colonel Castillo Armas was a man of good taste," the Generalísimo said in his reedy voice, examining every inch of her. Immediately afterward, he congratulated her for her speeches on La Voz Dominicana.

"It's good that you're attacking the Liberationists' lies. It goes without saying, they were Castillo Armas's true killers," Trujillo said to her. "But now it's important that you support General Miguel Ydígoras Fuentes's government. He's a good friend, and he's doing what has to be done in the country. The Liberationists are trying to cut him off at the knees. In essence, they're weaklings, and they're allowing the communists to infiltrate their ranks. Ydígoras Fuentes has more than enough courage, though, and I'm sure he will soon punish Castillo Armas's murderers."

Before leaving, Martita kissed El Jefe's hand. On every program afterward, she championed General Ydígoras Fuentes without reserve. The president, who took office on March 2, 1958, was the only one capable of emulating in Guatemala the work Generalísimo Trujillo had carried out in the Dominican Republic, she said, putting the country in order, bringing economic progress, and putting an end to *red sedition*.

What role had Abbes García played in the murder of Carlos Castillo Armas? The question brought uncertainty and grief to Miss Guatemala for years. The way things had happened pointed to the Dominican as a link, if not the intellectual and perhaps even material agent of the assassination. Wasn't his main reason in approaching her to get a private appointment with Castillo Armas? Had she not seen and heard Abbes García offer to murder Arévalo and Árbenz in the name of Trujillo? Had the then–lieutenant colonel not fled Guatemala two days before the crime? Was this to conceal all traces of his links to it? Marta had doubts about it all: the night she reached San Salvador, it seemed to her that Abbes García had arrived just a few minutes before her. And hadn't Gacel let slip that Abbes García was escaping Guatemala just as they were? Every time she raised the matter, the chief of the Military Intelligence Service cut her off, forcing her to change the subject. Why did it make him so uncomfortable? She had her suspicions about him, but she didn't dare accuse him, because she was dependent on him so long as she was in Ciudad Trujillo. Over the years, whenever he mentioned Castillo Armas, Abbes García would adopt a contemptuous tone, calling him a *weakling*, characterless, a bad choice for the CIA to head the Liberationists' revolution against Árbenz, a mediocrity, without authority or any vision of the future, an ingrate who had treated Trujillo badly, despite the money, weapons, and men the latter had supplied him with for his army before the coup. And hadn't Castillo Armas started handing land out to the peasants after revoking the Agrarian Reform law, the Trojan horse of communism in Guatemala? In human terms, his murder was unfortunate, but whoever had killed him had salvaged the anticommunist movement in Guatemala. Thankfully, General Ydígoras Fuentes was now in power, a man who was following Trujillo's model in the Dominican Republic to his country's benefit.

Marta sang Ydígoras Fuentes's praises daily on her program, which came through loud and clear in Guatemala. La Voz Dominicana's studios were the most powerful in the entire Caribbean, and their broadcasts reached Venezuela, Colombia, Puerto Rico, Miami, and all of Central America.

One day, coming out of the booth after finishing her program, Marta found herself face-to-face—what a surprise—with the gringo whose name wasn't Mike. He was little changed, a bit thinner than she remembered, but still in his jeans, boots, and plaid shirt. They hugged like old friends.

"I thought I'd never see you again, Mike."

"You've made quite a name for yourself in the Dominican Republic. Congratulations, Martita," he said. "Everyone's telling me about your program. And not just in Ciudad Trujillo. All over the Caribbean. All over Central America. You're a famous political commentator now."

"I've been waging the battle for years," Miss Guatemala said. "I'll never be able to thank you for your help back there, when Castillo Armas's killers were about to murder me."

"Let me take you for a bite to eat," Mike said. "They just opened a new pizzeria, Vesuvio, here on the esplanade."

They went to the restaurant, and the gringo treated her to an excellent pizza margherita with a glass of Chianti. He was there to tell her he was spending a lot of time in the Dominican Republic now, and he would like to resume their regular conversations, the same as back in Guatemala.

"Are you going to pay me?" she asked him point-blank. Then she continued: "You see, back in Guatemala, I had someone taking care of me, so those little extras you gave me were just that. Here I have to earn a living on my own. It's not easy, I can assure you."

"Of course, of course I'll pay you," Mike said, reassuring her. "I'll take care of it, you can count on it."

After that, if Mike was in Ciudad Trujillo, they would meet once a week in different places—restaurants, cafés, parks, churches, at Marta's pension, or at the elegant hotels where the gringo stayed. Their conversation was exclusively political. Martita would repeat for him everything she talked about on the radio and, most importantly for Mike, whatever Abbes García told her about the stability of the regime and his own work for it. At the end, just as before, he would hand Marta an envelope of dollars. When she asked once if they were both working for the CIA, he smiled and told her in English: *No comment.*

Not only did the two of them talk; Mike gave her little jobs, finding out something about someone, taking messages to men and women she didn't know, usually military figures.

"Am I risking my life doing this?" she asked him once when they were walking along the pier looking at the sea, which shimmered almost white at that hour.

"Under Generalísimo Trujillo, everyone in the country is risking their life just being here," he responded. "You're perfectly aware of that, Martita."

It was true. In recent years, the situation had deteriorated progressively. Marta realized it when she saw the growing worry of Johnny Abbes, who seemed more anxious on those few occasions when she saw him. According to him, there had been new attempts at invasion, and deaths as a consequence. All over, there was talk of raids and roundups, people disappearing without a trace, firing squads at the military bases, the murder of members of the opposition, whose bodies were left spread-eagled in the street or else fed to the sharks, according to some. Even at La Voz Dominicana, the regime's own station, Marta often heard murmurs from employees, announcers, and journalists about the ongoing decline in the political situation. She began to feel something like panic. What if Trujillo fell and the communists took over, like in Cuba? She had nightmares of being trapped in a country where the Catholic religion would be forbidden—she had become deeply devout, never missed a Sunday Mass, and took part in processions in the colonial city clad in a veil and shawl. The prisons and concentration camps would fill up, and she would certainly end up in one, too, as a known anticommunist and champion of Trujillo and all the strongmen and military dictators throughout Latin America.

It was in these circumstances that she received the invitation of General Héctor Trujillo, President of the Republic, to visit him in his office at the National Palace two days later, at seven in the evening. It arrived in the hands of a uniformed motorcyclist, and her workmates joked with her about it. Why was she only being invited to see the president now, when she'd been nearly three years in the Dominican Republic?

Marta smartened up as best she could—she hardly had dresses to choose from—and took a taxi to the National Palace at the appointed hour. An official walked her through the many rooms and chambers, which were now beginning to empty out, and left her in an anteroom, where she had to wait for a few minutes. Finally, the door of the president's office opened, and she was shown in. Negro Trujillo was dressed in a general's uniform, with an array of medals pinned to his chest, and as soon as she entered, Martita felt the blast of the airconditioning, which kept the sumptuous office almost freezing. Her first impression of him was horrible. He was talking on the phone, and motioned for her to sit down; she detested the insolent way he gawked at every inch of her with his lascivious yellow eyes while continuing his conversation. Things went on this way for several minutes; as he spoke, the president stripped her naked with his stare, shamelessly and impertinently. She was starting to be irritated.

When he hung up, he smiled, his lips peeling away from his teeth. He walked over to shake her hand and sat down across from her. He was a stocky mulatto, a bit on the short side, with a swollen belly.

"I was very excited to meet you," he said, still examining her crudely. He was dark-skinned, with a broad, meaty face and tiny, overactive hands. "I've been listening to your programs on La Voz

Dominicana for a long time. Allow me to congratulate you. Naturally your ideas are the same as mine. And the rest of the regime's."

"Thank you very much, Mr. President," she said. "May I ask you to what I owe the honor of this invitation?"

"They told me you were not just a good journalist, but also a very beautiful woman," the president said, his obscene, smiling eyes taking on a capricious expression. "And I must confess, I have a weakness for beauty."

Marta felt less flattered than offended. She didn't know what bothered her more: his stare or his metallic voice, noxious and lustful.

"Let's not beat around the bush," he said brusquely, rising to his feet. "I'm a very busy man, as you can well imagine, Martita. So we will get straight to the reason you are here."

He walked to his desk, picked up an envelope, and handed it to her. Baffled, unsure what to say, Martita opened it. There was a check signed *Héctor Bienvenido Trujillo Molina*, with the amount left blank.

"What is this all about, Mr. President?" she asked softly, knowing and not wanting to know what it meant.

"You can write the amount in yourself," Negro Trujillo said, devouring her with his greedy eyes. "Whatever you think you're worth, that's what I think you're worth."

Martita stood up. She was ashen and trembling.

"I don't have time to waste on these things," he explained, speaking without hesitation, firing off words. "I mean, I don't have time to waste on romance. That's why I said we shouldn't beat around the bush. I want to have sex with you. I want us to have a good time together. And why should I get you a present when you can get one yourself . . ."

He couldn't finish the phrase before Marta slapped him hard enough to send him wobbling. Nor was that all. Without giving him time to react, she pounced, striking him with both hands and shouting, "No one treats me like that, not you or anyone else," biting his ear and ignoring the blows he answered back with. She wouldn't let go, she had sunk her teeth in with all her strength and the indignation that was now seeping from her pores. She heard him howling something, a door opened, men in uniform entered, they grabbed her, pulled her away from the president, and she watched him bring both hands to his ear in shock—she'd almost torn it off—roaring:

"Jail! Take that crazy bitch to jail!"

She must have fainted from the punches and kicks that fell on her as the president's guard tried to separate her from him. Only vaguely, as if it were a dream, did she recall them dragging her down several hallways and a flight of stairs. When she came to, she was in a kind of cell, a windowless room with a single chair. It was lit tenuously by a bulb with flies and mosquitoes buzzing around it. Her watch had fallen off in the scuffle. Or had they stolen it? The worst part of the forty-eight hours she spent closed up in the basement of the National Palace wasn't the lack of food and water, but not knowing the hour, if it was day or night, how quickly or slowly time was passing. All around her was an overbearing silence, interrupted only occasionally by distant footsteps. She must have been in the remotest part of the vaults under the building. Not knowing what time it was somehow worried her more than her future. Were they going to kill her? How horrible it would be to remain shut up in there, in this room with one chair, unable to go to the bathroom or otherwise attend to her needs, dying little by little from starvation and thirst. The hunger she could handle, but the dryness in her throat was driving her mad. Her tongue felt like sandpaper. She lay on the floor, but the discomfort and the pain from the beating the guards had given her made it impossible to sleep. She took off her shoes and noticed a dreadful swelling in her feet. Not for a single moment did she regret the fury she'd unleashed on Negro Trujillo or clawing and striking him and biting his ear with all the strength her jaws could muster. She'd heard that mulatto bastard shrieking like a crushed rat and had seen the fear and surprise in his yellowy eyes. He could offend a woman, sure, but he couldn't defend himself. How that bastard cried—she had scared him. Even if they killed her for it, she had no regrets, and would gladly do the same thing again. Never in her life had she felt so offended, brutalized, humiliated as when that son of a bitch passed her that envelope and she saw the check inside and realized what he was proposing. The thought that she'd be willing to write down how much she wanted to make in exchange for being a whore! She smiled in the midst of her pain and uncertainty, remembered her teeth sinking into his gelatinous flesh.

She managed to sleep at times, and when she did, she dreamed that all that had been a nightmare. When she woke, she understood the nightmare was real. A sensation of doom invaded her, the certainty that those degenerates would leave her there to starve and that the worst moments would be the last ones, still to come. Then she would remember Guatemala City, Dr. Efrén García Ardiles, and the son she'd abandoned just a few years after his birth. Had his father talked to him about her? She dreamed she was urinating, and when she awoke, she noticed her underwear and skirt were damp. Would she eventually shit herself, too? She thought nebulously about her father, her housemaid Símula, who had taken such good care of her. Was the child she gave birth to still alive? He would be ten now. Could Efrén García Ardiles have left him at an orphanage? Trencito—was he alive? She hadn't heard a word about him. Once in a while, Símula would send her a few lines about her father, who remained confined to his home and sunk in despair. Her stomach hurt. The father who had adored her when she was a girl only later to reject her was now prey to bottomless rancor. Was Arturo Borrero Lamas still alive? Her thirst began to torment her, and she dragged herself to the door, pounding and screaming for a glass of water. But no one answered. There were no guards nearby, or if there were, they'd been ordered not to communicate with her. With time, weariness and weakness overtook her, and she lay there on the floor counting—her secret since girlhood for falling asleep.

When the door finally opened, men in uniform came in, lifted her up, smoothed out her clothes, and dragged her down several hallways and up some stairs. She was weak, and could only ask, for the love of God, for a little water, please, she was dying of thirst. They seemed not to hear her. They hauled her dead weight across corridors and through various rooms, stopping before a door that flew open immediately. She saw Generalísimo Trujillo himself in front of her, along with Negro Trujillo with a bandaged ear and Johnny Abbes García. The three of them observed her, alarm in their eyes. The soldiers tugged her over to an armchair and let her fall. Finally, Marta was able to get out one phrase:

"Water, please. Water. Water."

When they gave her a glass, she drank from it in small sips, closing her eyes, feeling how the cold liquid entered her body and brought her back to life.

"In my own name and in my brother's, I beg your forgiveness for what has happened," she heard Generalísimo Trujillo say in his solemn, reedy voice. "He will personally ask your forgiveness as well."

And since the puppet president of the Dominican Republic was dawdling in making himself heard, the Generalísimo, in a firmer tone, asked:

"What are you waiting for?"

Then, making the best of a bad situation, Negro Trujillo sputtered, "I beg your pardon, miss."

"That's a sorry, mediocre way of asking forgiveness," the Generalísimo said. "You ought to have told her: I acted like an ill-mannered pig and a thug, and I kneel before you now to apologize for having offended you with my uncouth behavior."

El Jefe's words were followed by an ominous silence. Martita had been handed a second glass of water, and she continued drinking it drop by drop, feeling the gratitude in her body, her veins, her bones as it seemed to restore her from within.

"You can go now, Negro," Trujillo said. "But first, you'd better remember one very important thing. You don't exist. Don't forget that, especially when you get the urge to do something stupid, like your actions with this lady here. You don't exist. You are my invention. And just as I invented you, I can uninvent you whenever I feel like it."

She heard steps, the opening and closing of a door. The puppet president had gone.

"I can see the lady is in a terrible state," the Generalísimo said. "Have her put up in the finest hotel in Ciudad Trujillo. A doctor should look at her right away. Be sure they do a thorough examination.

She is the government's guest and will be treated with the utmost attention. Now."

"Yes, Jefe," Abbes García said. "Right away."

He bent down and gave her his arm, and with great effort, she managed to stand. She tried to thank the Generalísimo, but she had lost her voice. She wanted to vomit and go to sleep. Tears flowed from her eyes.

"Be strong, Martita," Abbes García told her as soon as they were through the door.

"What's going to happen to me now?" she babbled, holding on to the colonel's arm with both hands and stumbling through the rooms and hallways.

"First, you'll spend a few days at the Hotel Jaragua, getting treated like a queen thanks to the Generalísimo," Abbes García said. Then he added, lowering his voice, "As soon as you're better, you need to leave. El Jefe has offended Negro Trujillo, and that mulatto bastard can hold a grudge, he'll try to have you killed. For now, be calm, rest, and try to recover. I'll talk to Mike and we'll figure out how to get you out of here as soon as possible."

XXIV

TAKING CARE OF AHMED KURONY's clandestine gambling dens gradually resuscitated Enrique Trinidad Oliva's will to live, his ability to sleep, his taste for food and fine clothes. And, slowly, for women. He gave himself over to his work with passion and gratitude to his employer, the man who had returned to him a humanity he thought he had lost in those five years of horror.

It wasn't an easy gig. The Turk's dives attracted dangerous fauna in a Guatemala City where criminal and political violence was on the rise every day: once-rare kidnappings, murders, and assaults were more frequent than ever. Enrique had his goons go carefully through the pockets of every customer and hold on to their weapons for the time they were in the building. Occasionally they had to break up bar fights, separating the belligerents quickly, calming the spirits of the customers to keep the place from falling into ill repute.

Hiring the muscle and keeping an eye on them was a job of its own—these weren't people you could trust. Lots of them had been to prison, and if they weren't born criminals, they'd picked up nasty habits in the slammer. Enrique had the nerve to stay on top of them, though, and would fire them at their first slipup, reminding them constantly: *Whoever messes with me will pay for it, with interest.*

He had changed his face and name. Now he went by Esteban Ramos. A trim beard covered his face and concealed his features. He rarely removed his dark glasses and had changed his haircut. He devoted all twenty-four hours of the day to his job: even when he was asleep, he was dreaming of how to improve things. He had moved not far from the Yurrita church, to a pension where they thought he was a telegraph operator and where the cat, Micifuz, had taken a liking to him and slept at the foot of his bed.

The Turk invited him once in a while to lunch or to have a drink. One day, after congratulating him for his devotion to his work, he offered him *more responsibility.* The Turk was a thickset man, half bald, in his fifties, who liked to wear rings and kept his dark glasses on day and night. *A higher salary comes with it, of course*, he added, clapping him on the arm. He warned him there would be risks involved. Enrique thus confirmed what he had already suspected: that the Turk's main income was from contraband, not gambling.

Henceforward, he would work double time, as security in the gambling clubs and receiving or sending off trucks and motorboats across all the country's borders, never asking the nature of the merchandise the Turk distributed or collected, though he had a good sense of what it must be.

He knew that by doing this he was stepping into quicksand and could wind up in jail or shot in the back at any time. But he was earning good money now, he could buy nice clothes and eat better, and one happy night he'd even paid for a whore at one of the bars around Parque Concordia. When he took her to a nearby hotel, he was reassured: he had recovered the sexual feelings he thought had been snuffed out.

With more money, he could rent an apartment in Zone 14, where the best places were being built. He got a butler and a cook, and even bought a secondhand Ford, like new. There were no problems with his papers. The Turk had connections, friends in high places, and he paid good money to people in the administration. They arranged an up-to-date identity for him as Esteban Ramos, industrial engineer. He knew he had made it to the upper echelons of the Turk's organization when, after a lunch washed down with copious beer, the Turk proposed sending him to Bogotá. He didn't mince words: it had to do with the price of cocaine. The producer in Colombia was trying to raise it exorbitantly. Enrique's mission would be to convince him to accept a discounted price; if he didn't, the Turk would lose the Guatemalan market.

Enrique couldn't believe it. He held in his hands a passport with all the necessary stamps, a photo, and his new name and profession: Esteban Ramos, industrial engineer. He left and took a room at the Hotel Tequendama in Bogotá. The altitude gave him palpitations. He got the producer to accept a reasonable price, went home, and the Turk was happy with his success.

Sometimes—at a restaurant, café, or show, or in the late hours at Ciro's, the only nightclub in the city until the Casablanca opened—he would recognize someone from his previous life, when he was a military man with a hunger for power who hadn't yet gone to jail. They never recognized him, and he never said hello. He hadn't seen anyone from his family, he didn't know anything about them. That didn't bother him: he was another person now.

But he was worried by the violence that had been spreading all over Guatemala. There were guerrillas in Petén and in the east, assassinations, kidnappings, curfews, so-called *expropriations* of banks. Crime often masqueraded as politics. And then, the military coups came one after the other. Life was more dangerous than before, for everyone. Which was also bad for business.

XXV

O N JUNE 18, 1954, when Castillo Armas's troops from the Army of Liberation crossed the border with Honduras in three places, John Emil Peurifoy, the United States ambassador newly appointed by the Eisenhower administration, had been in Guatemala for seven months. With his effervescent vigor, it could be said without exaggeration that he had not stopped working for a single day on what his boss, Secretary of State John Foster Dulles, had informed him was his mission: to destroy the regime of Jacobo Árbenz.

John Emil Peurifoy was forty-six years old, had the build of an orangutan, and had reached his post through immense labor and at the cost of many misfortunes. He had been born in 1907 in Walterboro, a small town in South Carolina, and after his parents' very early deaths, he had lived in the homes of relatives and scrounged for low-paying jobs to survive. He dreamed of being a soldier, and was admitted to West Point, but for health reasons, he soon had to leave. In Washington, he had made his living as an elevator operator. In 1936, he married Betty Jane Cox, and soon afterward he took a lowly position at the State Department. Thanks to his tenacity and ambition, he rose from the very bottom to become ambassador to Greece after the war, at a time when communist guerrillas had the country in flames and were near to overthrowing the monarchy and taking power themselves. He spent three years there.

Those were his glory days. Mixing threats with an unprecedented capacity for intrigue, a keen nose, a practical spirit, and courage bordering on recklessness, he put together a military junta supported by the crown and supplied with weapons from the United States and Britain. They defeated the guerrillas and installed a repressive, authoritarian regime. It was then that he received the nickname the Butcher of Greece. John Foster Dulles and his brother Allen, the head of the CIA, felt a man of his qualities was the ideal diplomat to represent a country that had decided to get rid of Jacobo Árbenz's government by hook or by crook. As soon as he set foot in Guatemala, in his inevitable Borsalino hat with a feather tucked into the band, he began to work energetically to demolish said government, never bothering to verify on the ground whether the accusations that Árbenz's regime was in thrall to communism were exaggerations or outright fabrications, as his second-in-command on the staff had suggested.

From the day he presented his credentials at the daunting, immense National Palace in Guatemala City, the new ambassador made it clear to President Árbenz that life for him in that country would soon be difficult. When the formalities were over, the government leader invited the ambassador to a private room. Before they toasted with glasses of champagne that a waiter had just served them, he watched Peurifoy hand him a paper with a numbered list of forty people.

"Qué es esto?" President Árbenz, a tall and handsome man, ordinarily of elegant bearing, struggled to express himself in English, and always kept an interpreter nearby. Peurifoy had his own with him as well.

"Forty communist members of your government," the ambassador said with extremely undiplomatic curtness. "I am asking you in the name of the United States to remove them from their posts immediately as infiltrators in the service of a foreign power working against the interests of Guatemala."

Before answering, Árbenz took a glance at the list. Some of the men were self-declared leftists, some good friends and close collaborators. Many were no more communist than he was. What nonsense! Smiling amiably, he turned to his visitor:

"We're starting off on the wrong foot, Ambassador. You've been badly informed. The only avowed communists on this list are the four deputies from the Guatemalan Party of Labor, and even then, most of its leaders and its handful of supporters don't have the first idea of what communism really is. As for the rest, they're as anticommunist as you are." He paused, then added, no less affably, "Have you forgotten that Guatemala is a sovereign nation and that you are an ambassador, not a viceroy or proconsul?"

Peurifoy cackled, opening his mouth wide, and a bit of foam flew out. He then spoke, slowly, to ease the work of the two interpreters. He was a large, strong man, with very white skin and dark, aggressive eyes; there was a bit of early gray hair in his bushy eyebrows and sideburns; sweat was glistening on his forehead. From that day onward, whenever he saw the ambassador, the president saw him as a man on the verge of exploding in a fit of rage.

"I had assumed that I could shoot straight with you from day one, Mr. President. You're not going to tell me this thing about your government being rife with communists is a Yankee fantasy? You've got the proof right there that it's not."

"May I know who the imaginative person who put together this list is?"

"The CIA," the ambassador responded with another insolent smile. "It's a very efficient institution, the Nazis found that out during the war. And now, thanks to Senator McCarthy, they're cleaning up the administration in North America. We've had a good number of reds there, too, just like in your government. So are you saying you won't dismiss them?"

"No, I'll be confirming them, actually," the president said jovially, taking the whole thing as a joke. "If the CIA considers them enemies, that means I can trust them. I thank you for your impertinence, Ambassador."

"It appears you and I see eye to eye, Mr. President," the latter said with a grin.

That night, at Villa Pomona, President Árbenz told his wife, María Vilanova, "The United States has sent us a chimpanzee as ambassador."

"Why not?" she replied. "Don't the gringos consider us a zoo as it is?"

The first actions undertaken by the soldiers of the Army of Liberation on June 18 and 19, 1954, were hardly auspicious for Colonel Castillo Armas. The troops who departed for Zacapa from the municipality of Florida in Honduras, one hundred twenty-two men, came upon a small Civil Guard outpost in Gualán, with thirty soldiers under Second Lieutenant César Augusto Silva Girón, a young, energetic officer ready for action. His soldiers were prepared for war, posted on the tops of the surrounding hills. They ambushed the Liberationist troops, catching them off guard and forcing them to fight tenaciously to cover their retreat. The ground was littered with dozens of dead, among them the commander, Colonel Juan Chajón Chúa, along with many more wounded. Only thirty rebels escaped death or capture.

Hatchet Face himself was traveling with the Liberationist forces led by Colonel Miguel Ángel Mendoza. They left from Nueva Ocotepeque and crossed the frontier at dawn en route to Esquipulas. There they encountered a garrison better equipped than they'd expected, spirited and anxious to fight the invaders, just as in Gualán. The Army of Liberation was saved from a humiliating defeat thanks to the emergency air reinforcements sent from Nicaragua, and particularly to the derring-do of Jerry Fred DeLarm, who dropped fragmentation bombs on the Esquipulas barracks and was lucky or accurate enough to blow apart the two cannons from one of the artillery units that was devastating the attackers.

The majority had departed from Macuelizo: one hundred ninety-eight soldiers who approached Puerto Barrios on two fronts, one on land and one by sea in the schooner *Siesta*, sent by Generalísimo

Trujillo and captained by Alberto Artiga. The plan was to pursue a pincer movement that would suffocate the troops concentrated in the military zone of Guatemala's major Caribbean seaport. But they were greeted on both sides with thick volleys of rifle fire and active rebellion from the civilian population. Brigades of port workers, armed in the previous days by the union and the government, joined the soldiers in the defense of the military base. This was the only time the so-called popular militias, which had caused so much alarm among the opposition despite their merely hypothetical existence, showed any signs of life. The Liberationists had to flee, leaving behind their dead and wounded on the battlefield surrounding the harbor. The Puerto Barrios garrison was well supplied, and the officials and soldiers were aided by the civil population, which pitched in with hunting rifles, clubs, stones, and knives. The battle dragged on for several hours, and when the attackers were defeated, the multitude executed several of them who'd been taken prisoner. In their first sally, the Army of Liberation lost everywhere it fought.

A small group of invaders decamping from Santa Ana, El Salvador, didn't even manage to reach the border: the Salvadoran army arrested them and stripped them of their arms, for which they lacked the requisite permissions. Only two days later, after frenetic activity on the part of the American Embassy, were the prisoners freed, with the order to go directly to Honduras, because the president of El Salvador, Óscar Osorio, was opposed to letting Castillo Armas's followers use his territory to plot against the government of Guatemala.

But the worst of all the rebels' disappointments during those first two days of the invasion was the utter failure of the Liberationists' air force to supply armaments to the rebel commandos who their informants had told them were already operating in Guatemalan territory. That was a lie—pure propaganda. Colonel Brodfrost sent the Douglas C-124C cargo planes at the agreed-upon time, but the teams that were supposed to receive the loads of weapons, food, and medicine parachuted in never appeared. The North American pilots flew over the drop sites and the surrounding areas for a long time, until they received the order to return to Managua, either leaving their consignment on board or dumping it into the sea. Allen Dulles, the head of the CIA, authorized a fourth Douglas C-124C in addition to the other three, and supplied the funds for its purchase. The fleet continued to grow in the succeeding days until, on the eve of the invasion, it had six C-47 (DC-3) cargo planes, six F-47 Thunderbolts, a P-38 fighter, a Cessna 180, and a Cessna 140. The pilots, all of them gringos, made two thousand dollars a month plus bonuses for every successful mission.

In meetings with Peurifoy over the course of nearly eight months, President Árbenz tried to explain to him the country's true situation. He insisted that the measures his government had undertaken, including the Agrarian Reform, were meant to turn Guatemala into a modern, capitalist democracy like the United States and the other nations of the West. Were there any *collective farms* in the country? Had any private companies been nationalized? The fallow lands the government had nationalized and disbursed among the peasants and the poor were individual plots to be used to develop private agriculture in a free market. *Yes, listen clearly, Ambassador, ca-pi-ta-list*, the president hissed, and the interpreter did the same. If the government wanted to tax United Fruit the same way it taxed every other grower in Guatemala, it was in order to provide the country with schools, highways, and bridges, to pay teachers better, to attract competent government workers and finance public works that would pull the indigenous communities, the immense majority of Guatemala's three million citizens, out of isolation and poverty. President Árbenz insisted on all this, though he had realized quickly that Ambassador Peurifoy was a man immune to all reason and argument. He didn't even listen. He simply repeated, like a ventriloquist's dummy, that communism was making inroads all over the country. Hadn't the archbishop himself, Monsignor Mariano Rossell y Arellano, said so in his famous pastoral message? Hadn't it been clear since the formation of the unions back in the days of Juan José Arévalo? Weren't there agitators out spreading the spirit of rebellion among the peasants and workers? Were there not land thefts, farms being invaded?

Didn't the businessmen and large growers feel threatened? Hadn't many of them left the country? Didn't the radios and newspapers talk about it every day?

"Aren't there unions in the United States?" Árbenz replied. "The one place there aren't free and independent unions is Russia."

But the ambassador didn't care to understand and repeated, sometimes in a calm tone, sometimes in a menacing one, that the United States wouldn't allow a Soviet colony between California and the Panama Canal. That was the reason—*no intimidation implied*—that the Marines were already surrounding Guatemala, stationed across the Caribbean and the Pacific.

"Do you know how many Russian citizens there are in Guatemala at this very moment?" Árbenz asked. "Not a one, Ambassador. Would you mind telling me how the Soviet Union plans to turn Guatemala into a colony if there is not a single Soviet citizen in the country?"

Árbenz's protests against the worldwide press campaign spawned in the United States were equally pointless. How was it possible that newspapers and magazines as prestigious as *The New York Times*, *The Washington Post*, *Time*, *Newsweek*, and the *Chicago Tribune* could invent something as fantastical as communism in Guatemala?! It was a lie through and through, an indecent caricature of reforms whose entire point was to prevent poverty, injustice, and social inequality from pushing the Guatemalans *toward* communism. The diplomat responded dryly that the United States was a democracy with a free press, and the government didn't get involved with it. With a wealth of details, Árbenz explained that the Agrarian Reform hadn't nationalized a single plot of land La Frutera had cultivated—nothing from United Fruit, nothing from the Guatemalan latifundistas. The only lands affected were unused, unplanted. And when they did nationalize them, they paid the owners the same value they had assigned these parcels on their tax declarations.

The president asked the ambassador to stop meeting with soldiers and encouraging them to try to overthrow his government—Peurifoy didn't move as he said this—and to tour the country instead, to see with his own eyes how a half million Indians finally had lands of their own that could help them become homeowners—*yes, Mr. Ambassador, home-ow-ners*—prospering and making Guatemala a society without hunger, exploitation, or poverty, following the model of the United States. Shielded by insensitivity, obsessed with his mission, Peurifoy never bothered to travel outside Guatemala City. And in all his interviews with the president, he kept repeating a single question:

"Why is your government so dead set against a North American company like United Fruit, Mr. President?"

"Do you believe it's right, Mr. Ambassador, that La Frutera has not paid a single cent in taxes in more than half a century operating in Guatemala?" Árbenz responded. "That is correct: never in its history. Not one cent. True, it did bribe dictators, Estrada Cabrera, Ubico, so that they would sign those contracts exempting it. But now I'm here, and they can't bribe me, they're going to have to pay, the same way businesses do in the United States and in all the Western democracies. Don't companies in your country pay taxes? Anyway, here it's only half of what they have to pay there."

The president knew he was wasting his breath. He knew Ambassador Peurifoy wouldn't give up his efforts to push the army to rise up against his government in a coup. He had asked his ministers if he could censure him and throw him out of the country, but Chancellor Guillermo Toriello was against it, saying it would only aggravate the crisis with the United States and might even be the pretext for an invasion of Guatemala by the Marines. This supposed invasion was talked about constantly on all sides. Árbenz knew it was a source of dread for the officers in the Guatemalan army, who feared they would be pulverized. Confidential surveys conducted by the government indicated that in the case of a Yankee invasion, between half and two-thirds of the Guatemalan army would go over to the enemy side. This was his greatest worry. He had managed to keep his colleagues in the military under control, but he knew that as soon as the Marines set foot here, the armed forces would crumble. At these moments of tension, he felt a kind of itch throughout his body—the need for a shot of whiskey or rum. But he never gave in to temptation.

When Árbenz told Peurifoy he was the first anticommunist in Guatemala, he saw the other man smile wryly. When he asked—leaving aside the total absence of Russians in the country—what kind of Russian satellite had never had commercial or diplomatic relations with the Soviet Union and moreover boasted a constitution that prohibited international political parties, Peurifoy didn't bother answering. Nor did he reply—even if his expression grew more skeptical—to Árbenz's assertion that the Guatemalan Party of Labor, which at least did call itself communist, was a risibly small organization. On various occasions, Peurifoy had suggested that though they had only four congressmen, they controlled all the unions, and that was a reality that had sowed terror among the landholding families and businessmen, many of whom had been forced to move elsewhere after their properties were taken over. *There's nothing to be done*, Árbenz thought. *They've sent us an imbecile.*

And yet, John Emil Peurifoy wasn't an imbecile. A fanatic and a racist, yes, a McCarthyite, a somewhat dense man who took a long time to grasp things intellectually, as Árbenz's wife, Mrs. María Cristina Vilanova, had repeated day and night to anyone who would listen from the first time she had met him. But he was efficient, he would hammer blindly until he had destroyed whatever obstacles stood between him and his objectives. He'd been bold enough to try to buy off the head of the army, Colonel Carlos Enrique Díaz (Little Árbenz the Second), whom a CIA messenger had offered two hundred thousand dollars on a trip he took to Caracas for the purposes of *collaboration with the United States*. Colonel Díaz rejected the offer, and when he returned from Venezuela, ran to tell President Árbenz the story. He confessed that he was *terrified* in Caracas, thinking his wife had asked someone to tail him—he'd taken his lover with him on the trip.

Ambassador Peurifoy closely followed the same strategy he had employed in Greece, convincing the military chiefs that Árbenz's policies were harmful not just to the country, but to the armed forces—the very institution the communists would destroy as soon as they were in power, replacing them with popular militias led by the party, just as they'd done in Russia and in the people's democracies they had co-opted after the Second World War. The ambassador made no effort to cover his tracks, and Árbenz and his government knew his every move. The president saw them as *provocations* meant to force him to expel the ambassador and give the U.S.A. a pretext for invading the country. Peurifoy met with the colonels and majors with troops under their command, starting with the head of the army, Colonel Díaz; Colonel Elfego H. Monzón, the head of the Civil Guard; Colonel Rogelio Cruz Wer; and Major Jaime Rosemberg, who oversaw the Judicial Police. They conferred at the embassy, or at the casino, or in the private homes of landowners and businessmen horrified at the reforms—particularly Decree 900, the Agrarian Reform Law—some of whom were enraged at having to pay taxes for the first time in their lives. The ambassador advised them that if things continued to get worse, the United States would have no choice but to intervene. Were they willing to face off against the most powerful army in the world? Then he reminded them that since 1951, when these communist strategies Árbenz referred to as *social measures* first appeared in the country, the United States had been obliged to respond with an embargo that prohibited Guatemala from importing armaments, munitions, or parts for their military equipment from any country in the West. The boycott had the support of numerous European countries, and it had caused great damage to the Guatemalan army. Were they not well aware of that? And was this not reason enough to take action and depose the present government?

Nonetheless, the ambassador noted on June 18, as Castillo Armas's forces were crossing the border with Honduras, that the reaction of many of the officers he had met with periodically was one of contempt. They found it *intolerable*, an *act of betrayal*, that this piddling soldier, this insignificant milksop, would rise up against his own country with a band of mercenaries, many of them foreign. The exasperation throughout the armed forces led Peurifoy to change strategy and ask first that the State Department and the CIA make their support of the *traitor* Castillo Armas less explicit, and second that Washington admit the virtues of the *institutional coup* he himself had advocated from the beginning.

Thanks to Peurifoy's efforts, the embassy now had contacts among Guatemala's officer class. They were *much more economical than the Greek officers*, he informed his superiors at the State Department. Not all of them were as scrupulous as Colonel Díaz. Ambassador Peurifoy sent daily reports to Washington, worked to disparage Castillo Armas's actions in exile, and defended his conviction that it was best for the armed forces to rise up and depose Árbenz on their own. This, he argued, would be more effective than the invasion, which had dragged on long enough to more than justify the immense skepticism on the part of the military and civilian population.

His reasoning was confirmed on June 18 and 19, 1954, after Castillo Armas's troops (or *gangs*, as Peurifoy called them) crossed the border. Had it not been for the Liberationist air force, the invasion would have been an outright disaster; the planes were the only thing that kept the opposition forces from being exterminated after their defeat in Gualán and Puerto Barrios. Thanks to a miracle, they even saved the ones who had tried to occupy Zacapa. The air power available to Árbenz's government was a joke, consisting of five Beechcraft AT-11s, and they lost one of them the very first day, when the pilot deserted, flew to Honduras, and joined the rebellion. Árbenz refused to let the rest of them go into combat, fearing the other airmen would do the same. This left the airspace open for Colonel Brodfrost's Liberationists.

The gringo pilots made good use of their monopoly. In Chiquimula, especially, the rebel fliers wrought destruction, with Jerry Fred DeLarm at their head. With his suicidal dive-bombing of the courtyard at the base, he destroyed their heavy artillery and killed and injured many men, inducing the rest of the soldiers to give up on June 23 and rendering their initial victory meaningless. The Liberationist troops then occupied their base. This raised the morale of the invaders, who were considering retreating to Honduran territory after the catastrophe of the previous two days. Radio Liberación presented Castillo Armas's taking of the outposts at Esquipulas and Chiquimula as the *beginning of the end* of the Árbenz government.

At that point, Ambassador Peurifoy encouraged the State Department and the strategic planners of the Liberationist invasion (overseen by two CIA men, Robertson and Wisner) to bomb Guatemala City. There would have to be unrest in the capital to spur the army to action. He justified this by referring to what he had told the senior officers, including Colonel Monzón and the head of the army, Colonel Díaz, explicitly: *Noncombatants will have to die. Panic will have to break out among the civilian population. That is the only provocation that will allow us to intervene against Árbenz.* His plan was confirmed when Colonel Elfego H. Monzón appeared at the embassy escorted by Colonels José Luis Cruz Salazar and Mauricio Dubois to specify that the target of the Liberationists' bombings would be the Fort of Matamoros in the heart of downtown.

The attack took place on June 25, just before dusk. The Liberationist air force had grown by then. The two Thunderbolts piloted by Williams and DeLarm strafed Chiquimula and Zacapa before proceeding to the capital, destroying a train with government reinforcements heading toward those bases and demolishing a bridge to impede the progress of the survivors, who were advancing on foot.

The two planes reached their destination at 2:20 p.m. Williams was the first to fly over the Fort of Matamoros, but his 275-pound fragmentation bomb remained lodged in the latch mechanism. Flying behind him, DeLarm managed to drop his own 555-pound bomb atop the explosives depot, which was blown to pieces. There was a succession of detonations and countless dead and wounded inside and outside the base. Both planes took on artillery fire as they swept down to machine gun the survivors. They flew back, but not before Williams had dropped two weaker bombs elsewhere in the city. One of them landed in the ceremonial courtyard of the Military Academy. This satisfied the officers, with Colonel Díaz and Colonel Elfego H. Monzón at their head: among the general population, there were many dead and wounded, and panic had sent thousands of families into the streets, escaping from a city that was now in flames, bearing bundles of clothing and cradles, with their dogs in tow, fearing the Liberationist pilots would return to bomb them again.

Twenty-four hours after the bombardment of the Fort of Matamoros, with the city in chaos, still shaken from the attack, with rivers of people fleeing to the countryside and the dead and wounded lying abandoned in the street, President Árbenz received an urgent plea from the head of the army, Colonel Enrique Díaz, *in the name of the armed forces, which I have the honor of presiding over,* to meet with him and the leadership of that institution *in view of the very grave events of yesterday, the bombing of the Fort of Matamoros and the surrounding area by the enemies' planes.* Díaz, Monzón, and many others among the General Staff were personal friends of Árbenz and colleagues of his from the Politécnica. The president had even used his influence to help Díaz rise to his position of leadership. Nonetheless, the tone of that request led him to suspect that Colonel Díaz was no longer the man he was familiar with, the friend and companion he'd known since their youth. Until two days ago, he'd informed the president regularly about the pressure Peurifoy was placing on the army officers to drive them toward a coup. Was it happening now? Had they bought off Enrique, too? He responded immediately, agreeing to see Díaz and the rest of the General Staff that afternoon in his offices.

Afterward, he called in three of his civilian advisers and friends, Carlos Manuel Pellecer, Víctor Manuel Gutiérrez, General Secretary of the Confederation of Workers' and Farmers' Unions, and José Manuel Fortuny, leader of the Guatemalan Party of Labor, all of whom had collaborated with him on the drafting of the Agrarian Reform law and on its implementation once it had passed Congress. Fortuny had also been in charge of a secret arms purchase from Czechoslovakia in 1954 to bypass the U.S. embargo against Guatemala, which had become a source of great concern to the army. Fortuny succeeded, and Árbenz got the weapons into the country on a Swiss vessel, the *Alfhem,* which made it through Puerto Barrios without being detected by the United States. What better proof was there that the Soviet Union had no interest in what was happening in Guatemala, Árbenz had thought many times, than the fact that his government had been forced to pay for these weapons in cash, at an exorbitant price, without discounts of any kind. The Yankee press had made a scandal of that purchase of rifles and bazookas which, it was broadly assumed, the army would let fall into the hands of the then-nonexistent civilian militias.

Without saying a word about Díaz's message, Árbenz asked them how the formation of the militias was progressing. Their answers were deeply pessimistic, those of Fortuny in particular. It was slow; not all the peasants' unions wanted their members enlisting; others, though willing to collaborate, had met with resistance in their own ranks. They had just gotten their small holdings and wanted to devote their time to cultivating them, not to becoming militiamen and waging war. Fortuny, who had been a close friend of Jacobo and María Árbenz before the elections, assured him that the greater problem was reluctance among the army officials in charge of training the recruits; they feared this *civilian army* and saw it as a threat to their own survival. Or perhaps they had received orders from above to sabotage its formation. No more than a few dozen volunteers had shown up at the stadium in Ciudad Olímpica, not the thousands they had hoped for, and the officers assigned to them had made excuses, failed to appear in the places reserved for training, or found pretexts not to hand over the rifles as promised. This much was clear: the Guatemalan army took a dim view of the popular militias meant to defend the revolution. Ambassador Peurifoy had convinced the doubters that once formed, these so-called militias would liquidate the legitimate armed forces. Fighting, waging war, those were jobs for the army, not for unions and peasants. José Manuel Fortuny would be rewarded for his forthrightness with an accusation of *conduct unbecoming his position* and expressing *erroneous and pessimistic political ideas* by the Central Committee of the Guatemalan Party of Labor, in which he was the secretary general. After being subject to *disciplinary proceedings*, he was removed from the leadership of the PGT.

Árbenz didn't tell the three men about the meeting he was having with the General Staff that afternoon. Their report left him deeply pessimistic. What they told him confirmed his worst suspicions. It was possible that the officers had received orders from above to prevaricate and make excuses, or that they had decided on their own. There may have been enlisted men in favor of the social reforms, but esprit de corps was paramount. The president had always known the army would never accept a confrontation with the United States. However much they detested Castillo Armas, war with the Marines was out of the question. And who could say they were wrong?

Twenty or so military leaders, some of them from garrisons in the country's interior, entered the president's office at eight in the evening. All were in their ceremonial uniforms with medals pinned to their chests. The president allowed the head of the army to speak first.

Despite the deferential repetition of the words "Mr. President" throughout, Jacobo Árbenz saw what was coming as soon as the astute, prudent Colonel Carlos Enrique Díaz began speaking. The October Revolution had to be defended, along with its reforms, the Agrarian Reform law, the distribution of land to the peasants. This was imperative, of course it was, of course, Mr. President, Díaz insisted. The army understood and supported these reforms. And of course, they couldn't tolerate an armed rebellion hatched by a traitor like Castillo Armas, a rebellion supported by mercenaries from abroad and backed by a hostile and uncomprehending foreign power, the United States. That rebellion, that *invasion* from Honduras, valiantly rebuffed in Gualán and Puerto Barrios, must be defeated. About this there was no doubt. The eight thousand soldiers and officers of the Guatemalan army were of a single mind in this respect. But naturally, the Guatemalan army could not risk war with the United States, the most powerful country in the world. Further: America's hostility *toward you, Mr. President* (Árbenz interrupted him: *toward Guatemala*), *yes indeed, toward Guatemala*, Díaz corrected himself, had done a great deal of damage to the armed forces, there was the embargo, they couldn't buy armaments, munitions, even spare parts, the United States had swayed virtually every country in the West to go along with this, and now the army was at an extraordinary disadvantage, as the past few days had shown, compared with Castillo Armas and his anti-patriotic invaders, his band of mercenaries and traitors. And evidently the countries in the East could never replace the United States as a chief supplier of arms, the purchase of weapons from Czechoslovakia a few months before had made that clear, the ensuing scandal overseas had nearly provoked an invasion of Guatemala by the Marines. All that for old equipment with obsolete parts, almost impossible to use effectively.

During a long pause, sepulchral silence reigned, and no one present moved. *Here it comes*, Árbenz thought. He wasn't wrong.

"For these reasons, Mr. President, the high military authorities, wishing to preserve the achievements of the revolution and defeat Castillo Armas as quickly and efficiently as possible, ask, as an act of generosity and patriotism, that you submit your resignation. The army will take power and will commit to salvaging your achievements, especially the Agrarian Reform. And to driving back Castillo Armas and his mercenaries."

Colonel Carlos Enrique Díaz concluded, and another long silence followed. Finally, President Árbenz asked:

"Do all the officers present subscribe to what the head of the army has just said?"

"There is universal agreement, Mr. President," Colonel Díaz replied. "The General Staff voted unanimously, and the leaders of every garrison and region in Guatemala followed suit."

Another electric silence. Jacobo Árbenz rose from his seat and remained standing as he spoke in a firm voice:

"I will not cling to the post I was chosen for by the vast majority of Guatemalans in free and fair elections. Being here has allowed me to carry out social and economic reforms that are indispensable for correcting the centuries of injustice the peasants in this country have endured. If stepping down will suffice to preserve these reforms, I have no reason to continue on as president. Above all, if it is a question of defeating and punishing the traitor Castillo Armas."

"We swear to it on our honor, Mr. President," Colonel Carlos Enrique Díaz assured him, clicking his heels.

"The chairman of the armed forces is to stay with me," the president said. "The remaining officers should return to their posts. Colonel Díaz will give you official notice of my decision."

The officers departed one by one. Each of them saluted him, raising a hand to their peaked cap before stepping out.

When Árbenz was alone with Díaz, he asked him, noticing his pallor:

"You really believe my resignation will placate the United States?"

"I don't know about the United States," Colonel Díaz said. "But it will satisfy the army, Jacobo, and they're on the verge of an uprising. I promise you that. I've worked miracles to keep it from happening. Ambassador Peurifoy has assured me that if you do resign, the U.S. will respect your measures, especially the land reform. All Washington wants is the communists out of power.

"Did he ask you to have them shot?"

"For now, he just wants them jailed. And expelled immediately from the public administration. He's made very thorough lists."

"What will happen to Castillo Armas?"

"That's been the toughest thing to deal with," Colonel Díaz said. "But I've been emphatic about that, I haven't given an inch. We refuse to deal with a traitor and a subversive. Ambassador Peurifoy assured me that if the army takes power, jails the communists, and outlaws the Guatemalan Party of Labor, the U.S.A. will let Castillo Armas fall. And I've repeated myself to the point of exhaustion: he's a turncoat, he must be defeated and put on trial for his betrayal of his uniform and his country."

"That's good, Carlos," the president said. "I'm sure you're telling me the truth. I hope you really can safeguard the social and economic reforms we managed to push through. And keep that son of a bitch out of power."

"I swear it to you, Jacobo," the head of the army said with a salute.

Árbenz watched him leave the office, shutting the door behind him. His entire body was trembling. He had to close his eyes and take a deep breath to calm himself. Was the decision he was about to take the right one? It would be if Colonel Carlos Enrique Díaz and the army respected their commitments and didn't cut a deal with that deserter and his band of opportunists. But he wasn't sure the soldiers would follow Díaz. If all the officers had been loyal, the invaders would already have been driven back, but they were still out there assaulting the government's troops. The latest news coming in was of a horrifying slaughter the rebels had inflicted on the civilian population of Bananera. He was afraid that after his resignation, the officers' duplicity would grow and that they would wind up overwhelming Carlos Enrique, no matter how much Árbenz trusted his word.

He spoke with Fortuny on the phone and informed him of his decision to step down. Confused and alarmed, Fortuny tried to dissuade him, but when the president shouted that it was final, and nothing else could save the revolution and prevent Castillo Armas from taking over, he fell quiet. It was the only way, Árbenz continued, to avoid a Yankee invasion that would decimate the civilian population. Before hanging up, he told him that this time, unusually, he would write his own speech to declare his resignation, and that, since there was a witch hunt coming against real and alleged communists, his friend should take immediate precautions. Then he hung up.

He gave instructions for Radio Nacional to make preparations for an address he would deliver to the entire country in the next few hours. He called the Mexican ambassador, Primo Villa Michel, whom he had been in close contact with in recent days, and told him that after reading his speech that night, he and his family would be seeking asylum at the embassy, if the Mexican government was willing to take them in. The ambassador assured him that they were, and told him he would send confirmation within the hour. He called his wife on the phone, uttering five simple words:

"Get our suitcases ready, María."

After a pause, María Cristina Vilanova replied: "They already are, dear. For when?"

"Tonight," he said.

The president told his assistants he didn't wish to be interrupted. He closed himself in his office to organize his papers in his briefcase and destroy those he wouldn't be taking with him. As he did, he served himself a half glass of whiskey, his first after three years of sobriety. He drank it in one swallow, closing his eyes.

XXVI

H E HAD GONE TO BUY A GIFT for his cook—today was her
birthday—at one of those gigantic stores they had opened
in the south of Guatemala City, and when he came out,
he heard someone call him by his first name: *Enrique?* He stopped,
turned, and saw a young girl in blue jeans and one of those long,
military-style jackets that had become fashionable among the younger
generations. She was wearing a blue beret, had pretty eyes, and smiled
as if they knew each other.

"You're Lieutenant Colonel Enrique Trinidad Oliva, no?" The
girl took a step toward him, her hand outstretched, maintaining her
smile.

He turned serious and replied gruffly: "You're mistaken, I don't
know who that is." He tried to moderate the bitterness in his tone
by smiling back. "My name's Esteban Ramos. At your service. And
you?"

"I must have gotten confused," the girl said, smiling again. "A
thousand pardons."

She turned around and walked away with an elastic gate, her hips swaying slightly.

He remained immobile, the gift tucked under his arm, paralyzed by surprise and cursing himself for reacting so ineptly. His legs were shaking, his palms damp. In his mind, he reproached himself. He had committed three serious errors: stopping when he heard his former name, getting mad when he denied being Lieutenant Colonel Enrique Trinidad Oliva, and acting at once too distant and too familiar. He should have gone on his way without stopping, then the girl would have thought she had the wrong man. *You gave yourself away, idiot*, he thought. As he drove his car back home, he felt a sort of vertigo, and a thousand questions consumed him: Who was the girl? Had they run into each other by chance? Had she been following him? He was certain they'd never met: she couldn't have been more than seventeen or eighteen, so she would have been eleven or twelve when he went to prison. She couldn't have remembered him—he had changed a great deal. Besides, he didn't recognize that face, those eyes, that breezy attitude. No, she had never met him before, and yes, she was following him, trying to confirm his identity. And thanks to his incompetence, she had. Could she be a cop? Doubtful. Military intelligence? Unlikely. She looked like a student, from San Carlos University maybe, a humanities or law major, from one of the departments the radicals had taken over. She must have been a member of some extremist group, communist, the type that plants bombs in a bank or in a general's house. Those were the only kind of people who could be interested in finding out if the former chief of the intelligence services for Castillo Armas's Liberationist government was still alive and working in the civilian world under an assumed name.

He told the Turk what had happened that same afternoon. The Turk didn't seem to make much of it, but he told him he could find out through his contacts in the government if the police or the Secret Service were on his trail. Two days later, Ahmed Kurony said no, his informants had left no room for doubt: nobody was keeping tabs on him, not the cops and not the army. For that very reason, he couldn't banish the thought that, if the meeting hadn't been a chance occurrence, one of those terrorist groups cropping up all over the country was determined to chase down the former officer accused of so many horrors during the period of the Liberationist revolt.

From then on, Enrique took precautions. He went back to carrying a gun. He had quit because, with all the unrest, terrorism, and petty crime, police and military patrols were now stopping people on the streets to search them or ask for their ID. After inadvertently revealing his true identity, Enrique never left home without his revolver tucked into his belt—a gift from the Turk himself. Wherever he was, he always kept his guard up. The sensation that someone was following him, spying on him, persisted. He tried not to spend much time outside, to go from meetings to home without stopping off, avoiding bars and restaurants. He hadn't set foot back in Ciro's or the Casablanca, not even the night the Turk invited him to see Tongolele, the famous rumba dancer with the white streak in her long black hair. When he visited the Turk's casinos, he now did so with Temístocles, his most trusted bodyguard.

One night, when he was making his rounds of the gambling joints, he thought he saw confirmation that he was being trailed. It was stupid, the way it happened. He had just strolled through a casino in a hidden room in the back of an antique store on Pasaje Rubio in the old city, and he saw a flash coming from behind him. He turned around swiftly and ordered his bodyguard to stop whoever had taken the picture. He and the security guards grabbed a young man, but he must not have been the photographer, because he didn't have a camera on him. He turned out to be a traveling salesman, and he had been a regular there for years. Enrique himself had to apologize to him. And yet, despite the evidence, despite the denials of the bouncers and his bodyguard, he continued to believe that someone had taken a photo behind his back. Was he losing his mind? Having visions? No, it wasn't paranoia—it was instinct. He'd heard the click and seen the glimmer from the flash. Probably the photographer had been faster than security. He slept badly, had nightmares, and during the day the thought tormented him that the life he'd managed to rebuild after the bottomless pit of prison could fall apart like a house of cards.

One morning, his butler, Tiburcio, came to wake him, one finger over his lips to keep him from making any noise. It was the crack of dawn, and there was little light in the sky. He got up and walked to the window, pulling the curtain slightly aside. Enrique saw a man taking photos of his apartment and the building's front door. He wasn't making a secret of it, and snapped pictures from all angles. Then he walked to a corner where a car was waiting for him. As soon as he got in, it took off.

Now there was no doubt. Here was the evidence. They were following him and they could kidnap him or kill him at any moment. Even today. They couldn't be common criminals. Why would they want to kidnap him? He wasn't a millionaire, he wouldn't even be able to pay a ransom. He talked that same evening with the Turk and asked him to get him out of the country for a while. At first, Kurony was hesitant. He needed him there, in Guatemala. He'd given him high-level responsibilities in the businesses. Most likely he was just seeing things. People often took pictures out on the street in the morning. Maybe the guy was a tourist, one of those camera nuts out looking for just the right light at sunrise. But since Enrique insisted, he eventually told him okay. He would send him to Mexico City for a few weeks to see if he'd forget his so-called pursuers. In that beehive of a city, he could hide out and feel safe for a while.

XXVII

T HOUGH NEARLY THE WHOLE COUNTRY LISTENED to President Jacobo Árbenz's resignation on the radio, the two most extreme reactions must have been Ambassador Peurifoy's euphoria—wasn't this proof that his strategy of an *institutional coup* had been a success, and had gotten the communist out of office swiftly?—and Colonel Castillo Armas's unfettered rage from his headquarters in Esquipulas, cursing and ranting while his subordinates listened in silence.

Ambassador John Emil Peurifoy hurriedly wrote a report to the State Department: Árbenz's resignation meant that the entire army had turned its back on him. The army's rise to power would facilitate the elimination of all those subversive elements entrenched in the administration, the disbanding of the belligerent unions, and the immediate revocation of the policies that discriminated against United Fruit. He would meet immediately with Colonel Carlos Enrique Díaz, the new president, to demand these measures be carried out.

Castillo Armas's message to the CIA (or rather: to Mr. Frank Wisner, with a copy sent to Colonel Brodfrost) was very different in character. He was not in the least pleased with what had happened, and considered the Mute Árbenz's stepping down to be a travesty meant to safeguard the worst excesses of the October Revolution—a farce carried out with the aid of Árbenz's servant and accomplice, the chief of the army, Colonel Little Árbenz the Second. The proof was that he had allowed the president to broadcast that message on the radio insulting the Army of Liberation and Castillo Armas himself and accusing the United States of planning, supporting, and directing the invasion—repeating all the communists' slander. He wouldn't play along with this kind of political nonsense. If the U.S.A. was stupid enough to support Colonel Carlos Enrique Díaz, he would denounce the situation and return immediately to Honduras. From there, he would let the world know that once more, Guatemala's communists had triumphed—now with Washington's support!—with this pantomime of Árbenz's resignation, which would allow everything to stay the same and permit the reds to go on destroying Guatemala. Hatchet Face urged the CIA, the State Department, and President Eisenhower not to let Ambassador Peurifoy deceive them and to demand the immediate abdication of Little Árbenz the Second. He would never negotiate with that communist, and would continue as long as it took as the head of the Army of Liberation. Last, he informed them that, after hearing Árbenz's resignation, numerous Guatemalan officers had gotten in touch with him offering a truce and some even declaring their open support of the invasion.

Castillo Armas's bluster wasn't entirely idle. Hearing Árbenz's resignation over the radio diminished faith in the revolution, which the majority of the officers in the armed forces had resigned themselves to more out of obedience than conviction. They felt they were free to choose. And the majority happened to believe that in this dawning period of disorder and uncertainty, joining Castillo Armas's invasion, which had the support of the United States, was preferable to continuing to support a revolution whose victims would, sooner or later, as the indefatigable Ambassador Peurifoy assured them, include the Guatemalan army itself. For this reason, Colonel Víctor M. León, who oversaw the government forces defending Zacapa and had, up to then, resolutely fended off the invaders, sent an emissary to Castillo Armas on the night Árbenz stepped down asking for a truce to open peace negotiations. This decision, he conveyed, had the support of all the officers under his command.

Ambassador Peurifoy didn't have the chance to celebrate his presumptive victory. Just a few hours after sending his report, he received a message in code from his boss, John Foster Dulles, who stated in the harshest terms that he was under no circumstances to accept Colonel Carlos Enrique Díaz stepping in to replace Árbenz as president: there was clear evidence of collusion between them, otherwise Díaz would never have allowed the former leader to depart from office with an address that insulted and defamed the United States and disparaged Castillo Armas and the Liberationists. The ambassador would have to demand that Colonel Díaz abandon the post, stepping aside for a truly independent military junta without ties to Árbenz; and he should pressure them, with the threat of a military invasion if need be, to negotiate with Castillo Armas, who was committed without reservations to repealing each and every one of the communists' reforms.

Ambassador Peurifoy changed his position, adopting John Foster Dulles's thinking as his own. He hastily requested an appointment with Colonel Díaz; he had a message from Washington he needed to convey in person. The new president agreed to see him at ten in the morning (it was already dawn on that endless day). Before going, Ambassador Peurifoy put on his thick shoulder holster with the ostentatious revolver that had always accompanied him on his negotiations with the Greek officers, who, incidentally, had struck him as more civilized than these Indians in uniform.

Their encounter took place in the General Staff's main offices. Colonel Díaz was there with two other officers, Colonel Elfego H. Monzón and Colonel Rogelio Cruz Wer, head of the Civil Guard, a man unknown to the ambassador before then. The three of them received him in a celebratory mood: *We've finally done what you wanted, Ambassador, Árbenz is gone and the hunt for the communists is underway.*

Once the greetings were over, Colonel Díaz told Peurifoy he had given orders to arrest the union leaders, affiliates of the Guatemalan Party of Labor, and other subversives throughout the nation.

"But unfortunately," he added, "certain leaders of the Guatemalan Party of Labor managed to seek asylum at the Mexican Embassy. Ambassador Primo Villa Michel is in cahoots with them, and he granted it."

"That's your fault, Colonel Díaz, you've done your job poorly," Peurifoy scolded him, convinced that he had to break the officers' morale right from the first or he would lose. When the three men heard this, the joy drained from their faces.

"I don't understand what you mean, Ambassador," Colonel Díaz finally replied.

"You will soon, Colonel," Peurifoy replied shrilly, wagging his index finger in the Guatemalan's face. "Our agreement did not include Árbenz stepping down after giving a speech heard all over Guatemala that lavished insults on the United States, accusing us of conspiring against social reforms on behalf of United Fruit, attacking Castillo Armas and his men, 'a band of mercenaries' as he called them, one that had to be defeated—and that is something you have apparently agreed to do."

Colonel Díaz turned ashen. Peurifoy didn't give him a chance to speak. The other officers, very pale, said nothing. The interpreter translated the ambassador's words swiftly, imitating his energy and his menacing gestures.

"Nor did we agree," the diplomat proceeded, "to give Árbenz time to alert all the communists in the regime so they could seek asylum, not just in the Mexican Embassy, but also from Colombia, Chile, Argentina, Brazil, Venezuela, etc., etc. They've been going into hiding since last night, and neither the army nor the police have done anything to stop them. That was not what we agreed on. My government is offended and insulted by what has happened, and we will be taking all appropriate measures. Colonel Díaz, listen very closely. The United States does not find you acceptable as president of Guatemala. You cannot replace Árbenz. I'm telling you this in my official capacity. If you refuse to stand down, you will face the consequences. You know perfectly well what the situation in your country is. The United States Navy has Guatemala hemmed in on the Caribbean side and on the Pacific. The Marines are ready to disembark, and they'll do in a matter of hours all that you've proven incapable of. Don't drag your country into the flames. Renounce your right to preside over the military junta immediately and look for a way out of this impasse. You don't want an invasion or a military occupation: if you get one, blood will flow, and the damage to Guatemala will be tremendous."

He stopped talking now, and looked at the faces of the three colonels. They were rigid, mute, alert.

"Is this an ultimatum?" Colonel Carlos Enrique Díaz finally asked. His voice was quavering, and tears gleamed in his eyes.

"Yes, it is," the ambassador replied resolutely. But then his expression and his words softened. "I am encouraging you to be a patriot, Colonel. Step down, and save Guatemala from an invasion that will leave thousands of dead and a country in ruins. Don't wind up in the history books as a soldier so proud he allowed his country to be annihilated. With your resignation, we can try to agree on a junta of three or four men willing to negotiate with Castillo Armas and reach a deal acceptable to my government. One that will allow the United States to collaborate in Guatemala's democratization and reconstruction."

The three colonels were white-faced and silent, and Ambassador Peurifoy knew that he had won the game, just as he had in Greece. After looking back and forth at each other, the men nodded and forced somewhat macabre smiles. They asked the ambassador to take a seat, ordered coffee and mineral water, brought out their cigarettes. They smoked and talked, blowing the fumes in each other's faces, and an hour later, they had agreed on the members of the junta, on the country to which they would send Colonel Carlos Enrique Díaz as ambassador, and on the text of the declaration that would inform Guatemalans of the nomination of a new military regime willing, in the spirit of peace and brotherhood, to negotiate an agreement with Colonel Castillo Armas in which neither party was winner or loser, thereby inaugurating a new era of freedom and democracy in Guatemala.

The diplomat departed the offices of the General Staff, and as soon as he'd reached the embassy, he called Washington and informed them of the meeting in detail. Clearly the problem now was Colonel Castillo Armas. He had demanded the immediate surrender of the government's army and was trying to enter Guatemala City in a military parade, marching at the head of the Army of Liberation. *That bastard's the next one we're going to have to bring to heel*, Peurifoy told himself. *He's let this get to his head.* He was exhausted, but as always, crisis exhilarated him, awakening a physical need for action and risk.

Following President Árbenz's abdication, there were five military juntas, each of them closer to the United States than the last, all buckling under Peurifoy's demands and machinations, each trying to outdo its predecessor in its willingness to persecute, capture, torture, and execute the communists. The leaders of the Guatemalan Party of Labor who hadn't sought asylum at one of the embassies were able to hide out or flee to the mountains or the jungle thanks to warnings from Árbenz and Fortuny, but many others couldn't, particularly the union leaders, the schoolteachers, young students, and mixed-race professionals who had mobilized—many of them brought into politics for the first time—after the October Revolution. The number of victims was never known, but there were hundreds, perhaps thousands, people from the hills, peasants without names or histories for whom a plot of nationalized land had been like a gift from heaven, and when the Agrarian Reform was repealed and they had to hand back what they already thought of as their property, they were left reeling. Some acquiesced, but others defended their holdings with bared teeth. They were tortured or killed, or spent long years in prisons without ever really grasping those strange shifts of fate of which they were first beneficiaries, then victims two or three years later.

The junta that endured the shortest time—no more than a few hours—was composed of Colonels Carlos Enrique Díaz, José Ángel Sánchez, and Elfego H. Monzón. When Castillo Armas failed to recognize them and refused to have any dealings with them, they lost all authority. He had grown arrogant because, after Árbenz's resignation, many government troops sent to fight him near the Honduran border had gone over to his side instead. The more self-assured he felt, the more defiant he acted with the North Americans. Since the night Árbenz sought asylum, Peurifoy had been applying pressure, dangling the threat of an invasion by the Marines over the officers' heads. Slowly, they all gave ground. Castillo Armas wasn't satisfied with Díaz's resignation. He demanded a big military parade, with him at the head, to welcome the Liberationist troops into Guatemala City. If he didn't get it, there would be no negotiations between the government's troops and himself. Ambassador Peurifoy went days without eating, nights without sleeping, in endless discussions, reaching agreements that would last hours or even just minutes before one or the other side rebelled violently against them, communicating with Washington to fine-tune accords, only to start over from the beginning.

While all this was happening, the soldiers, the police, and the officers in charge had unleashed a witch hunt unprecedented even in Guatemala's violent history. The closures of the union halls and Agrarian Reform offices that had opened in all the villages were carried out in a hail of bullets, with the imprisonment of whoever was found inside at the time; there were blacklists with names supplied by anonymous informants. Many of those arrested, humble persons without influence or allies, were tortured, often to death, their bodies buried or burned and their families never told of their end. Panic seeped into every crack in Guatemalan society, particularly among those without means, and violent excesses went beyond any horror ever before seen. In the months that followed Castillo Armas's rise to power, approximately 200,000 Mayans, terrified by the slaughter, managed to flee to Chiapas in Mexico. This is virtually the only figure verifiable from the days of repression, and it came to light through information issued by the Mexican authorities.

Not since the era of the Inquisition had political repression in Guatemala taken the form of burnings of *pernicious and subversive documents*, which occurred now on the military bases and in the public squares. Pamphlets, flyers, newspapers, magazines, and books—from an inscrutable selection of authors that included Victor Hugo and Dostoevsky—smoldered on bonfires around which children danced as if celebrating Saint John's Eve.

The final negotiations between the Liberationists and what was left of the military on the government's side took place in El Salvador, where president Óscar Osorio had, at the urging of Washington, offered to host the two parties. With his loaded revolver under his left arm, Ambassador Peurifoy was in attendance, not as an observer but as an "implicated witness" (to make a distinction he insisted on and only he understood). The Secretary of State had selected him to represent the United States in the talks, ordering him to take all necessary steps to assure Castillo Armas's conditions were met. Guatemala had been severely damaged by events in the foregoing decade, and it was important to Eisenhower's government that the country be led by someone whose political convictions and temperament would make him friendly to Washington and amenable to the North American companies operating in Central America.

The U.S. ambassadors to Nicaragua, El Salvador, and Honduras were there to offer their assistance, but Peurifoy took the active role in the discussions. In truth, he dictated them, supporting Castillo Armas against Colonels Elfego H. Monzón and Mauricio Dubois, who were there as representatives of the Guatemalan army. Eventually a deal was struck. A *temporary junta* was put in place, consisting of Castillo Armas, Monzón, José Luis Cruz Salazar, Mauricio Dubois, and Enrique Trinidad Oliva. It would be dissolved as soon as a new constitution was in place. There would be a *unity parade* in which the Liberationists and the armed forces would celebrate Victory Day together.

Castillo Armas had greeted the Cowboy coldly in San Salvador, but was cordial with him on the plane ride back to Guatemala, and thanked him for his support in the negotiations. *You'll be greeted as a hero in your country, Colonel*, Peurifoy predicted. And so he was. But the United States ambassador, not the rebel colonel, was the first to step out of the plane at the airport in Guatemala City. During the enormous celebrations, with 130,000 people in attendance, Castillo

Armas asked Peurifoy to address *the Guatemalan people*, and the diplomat showed a timidity unusual in a man best described as a human bulldozer, limiting himself to toasting to the country's future. A huge mass of people, exhausted from the insecurity and violence of recent months, gathered at the airport and in streets across the city to salute Colonel Castillo Armas, who would thenceforth be recognized as the undisputed superior of all his colleagues and adversaries in the army. Washington had instructed Peurifoy to persuade the members of the junta chosen in San Salvador to step down and let Castillo Armas lead. It wasn't easy. Colonel Cruz Salazar asked for the ambassador's post in Washington and a large amount of money in exchange. Mauricio Dubois was no different. Both received a hundred thousand dollars in compensation. It is not known how the other members were rewarded, but all of them stood aside for the new leader.

In this way, following a hasty plebiscite in which he was the unequivocal victor, the head of the Army of Liberation became the new president of the Republic of Guatemala, with the mission of eliminating those lunatic antidemocratic measures put forward by the governments of Arévalo and Árbenz in their quest to turn Guatemala into a satellite of the Soviet Union. (Only once the imposing parade was over would Hatchet Face learn of the behavior of the cadets from the Politécnica who were in attendance, who had come to blows with the fleabag Liberationists.)

On July 4, Ambassador Peurifoy and his wife, Betty Jane, held a memorable reception for five hundred people at their residence in Zone 14, Guatemala's most elegant quarter, with singing, toasts, congratulatory hugs, and countless words of praise for the hero of the day—not Castillo Armas, but the ambassador himself.

But the weary diplomat could not yet rest. No sooner were the festivities over than the State Department ordered him to collaborate with the CIA to erase, now that Árbenz was gone, all signs of the U.S.A.'s participation in Operation PBSuccess. It was imperative that not a trace of it remain, to put an end to the international campaign led by communists and fellow travelers—with none other than France among them—which accused the United States of invading a small sovereign country and overturning its democratically elected government to defend the privileges of a single multinational, the United Fruit Company. Fighting through his weariness, unwashed, unshaved, without even changing his shirt, Peurifoy arranged a return to America for the six hundred operators the CIA had brought in from Nicaragua, Guatemala, El Salvador, Panama, and Honduras to prepare the invasion. He also had to make the twenty planes of the Liberationist air force disappear. Several of them were given to Anastasio Somoza in thanks for the assistance he had granted to Castillo Armas's mercenaries, letting them train in Nicaragua and offering them places to do so. Others Castillo Armas kept himself as the basis for a reconstructed Guatemalan air force.

Peurifoy and his family spent their last days in Guatemala (the State Department had made clear that a person as involved in Árbenz's fall as he should leave the country as soon as possible, and he agreed) mailing packages and packing suitcases for his upcoming assignment at the U.S. Embassy in Thailand. Numerous Guatemalan landowners and businessmen had them over to say goodbye in person, telling them they would miss them a great deal. Peurifoy imagined that in the far-off Orient, he could finally get a bit of rest.

Before leaving for his next destination, he was able to make a hidden wish come true: he convinced the Mexican ambassador to allow him entry into that building full of asylum seekers whose journey into exile the Castillo Armas government had complicated with any number of pretexts. He didn't see ex-president Árbenz, who refused to meet with him. But he did have the satisfaction of spending a moment with José Manuel Fortuny, a former member of Árbenz's party and later secretary general of the Guatemalan Party of Labor. They spoke for a few minutes before the Guatemalan recognized the ambassador and went silent. He confessed he was still friends with Árbenz, and had collaborated closely with him on the drafting and execution of the Agrarian Reform law. Peurifoy saw him as a man defeated, his morale devastated. He had lost many pounds and spoke without looking, eyes red from sleepless nights and haunting visions. He stopped answering questions, as if he didn't understand or hear them. In his report to the State Department, Peurifoy described how his old and dangerous adversary—a Soviet agent, without a doubt—was now a ruin, a man consumed by neuroses and probably secretly remorseful for his actions.

Wagging tongues said that Ambassador Peurifoy asked, when the State Department informed him his next stopping-point would be Thailand: "Is there a coup d'état on the horizon?" Whether he spoke in jest isn't known. He had promised his children and Betty Jane that once there they would finally have the calm needed to live like a proper family. And they did enjoy a few months—not more—without political upheavals, and the ambassador at least learned something of the country's famed traditional massage, a practice linked to the religious beliefs, the sports, and the sexuality of Thailand, and one of its national passions. On August 12, 1955, after less than a year at his post, Ambassador Peurifoy was driving, very fast as usual, with his two sons in his brand-new blue Thunderbird through the out-skirts of Bangkok when a truck traveling in the opposite direction seems to have collided with him on a bridge. The ambassador and his younger son died instantly. A government plane was sent from America to repatriate their remains, and the State Department ex-erted no pressure to pursue the investigation into whether his tragic death had been a communist plot to punish the man who had fought so successfully against the expansion of the Soviet Union. The United States preferred that the matter be quickly forgotten. It was disturbed at the time by an international campaign denouncing Washington's intervention in Guatemala and its role in the fall of the Árbenz gov-ernment, which some had begun to defend, recognizing that Árbenz hadn't been a communist of any sort, but rather an unsuspecting, well-intentioned man whose only wish was to bring progress, democ-racy, and social justice to his country, even if his methods were erratic and his advisers at times led him astray.

Peurifoy's widow, Betty Jane, published a diary with many exam-ples of her husband's diplomatic achievements, presenting him as a hero. It sold modestly and wasn't widely reviewed. The United States government paid it no attention whatsoever.

Meanwhile, in Guatemala, President Castillo Armas, elected in a plebiscite with no opponents on the ballot—his colleagues in the military junta had already resigned in his favor—worked to put an end to all the unpleasantries occasioned by the October Revolution. He abolished the unions, federations, foundations, and peasants' and workers' associations, closed the National Indigenous Institute, gave back to the landowners and United Fruit the *fallow lands* that had been nationalized, abrogated the law that required companies and latifundias to pay taxes, and filled the prisons with unionists, teachers, journalists, and students accused of being *communists* or *subversives*. In the countryside, there were scenes of violence, with massacres in some places equaling or perhaps exceeding in brutality those that had occurred in Patzicía (San Juan Comalapa) in the early days of Arévalo's government in the fierce clash between the ladinos and the Kaqchikel Maya. Following the State Department's instructions, the new U.S. ambassador, a more prudent man than John Peurifoy, tried to moderate to some degree Castillo Armas's anticommunist fervor, and this led to friction, disagreement, and minor clashes between the U.S. and the leader the Eisenhower administration had made such efforts to enthrone. Around that time, people in Guatemala began to say that the United States had erred in choosing Hatchet Face as the new standard-bearer for freedom in Central America and the world. He was too extremist, and aroused less sympathy among the armed forces than they had earlier believed.

XXVIII

WHEN HE WOKE, it was still dark out. The clock read 4:30 in the morning. He had only slept three and a half hours. The night before, he'd been packing his bags until 1:00 a.m. There, in those two suitcases and one small briefcase, was everything he now possessed in the world. He had given his used clothes to the cook and the butler: many ties and pairs of shoes, handkerchiefs and underwear, still-new garments he no longer had room for. He had canceled the lease, and the owners would pick up the keys at noon. They were there the day before, taking a last look at the apartment. They saw that it was in better condition than when he'd rented it, with a fresh coat of paint and his furniture, which he was leaving behind as a gift.

He'd withdrawn all his savings from the bank and converted them to traveler's checks, which he could exchange for cash in Mexico. Before going to the airport, he would pass by the Banco Popular to close the last of his accounts, which no longer had much money in it.

At that moment, a thought frightened him. Many people knew he was leaving: the cook, the butler, the tellers at the two banks who had attended to him. Had he been imprudent? Would it not have been better to leave without saying anything, to disappear from one day to the next? He immediately vanquished his doubts. Those apprehensions were absurd. He had hesitated, thinking it might have been preferable to travel to Mexico by land instead of by air. Maybe so, but he wasn't sure his old, secondhand Ford, which he had gone on using through the years, would survive on the patchy roads, especially when he'd have to turn off into the jungle headed for the border in Tapachula, Chiapas. Ah—it was too late to worry about it. Temístocles, the best of his bodyguards, would soon be there; he'd promised to sell the Ford and send half of the purchase price to Mexico (the other half he could keep as a commission).

What would his life be like in the Mexican capital? He didn't know anyone there, though at least a part of his family from before had settled there several years ago. He didn't want to see them, they were dead to him and had been since before he got out of prison. The ingrates. He'd placed all his hopes in the Turk, Ahmed Kurony. He had promised to find him work, and he knew he could trust him. The Turk had helped him survive all those years and build a new life for himself. He would adapt and get ahead. Living there meant not having to spend every day looking over his shoulder, afraid of being recognized by people who wanted to kidnap or kill him. The important thing, now that he knew they were looking for him, was to evaporate, vanish, forget Guatemala forever—or at least for a few years. He had thought a great deal in those past few days and had decided that, if they did find him, the best thing would be if they murdered him. If they kidnapped him, looking for ransom, he was lost: he couldn't pay and there was no one who would pay it for him. They'd take their time torturing him horribly, and then they'd end up doing him in. Who were *they*? One of those little revolutionary groups that had appeared in Guatemala recently? But their militants were young, they couldn't remember the things he'd done as Castillo Armas's director of security. Maybe children or relatives of the people who wound up in prison or lost their lives during those years.

He thought vaguely about his ex-wife and the two children he'd had with her. The three of them would now be Mexican citizens, with the accents and whimsical turns of phrase they had picked up from the movies. If he ever ran into them in the street, they wouldn't recognize him, probably, and he wouldn't recognize them. He'd have to find a wife there. He had been alone too long, devoted to the difficult task of getting by. Hopefully he could find a nice, pretty Mexican he could remake his life with, feel the warmth of a family. He was tired of what his existence had become since he'd left jail, with no companion, no love, no friends, no one to have a Mass said for his soul if they killed him.

At five he got up and went to the bathroom to shower and shave. He did it slowly, letting time flow past. Once dressed, he made coffee with milk and toasted the bread the cook had left sliced for him. After breakfast, he turned on the radio to hear the news of the day. But instead of listening to the programs, he ruminated on the injustices committed against him. He wasn't usually someone to waste time pitying himself, but lately, especially since he'd discovered he was being followed, he had been susceptible to it. Everyone had treated him badly, Castillo Armas above all. He had helped him, agreed to give up his place in the military junta that they'd decided on in San Salvador so the other man could rise to the presidency. And in return for his service, he'd been pushed to the margins, sold short, given a ridiculous, meaningless post as director of security. How many officers had made a commitment to him, only to turn their back and plot with the army chiefs to leave him rotting in prison for five years? Never letting him explain himself before a judge or jury, because they were afraid he would talk and put all of them in danger.

In Mexico, he would forget all that. A new city, a new job, a new wife, a new life.

He turned off the radio and sat there still, dozing on the sofa in the living room, until his bodyguard, Temístocles, arrived at 8:00 a.m. He was a young guy, always dressed the same, in jeans with a thick belt, a button-down shirt, and a loose black jacket with a pair of revolvers hidden inside it. He'd been a soldier and they'd taught him how to handle a gun. He'd been working for the Turk for several years. Temístocles had always seemed to him the most skilled of his men, and the one he could place the most trust in. He offered him a cup of coffee, but the kid had already had breakfast. The two of them took the suitcases down to the old Ford, parked at the entrance to the building where he had lived.

He locked the apartment door and tossed the key through the mail slot, as the owners had asked.

They drove to a branch office of the Banco Popular. It was still closed, but that was fine, they had more than enough time. They waited in the car, talking and smoking a cigarette, parked a few feet from the door. His plane left at 11:00 a.m. If he was at the airport an hour before, that was enough. The offices opened at 8:30.

Temístocles walked inside with him and stayed by his side, hands stuffed into his black jacket, while he spoke with the teller and finished his business. He slid the money into his wallet. Then they left. They got in the car, and just as Enrique grabbed the key to turn it in the ignition, he saw the girl. Her, the one from the department store, dressed more or less the same as she had been the last time, in jeans, a military shirt, and a blue beret. She was standing a hundred or a hundred fifty feet away, leaning against a lamppost, looking at the car. She seemed to be smiling at him.

Nervous, frenzied, he turned the key. At that moment, the bomb exploded. On the radio that afternoon, and in the papers that next day toward the end of March 1963, not long before the coup that would depose General Miguel Ydígoras Fuentes and bring to power Enrique Peralta Azurdia, there was news of a terrorist attack that had killed two people and wounded several others in the capital. Only long afterward did two reporters' investigation for *El Imparcial* reveal to the broader public that one of the deceased victims, a certain *Esteban Ramos, industrial engineer*, was actually the former chief of security, Lieutenant Colonel Enrique Trinidad Oliva, expelled from the army for human rights violations and for his involvement, in some way that was not quite clear, in the assassination of President Carlos Castillo Armas.

Journalists speculated about his subsequent life in hiding, and he was the subject of much suspicion—some thought, for example, he'd belonged to an extreme right group called the White Hand, which was preparing to overthrow the government. What no one imagined was that he had been working as a smuggler and right-hand man to a pit boss.

XXIX

W HEN SÍMULA TOLD EFRÉN GARCÍA ARDILES that Arturo
Borrero Lamas was on his deathbed, he was briefly uncertain what to do. But then he made a decision. He told
Marta's former maidservant to ask his onetime friend for permission
to pay him a visit. To his surprise, Arturo agreed. He even set a day
and time: Saturday at five in the afternoon. Efrén remembered this
was the same day Borrero Lamas's friends used to gather in his home
long ago to play a card game, *rocambor*, now unknown elsewhere in
the world. Only a few years had passed, and yet how Guatemala had
changed. And his life, too. How might Arturo be?

He was worse than imagined. He lay in bed in what was now like
a makeshift hospital room, with tablets and salves strewn all over and
a round-the-clock nurse who discreetly left the room as soon as he'd
entered. The curtains were pulled and the room sunk in shadows—
the light bothered the sick man. There was a stench of medicine and
illness that reminded Efrén of the profession he had abandoned. The
old servants, Patrocinio and Juana, were still there. Arturo was gaunt
and bony, his voice and the gaze in his sunken eyes suffused with

weariness. He spoke in a low tone with long pauses, barely moving his lips, as if overwhelmed by the effort.

They didn't shake hands, but Efrén did clap him a few times on the shoulder, asking him:

"How are you doing?"

"You know perfectly well that I'm dying," Arturo responded dryly. "Otherwise I wouldn't have had you over. But at the hour of his death, a Christian must leave his malice behind. So please, sit down. I'm happy to see you, Efrén."

"I am, too, Arturo. How are you?" he asked again.

His former friend lay beneath a blanket and a counterpane. Was he having chills? Efrén himself was hot. There were old paintings on the walls, and behind the bed hung a cross with Christ in his agony. The invalid's bloodless face spoke of long days without exposure to the sun.

"I don't know if you know this, Arturo, but I'm no longer practicing medicine. They threw me out of San Juan de Dios General and little by little every other door closed to me. With Castillo Armas in power, I had to close my office, I didn't have any patients left. Now I'm giving classes at a private school. Biology, chemistry, physics. Believe it or not, I've found I like teaching."

"You must be going hungry," the invalid whispered. "Being a teacher in Guatemala means living like a beggar, or not much better."

"It's not so bad," Efrén said with a shrug. "I make less than I did as a doctor, obviously. But when my mother died, I sold the house. With my savings, I make it to the end of the month."

"So in the end, we're both more or less fucked," Arturo grunted. "We didn't even make it to sixty. What a couple of failures!"

To hear him, Efrén had to crouch and lean in toward the sick man's bed. After a long pause, he finally dared to say:

"Aren't you going to ask me about your grandson, Arturo?"

"I don't have any grandson," he responded. "I can't rightly ask you about someone who doesn't exist."

"He's eleven now, and raucous as a squirrel," Efrén said, as if he hadn't heard. "Sweet, curious, cheerful. Símula nicknamed him Trencito. He gets good grades and he plays all the sports, even if he's not much good at them. He's happy. I've really grown to care about him. I'm doing double duty, of course, mother and father. I tell him stories, sometimes from memory, sometimes out of books. He's a hell of a reader, despite his age. Give him a book, and he'll sit there fascinated, his eyes as big as saucers. He asks me lots of questions, sometimes I don't even know the answers. If there's anyone he resembles, it's you."

Símula came in to bring Efrén a lemonade. She asked Arturo if he needed anything, and he shook his head. She no longer worked there since Miss Guatemala left, but she came by once in a while to lend a hand to Patrocinio and Juana and to see Arturo, especially after they diagnosed him with cancer. *I'm going to make Trencito's meal,* she whispered in Efrén's ear before leaving the room. He hadn't cared much for the nickname at first, but there was no getting the maid to call the boy by his name, and in the end, he'd got used to it.

"Cancer of the pancreas," the sick man blurted out with a jolt. "The worst kind. They found it very late, when it had already metastasized. The pain is awful, but they keep me sedated most of the time. My friend Father Ulloa, the Jesuit—I guess you remember him—won't allow me to help things along. He says it would be suicide, he wants me to hold out till the end. I tell him that's pure sadism on the Church's part. He talks to me about God and the infinite mysteries of Christian doctrine. Until now I've respected his opinion, but I don't know that I'll go on obeying much longer. What do you think?"

"I don't believe in God anymore, Arturo."

"So you've turned atheist then. First communist, then atheist. There's clearly nothing to be done with you, Efrén."

"Agnostic, not atheist. That's what I am nowadays: perplexed. I don't believe, I don't not believe. Confused, maybe that's the better word. I'll tell you another thing: remember how, when we were boys, we used to anguish over the thought of death, of whatever it was that came afterward? I've changed in that regard, too. Maybe it seems like a lie to you, but I don't care anymore whether or not there's life in the next world."

"You killed me before cancer could, Efrén." He had sat up slightly

227

to interrupt him, and was looking him straight in the eyes. "But I don't hold it against you. You know when I stopped? When I found out Martita had become Castillo Armas's lover. That was even worse than learning you'd gotten her pregnant."

Efrén didn't know what to say. Arturo was leaning his head on the pillow again with his eyes closed. He was paler now. The walls of the old colonial house must have been made of thick stone, because not a single sound from the street penetrated them.

"Yes, far, far worse," the sick man continued, eyes still shut, drawing a deep breath. "A daughter of mine whoring herself to a pathetic little colonel barely worthy of the name. A bastard even, you believe that?"

Efrén still didn't utter a word. He was shocked: he'd never imagined Arturo would touch on this subject, let alone so openly.

"There are rumors, even, that she had some kind of role in Castillo Armas's assassination." Borrero Lamas seemed at a loss for words, but then, slowly, he relaxed. "Tell me the truth, Efrén, for the sake of our old friendship. This is something that's been tormenting me ever since talk of it began. Do you think it's possible? That she was caught up in the killing?"

"I don't know, Arturo." Efrén was uncomfortable. He had wondered the same thing often, and the thought of it tormented him on certain nights like a bad dream. "It's hard for me to believe, just as it is for everyone we know. But I have the sense that the Marta you and I remember isn't the same as the one who came later. There are all kinds of conjectures about the murder, some of them frankly absurd. Just as with so much else in Guatemala's history, it's likely we'll never know the answer. You know what conclusion I've come to with all that's happened to me, Arturo, with all that's happened in this country? That a human being is something contemptible indeed. It seems that deep down, a monster dwells in each of us. As if it were just waiting for the right moment to emerge into the light and wreak chaos. Of course, it's hard for me to imagine Marta caught up in something so terrible. Given her situation, the fact that many people despised her and hoped to get on Odilia's good side, all that could be the invention of backbiters. Or a way of distracting attention from those who are truly guilty. But I don't know. Forgive me, I just can't give you an answer."

There was a long pause. An insect had begun buzzing through the room, a wasp, appearing and disappearing beneath the light shed by the lamp.

"You know what?" Efrén asked. "There's something I've always wanted to ask you. The way we used to play *rocambor* every Saturday in this very house—how did that start? Nobody remembers that game, no one plays it anymore."

"My father used to play it with his friends, and I was always a man who respected tradition," Arturo replied. "That used to be lovely. But all good things come to an end, or so it seems. Even *rocambor*. Now you tell me something. Are you still in thrall to your crazy political ideas? Are you still a communist? I know Castillo Armas had you imprisoned. And that you were a pariah when you came out."

"You're wrong, I never was a communist," Efrén said. "I don't know where that absurd idea came from, but it ruined my life. Not that I care much anymore. My ideas haven't changed much. The truth is, I was hopeful with Arévalo and particularly with Árbenz. But you know how all that turned out. More killings and exiles. The U.S.A. put an end to whatever optimism I had, and now we're back with the same thing we've always had: one dictatorship after another. You think it's a good thing, having General Ydígoras Fuentes for president?"

"Sickness has turned me into a fatalist," he responded, dodging the question. "What's certain is America will go on making the decisions for us. But maybe the alternative would be worse. I mean, if Moscow ran our lives instead of Washington. Whenever we get to run free, we do even worse. It would seem the lesser evil would have been for us all to remain slaves."

He laughed for an instant, a cavernous laugh.

"So for you, it's better to be a slave than a leftist. You haven't changed a bit, either, Arturo," Efrén said, shrugging. "In your heart, you believe, like lots of other Guatemalans, that we've gotten what we deserve with Ydígoras Fuentes. A murderer and a thief. You're not really a fatalist, despite what you say. It's just that you're still committed to making the bad choice."

"If you want me to tell you the truth, Efrén, I couldn't give less of a damn about politics," Arturo said. "I was just trying to provoke you. I used to get a kick out of that in the old days, remember? Riling you up, so you'd launch into one of those ideology lessons you used to like to give on Saturday afternoons."

He seemed to be smiling again, but he stopped talking, and the subsequent silence went on a long time. Efrén sipped his lemonade. Had he been right to come? This house made him sad, it reminded him of the beginning of the end. This would be the last time he saw Arturo. You couldn't say they had patched things up. Their political ideas remained irreconcilable. And the saga of Miss Guatemala was still there in the background and would always come between them. He went to stand up and say goodbye, and as he did, he heard Arturo's voice again:

"I've left this house to charity. Father Ulloa will manage it. I also set up a trust to pay for the running of it. It will go to abandoned children, single mothers, old people out on the street, that sort of thing. The Chichicastenango estate, which is just a source of painful memories to me, I'm handing over to some Catholic sisters. I've arranged things so that once I die, they'll take Marta in at the finest residence in Guatemala. They'll care for her to the end. If she ever does die, I mean. Because up to now, she's managed to bury all of us."

Who was Arturo talking about? Ah, Marta senior. Efrén remembered Miss Guatemala's mother, who was still alive, if out of her mind, and knew nothing about what was currently going on. *Better for her*, he thought.

"With all these donations, I'm sure you'll go straight to heaven, Arturo," Efrén joked.

"I hope so," Arturo replied, playing along before turning sorrowful. "The problem is, even I'm not so sure heaven exists, Efrén."

Efrén made no reply. He thought for a second about Father Ulloa, the man who had married him and Martita. He looked at his watch.

It was nearly time for little Efrén's dinner. Today, Símula would be preparing it, and she would want to stay there to watch him eat, telling him stories about his grandfather and his mother, subjects otherwise never touched on. Trencito was a lively boy, and inquisitive. A young, normal, healthy boy, with Marta's same mysterious big blue eyes. He had no memory of his mother, since she left when he was only five. What would happen to him in the future? Arturo could have left him something, a little fund so he could study and have a career. He wouldn't inherit a cent from Efrén, who spent every cent he made. That was what preoccupied him most these days. Living long enough to see his son's future assured; educating him and preparing him to get ahead. He didn't have close relatives who could care for his boy if he had an accident or fell mortally ill as Arturo had. There was nothing to be done: he would have to survive and make it to old age. He remembered that, when they were young, he and Arturo represented great hopes for the respective families. *You two will both go far*, his mother used to prophesy. *You were wrong, Mother. We didn't get anywhere. Arturo will die bitter and frustrated and I will never again raise my head and this country will never allow me to raise it.* He reconsidered and told himself these thoughts were ridiculous and would only work to paralyze him. It was better to shake them off. To go eat with Trencito. To talk awhile with Símula, if she was still around.

He got up and left on tiptoe to keep from waking Arturo, who had fallen asleep. Patrocinio and Juana accompanied him to the door, and he hugged them both.

XXX

H E HAD SLEPT IN THE OFFICES of the SIM, the Military
Intelligence Service, a well-guarded building in Ciudad
Trujillo on the corner of Avenida México and Calle 30 de
Marzo, because he was afraid they'd kill him at his home. Some of
the SIM administration had fled, but the bodyguards, informers, in-
spectors, and collaborators he was closest to hadn't known what to
do or where to go. For now, at least, the regime could count on them.

But him—who could he count on? He didn't know, and that was
what tormented him and kept him up at night, despite the Nembutal
he took each day before bed. Since El Jefe's murder on May 30, 1961,
his life had fallen into a pit of anguish and uncertainty. The day before,
General Ramfis Trujillo had gotten word to him through intermediaries that there was no point in trying to get an appointment, because he
would never agree to meet with him. But almost simultaneously, Joaquín Balaguer, president of the republic, had requested his presence
in his office at the National Palace at ten the next morning. What was
in store for him?

At 6:00 a.m., he got up from the cot he kept next to his desk, showered, dressed, and went for a coffee in the canteen, where the waiters and the few guests greeted him with questions in their eyes: What was happening in the Dominican Republic? What was coming now that El Jefe had been assassinated? He didn't know, either. Since that catastrophe, he'd thought of only one thing: finding the assassins. But that was done. Only two of the people who had ambushed El Jefe on the road leaving Ciudad Trujillo toward San Cristóbal were still in hiding: Luis Amiama Tió and Antonio Imbert. People were on their trail, they'd both be caught soon, and they'd wind up with their comrades in prison or in their graves. The one certain thing, he thought, was that Ramfis would make them pay dearly for their crime. According to everything he'd heard, he was enraged, almost insane after his father's death. The night after his arrival from Paris on a plane rented from Air France, he had taken the senior cadets from the Military Academy to La Cuarentena Prison and ordered each of them to choose one of the *communists* incarcerated there and execute them personally with a bullet to the head. Why was he refusing to see him? He knew Trujillo's oldest son had never liked him. Why? Jealousy, maybe, because El Jefe had always shown more affection for him than for his own children. It pleased Abbes García to think that Trujillo might have loved him more than Ramfis or Radhamés.

After a meager breakfast, he returned to his office, where the day's newspapers waited for him on his desk. He didn't read them, he just paged through them, stopping now and then at certain headlines. They didn't have much to say about the Dominican Republic's future, just that the U.S.A. and, obviously, Betancourt, Figueres, Muñoz Marín and untold other Latin American leaders were demanding democracy return to the country before lifting the embargo. No, they didn't know much: the press, like everyone, was confused, frightened, blind, unaware of what awaited the Dominican people after those bastards had slain their supreme leader, their figurehead, the Generalísimo who had turned that backward republic into what was in 1961, a solid, prosperous country, with the finest army in all the Caribbean. Ingrates! Dogs! Bastards! Sons of bitches! At least Ramfis would make them pay dearly for their crime—very dearly indeed.

At nine thirty, he put on his tie, his hat, and his dark glasses—he was in civilian garb, not his uniform—and walked outside. A chauffeured car was waiting for him by the door, on the corner of Avenida México and Calle 30 de Marzo, in accordance with instructions he had given the night before. While the car drove through the packed streets of Ciudad Trujillo (Would they change the name of the capital now that the Generalísimo had died? Most likely yes.) toward the National Palace, he thought it had been wise of him to send his new wife, Zita, to Mexico. An opportune decision. She should wait there until things cleared up.

They recognized him at the National Palace, but they still made him pass through the humiliating ritual of opening his briefcase, riffling through his papers, even patting down his jacket and pants. What a change! Before, when he'd gone to the palace, the guards were all adulatory smiles and no one had ever searched him.

In the waiting room of the office of Dr. Joaquín Balaguer (a puppet president until the day of the assassination who now thought his authority was bona fide), they humiliated him again, making him wait an hour before the head of state would receive him.

The president, normally a well-mannered man, didn't stand up to greet him, and when Abbes García walked over to his desk, he extended him a cold hand and murmured an almost inaudible hello. He finished looking through some documents, then rose, gesturing curtly for Abbes to take a seat in one of a row of armchairs. He was a short, simply dressed man with gray hair, his eyes almost hidden behind the thick lenses of his glasses. But Abbes García knew perfectly well that his benign appearance concealed sharp wits and extraordinary ambition.

"How are things, Mr. President?" he finally asked, trying to break the nervous silence.

"You must know that better than I, Colonel," the president said, a quick grin passing like a breath across his face. "They say you're the best-informed man in the country."

"I don't want to waste Your Excellency's time," Abbes García said after a moment. "Just tell me what you've called me here for. Are you firing me?"

"Hardly," Balaguer responded, again with that fleeting smile. "Actually I'm offering you a safer and more tranquil post than the one you have now."

At that moment, an assistant entered the office begging pardon, and said that Mrs. María Martínez de Trujillo, El Jefe's widow, was on the phone. It was urgent.

"Tell her I'll call back in a moment," Dr. Balaguer replied. And when the assistant was gone, he turned to Abbes García, his face now very serious. His voice changed as well. "As you can see, Colonel, I don't have a free minute for anything. So let's not waste time. This is a very simple matter. After the assassination, everything in the Dominican Republic has changed. And there's no reason for me to deceive you. You know perfectly well you're the most hated man in the country. And abroad, too. Unjustly, you are accused of the worst barbarities. Murder, torture, kidnapping, disappearances, every conceivable and inconceivable horror. You must also know that if we want to salvage any of Trujillo's many achievements, you cannot form part of our government."

He stopped talking, waiting for Abbes García's rejoinder, but since the latter remained mute, he continued:

"I'm offering you a diplomatic post. The Dominican consulate in Japan."

"In Japan?" Abbes García jumped back in his seat. Then he said sarcastically, "You couldn't find somewhere farther away?"

"There is no consulate farther from the Dominican Republic," President Balaguer responded very seriously. "You will leave tomorrow, at midday, passing through Canada. You already have a diplomatic passport ready, and your tickets have been purchased. You will be given both upon leaving this office."

Abbes García seemed to sink into his seat. His complexion was ashen, and his head felt like a volcano on the verge of erupting. Leave the country? Go to Japan? It took him a few seconds to say anything.

"Does General Ramfis Trujillo know about this decision, Your Excellency?"

"It took a lot for me to convince him, Colonel," he said in that soft voice, so mellifluous when he gave his speeches. "General Ramfis wanted to put you in prison. He believes you failed at your job. That with someone else at the head of the SIM, the Generalísimo would still be alive. I assure you, I worked very hard to get him to allow you to leave with a diplomatic post. That is my work alone. And you should thank me for it."

Now he laughed, genuinely, but only for a few seconds.

"May I stay a couple of days, to take care of my things?" Abbes García asked, knowing perfectly well what the answer would be.

"You can't stay even an hour longer than I've told you," Dr. Balaguer said, stressing each syllable. "General Ramfis could change his mind, take a step backward. I wish you good luck at your new destination, Mr. Abbes García. I was about to say Colonel, I forgot you no longer are one. General Ramfis has expelled you from the army. I suppose you've heard that."

He stood and returned to his desk without offering his hand, sitting down and looking through his papers again as if the other man weren't there. Abbes García walked toward the door and left without saying goodbye. He felt his legs trembling and thought he might faint, making a ridiculous spectacle. He slowly approached the exit, and in the hallway, an assistant handed him a folder, murmuring that inside was confirmation of his appointment, his diplomatic passport, and his tickets to Tokyo via Canada.

He ordered his driver to take him home, and wasn't surprised when he saw that the police who had stood guard there two days before were now gone. Desolate, he looked through the closets full of his suits and Zita's dresses, the ties and underwear, the shoes and socks. Before filling a suitcase with clothes, he emptied his safe of all the currency, Dominican and American, inside. He counted: it added up to two thousand three hundred forty-eight dollars. It would be enough to travel on. Once his luggage was packed, he looked through the desk in his office, and apart from a few bank statements, he burned all the papers, notebooks, and journals inside, with their notes on his work and politics. That took quite some time. Then he got back into the car, which had sat there waiting for him. The chauffeur asked him, "Taking a trip, Colonel?" He responded, "Yeah, for a few days, urgent matters." He realized he would probably never see that house again, and he wondered if he had forgotten to pack or burn anything important. He went to the Reserve Bank, where he kept two accounts in Dominican pesos. They told him they couldn't exchange his pesos for dollars, because the uncertainty following the president's killing had led to fluctuations in the value of the peso and all foreign currency transactions had been suspended. The bank director, who saw him in his office, told him quietly, "If it's urgent, you can exchange them on the street in Ciudad Colonial, but I don't recommend it, you'll end up paying a fortune for dollars. In all this chaos, everyone's started buying them up, just imagine . . ."

Abbes García gave up on the idea. If what President Balaguer had said was true, and Ramfis thought his irresponsibility was the cause of El Jefe's murder, then Trujillo's older son could change his mind and order him killed whenever he wished. It was better to keep those pesos in his wallet; he could exchange them overseas, if anyone would still pay anything for them . . .

It was past five in the afternoon when he returned to the Military Intelligence Service. The guards still stood at attention and saluted him at the building's front door. Was it true that Ramfis had expelled him from the army? In his office, he tore up and burned the documents, notes, and letters related to his government service; all he saved were a few personal papers he stowed in his briefcase. He looked at the walls, now bare except for a portrait of Trujillo, his look severe, his posture resolute, his chest covered in medals. Johnny's eyes watered.

He ordered two sandwiches brought to his office, one ham and one cheese, and an ice-cold beer. He ate and drank as he asked himself whether he should call Zita in Mexico to tell her about his trip or whether it was best to do it tomorrow from Canada. He decided on the latter. At the end of his only meal of the day, six of his collaborators appeared in his office—three civilians, one guard, and two soldiers. They were confused and frightened, and Lances Falcón, a small man, an accountant, with a salt-and-pepper mustache and dark glasses, asked him what would happen to them in the name of the rest of the group. They were disconcerted, frightened to death, and knew nothing about the situation. Was it true he was going overseas?

Abbes García listened to them without getting up, and decided to tell them the truth.

"I'm leaving, that's true. But not of my own free will. Balaguer's fired me. He's sending me to a diplomatic post on the other end of the world. All the way to Tokyo. As far as the Military Intelligence Service goes, I don't know. There's no way it will disappear, any incoming government will need it to survive, no matter who's president. Since Balaguer and Ramfis have divided power, with Balaguer taking the civilian side and Ramfis overseeing the military, most likely Ramfis will oversee the SIM. It's been wonderful working with you all. I thank you for your help. I know how much heroism it takes, and how great the sacrifices you've made are. Trujillo appreciated you all and held you in high regard. Now the rats are taking advantage of the instability to come out of their holes and accuse us of terrible crimes. I'm afraid there could be reprisals against you. So if you're asking me for advice, I say go! Hide. Don't become sacrificial lambs. Save yourselves."

He stood up and shook each of their hands. He could see tears in some of the men's eyes. They left the office more confused, frightened, and anxious than before. Abbes García was certain that all six would go into hiding as soon as they could.

When he was alone, he realized spending the night there was likely imprudent. If Ramfis wanted him arrested or killed, he would send people to find him at SIM. He decided to go to a hotel. He went outside. The car and the chauffeur were still there. He ordered his driver to take him to the Hotel Jaragua. Giving him a three-hundred-peso tip, he shook his hand and wished him luck.

"What should I do with the car, Colonel?" the man asked, chagrined.

Abbes García thought a moment, shrugged, and grunted, "Whatever you want."

The manager at the Jaragua knew him and didn't make him sign the guest registry. He gave him a suite, which he paid for in advance in cash, and ordered a car to take him to the airport in the morning. Abbes took a long bubble bath with mineral salts and lay down. Despite his customary pill, it took him a long time to get to sleep. He tried to think of women and the gashes he'd licked, to see if he could get turned on, but it was pointless. As it had every night since the 30th of May, the face of the murdered El Jefe came back into his mind, and he felt chills and unbearable loneliness at the thought that they had peppered Generalísimo Trujillo with bullets, and that he would never see him or hear his voice again. Then there was the terrible injustice, Ramfis accusing him of failing to protect him and therefore being responsible for his death, when for ten years he had lived for El Jefe alone, obedient to his every caprice, bathing himself in blood in the man's service, liberating him from all enemies at home and abroad, risking his life and his freedom. Those injustices had led to his fate.

He passed a short, distressful, sleepless night. He woke and ordered breakfast before shaving. Once dressed, he took the taxi the manager of the Jaragua had ordered for him. At the airport, there was a mob of journalists, photographers, and cameramen waiting, but he refused to make any statements, and thankfully, he was taken to the dignitaries' lounge, where he waited for his departure.

The last photograph that appears of him in biographies, press articles, and history books (though he lived years, maybe many years, longer) was taken that morning as he walked toward the stairs to the plane that would carry him to Canada. He is visible there in civilian clothes, a little thinner, less swollen than in earlier photos, wearing a hat and dark tie and a tailored jacket with one of its three buttons undone, holding a bulky suitcase, his bright white socks confirming the opinion of Generalísimo Trujillo that the head of the SIM hadn't the least idea what it meant to dress elegantly. His face is contracted into an uncomfortable grimace and his stare is evasive, unsettled, as if he knew he would never return to his country again. It was June 10, 1961, eleven days after the assassination of Trujillo.

He fell asleep not long after the plane took off and awoke in a daze just over an hour outside Toronto. Looking at his tickets to Tokyo, he saw there would be a six-hour layover before the next flight. Would he go directly to Japan? Of course not. He would call his wife in Mexico, his banker in Switzerland, and go personally to be sure his secret account in Geneva was still safe. He closed his eyes and thought about how uncertain life had become since El Jefe's death. His feelings for Trujillo were affectionate and grateful: El Jefe had trusted him, assigned him the most difficult missions, and Abbes García had always come through. His hands were stained with blood for him, but he'd been happy to do it, he'd loved that superhuman figure. And Trujillo had compensated him handsomely. He remembered his limitless generosity. It was thanks to Trujillo he had those savings in Switzerland—Trujillo himself had authorized the account. Could anyone have found out about it? No, no one but El Jefe, not even Zita, knew it existed. Just Trujillo, and now he was dead. There was no way Ramfis could know. How much did he have there? He couldn't remember. More than a million dollars anyway. He could get by with that for a good long while.

No sooner had he stepped off the Pan American Airways flight in Toronto than he changed his ticket to Tokyo to another with stopovers in Geneva and Paris, paying more than three thousand dollars in cash to do so. He called Zita, hoping to surprise her, but instead, she surprised him, telling him that morning the press in Mexico had published a photo of him departing from the airport in Ciudad Trujillo for an unknown destination. "They're sending us to Japan as diplomats," he said. "To Japan?" she replied with alarm. "What are we going to do there?" He answered: "We won't stay there for long. The important thing is, we're alive, and that's already a lot, given the way things in the Dominican Republic are going." Zita said nothing more, as always in these kinds of situations: she trusted him and was sure her husband would solve whatever problems arose. *She's a good wife*, he thought. Too bad she was so fixated on having children.

He called his banker in Switzerland right afterward, and luckily, he answered the phone himself. Abbes asked him to book him a hotel in Geneva and said he would visit him in his office two days later. When he hung up, he breathed a sigh of relief: his banker, who spoke very pure Spanish, had told him he now had one million, three hundred twenty-seven thousand dollars and fifty-six cents in his account. That meant no one had tried to break into his account: it had sat there, gathering interest in the Swiss citadel. For the first time since El Jefe's assassination, he was happy.

When he arrived in Geneva twelve hours later, he checked into a room at the same small lakeside hotel where he'd stayed three years earlier when he'd opened the account, which he'd added to regularly since; he filled the tub and took a long bubble bath with mineral salts, just as he had the day before. He felt a physical sense of well-being and tried to imagine his life in the future. He knew perfectly well the consular position in Japan wouldn't last long. Sooner or later, no matter what happened in the Dominican Republic, people would stop taking his calls. He would go on being the *most hated man*, and they'd pin all the murders, disappearances, tortures, and jailings on him, the ones he'd been involved in and the ones that were simply made up. So he needed to organize a future in another country, accept the idea of permanent exile. He noticed that he was sobbing. Tears had burst from his eyes and were draining into his mouth and leaving his lips humid and salty. Why was he crying? For El Jefe. There would never be another Trujillo in his lifetime. A man so admirable, so intelligent, astute, and energetic, a man who had, as he told him one day, bagged more than a thousand women, *taking them from the front and from behind.* A man capable of breaking through any and all obstacles. He had entered his life like an act of providence. It was a miracle that Abbes had written him that letter, asking for funding to go to Mexico to study police science. That had brought him a power he'd never dreamed of. Did they not say that after El Jefe he was the most feared man in the Dominican Republic? Yes, asking for help from Trujillo had been a before and after. Whatever happened, he'd been lucky to enter El Jefe's employ. What a miserable couple of traitors Balaguer and Ramfis were. Selling out to the Americans while El Jefe's body was still warm!

His conversation with his banker the next morning calmed him down. His account was still there, still secret, still perfectly protected,

even if he couldn't exchange his Dominican currency: amid so much
political instability, the international money markets had stopped ac-
cepting Dominican pesos. The banker recommended he leave them
in a safe at the bank until things changed. He did so and walked out
with a bundle of fifty thousand dollars and twenty thousand French
francs to spend in Paris.

In the French capital, he stayed in a suite at the George V and
hired a car and driver that same night to take him to a brothel. He'd
never licked a French whore's gash, and the prospect excited him. The
chauffeur took him to a little bar in Pigalle where he could choose a
girl, he told him, and take her to one of the little hotels nearby. He
did, and he wound up in bed that night with a chick from Algeria
who spoke a bit of garbled Spanish and who made him pay double
because, in her words, she got paid to blow the horn, not to get eaten,
that was something she wasn't used to. The night didn't end well: he
got an erection quickly, but he couldn't come. It was the first time it
had ever happened to him and he tried to play it down, blaming his
failure on the nervous tension he'd felt since El Jefe's death. *Don't
worry*, he told himself, *you're not impotent.*

The next day, he thought he would go to the Louvre—this was his
second visit to Paris, and on the first, he had been to no museums—
but when he got into his rented car, he instead asked the driver if he
knew of any Rosicrucian temples or monasteries in the city. The man
gave him an uncertain look: *Rosicrucian? Rosicrucian?* He ordered
him to take him to that dock on the Seine where the little boats go
back and forth and you can see the bridges and monuments of Paris
from the water. The ride lasted two hours, and he was able to distract
himself a bit. Afterward, he asked the chauffeur to take him to have
lunch at the best restaurant he could think of. At a traffic light, he
saw a woman's face that looked familiar. Cucha! Cuchita Antesana!
His girlfriend from a million years ago. He told the chauffeur to turn
around and pick her up where they'd seen her. He got out and hurried
over to the woman who reminded him of his long-lost love. Unbe-
lievably, it was she. She was the same, despite the fifteen years that
had passed. Cucha looked at him, surprised, disconcerted, amazed.

Johnny! Is that you? In Paris? Cucha had lived there for six months now, and was learning French at the Alliance Française in Boulevard Raspail. Was she free to have lunch? She certainly was. They went to La Coupole on Boulevard Montparnasse. Abbes hadn't seen her again since back when they were in love, when she had just finished secondary school and he was still a young journalist covering horse races, with an uninspired radio show that paid pennies.

When Cuchita saw him take out his red handkerchief, she asked him if he was still Rosicrucian. "Yeah, or halfway," he responded as a joke. "You wouldn't happen to know if there's a Rosicrucian temple in Paris, would you?" She hadn't had another companion since the breakup with Johnny. After her parents' death, she had used the inheritance to spend a year in the United States learning English. And now she would spend another year in France. So what was he doing here after General Trujillo's death?

"I'll be spending some time outside the Dominican Republic," he told her. And he started inventing fairy tales: "I'm going to devote myself to bringing together the governments of the right in Latin America, to get them to work together. So what's happening in our disgraced country doesn't happen to them. It's fallen into the chaos of democracy, it's selling out to the United States, and sooner or later, that's going to give the communists the upper hand. They know troubled waters make for good fishing. They'll end up taking over the Dominican Republic and turning it into a people's democracy, which is just another term for a Soviet satellite."

As he spoke, he started to convince himself that these words could be a reality. Why not? Wasn't every dictator in Latin America threatened with the same fate that had befallen El Jefe? They needed to come together, to be convinced to exchange information, to develop strategies to crush all those *democratic* conspiracies, which were nothing more than a Trojan horse for the communists. And who was better suited to serve as the link between those governments, to defend them against their enemies, the same men who were now running Guatemala with Washington's blessing?

By the time he left Cuchita at her hotel in the Latin Quarter, he had convinced himself that he would become what he had been for Trujillo for all the right-wing governments in the Caribbean and Central and South America: a strongman, a motivator, a bridge of solidarity, a lookout.

The rest of the afternoon, while he bought himself clothes, shoes, and ties in the finer shops near La Madeleine and the Champs-Élysées, he ruminated on that future trajectory he had invented to enrapture his girlfriend from his teenage years.

That night, he returned to the same bar in Pigalle, but instead of the Algerian from the night before, he took an African to the hotel. She didn't put up any objections. Her gash was reddish and rank and it turned him on immediately, and he was satisfied when he ejaculated onto the bed while he licked her. Thank goodness, his dick was still in working order.

Two days later, he was in Tokyo, where Zita had already arrived. At the minuscule embassy, the chargé d'affaires told him they couldn't give him an office, there wasn't enough space available. The ministry had informed them that his consulship would be merely *formal*. Abbes García didn't ask what exactly *formal* meant. He already had a clear enough idea.

XXXI

CRISPÍN CARRASQUILLA WAS THE SON of a railroad employee who had dreamed of being a soldier as long as he'd had the power of reason. His father encouraged this dream, even if his mother would have preferred engineering or medicine. He was born in a village, San Pedro Nécta, in Huehuetenango, close to the Mexican border. He spent much of his childhood moving from place to place. Eventually, they gave his father a stable post at Estación Central in Guatemala City, where Crispín attended a public school better than the grammar schools he'd gone to in the provinces.

He wasn't very studious, but he was a good athlete. He swam from a young age, almost from boyhood, because he'd been told doing so would help him grow; he'd been afraid his small stature would make it hard for him to get accepted at the Politécnica, because all candidates had to meet a height minimum. This troubled him, because he was still a few tenths of an inch short. The happiest day of his life must have been when he found out the Military Academy had accepted him—he wasn't one of the top applicants, but he wasn't at the bottom, either. His first three years as a cadet followed those same lines: he was neither an excellent nor a horrible student, always somewhere in the middle, studying dutifully and making an exemplary effort in military maneuvers and physical education. He was a good kid, artless, maybe a touch dim, easy to make friends with. He got along with everyone, from his fellow students to his superiors, was obedient, obliging, unaffected by the rigors of discipline, preferring to serve rather than follow orders, and his classmates thought highly of him, but without feeling any particular admiration.

His somewhat indefinite personality changed during the war in the last months of Jacobo Árbenz's government, when one of the sulfates dropped a bomb on the ceremonial courtyard of the Escuela Politécnica. No one was killed, but several were wounded, some even gravely, among them Cristóbal Fomento. Crispín Carrasquilla was walking out of Physics and watched, appalled, as the bomb exploded on one of the rooftops surrounding the courtyard and sent pieces of it flying; a rain of stone and rubble flew in all directions, breaking the surrounding windows and sending him rolling away on the ground. As he got up and made sure he was unharmed, he heard screams of pain from the injured and saw cadets, officers, and service employees run past covered in dust, some of them bloody. After a few minutes the shock and chaos were over and the entire school mobilized to take the casualties—including his friend Urogallo—to the infirmary, which, fortunately, hadn't suffered much damage.

Until then, Crispín had never cared about politics. He'd heard talk about the October Revolution that had ended General Jorge Ubico Castañeda's military dictatorship and about the junta overseen by Colonel Ponce Vaides, but he had never paid that much mind—he was just a schoolboy back then. He'd heard about the election of President Juan José Arévalo and his successor, Colonel Jacobo Árbenz, at the time when he was entering the Politécnica. He saw all that as something distant, matters that didn't concern him. And this was the same attitude the other cadets had. He didn't take part in any of the arguments that sometimes occurred in his presence when Colonel Castillo Armas first rose up in Guatemala and accused Árbenz's government of being communists. But his neutrality—or rather,

his indifference—to politics vanished when the sulfates started flying over Guatemala City, throwing down leaflets of propaganda or
bombs that brought devastation, victims, panic, especially since the
day one of them shelled the Military Academy. Gringo pilots attacking Guatemalans, military forts like Matamoros or San José de Buena
Vista, even the Politécnica itself—this touched his pride and his idea
of what patriotism meant, and it turned him into another person. It
was a crime against the country, he thought, and no one who loved
Guatemala could accept it and keep even a bit of their dignity, let
alone a cadet training to be an officer in the army.

After that, he took part in every discussion of politics at school,
sometimes even starting them. Neither the cadets nor the officers had
a single position: they were divided over the Árbenz government and
its reforms, particularly land reform; but almost to a man, both groups
were withering about Castillo Armas, who had broken the unity of the
armed forces and attacked his own country with support and financing from the United States.

That his friend and classmate Cristóbal Fomento was one of the
wounded in the bombing of the ceremonial courtyard affected him
deeply. Cristóbal loved animals and was forever talking about exotic
species unknown in Guatemala. One fine day, he showed up with a
magazine with photos of something that looked a bit like a rooster and
was called *urogallo* in Spain; the images had so excited him that the cadets had called him that ever since. When Crispín went to see him in
the military hospital, where they'd transferred him from the school's
infirmary, he found his friend looking sad as can be. The doctors had
been unable to save one of his eyes; that wasn't as bad as it could have
been, but it was incompatible with a career as a soldier. Urogallo would
have to leave the Academy and look for another profession. The two
friends' long talk was painful, and at one point, Crispín saw the tears
streaming down Cristóbal's cheeks when he told him he would devote
his life to agriculture, because an uncle of his had offered to take him
to work on his coffee estate in Alta Verapaz.

After the day the bomb fell in the ceremonial courtyard, all
the cadets, not just Crispín, had begun to talk a lot about politics.

Surprisingly, Crispín's personality changed. He became a leader, someone his classmates listened to in the stables, on the fields, or at night, after lights-out, when they would exchange ideas lying on their bunk beds in the dark. He would inveigh heatedly against those *traitors to the Fatherland* who had obeyed the Yankees and risen up against their own army to overthrow President Árbenz, as if Guatemala were a colony and not an independent country. His ideas were naturally confused, more emotional than rational, and they mingled love (for the land of his birth, for his comrades, and for his army, all of which, for him, were shrouded in sanctity) and hatred, even rage against anyone willing to let political interests compel them to attack their own country, like the leaders of the Army of Liberation, which was largely made up of mercenaries, many of them foreigners, who were bombing Guatemala City with planes piloted by Yankees and had sent a sulfate to drop a bomb on the Military Academy.

When the cadets were informed, at the beginning of July 1954, that all were to go to La Aurora airport to receive Castillo Armas, who was returning from El Salvador with the Yankee ambassador John E. Peurifoy and the military chiefs the Liberationists had signed a peace treaty with, naming a junta that would run the country with Castillo Armas as a member, Crispín Carrasquilla and his companions declared a boycott.

That same day, the director of the Military Academy, Colonel Eufemio Mendoza, summoned him to a meeting.

"I should have sent you off to the brig instead of calling you to my office," the colonel said, grimacing, in a voice that blended rage and bewilderment. "Have you lost your mind, Carrasquilla? A boycott at a military institution? Don't you realize that's the same thing as sedition? You could be expelled from the academy and imprisoned for nonsense like this!"

Colonel Eufemio Mendoza wasn't a bad person. He exercised frequently and had an athlete's build. He was always scratching his mustache. He, too, was livid over the bombing at the academy and understood that the cadets were scandalized by it. But the army wouldn't exist without discipline and a respect for hierarchy. The principal reminded cadet Carrasquilla, who listened to him at attention, unblinking, that in the army, orders were orders, you obeyed them and didn't hesitate or complain; otherwise the institution wouldn't function and then it couldn't fulfill its mission, the defense of the nation's sovereignty, in other words, of the Fatherland.

It was a long sermon, and toward the end, the colonel softened a bit, saying he understood the cadets were hurt and enraged. That was only human. But in the army, if a superior gives a soldier a command, he follows it, whether he likes it or not. And the order from above was clear as day: the cadets were to go to La Aurora airport in formation to greet the military leaders, Castillo Armas, and the Liberationists who had signed the peace accord in San Salvador.

"I don't care for it either," Colonel Mendoza confessed suddenly, lowering his voice to a whisper and looking knowingly at the cadet. "But I'll be there, in front of the school's committee, carrying out the orders I received. And you'll be there, too, in formation, in your parade uniform with your rifle clean and well oiled, unless you can't figure out a way to forget this idiotic idea of proposing the cadets boycott the commands of their superiors."

Eventually, Crispín apologized, admitting Colonel Mendoza was right. He had acted irresponsibly, and would admit as much in front of his classmates that very afternoon.

The cadets accompanied numerous military battalions and the police to La Aurora airport to welcome Castillo Armas and his retinue. There, in the enormous crowd saluting him—who were celebrating, more than the agreement between the army and the Liberationists, the end of the war, of insecurity, of uncertainty and fear—few sensed that a grave incident was on the verge of taking place between the cadets of the Military Academy and the platoon of militiamen and Liberationist soldiers, who were likewise standing on the tarmac to salute the men coming off the plane. The majority of those in that huge sea of people didn't even notice what happened. Nor did the journalists from the newspapers and radio stations, who were enthralled now with Castillo Armas, say a word about the events, which only became known through the testimony of the participants.

It was one of the first Liberationist contingents to reach the capital. They had lined up alongside the company of cadets from the Military Academy in their dirty, torn uniforms, which they wore carelessly—a herd of undisciplined grifters with ragtag armaments, rifles, shotguns, revolvers, and automatics, looking shabby in their hats and peaked caps and patches. Despite all this, they thought they could crack jokes at the expense of the cadets, impeccable in their freshly washed and ironed uniforms, who stood rigid in ordered rows listening to the jokes and insults of that gang of thugs in which true-born Guatemalans mingled with others from Central America who saw all this as nothing more than a payday. And now they were there, daring to mock and offend the future officers of the Guatemalan army.

The lieutenants standing at the head of the companies of cadets kept them from responding to the Liberationists' insults and provocations, but not for long. When the doors of the airplane that had just come from San Salvador opened, and Ambassador John Emil Peurifoy appeared with Castillo Armas behind him, the multitude rushed forward and broke the barriers to get close to the new arrivals. There was disorder, a melee, and several of the cadets and even a few of the officers took advantage of the chaos to confront the Liberationists, punching, kicking, and headbutting the men who had scorned them and called them followers of Árbenz. Crispín joined them, though before this he had never been prone to violence against anyone. With his new personality, as soon as disorder broke out, he was there shouting insults on the front lines, raising the butt of his rifle to strike whatever mercenary was nearest to hand.

All this aggravated the tension and animosity between the Military Academy and the Liberationists. The same day, the students from the Politécnica had been given leave to spend the night with their families, and there was another violent incident with a group of cadets in the Cinema Capitol on Sixth Avenue in Zone 1. As they were leaving the theater, they bumped into a half dozen invaders who had been waiting there to harass them. In the resulting fracas, two senior cadets were wounded and had to go to a public clinic for treatment. Crispín wasn't there, but he heard the details of what had occurred; it was the only thing anyone at the Military Academy was talking about. And so the idea began to spread among the cadets—several pushed for it at the same time—of settling accounts with the Liberationists concentrated around Roosevelt Hospital, which was still under construction. People were talking about it in low tones, and not especially clearly—was this supposed to be a military operation, or a clash between guerrilla groups?—when another, still more violent episode fired the spirits of the cadets and, this time, of several of the officers, too.

It happened in the brothel in the Gerona neighborhood overseen by Miss Miriam Ritcher, the gringa who tried to pass herself off as French (actually she'd been born in Havana) and sported a shimmering blond dye job. Three cadets were there having a drink at the bar when a group of Liberationists approached them; insults flew, bottles and glasses were shattered, and when the cadets held their ground, the Liberationists sent for reinforcements from their base at Roosevelt Hospital. Things seemed to have calmed down when six more Liberationists burst into the brothel armed with machine guns. Pointing their weapons, they submitted the three cadets to endless humiliations. They stripped them naked, made them dance and sing and cavort like pansies and spit and pissed on them while they did.

The final straw was August 2, 1954, the so-called Victory Parade. It had been conceived as a military affair, with the Guatemalan army's soldiers marching alongside the Liberationist brigades in a show of unity for the two forces. But in his speech, President Castillo Armas reserved his words of homage for the anticommunist forces, and awarded medals and other recognitions to the winning side alone. The better part of the public even went so far as to hiss and catcall at the cadets in the midst of the parade.

That night, the cadets from the Military Academy, with the backing of several young officers, attacked Roosevelt Hospital. By general agreement, the senior cadets, who were on the verge of graduating, would not participate, to keep from endangering their careers. But two of them insisted on taking part in the expedition, and the others did, too. They locked the principal, Colonel Eufemio Mendoza, and the rest of their superiors who had chosen to sit out the attack in the operations room with their agreement; then the cadets and the officers who had volunteered to go with them loaded their weapons, put on their helmets, and climbed into the buses that would take them to Roosevelt Hospital, where a reconnaissance group had been casing the area and spying on the Liberationists' activities. Crispín Carrasquilla by now was an undisputed leader of the group, and that night he directed their movements, after a fashion. Even the small clique of officers listened to his opinions, arguing about them but generally acquiescing. He had been the one to propose they ask all the new cadets individually whether they were willing to participate in the attack. All of them said they were.

Combat began at 4:30 a.m. The attackers had the advantage of surprise: the Liberationists didn't expect them and were stunned when fire from the rifles, bazookas, and cannons started to pummel them on that dark, rainy morning. Crispín was at the front, on the right flank of a column attacking Roosevelt Hospital in a pincer movement. Immediately, men began to fall, dead and wounded, all around him, and his comrades struggled to hear the orders he was shouting over the gunfire, cries, and groans. Amid the exhaustion, elation, and deafening explosions, he felt he was now doing what he had always dreamed of. He didn't even realize when, as he led the charge against the front door of Roosevelt Hospital, two bullets pierced his torso.

Stupefied at first by the cadets' attack, the Liberationists soon responded in kind. For much of the morning, while the sun rose in the sky, the rain ceased, and the dawn shone over that remote corner of Guatemala City, the shooting would die down, then resume with greater ferocity, and families in the neighborhood would run from their homes, carrying their children and suitcases and bundles filled with the essentials, horrified that something like this could happen at the very moment when they thought peace had finally arrived in the country.

At midday, the cadets received a shipment of mortars from the military base at La Aurora. But not long afterward, they heard the roar of motors and saw a North American sulfate sweeping in overhead, newly arrived from Nicaragua to come to the Liberationists' aid. Later they would learn the pilot had been the madman Jerry Fred DeLarm. He did little harm to the cadets, as his fuel soon ran out, and he was forced to land at La Aurora airport. There he was detained by a military garrison, which refused to let him go, claiming they were awaiting instructions from their superiors. By the time he took to the air again, the hostilities had ended thanks to the mediation of Archbishop Rossell y Arellano and Ambassador Peurifoy. Both of them were declared enemies of President Árbenz, and both had applauded Castillo Armas's insurrection from the beginning, and so the cadets, and especially Crispín, had doubts as to their good faith. But the officers ordered them to accept the men's intercession. The archbishop—a very thin, almost skeletal man, spreading benedictions all around him, with his very long fingers and his eyes full of contrition and serenity— promised he would be absolutely neutral. His only mission was to stop the blood from flowing and to guarantee a resolution that would do honor to both parties. He would—he swore on his blessed mother's name, she was in heaven looking down on them right now—reach a verdict with neither winners nor losers.

While they were discussing the truce, Deputy Lieutenant Ramiro Llanos approached Crispín, who saw the alarm in the officer's eyes. Llanos offered to take the boy to the field hospital they'd set up in a nearby bakery.

"The field hospital? Why?" Crispín asked. He hadn't yet realized he was soaked in blood. Not once in the hours of shooting had he felt any pain, and only now did he notice the wounds in his chest and left shoulder.

Deputy Lieutenant Llanos took him by the arms—Crispín could sense he was about to faint—and called over two more cadets. They must have been in their first year, because their caps sat loosely over their heads, and their faces were coated in dust and sweat. They helped carry Crispín off. He realized he was no longer holding his rifles, and that everything had begun to look hazy. His mother's and father's faces appeared, there they were, looking at him with affection, admiration, and grief; he would have liked to tell them something nice, something loving, but he didn't have the strength to speak. When they entered the bakery they had emptied to give the soldiers first aid, Crispín could no longer see. But he still heard the rumor of voices, mingled hopelessly now and fading inexorably into the distance.

Crispín neither witnessed nor heard word of the negotiations in which Guatemala's wily archbishop, Monsignor Mariano Rossell y Arellano, arranged to have a unit of cadets sent to the National Palace. President Castillo Armas received them in person. The cadets told the president that they could no longer tolerate humiliations of the kind the Liberationists had perpetrated in the foregoing days. They demanded that the mercenaries, whom they had defeated in the battle, admit defeat and leave Roosevelt Hospital with their hands up, turning their weapons over to the authorities. Scowling, Castillo Armas gave in to their demands. Crispín didn't watch as the Liberationists emerged from the half-built hospital with their hands raised in the air, and didn't see them turn over the rifles, shotguns, mortars, and pistols to the cadets.

Three conditions were agreed to and were immediately violated: the defeated, upon giving up their weapons, would return to their home villages or countries; the rebel cadets would suffer no reprisals for their actions that day, which would not appear on their service record, and would return to the Military Academy and finish their studies in normal conditions; and finally, the officers and enlisted men who had supported them would continue to serve in the army without prejudice, and their participation would likewise be expunged from their records.

Since he died that afternoon before they could transfer him to a hospital, Crispín Carrasquilla never learned that this accord, upon signing, became so much useless paper, just as he and the other cadets had feared. His side had won on the ground, but the Liberationists were the real victors in the conflict, which would hardly appear in the press or the history books, as if it were an event without any importance. The Military Academy was immediately closed for several months, for reorganization. The officers and enlisted men who had supported the rebels were expelled from the army and stripped of their pensions. Of the cadets, only six whose relatives had a degree of influence in Castillo Armas's government were allowed to continue their studies, in military schools in allied countries like Somoza's Nicaragua and Pérez Jiménez's Venezuela. The others were dismissed from the institution and refused readmission when the Politécnica reopened under a new principal with an entirely new staff of officers.

Not long afterward, President Castillo Armas awarded the country's highest honor to Archbishop Rossell y Arellano in a ceremony held at the cathedral, calling him—in a speech written by Efraín Nájera Farfán—*an illustrious patriot, a hero, and a saint.*

Crispín Carrasquilla's parents tried in vain to recover their son's body. The military leaders informed them he had been buried with other victims from that revolutionary ploy in a common grave, the location of which would be kept secret to prevent it from becoming a place of pilgrimage for communists in the future.

XXXII

H E WAS SWEATING COPIOUSLY. It wasn't the heat: from his bed, he could see the blades of the fan whirling over his head, giving off a breeze that blew against his face. It was fear. He had never felt a fear like this before, not that he remembered anyway, not even the day he found out they'd assassinated El Jefe and that his own future had collapsed and that from then on he'd have to get by on his wits, if he was lucky. Fleeing overseas, maybe. What he'd felt back then had been sorrow, rage, loneliness, not fear. Fear was the thing he was feeling now, a fear that was making him drip cold sweat that soaked through his shirt and underwear and made his teeth chatter. Chills paralyzed him, and he had to struggle to keep himself from screaming, asking for help. From whom? God? Did he even believe in God? From Brother Cristóbal, then?

The sun was coming up; he could see a blue band of light far off on the horizon that grew and illuminated his home in Pétion-Ville, its fruit trees, its jacarandas and creepers. Soon the hens would start to cackle and the dogs would set to barking. With the light of day, the fear would diminish and he would have to get hold of himself and depart for the Dominican Embassy, where he had an appointment at 11:00 a.m. Would the ambassador agree to see him, or would he be stuck once more with that consul in the trim suit with the reedy voice and round-framed glasses? Had Balaguer finally given him an answer? He had never imagined, he thought with embarrassment, that one day he'd be so scared he'd have to turn to that petty little man, that godforsaken President Joaquín Balaguer, begging him to save his life and the lives of his wife, Zita, and their two young daughters. Would Balaguer answer him in person? Would he make the magnanimous gesture of *pardoning* him and repatriating him with his family? Balaguer might be a traitor, but he was an intellectual, too, he had a sense of history, and he wanted his place in posterity. That might suffice to convince him to save the *most hated man in the Dominican Republic,* as he had called him in their final conversation in Ciudad Trujillo, from a certain and atrocious death when he'd forced him to leave the country with that story about a consular job in Japan.

What a load of rubbish! he thought. A filthy lie. He remembered his horrible days in Tokyo. They hadn't even given him an office. He'd been living with Zita in a hotel that cost an arm and a leg, and the money for his expenses as a newly installed diplomat never came, let alone his first paycheck. After a few weeks, the chargé d'affaires informed him that *for budgetary reasons,* his assignment had been revoked, and that the Japanese authorities were giving him and his wife just two weeks to leave the country, since they no longer had a reason for being there. They'd had to return to Paris, where they lived for nearly a year. It was there that Zita gave birth to the first of their daughters, and they spent a good part of the million-plus dollars he'd had tucked away in his Swiss account. It had seemed like a lot of money when he never touched it and it was earning interest, but in a life without income of any sort, it melted like butter in his hands.

What did Abbes García do in those years of exile? Conspire. Write letters and make phone calls to every Dominican official and cop he knew to try to make friends and wrangle them into scheming against Balaguer. They said yes, but none of them lifted a finger. They all wanted tickets to Europe or Canada to see him, of course. But nothing serious ever came of these intrigues. One day, Abbes García realized that none of this would get anywhere if he couldn't get Ramfis Trujillo on his side. So he wrote him on bended knee, and to his surprise, Ramfis himself responded. He was living in Spain at the time, and agreed to come to Paris to speak with him. He was cordial and open. His hatred for Balaguer rivaled Abbes García's own. He had finally realized that he, too—none other than Trujillo's eldest son!—had been manipulated by the sly, unscrupulous fox now sitting in the president's office. So hungry was Ramfis for power, so keen to be master of the country that had failed to appreciate his father and his family, that Abbes García gave everything in the following months to crafting a strategy that seemed viable, with El Jefe's son behind him. But this time, too, it failed to take off, because the officers who had once agreed to take part kept their distance, saying a coup could never succeed without the backing of the United States. They vanished, and since then Abbes García's only conspiracies took place in his imagination. He tried to spend less, because in just a few years his supply of dollars had been reduced by half, and he knew he would never find work. All he knew was torture, bomb making, spying, and killing. Who was going to hire him to do that in Europe?

When they decided to move to Canada in 1964, Zita was pregnant with their second child. He wanted her to get an abortion, but she refused, and in the end, she got her way. Life in Toronto was cheaper than in Paris, but their residency permit lasted only six months, and when they asked for another, they were denied it with the excuse that the money they had left was insufficient to guarantee another six-month stay in the country.

In these circumstances, entirely unexpectedly, Abbes García received an offer to move to Haiti as a security consultant for President François Duvalier.

At a friend's house in Toronto, he had met a Haitian who spoke very fluent Spanish, having lived for a time in the Dominican Republic. He recognized him immediately: "You're here? What is Colonel Johnny Abbes García doing in Toronto?" Johnny replied, "Business," and tried to slither away. The Haitian's name was François Delony, and from what they told him, he was a journalist. In reality he worked for Papa Doc, Haiti's indisputable leader since 1957. Delony asked for his number, and called a few days later to invite him to lunch. At the fish house where he took him, he made him the offer that had so surprised him:

"I've been learning a lot about you, Mr. Abbes García. I know President Balaguer threw you out of your country and that since then you've been roving the world like some kind of pariah. Would you be interested in a serious proposition? A move to Port-au-Prince, to work for the Haitian government."

Abbes García was stunned, and didn't answer for several seconds.

"Are you serious?" he finally said. "May I ask you if this offer comes directly from President François Duvalier?"

"From him personally," Delony replied. "Are you interested? Your role would be adviser to the president on security matters."

He accepted right away, without even knowing his salary or work conditions. *I was an imbecile*, he thought. It was daytime now, the hens were clucking, the dogs had begun to bark, and the three servant girls were moving around, making noise in the kitchen.

In a week, he, Zita, and the two girls were in Port-au-Prince at the Hotel Les Ambassadeurs. The first few days were the best ones, Abbes García remembered. The heat, the radiant sun, the scent of the sea, the luxurious vegetation, the merengues, all that reminded him he was back in the Caribbean. He imagined that soon those masses of people would address him in soft Dominican Spanish. But no—the blacks and mulattoes talked in French and Creole and he didn't understand a damned word. Two days later, they took him to see President Duvalier at his office in the National Palace. It was the first and last time he ever saw him. He was an enigmatic man, a doctor by profession, but more than that, people said, a shaman. The Haitians attributed his power to his practice of voodoo, which fascinated and terrified the people in equal measure. He was tall, slender, well-dressed, of an uncertain age. He received him affably in a dark suit with gleaming shoes, and addressed him in elegant Spanish. He thanked him for coming to collaborate with his government on security matters, in which he knew, he said, that Abbes was an *expert*. He had kind words for Generalísimo Trujillo, and said that fortunately he got on well with President Balaguer. Here he allowed himself a somewhat cryptic joke:

"Now when he finds out you're here collaborating with my government, President Balaguer will get a bit agitated, don't you think?"

A smile passed quickly over his dark face, and his deep-set eyes shone a moment behind his thick glasses. Then he explained that his minister of the interior would be in contact with him to discuss all practical matters. He stood up, gave him his hand, and that was that.

Abbes García hadn't seen him again in private in the two years he'd lived in Haiti, only from afar, at official events. He had asked for an audience on at least a dozen occasions, but according to the minister of the interior, the president was always busy and simply didn't have time to see him. Perhaps that was one reason Abbes García had been foolish enough to get into bed with President Duvalier's son-in-law, Colonel Max Dominique, husband of Dedé, Marie-Denise, Papa Doc's daughter. When he thought of Dedé, Abbes García felt a tingle in the tip of his penis. It had happened the few times he had seen that woman, so tall, so haughty, with her beautiful body and the cold, hard stare that perfectly conveyed the tyrannical, implacable temperament she was said to possess—very similar to the temperament of her father. How Abbes García had wanted to tongue the gash of that goddess of ebony and ice. The memory of Colonel Max Dominique brought Abbes García back to the reality of his situation. Again, he felt frozen with terror, and his entire body trembled.

He had met Max Dominique at the Military Academy in Pétion-Ville, where he gave classes on security matters. Many coveted the colonel's proximity to his father-in-law, Papa Doc. He had been cordial with the new arrival, and invited him one day to dinner at his home. That was where he met the woman with the long, beautiful legs, Dedé, the lady of the house, who so fired the longings of the security consultant that after dinner, he'd visited a squalid cathouse in the center of the capital to relieve his tensions between the legs of a hooker he could only communicate with through hand gestures. That was how his relationship with Colonel Max Dominique had begun. Slowly—*like an idiot*, he thought—he had gotten caught up in his conspiracy to prevent his father-in-law's son, Dedé's younger brother, Jean-Claude, also known as Baby Doc, from taking power after his father's death—this despite President François Duvalier's having chosen him as his successor. The conspiracy was perverse, in some ways ridiculous: in the multiple meetings that Abbes García had attended, the officers around Max Dominique spoke of it in almost ghostly terms, without dates, without specifying places or weapons, without considering the political ramifications, as if all that were in a gaseous or prenatal state. Then, all of a sudden, word began to get around, without a single line in the papers or a mention in the radio to prove it, that Papa Doc had ordered the execution of nineteen officers from the army for forming part of an attempted conspiracy.

When Abbes García had gotten control of himself, he stood up and went to shower. He spent a long time under the jet of water, which was tepid rather than cold. Then he brushed his teeth and shaved carefully. Finally he dressed in his finest suit and a collared shirt. If he was meeting with the Dominican ambassador, he would need to make the best impression he could. During breakfast—he left his plate of fruit untouched, said he didn't want eggs, limited himself to a small slice of black bread and a cup of coffee—he thought obsessively about the Dominican Embassy and Balaguer. He had barely eaten those past few days, and he'd had to ask his maids to punch a few more holes in his belt. It was just seven, so he decided to flip through the newspapers one of the girls had left on the table.

There was nothing in them about the dismantled conspiracy, even less about the shooting of the nineteen officers who were implicated, and not a word about the nomination of Max Dominique as the new ambassador to Spain. Nor about his journey to Madrid the day before to assume his post in the company of his wife, Marie-Denise.

Why had President Duvalier forgiven the head of the conspiracy, sending him to a diplomatic post in Spain instead of having him shot with all the army officers who'd plotted against him? It must have been out of love for his daughter, Marie-Denise. Did

Papa Doc know that Dedé was the one to put the idea of liquidating him and taking his place into Max Dominique's head? He had to. François Duvalier knew everything and he couldn't fail to see that Dedé was wounded and resentful—everyone in Haiti talked about it—because he had chosen her younger brother instead of her to succeed him. And yet, the witch doctor had forgiven his bloodthirsty daughter and was sending her and Max to Spain as diplomats after secretly shooting and burying the military men involved in the conspiracy.

Why hadn't Duvalier had him shot, too? Had he reserved a special punishment for him, featuring those exquisite tortures he'd been teaching the *tonton macoutes* at the Military Academy in Pétion-Ville for the last two years? Again, the shaking rose from his feet up to his head, making his teeth chatter. Again, he was sweating, and his once-clean shirt and pants were soaked. He needed to get a handle on his nerves, it wasn't good for the Dominican ambassador to see him like that, he would certainly pass word along to President Balaguer. And imagine the satisfaction he'd feel if he heard Abbes García was terrified of being punished by Duvalier for conspiring against him with his daughter and son-in-law!

At 8:00 a.m., he entered the room where Zita slept with the girls. His wife was already awake, eating the breakfast the maids had brought her in bed: a cup of tea, a plate of pineapple and papaya, and toast with butter and marmalade. How calm and carefree she seemed: Did she have any idea of the danger they were in? Of course, but she trusted him blindly, and thought he was capable of fixing anything. The poor woman!

"Why aren't the girls up?" he asked instead of telling her good morning. "Don't they have school?"

"You yourself said they shouldn't go," Zita reminded him. "Don't you remember? I hope this isn't the first sign of arteriosclerosis."

"Sure, right," he said. "Yeah, until things clear up, it's better if the girls don't leave the house. You either."

She nodded. He envied her: she could die a horrible death at any moment, but there she was eating her fruit as if this were a day like any other. He felt compassion for his wife. Through all those meetings he'd had at Dedé and Max Dominique's house, she had never gotten upset. When she found out François Duvalier had ordered the nineteen officers involved in the conspiracy shot, she didn't utter a word. Did she really think he was a superman, capable of emerging miraculously from this monstrous predicament they were in? Up to now, it was true, however bad things got, he'd always found a way out of the thorniest situations; but Abbes García had the sense that this time every door he might run through to escape his bad luck was closed. Vaguely, he remembered how Brother Cristóbal had told him the history of the Rosicrucians back in Mexico, and he missed the peace and serenity he had felt listening to his sermons.

"Are you going to the embassy? Do you think they'll repatriate us?" she asked as if it were a foregone conclusion.

"Of course," he said. "Hopefully Balaguer will understand me asking him this favor is a major concession."

"And if they don't?" she asked, her voice modulating slightly.

"We'll see," he said, shrugging. "Stay put. I'll come straight back from the embassy to let you know."

He walked outside. His chauffeur wasn't there. A bad sign: he had told him the night before to come early. Had he fled? Had they ordered him not to go? He grabbed the keys to his truck and drove himself. He traveled slowly, avoiding the pedestrians who walked back and forth in front of the vehicle with an utter absence of caution, as if avoiding an accident were his responsibility and not theirs. A half hour later, he was parked in front of the Dominican Embassy in downtown Port-au-Prince. It was a few minutes before the hour, and he waited inside the car with the air-conditioning on. When his watch told him it was eleven, he turned off the motor, got out, and rang at the embassy door. The same brown-haired girl greeted him who had done so three days before.

"The consul is expecting you," she said with a very friendly smile. "Please come in."

So he wouldn't be meeting with the ambassador this time, either. The girl took him to the same office as last time. The consul was wearing the same snug gray suit, which looked too tight to let him properly breathe. He smiled the same forced smile and looked at him with the same sparkling eyes. Johnny remembered them well.

"Any news, sir?" Abbes García asked, getting straight to the point.

"Unfortunately not, Colonel," the consul responded, motioning for him to take a seat. "We don't have an answer yet."

Abbes García felt sweat pouring down his face and his heart pounding in his chest.

"I was hoping I could speak to the ambassador," he burbled, and in his tone there was something imploring. "I'll only take ten minutes, five minutes of his time. Please, sir. This is a very serious matter. I need to explain it to him in person."

"The ambassador isn't here, Colonel," the consul replied. "He's not in Haiti, I mean. He's been called to Santo Domingo on business."

Abbes García knew the consul was lying. He was sure that if he kicked down the door to the ambassador's office, he would see him there, frightened, behind his desk, offering explanations that would just be more lies.

"You don't understand my situation," he added, struggling to get out his words. "My life, the lives of my wife and children are in danger. I explained all this in my letter to President Balaguer. If they kill us, it will be an international scandal and people will blame him. A scandal that could have grave political consequences for his government. Don't you understand?"

"I understand perfectly, Colonel, I swear," the consul said, shaking his head. "We've explained the matter to the ministry with a wealth of details. They must be studying your case. As soon as there is an answer, I will let you know personally."

"Either you don't understand or you're lying to me," Abbes García said, no longer able to contain himself. "Do you think there's time for that? They could kill us today, this very afternoon. I deserve protection under the law. We are Dominican citizens. We have the right to immediate repatriation."

The consul got up from his desk and sat down next to Abbes García. He seemed to be struggling to say something, but he didn't dare. His tiny eyes looked from left to right. When he spoke, he lowered his voice to a near-whisper.

"Let me give you a bit of advice, Colonel. Seek asylum. Don't wait. At the Mexican consulate, for example. I'm telling you this as a friend, not an official. You will not receive a response to your letter to President Balaguer. I am certain of it. I'm risking my job telling you this, Colonel. I'm doing so out of Christian charity, because I understand your and your family's situation. Don't wait."

Abbes García tried to get up, but his tremors had come back, and he let himself slump again in the chair. Did that advice make sense? Maybe. But they had expelled him from Mexico years ago as an undesirable alien. Argentina, then. Or Brazil. Or Paraguay. Despite the shaking in his legs, he managed to stand up on the second try. Not bothering to say goodbye to the consul, walking like an automaton, he turned toward the front door. He didn't respond to the farewell from the brown-haired girl. He sat in his truck without turning on the motor until his twitching stopped. Yes, he would try to seek asylum in a Latin American embassy. But not Mexico. Brazil, yes, Brazil. Or Paraguay. Did those countries have embassies in Port-au-Prince? He would look in the phone book. The son of a bitch—Balaguer had gotten his letter and hadn't bothered to answer. To cover up the traces. He wanted Papa Doc to kill him, obviously. Maybe President Duvalier had even consulted with him about it. *What should I do with him, Mr. President?* And that fox, who never committed himself, must have responded: *I will leave that to Your Excellency's wisdom.* He was terrified of seeing Johnny show up in the Dominican Republic to mobilize the many followers El Jefe still had, not only inside the military. He wanted Papa Doc to do his dirty work and get rid of him.

When he passed the Pétion-Ville Military Academy, he remembered the work he had done those previous two years, the talks he used to give the cadets on security, the special cases he described to the officers and the auxiliary squads of ex-prisoners and delinquents with a rap sheet known as the *tonton macoutes.* He spoke slowly, using notes that the interpreter would translate into Creole. Were they

useful for something? At the very least, the officers, cadets, and auxil-
iaries seemed interested. They asked him lots of questions about how
to make a prisoner talk. You use fear, he had told them a thousand
times. You've got to make them very scared. Of being castrated. Of
being burned alive. Of having their eyes gouged out. Of getting a
broomstick or a bottle shoved up their ass. They need to feel panic,
terror, the same kind he was feeling just then. He'd even had them buy
an electric chair like the one in La Cuarentena back in Ciudad Trujillo, like the one General Ramfis had at the Aviation Academy. With
a difference: the electric chair in Pétion-Ville never functioned as it
was supposed to. The electricity couldn't be dosed out, and it killed the
prisoners immediately instead of frying them little by little till they
talked. All that money just to char a prisoner to a crisp. He laughed
reluctantly at the memory of his students' giggles when he told them
how, during interrogations back in Ciudad Trujillo, while his prisoners shrieked and pleaded, he liked to recite sentimental poems by
Amado Nervo or sing songs by Agustín Lara.

It had been madness to conspire with Max Dominique. Stupid,
insane, shameful, and now he would probably end up sitting in the
electric chair at the Military Academy in Pétion-Ville. It had all been
a tremendous mistake, starting with coming to Haiti, a third-rate
country where everything always went to hell. Why hadn't Papa Doc
put him in front of the firing squad along with the rest of the officers?
What tortures did he have planned for him? Of course his friend
Balaguer was in on it. When he entered his home in Pétion-Ville,
Abbes García's pants, shirt, jacket, and even tie were soaked with
sweat.

Zita was in the living room with the children reading them a
story. When she saw him in this state, she turned pale. He shook his
head.

"The ambassador didn't see me, just the same flunky as always."
His voice was wavering, but he thought that if he cried in front of
his wife, he'd terrify her as well as the two girls. With superhuman
effort, he restrained himself. He added very slowly, feeling how his
voice betrayed his fear: "Balaguer hasn't responded to my letter. We

need to seek asylum. I'm going to call the embassy in Brazil right now. Bring me the phone book, please."

While Zita went to look for it, the girls remained sitting on the sofa. They both looked like their mother; neither looked like him. They were well-dressed in blue smocks and little white shoes. In their motionlessness, their serenity, their seriousness, there was something like a premonition of the grave things that were about to occur, and they seemed to think it best not to ask their father what might happen.

When Abbes García saw Zita return to the living room, he noticed there was no phone book in her hands, and he was about to upbraid her when his wife's pallor and the look of terror in her eyes stopped him. She was tall and shapely, but she had grown thin in the preceding days. She had raised one arm, and was pointing outside. *What is it?* he murmured, taking a few steps toward the large window that looked out onto their garden and the street. Trucks were parking in front of their door. First there were three of them, then a fourth pulled in behind them. Men jumped out in overalls, T-shirts, and black berets—the uniform of the *tonton macoutes.* He counted at least twenty of them. In their hands, they held clubs and knives and—he was sure, even if he couldn't see them—automatics and revolvers were tucked into their thick black belts. They lined up in front of his house, waiting for an order. *They're here,* he thought. He didn't know what to do or what to say.

"What are you waiting for, Johnny?" Zita exclaimed behind him. He turned and saw his wife embracing the two girls, who were hanging on their mother and crying. "Do something, do something, Johnny."

My revolver, he thought, and ran to the bedroom to take it out of the drawer in the nightstand where he kept it locked up. He would kill Zita and the girls, and then he would kill himself.

But in the bedroom, he looked out the window and saw that the *tonton macoutes* (how many of them had been his students at the Military Academy in Pétion-Ville?) were still there in formation in front of the railing and the door that led to the garden. Why weren't they coming in? Now they did. One man kicked the wooden door and sent it flying, and they stomped in, passed through the garden in a platoon and walked toward the henhouses, ignoring the barking of the dogs that rushed forward to meet them. Believing and yet disbelieving all he was seeing, Abbes García, revolver in hand, watched the *tonton macoutes* take over, crushing the flowers and vegetable beds, beating and stabbing the two dogs to death, then stomping and kicking them until their bodies were coated in blood.

He ran to the living room and saw that the three maids were there, too, holding each other, their eyes not shifting from the window. Zita didn't even try to calm the girls, who were holding on to her and shrieking: what was happening in the garden had hypnotized her. After the dogs, the invaders had turned their rage on the chickens. Feathers were flying, and the cackles of the birds and the howling and cursing of the raiders was deafening.

"They've killed the dogs and the chickens," Zita said. "Now they're coming for us."

The three maids were on their knees alternately praying and weeping. The slaughter and the shouting wouldn't stop. Absurdly, Abbes García ordered the women to lock the door, but they didn't hear or didn't have the strength to obey him.

When he saw the front door of the house give way and the first faces, black with glassy eyes (*they've been drugged*, Abbes thought) peeked in, he lifted his revolver and fired. But instead of recoil, what he felt was the thud of the hammer against an absent cartridge. He'd forgotten to load it, and would die without defending himself, without killing even one of those repulsive black bastards who, following very clear instructions, left him and Zita and the children standing there, turning their clubs and knives on the maids and beating and stabbing them as they shouted an incomprehensible babble of insults and curses. He hugged Zita and the girls, who were shaking as they pressed their heads into his chest, no longer strong enough to cry.

The *tonton macoutes* jumped now on the bodies of the maids, or what was left of them, in a strange dance. Abbes García saw blood on their hands, on their faces, on their clothes, on their clubs, and more than a massacre, the thing seemed like a primal, barbarous feast, a ritual. Never in his worst nightmares had he imagined that he would die like this, butchered by a horde of niggers who could have used their pistols but preferred more primitive weapons, the clubs and knives mankind had used in caverns and forests since prehistoric times.

Neither Johnny Abbes García nor Zita nor the girls saw the end of all that. It was instead seen by a witness, the born-again Christian Dorothy Sanders. She was a neighbor, and they had exchanged no more than the barest greetings despite living on the same street. She would say later, taking tranquilizers for her nerves and determined to give up her missionary job and return to the United States as soon as possible, that once the horrible slaughter was over, the blacks had emptied cans of kerosene on the dwelling and had set it on fire. She had watched the house burn to a mound of ash while the murderers and pyromaniacs got into their trucks and left, satisfied, surely, at a job well done.

AFTER

S HE LIVES BETWEEN WASHINGTON, D.C., AND VIRGINIA, not very far from Langley, where—and this could be mere coincidence—the CIA headquarters are located, in a gated residential community where one needs ID to enter. There are tall trees all around, and the place gives the impression of an island of tranquility, particularly on this spring afternoon, with its clear sky and soft sun gilding the leaves and tinting the flowers in the neighborhood. Invisible birds chirp everywhere, and bigger ones, seagulls in from the coast, maybe, cross the blue sky now and then. The houses are spacious, with big yards and luxury cars in the garages; at one of them, a ranch with stables, a young Amazon, her loose curls flowing in the wind, is riding a pony. But Miss Guatemala's dwelling is small, and is the most original and eccentric I've seen in my life. Outside and in, it reflects like a mirror the personality and tastes of its owner.

Soledad Álvarez, an old friend from the Dominican Republic who is, moreover, a magnificent poet, and Tony Raful, a Dominican poet, journalist, and historian, have managed, through months of acrobatic wrangling, to get me this interview, and both have warned me that more than one surprise lies in store for me this afternoon. Tony was here before, and is a good friend of Marta, this Guatemalan in exile, assuming she has ever truly been friends with anyone. Outside, her house is decorated with an abundance of plants on all four sides, herbs and creepers that must be made of plastic, like the flowers amassed inside, which give its interior the character of an indescribable jungle. Amid that artificial vegetation are tiny animals of cardboard, wood, or plush fabric that climb the scarlet walls and the gleaming tiles of the roof. There is also a great deal of mauve and hot-pink bougainvillea; this, however, seems to be real.

As soon as I enter, I am disconcerted by the clamorous chirping of birds. They are in cages, and their voices enliven, over the course of several hours at least, my conversation with Miss Guatemala (who never was such a thing). I confess that I'm somewhat nervous. I've spent two years imagining this woman, inventing her, attributing to her adventures of all kinds, distorting her so that no one—not even she—will recognize her in the story I've dreamed up. I expected many things, but not this gigantic, strident aviary. There are African canaries here, collared doves, parrots, cockatoos, macaws, and other species I can't identify. A sort of horror vacui has filled every corner, leaving not a single space empty. No one can move through Marta's house without knocking down some object posed amid the dozens or hundreds of flowerpots that abound here, some holding large plants, some small ones. Statues, busts, and religious figurines—Buddhas, Christs, virgins, and saints—alternate with mummies and Egyptian catafalques, photos, paintings, and homages to Latin American dictators like Generalísimo Trujillo and Carlos Castillo Armas. The latter was *the great love of my life*, as she will confess to me momentarily, and she has dedicated an entire wall to him, with a gigantic photo and a votive candle that flickers for him day and night and must be made of plastic, too, like the vertiginous throngs of flowers—roses, gladiolas, carnations, mimosas, orchids, tulips, geraniums—and the toys and keepsakes from all the places Marta Borrero Parra has had occasion to visit. From what I can see, she must have been around the world several times.

Our conversation will resemble that implausible dwelling, in a way: anarchic, original, confused, surprising. According to all the testimony I've managed to track down in books and newspapers and in the biographies of people who knew her in different phases of her dauntless life, she was a very beautiful and unsettling woman, with a verdigris stare that seemed to bore into the brains of those who spoke with her, leaving them rattled and unnerved. She is surely more than eighty years old now—I am not so imprudent as to ask her—and time has likely both shrunken her and filled her out a bit; even so, despite her maturity, something emanates from her that hints at her former glory, her seductiveness, the legends she gave rise to, the men who loved her and those she loved. She greets me in a black kimono full of pleats and folds, very carefully made up, wearing earrings and neck-laces, long-lashed, her fingernails painted jungle green. She is wear-ing an extraordinary pair of sandals of lime-green velvet. She must have gone under the knife more than once, because there is a great deal of tension in her face, where those eyes that once made so deep an impression on all the people she met, especially the men, continue to glimmer arrogantly, and with a certain mystery.

When we take our seats in a small clearing in that floral labyrinth, she tells me she knows that I *hate the seeds of fruits* (which is true) and that she is aware, moreover, that my favorite song since childhood has been "Alma, Corazón y Vida," a Peruvian waltz fashionable when I arrived in Piura at the age of ten in 1946, and which I heard sung for the first time by a Civil Guard who oversaw the prefecture where we lived (my grandfather was the prefect). When I ask her how she's come to know these very precise private details of my life, she smiles and responds laconically, as Símula would have done in my novel: *I have powers.* Her voice is warm and leisurely, with a slight Cen-tral American inflection neither time nor exile nor her travels has managed to erase. But what most captures my attention are her eyes, somewhere between green and gray, and her intense, bold, perforat-ing stare.

Almost without transition, she tells me she has had ten husbands and has buried all of them. She speaks softly and without ostentation, with pauses, rhythm, and music, always looking for the right word. She adds that, when she was a girl, she was raped by a Guatemalan communist, a doctor, and that since then, she's been a passionate and militant anticommunist. This I already know. But it surprises me to hear that the great love of her life was the Guatemalan colonel and president of the republic Carlos Castillo Armas, a *delicate, refined gentleman* who tried to divorce his wife, Odilia Palomo, to marry her, but was unable to, because *first, and perhaps to prevent him from it, they killed him.*

She speaks slowly, pronouncing every syllable, without waiting for responses or comments on what she's said, and at times she gives me the impression that she's forgotten I am here.

When she touches on her relations with the Dominican colonel Johnny Abbes García, chief of security for Generalísimo Trujillo, a killer and torturer and the author of a number of successful and attempted murders abroad—among them, the failed assassination of President Rómulo Betancourt in Caracas and, according to Tony Raful, the very successful one of Castillo Armas in Guatemala—Martita speaks with caution and evasively. He, too, she tells me, was another *consummate gentleman*, with exquisite manners, so considerate that when they dined together he would always slice her cutlets and steaks into little bites. He adored his mother, carried a photo of her in his wallet, and one night, when the lady had a fever, Marta saw him kneel at the foot of her bed and massage her feet. A son who cares about his mother that much—that's a good credential for a human being, isn't it? He had his manias, like everyone, his main one being his rambles all over the world looking for Rosicrucians. He could have indulged it to his heart's content here, in this country they're everywhere. Abbes García was deeply in love with her and constantly lavished her with attention and gifts, when they first met in Guatemala and later in what was then called Ciudad Trujillo, where she spent a few years in her early adulthood working as a political journalist. There, Abbes used to take her to the casinos, and one time he gave her three hundred dollars to bet on roulette and told her to keep the winnings. But, she assures me, she never responded to his advances and never slept with him.

When, however, I remind her of the many rumors according to which she had a child by Trujillo's henchman, a boy some even claim to have met in person before his untimely death in the Dominican Republic, she replies unfazed: *Preposterous fantasies without the least basis in truth.*

She is similarly far from forthright when I mention something abundantly documented in history books and journalists' reports: that Abbes García was the person who helped her escape from Guatemala on July 26, 1957, the night of Castillo Armas's murder, when his friends and colleagues among the Liberationists and in particular one of the likely assassins—Lieutenant Colonel Enrique Trinidad Oliva—pursued her in order to divert suspicions, accusing her of being an accomplice in the leader's killing:

Those things happened long ago, they're dust in the wind, forgotten, she says serenely, shrugging, then concludes with feigned indifference: *Why bring all that up again?*

Then there crosses her face one of those long, unfathomable smiles that must have been among her most seductive weapons in her youth.

"Is it true that the Cuban bandit Carlos Gacel Castro got you into a car and drove you from Guatemala City to San Salvador on the night of the murder?" I ask her. "And that the next day, Abbes García took you from San Salvador to the Dominican Republic in a private plane? All the history books say so. Is it true, or are these more preposterous fantasies without the least basis in truth?"

"Am I really that famous, that I show up in the history books?" she asks with a mocking smirk. She shrugs again, gracefully, coquettishly. "Well, there must be a bit of truth in all that. Don't forget I'm an old woman, and I can't remember everything I've lived through. We old people have memory lapses, we start to forget things."

And she giggles, refuting everything she's just said, covering her mouth with her hand.

She is healthy and vigorous despite her years, but she moves with some difficulty and with the aid of a cane. She gives me the occasional impression that the borders between reality and fiction dissolve in her mind without her being aware of it, but at other moments, it seems she is consciously administering these confusions. And that she knows far more than she is telling me, and that she's rambling, but deliberately. Like when she says she believes in extraterrestrials and assures me she has evidence of their existence, but refuses to be more precise, not wanting me to think she's insane, which, she adds with a broad smile that emphasizes her perfect set of teeth, is something *lots of people are going around saying.*

Finally I dare to touch on the real question, the thing that brought me here, a theory she alone has maintained in declarations, articles, interviews, and her chaotic online autobiography, which she updates every day:

"You claim it isn't true that Abbes García died in Haiti with Zita, his second wife, and their two daughters, at the hands of Papa Doc's *tonton macoutes*, who also killed his maids and dogs and chickens and then burned down his house. This is the account Balaguer gives in his autobiography (*Memoirs of a Courtier in the Era of Trujillo*) and an evangelical missionary, Dorothy Sanders, confirmed these events to the police. She was Abbes García's neighbor in Pétion-Ville and a direct witness of the events."

Martita is now listening to me with a very serious mien. She thinks a moment, and says finally, with her unalterably deliberate tranquility:

"That was a fiction cooked up by the CIA to keep Johnny from being pursued and to get him into the United States anonymously. Johnny started living here under an assumed name after having plastic surgery that changed his face, but not his voice. And he's still living here today."

"If he were alive, Abbes García would now be over eighty," I interrupt her. "In all likelihood, he would be closer to ninety."

"Is that so?" she asked. "I would have thought he was a bit older."

"Where did you come up with this story, Marta?" I press her. "Have you ever seen Abbes García in person here in the United States?"

Even here, she maintains her cool. She looks me up and down, as if wondering whether it's worth her time to try and convince me of something no one believes but that she knows is as true as life itself.

She sighs, and after a long pause during which the cackles and caws of the birds seem to grow louder, she continues:

"I only saw him once, many years ago now. But we talk on the phone with some frequency. He always calls me, from a phone booth, obviously. I don't know his number or where he's living. New York, California, Texas, who can say. He's very careful, as he should be. He had many enemies when he was working in politics, you know that as well as anyone. But worse than them now are the journalists, especially the ones from the gossip rags; they live for a scandal."

One winter night quite a few years back, she heard someone knocking on her door, in the same house where she lives now. She answered warily and saw a man outside in a long coat, with a scarf that hung to his feet. As soon as he spoke, she could identify him by his voice: *Don't you recognize me, Martita?* Astonished and on edge—how could she be otherwise?—she brought him into this very room, where there were fewer birds at the time. They talked for several hours, until dawn, drinking tea in little cups and reliving their adventures from time past. He confessed to her that she was the only one of his old acquaintances he had told he was still alive.

She pauses and recites in English a verse from a poem by Stephen Spender. It surprises me greatly to hear it coming from her lips: *Since we must part, let's part as heroes do.* (I'd never imagined her a reader of poetry of that caliber.) Before he left, he asked her to keep his secret. She did so for many years. Now there is no reason for such caution; every crime attributable to him has passed the various statutes of limitations, and his enemies are all dead and buried. Anyway, are there still people left who remember Abbes García? *Just you, Mario, so far as I can tell.*

She hasn't seen him again, but she's certain he's still alive and that he'll call her again one of these days. Or maybe even show up, knocking at her door at night the way he did the last time. Martita will tell him about our conversation and explain that I'm writing a novel full of lies and fabrications about both their lives. Will I have them marry at the end, the way people always do in love stories? She laughs a long time at her own joke, in a pleasant mood, and pins me with her verdigris stare.

Marta Borrero Parra lives with a Peruvian housemaid from Huancayo, a discreet, unflappable woman who disappears after serving us soft drinks. She returns only to have Marta take her medicines with sips of water, or when the lady of the house calls for her. She doesn't really seem like an employee, more like a secretary, a traveling companion, a close friend.

Marta soon forgets about politics and tells me, with an air of nostalgia, that her life here is tranquil, surrounded by all these keepsakes—she waves her hands to show off the flowers and objects around her—that attest to her travels across the wide world. I refrain from asking the question on my lips: *Are you still working for the CIA?* She takes her *little jaunts now and again*, but no longer gets around much, for obvious reasons. But thanks to TV and travel shows, she crosses the globe every night, for an hour at least, before bed. Some of those documentaries are wonderful. Last night she saw one devoted to Bhutan, with its pure mountains and its fat and inexpressive king, a living totem. She often thinks of Guatemala, her homeland, its forests, volcanoes, the indigenous peoples' multicolored costumes, the Saturday markets in the villages; but for half a century now she hasn't been back. She regrets never seeing a quetzal, that little bird that is her country's emblem, alive and flying through the air. She only knows them from photographs and drawings. The last time she was there, during an electoral campaign, she was saddened to see the misery her poor Guatemala had sunken into. It had gone to the communists in a rain of blood and fire, guerrillas marauded in the mountains and terrorists were planting bombs in the cities, killing and kidnapping decent people. At least the army was still there standing firm against them. What would have happened to Latin America if it hadn't been for the armies? That is why she renders them homage every day on her blog. The entire continent would have gone the way of Cuba if not for those brave underpaid soldiers the reds had slandered so mercilessly.

Tears come to my eyes when I think of them, she whispers. And she wipes her handkerchief theatrically across her face.

She is sitting next to a large photo of herself arm in arm with two generations of the Bush family: both former presidents of the United States and Jeb, the one-time governor of Florida. She tells me she has been an active supporter of the Republican Party, and is a registered member of both it and of the Cuban exiles' Orthodox Party. She still recruits Latino voters for the Republicans every election year, and loves the United States, her adopted country, every bit as much as Guatemala. She is pleased these days, not just because Donald Trump is in the White House, doing the things that have to be done, but also because a number of Chinese bonds she bought or inherited—it isn't clear which—have at last been recognized by the Beijing government. If everything turns out as it should, she will soon be a millionaire. It won't do much for her, with her accumulated years and afflictions, but she will donate the money to a fund dedicated to anticommunist organizations worldwide.

Tony Raful knows everything about her and has researched her past, and there is no doubt that much of what he's told me about her is true. Nor is there any doubt that from the time of her youth she was a woman to be reckoned with, audacious, brave, bold, capable of dealing with anyone or any unexpected surprise. An intrepid woman, hardened by a life in which she had survived terrible things. Tony himself, in the early pages of *The Rhapsody of Crime: Trujillo vs. Castillo Armas* (Santo Domingo, Grijalbo, 2017), tells how puppet president Héctor Bienvenido Trujillo Molina (the Generalísimo's brother, known to many as Negro) had her brought to his office in Ciudad Trujillo and tried to pay her to sleep with him, signing a blank check and telling her, *Write in the amount you like*, never imagining that she would leap at him in indignation, shouting *I'm not a prostitute* and nearly biting off one of his ears, before his guards appeared and dragged the ferocious Guatemalan away.

I ask her if the story is true. She nods, sprightly as a schoolgirl, and murmurs through her irrepressible laughter:

"I can still taste that ear that I bit into like a bulldog. It was a miracle I didn't tear it off!"

But she passes the buck when I ask her how the CIA managed to get her out of Ciudad Trujillo before Negro or his illustrious brother Rafael Leonidas could kill her:

"I don't remember how it happened. All that was so long ago!"

Back then, she tells me, changing the subject, she was *a very attractive woman. If you don't believe me, take a look at the walls.*

She points at various large-format photos in which she appears, young and beautiful, in colored tropical turbans or with serpentine locks of hair cascading over her bare shoulders.

I don't know how, but suddenly the conversation turns to Jacobo Árbenz, *a person I hated with all my heart when I was young*, as she confesses. But *now that he's dead and buried*, she sighs, he deserves her compassion.

"Those years of exile must have been terrible for him and his family." Another sigh. "Wherever he went, the leftists and communists reproached him for his cowardice, for resigning and going abroad instead of staying and fighting. Fidel Castro even permitted himself to insult him personally in a speech for not resisting Castillo Armas by running off to the mountains and forming bands of guerrillas. For not letting them kill him, in other words."

"So you realize now that Árbenz never was a communist?" I ask her. "That he was actually a democrat, a naive one, maybe, who wanted to modernize Guatemala, to turn it into a capitalist democracy? Even if, in exile, he became a member of the Guatemalan Party of Labor, he was never truly a communist."

"He was naive, indeed, and the reds found it easy to make him do their bidding," she corrects me. "I pity him and his family for what they went through in their years in exile. Going from one place to the next, never managing to put down roots anywhere: Mexico, Czechoslovakia, Russia, China, Uruguay. They were mistreated everywhere, and at times even had to go hungry. Then there were the family tragedies. His daughter Arabella, who was simply beautiful according to everyone who knew her, fell in love with a mediocre bullfighter, Jaime

Bravo, who cheated on her, and she wound up shooting herself in a nightclub he'd gone to with his lover. Apparently, even Árbenz's own wife, the famous aspiring intellectual and artist, ran around on him with a man from Cuba who was teaching her German. When Árbenz found out, he had to swallow it and keep his mouth shut. And then his other daughter, Leonora, was in and out of madhouses. She killed herself, too, a few years back. All that wound up destroying him. He turned to drink and on one of his benders wound up drowning in his own bathtub in Mexico. Or maybe it was a suicide. Oh well. I hope he repented of his crimes before he died and that the Lord was able to give him shelter."

She makes a show of sadness, crosses herself, and again takes several deep breaths.

I ask her if, with the years, she has come to see any of the merits of Juan José Arévalo.

"None whatsoever," she affirms categorically. She is furious now. "His presidency laid the groundwork to bring the Árbenz government into power. In his private life, at least, Árbenz was discreet, but Arévalo wanted every woman he could get his hands on. Don't you remember how he killed those two poor Russian ballerinas that he and a friend were out partying with? They had to have been quite drunk when they had that accident, and when the two girls ended up dead, not a single person bothered to hold Arévalo or that other bastard in the car accountable."

For a few moments, she falls silent while she takes her medicines. When her housemaid leaves the room, I ask her:

"Could you tell me, Marta, something about your relationship with the CIA? Many of Castillo Armas's friends believe you were working for the organization when the United States stopped supporting the colonel on the assumption that he lacked the ability to lead a true counterrevolution and decided to support a more energetic and charismatic man, General Miguel Ydígoras Fuentes."

"It's a touchy subject, we'd do best to leave it alone," she tells me, not irritated but firm, grave. Her eyes pierce me, as if she wanted to crucify me against the chair.

Nonetheless—and fearing the worst—I continue:

"The fact that you managed to get into the United States so quickly when you had to leave the Dominican Republic, and that they gave you a residency permit and citizenship almost immediately afterward, are arguments some have used to suggest your services were highly prized by the CIA, Marta."

"If you continue down this road, I'll have to ask you to leave immediately," she murmurs.

She hasn't raised her voice, but there is a deadly earnestness in the way she utters every word. Leaning on her cane, with great effort, she stands.

I beg her pardon, promise I won't discuss this exasperating matter any further, and eventually she sits back down. But I've plainly touched a nerve, and she is discomfited and irritable. From then on, her attitude changes. She loses her spontaneity, grows stiff, her glances are hostile, and the atmosphere turns cool. Does she consider me an enemy now? A communist lying in wait? Her responses will be artificial from here on out, and she won't make another joke for the rest of the conversation. When I see she's turned listless and that it will be impossible to get anything more of value from her, I simply thank her for seeing me and say my goodbyes. She accompanies me to the door, and says, as a sort of grace note:

"Don't bother sending me your book when it comes out, Mario. I will absolutely not be reading it. But I warn you, my lawyers will."

That same night, Soledad Álvarez, Tony Raful, and I will discuss the experience in a restaurant in Washington, D.C.: Café Milano, a place in Georgetown, always animated, full of noisy diners, with good pasta and excellent Italian wines. We've made a reservation and can talk there at our ease. Soledad and I agree that Tony was right not to send Marta a copy of his latest book. She would surely not have found it pleasant reading. Tony is gentle with her and grateful, but much of what he reveals about her are things she must have preferred left unsaid, or if not, at least discussed with less candor.

The three of us agree that my visit with the original Miss Guatemala was worth it, even if it's left me with more questions than answers. From what Marta told me, or didn't tell me, and above all her way of speaking and her irascibility at the end, I conclude that she did work for the CIA and that her services to the storied organization were significant. They concur. But our opinions differ on the degree of her participation in the assassination of Castillo Armas. Did she know beforehand, and did she consciously intervene in the preparations for the crime, or did her relationship with Abbes García and the CIA's man in Guatemala involve her in it, little by little? We talk this over for some time without reaching any conclusion. But all of us accept that, once she found out Lieutenant Colonel Enrique Trinidad Oliva meant to implicate her in the murder, her only choice was to flee, whether or not she was guilty, just like Abbes García and the man whose name wasn't Mike. Her proclamations of love for Castillo Armas were probably genuine and not just a later show of penitence for her possible involuntary involvement in his murder, though they, too, helped throw off any suspicions, clues, or investigations that might have pointed to her.

All three of us are certain that the United States erred terribly in preparing a coup against Árbenz with Colonel Castillo Armas at the head of the conspiracy. The victory was fleeting, pointless, and counterproductive. It helped foment anti-Americanism in Latin America all over again, and invigorated the Marxists, the Trotskyites, and the Fidelists. It radicalized Fidel Castro's 26th of July Movement and pushed it toward communism. Fidel learned the most obvious lessons from what had happened in Guatemala. We ought not forget that the other face of the Cuban Revolution, Che Guevara, was in Guatemala during the invasion, selling encyclopedias door-to-door to make ends meet. After meeting the Peruvian Hilda Gadea, his first wife, there, he tried to enlist in one of the people's militias Árbenz never managed to form just as Castillo Armas was invading. He had to seek asylum at the Argentine Embassy to avoid the raids the country's rabid anticommunism produced in those days. From all that, he likely drew a conclusion that would later prove tragic for Cuba: that a real revolution would have to liquidate the army to consolidate itself. This

287

explains the mass executions of soldiers and officers in the fortress of La Cabaña that Ernesto Guevara himself oversaw. It also sheds light on the notion that an alliance with the Soviet Union was indispensable for Cuba if the island wished to insulate itself from pressure, boycotts, and possible aggression from the United States. The history of Cuba might have been different had the United States accepted the modernization and democratization of Guatemala that Arévalo and Árbenz attempted to carry out. Democratization and modernization were what Fidel Castro intended for Cuban society when he assaulted the Moncada Barracks on July 26, 1953, in Santiago de Cuba. At the time, he was far from the collectivist and dictatorial extremes that would leave Cuba petrified to this day in an anachronistic absolutism stripped of all semblance of liberty. A testimony of this is his speech, "History Will Absolve Me," which he read before the judges trying him for that attack. No less grave were the effects of Castillo Armas's victory for the rest of Latin America (especially Guatemala), where for decades guerrillas and terrorists proliferated, and military dictatorships assassinated, tortured, and plundered their own countries, taking democracy off the table for half a century. When all is said and done, the North American invasion of Guatemala held up the continent's democratization for decades at the cost of thousands of lives, as it helped popularize the myth of armed struggle and socialism throughout Latin America. For at least three generations, young people killed and were killed for another impossible dream, still more radical and tragic than the dream of Jacobo Árbenz.

ACKNOWLEDGMENTS

To María Eugenia Gordillo, director of the Hemeroteca Nacional de Guatemala, who gave me access to newspapers and magazines from the period in which this novel takes place.

To Francisco Marroquín University in Guatemala, and especially to former vice rector Javier Fernández-Lasquetty, for the extraordinary favor of allowing me to work in their excellent library.

To my friend Percy Stormont, who knows his land so well, for the journey we made along the border between Honduras and Guatemala, visiting the places where Castillo Armas's rebels were engaged in fighting, and also for showing me the secrets of Guatemala City.

To Francisco Pérez de Antón, Maite Rico, Bertrand de la Grange, Jorge Manzanilla, Carlos Granés, Gloria Gutiérrez, Pilar Reyes, and Álvaro Vargas Llosa, for their generous assistance. And a very special thanks to the people this novel is dedicated to: Tony Raful, Soledad Álvarez, and Bernardo Vega.